RUSSELL JAMES

is a unique voice in modern crime writing. A writer's writer, he was called 'something of a cult' by *The Times* and 'the Godfather of British *noir*' by Ian Rankin.

There are no detectives in his books, and when the police do appear it is on the sidelines. James concentrates on the criminals, their victims and those caught up in events. When he started writing novels, he deliberately wrote counter to the spirit of the times – which was sex 'n' shopping and international conspiracy – and instead wr... ...rk, multi-lay... ... ... in char-
a ... ...a
fr... ... ..., though Russell James' novel remain emphatically British.

Russell James is Chairman of the Crime Writers Association, 2001/2. His previous novels include *Underground, Daylight, Payback, Slaughter Music, Count Me Out* and *Oh No, Not My Baby*.

A paperback original.

First Published in Great Britain in 2000 by
The Do-Not Press Ltd
16 The Woodlands
London SE13 6TY
www.thedonotpress.co.uk
email: thedonotpress@zoo.co.uk

C-format paperback ISBN 1 899344 62 4
casebound edition ISBN 1 899 344 63 2

British Library Cataloguing in Publication Data. A catalogue
record for this book is available from the British Library.

b d f h g e c a

Printed and bound in Great Britain by
The Guernsey Press Co Ltd.

Painting in the Dark

by
Russell James

BLOODLINES

For those whose belief in this book never faltered: Jim Driver, Jane Conway-Gordon, Chris and Tony Pickering, and, of course, my wife, Jill.

.

Book One

Ab uno non disce omnes

CONSEQUENTLY

She recognised the sound but couldn't place it: heavy cleaver on wooden block. Meat in a butcher's shop. Crunch of bone, squelch of flesh, thunk of wood. But she and Paul were walking in a forest, nine o'clock at night, and the wide pathway curved before them green and damp beneath a moon-filled sky. Trees hung darkly on either side.

Paul paused. She felt his hand quiver and stop. They glanced at each other and Paul frowned: whoever was making the sound was round the curve ahead.

Cool air clung at her ankles.

When Paul glanced at her she shook her head, and with a sideways nod indicated they should turn back. He smiled absently. On the cold mossy ground she stepped away from him, but he held her hand more tightly and raised his other to signal silence. In the growing gloom she couldn't read his face.

Laura tugged his hand but he did not react. The sound stopped. As they waited motionless on the wooded path it seemed to her that every tree was waiting with them. A subdued sigh came from the leaves.

She heard the clang of metal against stone. Before she could say anything, she heard a new sound – the chop of spade on forest floor. She heard a grunt. Laura's voice was barely audible: 'Let's go back.'

But Paul had moved ahead of her, was peering through the tangled trees to see around the bend. She pulled at him. 'I don't like it.'

He let go her hand. Incredulously she watched Paul walk forward, as if drawn by some mad male imperative which drew him on a dare towards the sound. Her feet seemed to sink into cold ground. When she reached toward his back she was like a sapling rooted in mud, one thin branch extended, shivering in the air.

No choice. She couldn't stay like this; neither could she turn back and go to the car. She had to follow him.

She scurried along the mossy path. The only sound was someone

9

digging. She caught Paul at the sharp curve of the path where cold grey gloom lurked between the trees.

The digging stopped. So did they. The unseen man cursed, threw his spade to the ground and muttered words they could not catch. Laura reached for Paul's hand but when she laced her fingers in his, Paul's hand was cold as stone. Perhaps he would change his mind. As they hesitated on the silent path she stretched up to whisper in his ear, 'I'm frightened. Please take me home.'

Then came that sound again, that sickening crunch they had heard earlier, the butcher's cleaver – but closer now. Each blow accompanied by a grunt.

'No,' she whispered. 'We must go back.'

The sound seemed to pull Paul forward. He walked steadily along the dim moonlit path, round where the curve bent back on itself, and Laura followed as if in a dream. They were in an s-bend. Moonlight illuminated the shadowed path and the chopping sound grew louder. Whoever was there was not chopping wood. The sound was muffled, dampened. The snake bend straightened, then they saw him.

Barely ten yards away a man stood chopping downwards onto a stump. Something glistened beneath his axe – something like meat. With a start she realised the man was tiny – a dwarf, she thought. She must not scream.

But he had seen them. The dwarf stood feet apart, half crouched, the large axe heavy in his hand. Suddenly he bounded at them. Laura stepped back – and tripped.

She screamed, and as she landed on her backside the dwarf shrieked, 'Get out! Get out – if you know what's good for you.' She squirmed in the dirt and saw Paul facing him. The dwarf was closer now, six feet away, his axe raised. Dimly lit, his face seemed distorted with hate and fury – it *was* distorted, there was something wrong with it. 'Go away!' he shrieked, swinging the axe. He lunged at Paul.

But Paul foolishly did not back off. Laura sat helpless as he stood his ground. 'No!' she shouted as Paul stepped forward. 'No!' again. The dwarf waved his axe.

'No!'

Paul's hand shot out. The dwarf turned and ran – like a spider, his jerky sideways run taking him back toward the tree stump. He scrabbled on the ground for a pad of material but as Paul approached he straightened and lifted the axe above his head. This time he'd throw it. His body stiffened. His short arm tensed.

'Move back!' he spat.

Paul hesitated.

'Back!'

The axe quivered in the dwarf's hand, and Paul gave ground. 'Further. Go past the girl.'

Paul would not retreat beyond her. But he was far enough. The dwarf snatched up a filthy sack and swung it across his shoulder. There was something heavy in it. Laura sat staring at him, too scared to move. He *must* be a dwarf. Perhaps he was a little larger than a dwarf, but his misshapen face was not made of flesh. Was it a mask?

'Get up,' he snarled.

She started clambering to her feet. Paul helped her. 'Are you OK?' She nodded.

The dwarf rasped, 'Can you walk – you? Try your ankle. Walk that way – back where you came.'

Laura tugged Paul's arm. 'Come on. Please.'

'That's right – *please*,' jeered the little man.

She and Paul began to edge away. While he held that axe they would not risk turning their backs on him. Paul stopped again, and Laura clutched at him: 'Come on.'

Suddenly a missile flew out at them – not from the dwarf, but from the trees beside them, hitting Paul on his side before it fell. A piece of wood – a branch. The dwarf leered. 'See? There's more of us. You're surrounded now.'

Paul peered into the trees. Another branch flew out, but missed them. They saw someone move between the trees, but it was too dark. The dwarf yelled, 'Start running!' as from between the trees came an unearthly howl. Laura was pulling at Paul's arm. 'I saw one of them,' he said. Another branch flew past his face.

He let her drag him slowly away. When they reached the bend they saw the dwarf bend quickly to collect his spade, but when he tucked it beneath his arm the spade tangled with the sack across his back. He cursed, raised the spade in fury but then lowered it and shook the axe: 'Keep going! Round the corner.'

Paul muttered, 'I'm going to get that—'

'Not now,' she whispered. 'We'll call the police.'

The dwarf waved his axe. 'Go on!'

They heard that howl again. Whoever was out there was moving through the woods. They could hear him. They almost saw him. Suddenly, the little man had slipped away. Paul ran after him. Desperately, Laura called for Paul to stop – and at the tree stump Paul did stop. The little man could be heard crashing through the undergrowth, cursing loudly and clanking his spade. Paul glared after him, then glanced down. He bent closer to the ancient tree stump, then stood up.

When Laura reached him he was standing by a shallow hole.

Laura didn't want to look inside. But perhaps the dwarf had been burying gold. Dwarves did that, didn't they – bury gold beneath a tree?

Laura stood at the rim and peered inside. She saw no gold glinting in the moonlight, only something that looked like meat trampled in the dirt. The grubby flesh looked pink and fresh. Human. Where the axe had smashed the bones their inner cores looked black with blood. The fresh dug pit held broken limbs and a piece of torso.

Laura glanced away, wondering why she did not feel sick. In the movies this was the moment when someone turned away to vomit into a handkerchief. But she felt calm. In the cool night air she lifted her face and glanced around. She saw, on the broad stump where the dwarf had been working, the lump of meat he had left behind. Almost a yard long, including fingers. The dwarf must have meant to halve its length to fit the hole. The unreal white arm lay across the chopping surface, broken at a peculiar angle, almost cut through. There was little blood. In the feeble moonlight the dead flesh seemed as white as candlewax, and the hairs on the surface appeared so delicate that the slightest breeze might blow them away.

She listened. There were no night sounds except shivering leaves. As he stood beside her, Paul muttered, 'There doesn't seem to be a head.'

ONE

Despite the Spring sunshine they talked of snow. In two reclining chairs on the veranda outside her summerhouse they sat with teacups in their laps. The low cane table between them bore a plate of biscuits, a simnel cake, an elegant teapot, with a jug of milk for him, lemon for her, and sugar in a matching bowl. In the afternoon sun her grey hair glinted like snow at dusk. His face had reddened out of doors.

'Eighteen months I'd been in London but I'd not seen snow – which seemed uncanny, after Edinburgh. The winter before, you see, had been so mild. I had seen snow falling – but only twice, and each time it came with rain. The soft flakes fell like scraps of paper battered by the droplets. Snowflakes fluttered down in a barrage of dirty water, melting to nothingness before they touched the streets. That previous winter, London had seemed to me a dark sodden city – not cold, certainly not cold enough for snow – but a wet and watery town.'

'It has its seasons,' Sidonie murmured. She sat with her head tilted to catch the sun.

As he leant forward to reach for his tea, Murdo winced. Though he found the long low chairs comfortable they were ruinous for his back. In recent years he had come to prefer harder, more upright chairs, and sometimes now he walked with a stick. When visiting Sidonie he made a show of fitness – he was ten years younger than her, after all. He hadn't brought his stick today.

She watched him raise the cup and saucer in trembling hands. His eyes were still attractively dark blue but the flesh around them was loose and wrinkled, a pale brown mauvish colour, like an old bruise.

She said, 'We remember snow and rain and sunshine, but never the grey days.'

'Not memorable enough.' His chair scraped on the wooden deck. 'Only extreme weather – storms and heat waves – can cut through our gloomy self-obsession—'

Sidonie laughed. 'I'm not gloomy, Murdo.'

13

'But from time to time real life leaps up and smacks us in the face – smacks us *back* to life – makes us notice things like the weather.'

Sidonie was watching the way today's dappled sunlight tinted the red cedar of her summerhouse. She could hear birds calling territory in the trees. 'I've seen enough dramatic events.'

'You have a sunny nature.' His blue eyes twinkled in their folds of flesh.

'And you have a flirtatious one. You never change.'

He leant forward carefully, picked up the teapot and refilled their cups. 'When I first came down to London I was not at all flirtatious. I was a sombre lad.'

'I bet.'

'Presbyterian upbringing, you see.'

'No one says Presbyterian quite like you.'

Murdo smiled. 'Aye, well. I was lucky enough to join the army when the war was ending, and they never really knew what to do with me. I served most of my time in Scotland, three hours from home. I never felt like a real soldier.'

'London must have seemed a big adventure.'

'Oh yes. I had been warned that it was sinful, and so it was – though it took me a year or two to discover the sin. I wandered about in all my Presbyterian sobriety—' He twinkled at her. 'And the weather gave back a reflection of my face: resolutely glum.'

'It refused to snow?'

'Aye. Then one morning I woke up early – very early, dawn light barely discernible behind the street lights – and from my attic window I saw the whole city mantled with snow.'

'Typical of you to live in an attic, Murdo.'

'I could afford nothing else. That day, I remember thinking the snow had *manifested* itself to welcome me. Snow meant home to me, d'you see? It lay on the pavements, collected on sills, and if there had been trees outside my window the snow would have weighed their branches down.'

'Oh, were there really no trees, Murdo?' She chuckled. 'Did you live in a slum?'

'Opposite where I lived was a bomb site, walls and rubble, and during the night, drifts of snow gathered in the gaping holes to purify them. The ugly landscape had been made clean.'

He finished his tea and sat back in his chair. When the old lady lifted the teapot he waved it away. 'I've had my fill. Aye, well, I went down the stairs and slipped out the front door to walk in the snow. I was utterly alone, because as I say, it was barely dawn.'

'London. A cold morning.'

14

'But I didn't feel alone. Every snowflake kept me company—'

'Oh Murdo, really! You're courting me with cheap poetry.'

'No, no, words can't convey the feeling. There was magic there. When I looked up into the glowing streetlamps I saw each separate snowflake dancing in the light. Snowflakes settled soft as dust upon my shoulders and I felt for the first time that London belonged to me. Remember that?'

'A book was it, or a song?'

'I've forgotten now. Do you remember those novelty glass balls we shook to make a snowstorm – what did we call them? They held a little scene, perhaps a Father Christmas on whom snow fell. Though the man was alone, he was secure in his compact globe.'

'That's how you felt?'

Sidonie smiled lazily, her eyes half closed in the warm afternoon sun.

'I felt alive. After a while I went back inside the house, up to my chilly attic, and I looked again at the street below. The bomb site seemed even softer – it could have been a park, a walled garden deep under snowdrifts. But d'you know what struck me most?'

'Tell me.'

'My footprints in the snow. Everywhere was white and smooth except for those two clear tracks of feet, walking out and walking back. At the end of the tracks was a little island where I had stood and trampled, that patch totally distinct, the only blemish in all the whiteness, and it seemed for the first time that I had left my mark on the huge city.' Murdo chuckled. 'Not an easy thing to do.'

'You're an incurable romantic. When was that – forty-eight?'

'1947. London was a crippled city then.'

'I remember.'

'Bomb sites everywhere, and scars across every building which still stood. Nothing in the shops.'

'And no gaiety. The dogged drabness of it all. Fifty years ago. You came down and I returned. But like you, in a way, Murdo, I felt lost. The London I'd known before had been full of life. Handsome shops—'

'Handsome men, no doubt?'

'London before the war was elegant and delightful – I mean genuinely delightful, full of delight.'

Murdo shrugged. 'I'd stroll through the West End and catch occasional glimpses of privileged folk like you. You stood out even more than you had in the Thirties – still the only ones who could afford a car.'

'Or could acquire petrol coupons. No, the people you saw were probably spivs and black marketeers. Don't give me that nonsense, Murdo, about rich and poor – you'll outstay your welcome.'

'I mustn't do that.'

His smile seemed strained now. Shakily, he rose to his feet and stood on the wooden flooring beside the table like a weary waiter for whom the last guest would not go home. 'I don't know why I remembered snow. That wasn't what I meant to say at all. I was going to ask you—' He grimaced. '1947. About Naomi—'

He looked suddenly aghast, as if he had inadvertently blurted out an indiscretion. His hand rose to his chest and he staggered, gasped, and fell crashing to the ground. As he fell he upended the table – teacups arcing through the air, milk, sugar, the simnel cake, all cascading to the wooden floor. He collapsed in a disappearing puddle of steaming tea. Sidonie rushed to kneel beside him, her hands tugging at his clothes – but Murdo seemed so heavy, so hard to move. When she rolled him on his back the lurching movement caused a slight flicker beneath the surface of his eyelids. His lips twitched and for a moment she thought he might try to say something, but the only sound he produced was a short rasping sigh like the whisper of wind in a rusty pipe.

'Don't, dear, don't.'

The old lady heaved his white head into her lap and stroked his cheek. Then she loosened his tie and with some difficulty undid the collar button to his shirt.

'Murdo, please.'

Helplessly, she looked around the garden, knowing there was no one there. No neighbours overlooked. No one lived with her in the house. In the greening trees beyond the flower borders, birds continued to sing. She heard a bee hum. Afternoon sunlight lay patterned across her lawn and the scent of blossom hung in the air

After a while she lifted Murdo's head from her flowing skirt and lay him prone on the summerhouse veranda. Tea had soaked into the planks, leaving a faint blurred stain that would soon disappear. A broken line of splattered milk ran to the edge and a dusting of sugar lay around his body like dry snow. Even as she watched, the first ant appeared from a crack in the wooden floor.

She bent towards Murdo and straightened his tie. His hair had become disarranged and she used her fingers to smooth it back in place. In life, Murdo had been so proud of his looks and dignity.

To stand up from the hard floor Sidonie used the fallen table for support. She seemed old and frail. Once on her feet she paused a moment to regain her breath. After one final glance at the unmoving Murdo she set off slowly across the sunlit lawn to telephone for an ambulance.

TWO

Gottfleisch took a third croissant and dipped it in his blue Delft mug of drinking chocolate. The corpulent, silk-shirted man had lingered so long over breakfast that his drink had cooled, and when he raised the croissant to his fleshy lips a shroud of chocolate skin hung from the sticky pastry like the folded wings of a desiccated bat. When he bit into the croissant the brown skein came unstuck and drooped across his mouth. He slurped at it, sucking the sweet fragments from his lips while keeping his eye on the conservatory door in case Turmold should return. The man was taking an unconscionable time in the lavatory. Perhaps he had been distracted by one of the porno books.

In his white cast-iron two-seater settee, Gottfleisch shifted his massive bulk forward to pick up the newspaper, its front pages dominated by the announcement of the 1997 General Election in six weeks time. John Major claimed to be 'confident' of turning round his party's huge deficit but the press, it seemed, had written him off. He was yesterday's man. Bright tomorrow lay with Tony Blair.

Gottfleisch scrunched the pages impatiently, looking for the short piece which had earlier caught his eye. Though buried deep inside, the story had been illustrated by a familiar painting. The article itself was captioned *Death Of A Keene Agent*. Five paragraphs. Gottfleisch hadn't realised that Murdo Fyffe was the Keene family's agent. He hadn't realised Fyffe knew the Keenes at all, though with hindsight perhaps he should have guessed. Miss Keene herself – what was her name? Sidonie – had approached Gottfleisch once directly in his role as art dealer, and had asked if he might be interested in a watercolour – one of Naomi's, naturally – which for some reason Sidonie wanted to sell. A straightforward, legitimate transaction – which made a pleasant change for Gottfliesch. Since Naomi's paintings were valuable and rare he had asked if there were any more, but the old lady had replied vaguely. There might be one or two somewhere, she had said, playing dumb.

And now Murdo had stiffened his brush in the old lady's back-yard. The newspaper didn't give her address— 'a secluded cottage in rural Surrey' was all it said. But because of the painting he had sold for them, Gottfleisch knew he must have her address recorded in his files. It was odd, really, that he had not followed up.

Having finished his croissant he lifted the Delft mug and shook it to gauge the viscosity of the remaining chocolate. Still quite fluid. No wrinkly skin. He took a sip. Littered across the white iron table before him were the remains of his continental breakfast: rye bread and skofa, several more croissants, one last brioche, an untouched plate of crispbread biscuits, a bowl of butter, three kinds of jam, a little muesli, a compote of fruit, some cheese and an empty carton of Greek yoghurt. In summer Gottfleisch preferred to breakfast lightly. He did not eat sausages till winter.

He leant back in his chair, belched, twisted round, and peered into the house for any sight of the absent Turmold. Bladder problem or constipation? The latter, at a guess. The man was so thin that every muscle in his puny body seemed permanently clenched.

So, Gottfleisch mused, Murdo Fyffe had croaked. When they had last met, Fyffe had seemed fit enough for his – what, three score and ten? Yet he had checked out, according to this article, half way through a pleasant afternoon having tea with Miss Sidonie Keene. Fancy that.

In the last ten years Fyffe had brought Gottfleisch *several* Naomi Keenes but until this story linking him with her sister, Gottfleisch had assumed that Murdo had acquired the paintings by means best not enquired into. Why else would the Scotsman bring them to *him* to sell? The obvious had not occurred to Gottfleisch – that Fyffe had a direct link to the family – though if the sister *were* the source, surely she could have achieved a better price on the open market? Though certainly she was wise to use a dealer rather than risk a public auction: prices were unreliable and the wait – three months before the actual sale, followed by at least a month before the auction house paid up – might not have suited her. Murdo always prefered cash on the nail. And in those transactions Gottfleisch had not behaved too dishonourably: he had helped himself to an inevitably generous commission, but it had been based on the price the paintings made. They were 'particular' and sold only to a limited clique of keen collectors (an old tired pun), and Gottfleisch was able to place them with minimal publicity. There were so few Keenes on the open market that as their scarcity increased, so did their price.

And by dealing privately one avoided tax. Taking things all round, old Murdo had been rather shrewd. Gottfleisch would not have been the only channel through which Keene paintings passed. Other dealers acquired them and occasionally a work appeared at auction: Property of a Gentleman. Perhaps that gentleman had been Murdo Fyffe? Perhaps he was the conduit through which the old lady slowly released a little hoard of her sister's paintings. If that were so and if the old lady had lost her conduit, who would she use now? Could there be many paintings left? Might there be a small hoard of previously undiscovered Naomi Keenes?

Gottfleisch plucked an apricot from the fruit compote. When he had sucked the syrup from his fingers he unfolded the newspaper and turned to a page of crime reports. The mention of the Blackheath burglary was bland and vague, suggesting that the police had found no clues so far. He inhaled complacently. Now that the morning sun had risen high above his conservatory, those stolen antiques should be on a freight ship out of Harwich for the Hook of Holland. Gottfleisch checked his watch and nodded. He hoped the police would continue to search most diligently – in Blackheath.

At last he heard a footstep. Turmold appeared in the doorway from the house – thin, sallow, with the anxious grin of a man who knew he had spent too long in the lavatory – rubbing his hands together and yanking at the bulky belt he wore on his grey flannel trousers. The leather strap draped around him like a kiddy's hoop.

'I'd better sally on to the jolly old office.'

'So soon?'

'Should have been at the desk by nine.'

'Hardly possible now.'

'The phone starts ringing, you know?'

'Who wants to talk insurance at nine o'clock?'

'You'd be surprised. Sometimes there's a queue on the doorstep, waiting for us to open.'

'Accidents in the night?'

'Or perhaps the occasional burglary.'

Turmold grinned and stepped further inside the heated conservatory. 'Sometimes one of ours.'

Gottfleisch waved him to a seat. 'A little more breakfast before you go. Those chairs you mentioned – they are accredited?'

'Oh yes, Queen Anne. Our client saw a set just like them on TV – the Antiques Road Show. He heard the price and… fell off his chair!'

Turmold laughed dryly, like a distant engine refusing to start. 'He's got ten of them in the house, you see? Two carvers.'

'But he has had them properly accredited?'

'He has now. Written. Lapada. For insurance – we *insisted*.'

'Who did you place him with?'

19

'Ecclesiastical. Recently we've done Cornhill, Sun Alliance, L&G, Commercial Union, all of those – but not Ecclesiastical.'

'Ten Queen Anne chairs…'

'By using different insurance companies no one spots the common thread. No reason to connect separate burglaries to one single broker.'

'You reckon twenty thousand pounds – that's insurance value, I take it?'

'Conservative.'

'Which is twelve to fifteen, say, at auction. I might manage to move them for seven or eight.'

'Oh, Mr Gottfleisch!'

'They are stolen goods,' Gottfleisch said reprovingly. 'Has he anything else?'

'Quite a good table—'

'Difficult to carry out through the door.'

'Some Georgian cutlery – he *thinks* it's Georgian.'

'Not Queen Anne?'

'Heavens, no. I advised him to have the cutlery valued.' Turmold smiled. 'I suggested a gentleman from Dorking – an irritating type.'

'Dealer?'

'Oh yes. I like a valuation before a burglary.'

'In case the cutlery's worth taking too?'

'The main thing is to get another dealer in before we lift the chairs. Then the police will smell a rat.'

'And look for the rat in Dorking? Very good, Turmold. Most dealers have a dodgy reputation – even in Dorking. Where does your client live?'

'Outskirts of Whyteleafe.'

'Perfect. Do have more breakfast.'

Gottfleisch selected a croissant and dipped it in his jam. 'There's a commuter train calls in at Whyteleafe which the police have nick-named the Burglar's Special. Apparently, thieves slip down from Victoria or Clapham, knock off a house or two which they have spot-ted earlier from the train, then catch the late train back. I've heard it said that on some evenings the wicked rascals do four or five houses in a row, all inside an hour. Pick a night when there's a decent programme on the telly.'

'Like the Antiques Road Show?'

'That's on Sunday, dear boy, when trains run less frequently. Tell me, can one see your client's house from the passing train?'

Turmold frowned at his untouched breakfast. 'I don't think so. I don't use the train.'

'Pity. The police are very keen on this trainspotting theory. That's a beautiful nectarine you have there.'

'Hm?' Turmold blinked at his plate as if he hadn't noticed it before.

'Don't you want it?'

Gottfleisch reached across and took the fruit. 'Your Whyteleafe client sounds rather fun. We can leave the police to ponder whether the dastardly deed was perpetrated by your dodgy Dorking dealer or by teenage trainspotters.'

'Ten large Queen Anne chairs—'

'Oh yes, quite, quite. The lads could hardly carry them back to town on a train. Bad news for the Dorking dealer, I'm afraid. It sounds as if he will be their man.' Gottfleisch spat the nectarine stone delicately into a spoon. 'A small red herring, nothing more.'

'The client did mention a Victorian painting which he thinks might be by Pinwell.'

'Thinks?'

Gottfleisch helped himself to a chocolate chip muffin.

'And a few pieces of Netsuke.'

'Ah. Where does he keep them?'

'I suggested he didn't bother to have them valued. Sometimes when an old buffer like this has a valuation and finds himself worth a couple of hundred thou' more than he had thought, it makes him act unpredictably. Starts installing burglar alarms.'

'A couple of *hundred* thousand?'

Gottfleisch studied Turmold, who looked away self-deprecatingly. 'It's possible. He said something about 'bits and pieces that had been in the family'. Porcelain, I believe.'

'Turmold, dear boy, you are dribbling out the details like a poacher setting bait. So there's a good deal more there than a set of chairs?'

'I've brought a copy of his inventory. And his holiday dates. They're taking a two-week Spring break in France. I arranged the Green Card for him.'

Turmold could not restrain his leathery smile as he handed the envelope across. 'I really must be leaving now.' He stood up. 'In the unfortunate event of my client having to make a claim I shall insist on giving it my *personal* attention.'

'So you can put an accurate figure on his losses?'

Turmold was all smiles now. 'The usual fifteen per cent?'

'You can trust me, Turmold. A drop more breakfast?'

'Goodness, I've had enough,' Turmold said, though he did not appear to have eaten anything. He shuffled to the door.

When Gottfleisch was alone with the remains of breakfast he glanced again at his election-dominated newspaper and skipped to where the photograph smiled back at him in smudgy black and white. The little story was there only because of its tenuous connection with Naomi Keene; any snippet linked to her allowed the press to resurrect highlights of her past. Gottfleisch blinked and blew out his cheeks. Since Murdo Fyffe had had access to someone's collection, and since he had been on tea-taking terms with Naomi's sister, there must be every chance that two and two made four. Or two and two made Fyffe. Gottfleisch smiled. Fyffe had always been circumspect – nay, secretive – about the paintings and because he'd have distributed them through several outlets, few people reading the article would realise its true significance. Few people. One or two, perhaps.

With surprising agility the huge man projected himself from the double seat, strode to the rear of his conservatory and gazed across his leafy Greenwich garden. Beneath the mature bushes the earth lay dark from overnight rain. The lawn looked lush and in need of mowing. But Craig could do that.

Gottfleisch returned to the metal table and picked up the telephone. This was not a job for Craig; he was better suited to healthy outdoor tasks. This job would suit another of his little helpers, one who at this time of morning was no doubt still swaddled in his disgusting sheets. As he punched the number Gottfleisch imagined the little tyke burrowing beneath his filthy bedclothes to ignore the phone. He let the phone keep ringing until there was no chance the man would reply.

Gottfleisch put the phone down and chose himself a pear – so ripe and perfect that it soothed his initial impatience. He would call back later. There was no real hurry. Ticky might be an irritating little toad, but he was useful.

THREE

When I describe Murdo at the end of his life you cannot realise how handsome he had been. I describe a gentle self-mocking old man and you won't sense his vigour and attractiveness, his innocent Scottish grit and unsophisticated smile. I was drawn to him from the start – drawn to him, by God, I buckled at the knees! I would hover attentively in his vicinity – and for ages it seemed that we only met in crowds – I would laugh at his jokes, agree with his arguments, accidentally touch his sleeve. It was over a year before I could persuade him to my bed – and I do mean persuade: he was extraordinarily resistant.

Military training, I suppose – he was dug in so deeply that I could *not* break him down. I stormed his trenches, made surprise advances, but couldn't lay my hands on his artillery. When I finally did break his guard – well, you know what soldiers are! – he stood erect and I was drilled. Until then he hid like a sentry in his box. He seemed practically celibate. Flattering offers came his way but he remained resolutely Presbyterian about them all. As a celibate he was prime target. He might laugh and jest and tell amusing Scottish tales, but when a woman pressed him he would switch to an infuriating diffidence and pretend not to understand. Perhaps we were too forward for him. In the land of claymore and kilt perhaps people approach each other with less subtlety.

He took me a year.

I wasn't his first. Mirabelle – you won't know her, she's been dead for years – Mirabelle had him before me. At least I think so: discretion was another of Murdo's sterling virtues. In all the years I knew him he never once broke a confidence. So it was Mirabelle, I *think*. She had been all over him for months until suddenly – overnight, you might say – she became hideously calm and smug. Proprietorial. She now stood beside him as if by right. – Which was quite the wrong tactic with Murdo, because within a week whatever *had* existed between them had turned to ashes. Poor Mirabelle.

My friend Patsy thought it an enormous hoot. I remember her taking me aside in – where was it? – oh yes, her fencing club. (I still kept in trim, and fencing was one of the few luxuries left to me from my more hedonistic youth.) Patsy pointed out in all seriousness that by dropping Mirabelle, Murdo had at least proved he was not a gigolo! (Mirabelle had money, you see, and Murdo, who clearly had not, hadn't been tempted to secure her as a wealthy wife.) Patsy thought it a double relief: if it hadn't been for his brief fling with Mirabelle we might have wondered whether he was a lady's man at all. But in their short week together, Mirabelle assured Patsy that she had given our Scottish soldier a rigid kit inspection.

I finally pulled down his barricades (I'm sorry, but once I've started this I can't stop – as the art mistress said to the gardener) one night after a party at The Colony. He had been drinking, not heavily, but enough to loosen up. We went to his flat, and shortly afterwards we went to bed. There I was, open and defenceless as the low countries, while he laid on a sustained barrage. (I told you I don't stop.) The way he handled his grenades! He invaded and occupied me. He assaulted my front and then he took me from the rear.

Does it shock you to hear an old lady reminisce? Well, since you are younger than I am – everybody is, my dear, don't worry – you can't believe that my generation enjoyed sex. I have news for you: we wrote the book.

What *was* shocking – I might as well admit it – was the difference in our ages. I was forty (not that I admitted that to him – or to anybody!) while he was under thirty. But I was wearing well and had *savoire faire* – those were the days, you see, of Simone de Beauvoir, Simone Signoret, Simone Simone – all those husky and mysterious French Simones of an intriguing age. The Fifties was not a decade for nymphets: men wanted women with experience who would *deliver*.

And we did.

My Scottish soldier and I engaged in front line action for several weeks. An exhausting campaign. But suddenly his mighty gun stopped firing – I don't know why; perhaps both of us were spent. He stopped turning up for duty, and went AWOL.

I was numb, the walking wounded. But we remained friends. Murdo took other lovers; I found less sterling men. We became like brother and sister, though I still thought him romantic and dashing. I still loved him, in an unpossessive way, and was happy for him to win countless women – until in '59 he married a bus driver's daughter. (She was only a bus driver's daughter, but she let Murdo ring her bell!) And despite that appalling marriage – I suppose everyone is allowed one mistake – Murdo and I remained in touch. Our bright young set became older. They married and settled down. I became too old to be the 'older woman' any more.

✳

Twenty years earlier, the scene was more exuberant. My sister Naomi and I were bright and gay (an allowable word then) and thought of ourselves as artists – Naomi the painter, Sidonie the pianist. Naomi had long blonde hair, while I wore my hair short. We were both talented amateurs and had money enough to indulge ourselves. In the early Thirties when we were coming out, Daddy had introduced us to Augustus John and Walter Sickert, to Coward, Belcher, Baddeley and Arnold Bennett. I don't suggest that these legends were part of our regular set, but we did meet them. Daddy pointed Bennett out to me once – I think it might have been in the Gargoyle Club; Daddy loved to show us off there – and I walked up to the famous one, as one does when cocky and young, to ask, 'I say, aren't you Arnold Bennett?'

But in a strange mock cockney accent he replied, 'I wish I wos.'

Puzzled, I returned to Daddy, who merely smiled, and when I turned round the famous author had slipped away. (I say 'famous author' in case you don't know who Arnold Bennett was; I take nothing for granted nowadays.) Daddy whispered to me that in the Gargoyle it was not the done thing to recognise *anybody*.

The Thirties: if those days seem unimaginably long ago to you, I assure you that they seem as long ago to me. The memories of youth are supposed to return crystal clear, but they don't. Old memories are like scenes from a film, reappearing fitfully in our minds. Some images remain clear, with snatches of dialogue, a treasured tone of voice – but today I watch a person who was never me perform in scenes for which I have no true memory. I see her interact with people I recognise but can no longer say I know. As the pictures drift across and fade I cannot always tell whether the particular sequence actually took place or was invented by what I choose to call my memory.

In the Thirties I had a friend who worked in films, painting back-cloths and illusions. 'The theatre,' he said, 'was yesterday. In the twentieth century, Cinema is theatre.' Imre Goth was Hungarian, and knew the Kordas, the gods of British cinema. He was a professional artist, and Naomi said she envied him. 'But I need money,' he told her. 'While you do not. I envy you that.'

He would condescend to sit with us in the Bullfrog or Gargoyle. (There are class divisions between artists, just as among their customers.) 'The most tempting of sisters,' he called us. 'Like two

25

apricots in a tree. You have beauty. You have money. You each have a talent. What an idyllic life lies before you.'

I can still hear the voice of the enforced émigré. I remember his encouraging smile. But my life has led where all lives lead, Imre: to death and disappointment – to the empty husk of my poor Murdo, cold and still on the summerhouse floor.

FOUR

Although morning sunlight warmed the pavement outside the amusement arcade, it had little impact inside, being confined to a rectangle at the entrance. The street outside looked bleached and faded as if on a distant cinema screen, while the throbbing machines inside blazed in bold primary colours – rich blues and gold and clashing reds. Video images competed with each other. Electronic jingles blended with the background music beat.

At this early hour, customers were few. The only players were a Chinese man of indeterminate age, two white men in their early twenties and little Ticky, somewhere near the back. As he scuttled furtively through the video cavern the lurid coloured lights flickered across his maimed face until it resembled a troll from one of the games. It was a year now since he had been badly burned in a fairground side-show, and although plastic surgeons had done their best he would be scarred for life. Not that little Ticky had been handsome before: barely five feet tall with thinning hair and no looks at all, people had quipped at the time that plastic surgery could only improve him. People who made these jokes never visited him in hospital. Only when he came out did they realise that the fierce fire had melted his pathetic face. After surgery it seemed covered with a film of wax.

One thing Ticky soon discovered was that not everybody averted their gaze from his changed appearance. Some people – well, some *strangers* – realised his face had been rebuilt and they felt sympathy for him. Because Ticky seemed small and harmless one or two strangers actually reached out to pat him. Except they couldn't bring themselves to pat his head. Their hand would hover in the air, then fall lightly on his shoulder. Ticky didn't mind. Not really. He appreciated any attempt at human contact. In fact, if he was honest with himself, Ticky would admit that he had more contact with people now than he had ever had before. Before the accident, people had shunned him, kept away. Maybe it had been due to his halitosis – in

27

the old days he had suffered mightily from that. Not that *he* could ever smell it, but people had ribbed him, which was how he knew. But since the accident they didn't sneer at him any more. Maybe being in hospital all that time, the regular diet that they served, had flushed out whatever had previously fouled his gut. Maybe regular eating was a good thing. Or maybe it had been the shock. Whatever brought about the cure – and Ticky was convinced that something had – when eventually he came out of hospital he resolved to stick to a healthy diet. He made a decent stab at it, though some of the mush they had fed him there – white custard, poached fish, several new kinds of veg – did not fit easily into a single life. No single man cooked custard. Or poached fish.

But Ticky tried his best.

Occasionally, he began to question whether the halitosis really had gone away. It was hard to tell: since reappearing on the streets with his remodelled face, people did not insult him casually as they had before. No one called him Shorty, Runt-face, or Human Dustbin any more. So in some ways his life had become easier. There were compensations.

For instance: before the disfiguring accident, this arcade near Piccadilly Circus could have been dangerous for him, a No Go Area. Now he found it possible – not easy, but possible – to hang about the bright machines looking for a new young friend. The Piccadilly Arcade had always been a place where kids fresh from the provinces met streetwise brats and older men. For Ticky to approach a kid in here before the accident would have been impossible – one look and they'd think, 'pervert' – but now he was so disfigured they assumed that he could surely do no harm. A face like his aroused their sympathy.

The point about kids who gravitated to Piccadilly Circus, if they weren't already on the game, was that they spent half their time looking over their shoulders – partly dodging the Law, partly dodging men like him. They weren't ignorant, they had heard about his kind. In Ticky's opinion, this was part of the reason they ended up in the wicked city – curiosity and fear, mixed with hope and confused desire. Will I like it or will it hurt? The great adventure.

In the dark corner where Ticky loitered, a house spider had begun its web. From an electric cable to a metal pipe it lay a sticky line. The spider wandered backwards and forwards along that line, laying down additional thread to strengthen it. Then it began a second line, allowing it to droop loosely below the first. From this slacker line the spider descended on a thread which it anchored to a lower point on the pipe. Then it pulled the slack line down to form a V. The base of this V would become the centre of its web. Once established, the web might remain undisturbed for months. In the dust and grime of that dark corner the web would hang unnoticed, apart from once in a while when a solitary fly might drift in from outside to circle the dark interior: all the while coming nearer to the hanging snare.

The two white men wandered out to the street, leaving only Ticky and the Chinaman. It was early in the day and Ticky was only here on the off chance that some kid exhausted from dossing in a doorway might have nowhere else to go. But it seemed that this was not to be his morning, though the place would get busier later on.

When Ticky finally left the corner, he caused a tremor in the web.

*

Murdo's house looked much as always, Sidonie thought, though in some curious way she had expected to find it transformed by his death. Yet here it was, the same old furniture, the same familiar pictures on the walls, the same Afghan carpet. And that same drop-out son of his, the wretched Angus, floppy hair still dangling in the nerveless non-style of the Seventies around his podgy Seventies face. He had grown slacker in the cheek and needed a shave. He would be approaching forty soon, she realised. She had not seen Angus for over a year. From time to time he reappeared to convalesce between 'relationships' or ill-fated business ventures, to hang around his father a few aimless weeks, and then to slither back to the great Who Knows Where. Murdo had always indulged Angus, almost encouraging him to live a shiftless life. Though today, to do Angus credit, he did look distressed at his father's death. He seemed lost in the empty house.

'We'll have to sell it.'

'We?' Sidonie thought Angus might be referring to one of the washed-out women he was entangled with.

'*I* will. I'll have to sell it.'

Sidonie nodded. At least that meant that Angus would not be moving in. He couldn't live in this semi-rural setting – with or without a washed-out woman. Nor would the well-ordered villagers want him here.

'You can think about that after the funeral.'

'Oh yes.' He coughed. 'I suppose when we've done the service and that, people might just as well come back here. No need to hire somewhere.'

'This was his home. It would be best.'

'There won't be many people.'

Sidonie ran a finger across Murdo's walnut side table. He used to place it at her side when they had tea.

29

'What d'you think, a dozen?' Angus asked.

'Hm?'

'Friends. There won't be many.'

'No?'

'Dad was always complaining they were dying off. Did you know he used to read the obituary pages? Said it was like a roll call for his generation.'

'Everybody dies eventually.'

'Yeah, well, all the old fuddy-duddies are dying off.' He hesitated as he realised her age, but then blathered on regardless. 'It's time for a new generation.'

She raised an eyebrow at the less-than-young hippy, but he didn't notice.

'This election will sweep all the stuffy old crap away. New Labour, right? A brand new start.'

Sidonie wandered across to the captain's chair where Murdo had liked to sit.

Angus said, 'Not many people, then. We could knock up some sandwiches and a spot of drink.'

The wooden chair was gently sculpted as if to cradle the occupant in its arms. The polished seat had a soft deep sheen.

'A few sandwiches. And maybe we ought to buy some cake.'

Angus was watching her. Perhaps he expected *her* to do the catering? A man in his late thirties, helpless as a schoolboy. She said, 'There's a woman in the village. She won't charge you much.'

'I hope not.'

He was such a wet rag. She said, 'Or you could buy it all from M&S. People won't expect a slap-up meal.'

'Right. Nothing fancy.'

She could no longer look at the captain's chair. She had to get away. As she moved to the door she said, 'Murdo had a lot of friends.'

'They're mostly dead by now. Are you leaving?'

'Yes.'

'Wanted to talk to you.'

She closed her eyes. 'About whom to invite?'

'No, not that. Though I suppose... Well, this is hardly the time, is it?'

Sidonie hesitated in the doorway. She didn't want to stay in the house with Angus, yet to leave him there was like leaving a workman in one's bedroom.

He said, 'Leave it a few days, maybe, after he's been buried.'

Sidonie wasn't listening. Everything about the cottage was

30

painfully familiar and she didn't know why Angus had asked her to call, unless it really had been to persuade her to prepare the food. He was like a stranger in his father's house – no, it was *his* house now, with his father dead. Fortunately he would never live here. Angus stood gaunt and dishevelled on the sitting room floor like an auctioneer's clerk come to price it up. She glanced again at her old friend's things. Her oldest friend.

Already the room had developed a slight smell of mould, as if it too had died. It was almost as if a mist had drifted across his furniture and paintings. There were none of Naomi's here, only a few pleasant, inexpensive things – and the one red chalk sketch of a young girl which Sidonie had given Murdo years ago.

'That picture,' she said. 'It's mine. I gave it him.'

'Gave it?'

'Lent it, really.'

'Well, if you gave it…' Angus grinned awkwardly. 'Oh, I don't know.'

'I'd better take it back.'

Angus frowned. 'Shouldn't we wait? I mean, it's like part of the estate.'

'Estate?'

'You know… inheritance tax. Won't you have to prove you lent it to him?'

Sidonie came back inside the room and marched straight to the chalk drawing. 'Look at it,' she said. 'Who do you think that is?'

'Huh?'

Sidonie took the picture from the wall. 'That's me,' she said. 'It was drawn by my friend Imre Goth. Can't you see that?'

'Imre who? Look, I'm not sure—'

'I'm taking it home.'

✳

We were a cosmopolitan crowd, back in the Thirties. Our native British stock had been invigorated with exciting new blood from middle Europe, countries that don't exist any more – Silesia, East Prussia, Saar – little states squashed between the borders of larger ones. The map of Europe at that time looked like a chart of sand puddles drying in the sun. Hungary, for example, had lost two thirds of its homeland, and Austria and Germany had shrunk as well. Throughout the continent, displaced people ran like ants. Imre Goth moved from Hungary into Germany – and initially he did well. By the early Thirties he was moving among the exalted of the land – he painted *Präsident* Goering's portrait several times – and yet he had to leave everything behind and flee to London. Perhaps he was Jewish. Or perhaps being Hungarian was enough. But Imre's life was a succession of highs and lows – which he embellished at every telling with more than a dash of verbal paprika. I remember Imre holding court at the Hambone and the Gargoyle, spinning anecdote after anecdote of catastrophe and success: how he had been acclaimed in Transylvania but had had to flee King Carol ('My father, you understand, was an Austro-Hungarian count'); how he had arrived with nothing in Wiemahr Germany ('Not even my paint brushes – and if I'd had charcoal I would have *eaten* it'); how he had been discovered penniless by the art patron Goering ('My portrait of his beloved Karin hung above the bed of his second wife'); how he had fled the Nazis to start again in London ('And I shall never leave this beautiful country').

He was an outrageously charming – and talented – man, to whom painting came quite effortlessly. Where Naomi was painstaking and slow, Imre was carelessly slapdash. In less than a minute he could scribble a portrait on the back of a menu card – a good one too – and offer it in payment for his meal. The waiters seldom accepted them at the time, though any still in existence would be worth hundreds now. He continued to behave like this even when well off, laughing and saying that at one time it was the only way he had survived.

Those wonderful evenings in fashionable clubs. Evenings? Nights would be more accurate. After the theatre I would go for late supper, then champagne at midnight, then dancing in the small hours with a correctly dressed young man. Perhaps I'd take in the latest revue and meet the cast afterwards at the Gargoyle – Coward, Baddeley, Hulbert and his little Cicely.

If Daddy was with us he'd insist on making introductions – me to obscure pianists and Naomi to uninterested artists. She was a mere amateur, they thought, one of those society girls who liked to dabble in watercolours. She felt belittled by the whole performance. Once, when Daddy put her through this degrading introduction business, she picked a public argument with Walter Sickert – *Sir* Walter, the foremost portraitist in the land. She tried to tell *Sickert* about the use of light, insisting that the changing qualities of natural light added reality to a painting, and that its luminescence gave new depth. Sickert disagreed. He was obsessed with light, he grandly informed her – which artist is not? – but he claimed that it was for the artist to control the light, using light to immortalise the subject. Light was too important, Sickert said, to leave to the erratic whims of nature, and so he no longer painted in natural light. In his studio the blinds were always drawn. The result, he said, was that he could paint at any hour, and the quality of his colours remained unchanged. Painted light was not daylight, he said, and a true perfectionist might take a week to pin down a moonbeam – so to blazes with Naomi's fickle *natural* light. Sunlight begone!

I can see her now – the young Naomi I remember – the lithe quick body, long blonde hair and sweet furrowed brow. I see her lecturing the elderly one-time rebel, standing perhaps as he himself had stood twenty five years before when he decried the standards of the Royal Academy: feet aside on the night club floor, long finger pointing, defiant eyes – confident and fearless as only youth can be. He let her rant at him because she was young. But he forecast that when she matured she would come to learn that art did not benefit from reality and daylight. In time Naomi too would paint in the dark.

✳

'But at her age, what's the old biddy want with stupid paintings?' asked Ticky cheerfully. 'She's probably bored of 'em.'

Gottfleisch sighed. 'She may have had them sixty years.'

'There you are then. Sixty years. Mind, she must be old.'

Ticky nodded inanely across the desk. It was an early nineteenth century partners' desk, a massive double-sided piece chosen by Gottfleisch to suit his bulk. Ticky stood at the other side like an errant schoolboy.

Gottfleisch announced, 'I have invited myself to a funeral.'

Ticky brightened up. 'Anyone I know?'

'A friend of Miss Keene.'

Ticky cocked his head: there must be more to come.

'While we are at the funeral, Miss Keene's house will be left empty.'

Ticky smiled. In his rebuilt face, that smile was as if a scarecrow had been jolted into life. 'Has she far to go, sir, to the funeral? I mean, will she be out long?'

'Most of the afternoon, I should imagine. First there's the funeral, then a small reception.'

'Ah yes, cakes and ale. You need a drink. I went to a funeral once—'

'Not now, Ticky. Now remember, I don't want you to take anything. I don't want any sign that you've been there.'

Ticky inhaled. 'Just suss it out.'

'Exactly.' Gottfleisch gazed severely from beneath his eyebrows. 'Miss Keene comes from a wealthy family—'

Ticky clapped his hands and seemed about to speak. But Gottfleisch cut him short: 'She has always lived in a cultured world, so there will be valuables.'

'Excellent. Might as well knock 'em off while I'm there, sir.'

'I am particularly interested in some watercolours by her sister Naomi. These paintings may not be on display, so I want you to scout about for a locked room or hidden safe.'

Ticky raised his eyebrow. He would have raised both eyebrows but after the accident only one had regrown.

Gottfleisch continued: 'It's possible the old lady may have hidden them away.'

Ticky nodded knowledgeably. 'Hidden what, sir?'

'Pictures, idiot! Her sister's paintings. Do listen, Ticky. In recent years, several Keenes have surfaced – often through a friend of hers. Now he's dead.'

'Oh, dear.'

'It's *his* funeral.'

'I'll say. – Oh, the one you're going to?'

Gottfleisch eyed him bleakly. 'I hope you're paying attention, Ticky?'

'Yes, sir. The bloke's died what was letting out the pictures, and you think the old lady might have some left.'

'Well done.'

'Not just a pretty face, sir.' Ticky caught himself. He and Gottfleisch stared at each other blankly until Ticky cleared his throat. 'These paintings, then, of her sister's – they do belong to the old lady?'

'Yes.'

'Right. And she's flogged a few, but she ain't flogged all of them?'

Gottfleisch had begun flicking a cake crumb across the empty expanse of his polished desk. 'I dare say, being her sister's, they had sentimental value.'

'She still flogged 'em, though, unless this friend you mentioned was nicking 'em behind her back.'

'I don't think he was.'

Gottfleisch had flicked the crumb off the edge, and he now gave Ticky his undivided attention: 'For some years after her sister's death, the paintings seemed of little value. Then gradually their value began to climb. Naomi Keene's pictures, you see, have always appealed to a specialist taste.'

Ticky gave a knowing grin which Gottfleisch ignored.

'What you must do, dear boy, while we're at the funeral, is scour the house for locked doors or immovable objects. Take a camera with you. Make a record. Don't forget to photograph every decent painting. I want a thorough search so we'll know exactly what is there when we go back. You're to take an inventory, in effect.'

34

Ticky inhaled doubtfully, and then shrugged. 'Just as you say, sir. But since I'll be in the house anyway it'd be a shame to come away empty-handed.'

FIVE

It had threatened to be a funeral in the rain. There was a shower in the night and another midmorning, but the dark panoply was now rolling away across the North Downs. In their place, clumps of burnt cream clouds scampered across a freshly washed blue expanse, and the sun appeared and disappeared intermittently. When it shone it drew vapour from the shrubberies, and when it disappeared a breeze shook water from the leaves. In the village churchyard, people either carried raincoats or wore them undone. Some had brought umbrellas, dark and sombre as the men's ties.

One or two mourners struck a jarring note. Sidonie was surprised to see the unmissably large art dealer Gottfleisch, impeccably dressed, carrying a long golf umbrella rolled into gaudy stripes. If he opened it he would look like a small marquee. She saw Angus in an outdated suit of brown velour, presumably the only dark suit that he owned; something kept at the back of a spare cupboard for occasions like this. Surely he could have found something more suitable for his father's funeral?

Sidonie wore a sober suit of navy blue. She had not worn a hat, because people didn't nowadays, but she felt wrong without one. A hat was necessary, she believed, for church, and was even more so for a funeral. People didn't bother nowadays, except for weddings. – *Most* people didn't bother, although the young could prove her wrong: Muriel's granddaughter had come, a girl of nineteen or twenty, in a dark wide-brimmed boater which made her look ravishing. Murdo would have approved.

When Sidonie had arrived at the village church she had deposited her own umbrella inside the porch, and after the service, during which Spring sunlight streamed through the stained glass windows, she left it there while they went outside. Hers had been the only umbrella in the stand – and now, around the grave, the mourners carried theirs awkwardly like unwanted gifts. Inside the church they had kept them clenched between their knees as if, being Londoners

36

unused to villages, they had not trusted the receptacle in the public porch. Metropolitan visitors. Had she been metropolitan once?

Apart from Angus and Mr Gottfleisch there were Muriel and Pansy from the old set; Muriel's grand daughter; a balding Kingsley Davis, who she thought had died; Max Ulvaston; two Scottish cousins (or perhaps nephews); a commercial artist friend of Murdo's; Miles Pendle (critic) who had brought an extraordinarily youthful wife and irksome child; and of less interest, eight neighbours from the village and five others to whom she could not have put a name. Angus appeared to have invited no one, which was just as well.

As the party shuffled into position at the graveside Sidonie thought how unusual it was for her to be among so many familiar faces. For at least a decade she had lived quietly, and when she did go out she blended unnoticed with the crowd. People meant nothing to her, nor she to them. Yet today, her emotions raw from the reality of the funeral, she felt almost drunk from the sudden closeness of old friends and the memories they brought. Dear Pansy, who for a while had been her staunchest friend, yet whom she had not seen for several years. Muriel, whom she might not have seen since the Eighties. Max Ulvaston, though, she had seen as recently as this January when he had stayed at Murdo's for a long weekend. Familiar faces. The sight of them on this miserable occasion was enough to make a weaker person cry.

Sidonie shook her head. She must not lose her dignity. So far, everyone had behaved decorously. In glancing away she saw the vicar scurrying after them from the church. It was odd, she thought, how a funeral could reinforce one's grip on life: meeting old friends not seen for years – some almost forgotten – shaking hands, laying cheek to cheek, hearing their voices and noting how they had changed. – Or how they had *not* changed in Muriel's case: she hardly seemed to age.

Among these few undemanding friends Sidonie could relax and almost be herself. For they had *been* her friends, back in the Fifties. In those difficult years, when Sidonie met survivors from her pre-war set they responded awkwardly, sometimes cutting her dead as if they didn't know who she was. Or they uttered a few stilted sentences and scuttled away. Those one-time friends had seemed ill at ease, uncertain how to behave with her, what to say. It was because of Naomi, of course, whom they never mentioned.

By the Sixties it had died down. In that fun-filled decade everyone was caught up in the thrill of modern times, and had no interest in history. Only in the Seventies did a few echoes of the past return. But by then Sidonie lived in a different world, and when Naomi's name was revived, she withdrew further into it. Her sister's infamy might be contagious – not to mention that her own behaviour, falsified in the swills of journalism, put *her* equally beyond the pale. It took decades for such wounds to heal.

✳

Cudham Wood: Ticky almost missed it. The white metal sign was half hidden among uncut branches at the verge. 'Cudham would what?' Ticky asked himself, and laughed. He regarded this motor trip as a chance to air the engine. His tatty green Fiat seldom did more than three miles at a trot, most of it in traffic, not above third gear. Today was a chance to decoke the pistons – or whatever it was that a good run was supposed to do. He wasn't hot on cars.

Gottfleisch had told him to go straight through the village, out past the church, then to look for a hard right. He was already looking. Here outside the church the lane was congested with empty parked cars – a nicker's paradise. Ticky squeezed carefully between the parked cars as if his scrubby Fiat were as wide as they. Hiked onto the grass bank beside the road were a couple of fat motors, big bulging tyres, rich and self-satisfied. Many a day, Ticky would cheerfully have scraped one with his Fiat – just a scratch on those gleaming sides. To repair the damage on their paintwork would cost more than his own little car was worth. Occasionally some idiot would park a car like this in Deptford, some punter strayed in from Greenwich, and when the twit got back he'd find it scruffed. Asking for it. Lucky to find it there at all. Anyone parking a car worth twenty or thirty thousand quid in Deptford was lucky to find it later in *any* condition.

But today he kept away from other cars. He was working, on his best behaviour. Ticky eased gently by the churchyard, beyond the village, past where the 'Vote Conservative' posters petered out – and turned down a narrow country lane with high hedges and earthy banks. Along the centre was a broken line of rubble, mud and weeds, the road surface worn away. Little traffic came down here, and Ticky was relieved: he didn't like working in daylight. Since the fairground accident he had become so striking in appearance he could be identified at forty yards. Someone who saw him only once could give a description accurate enough to fetch the filth round straight away. Easy for them.

Ticky preferred to work at night. But work was work, and he was grateful for it. Last year, lying alone in hospital, Ticky couldn't see how he was going to survive outside. Doctors had tried to reassure him, and at first while the bandages were still in place he thought: plastic surgery, a brand new phizog. Attached to the pipe and drip, he would squirm around the hospital bed and consider his future. He

38

knew he had been hospitalised a fair number of days – though he wasn't too sure how many because somehow he had lost a few. But he didn't mind lying there. He thought about the plastic surgery and how it might change his life, but before the bandages were removed he picked up an undercurrent in the doctors' voices. They used words like 'brave' a lot, and when they cut off the bandages they wouldn't let him have a mirror.

Ticky stopped the car at an unexpected crossroad which Gottfleisch hadn't mentioned. When he looked more carefully he saw that the other road was an unmade farm track, so he continued on. Not much further now.

Even before the accident, Gottfleisch had been the only person to employ him. Everyone else had been prejudiced about his lack of height. Or something. Whatever their prejudice had been, they wouldn't use him. Story of his life.

While recovering slowly in the hospital Ticky had tried to face the facts. If life had been difficult before, and if he were now to be scarred for life, what hope was there for him in future? In those bleak depressing days he had had no visitors – apart from police. They would meander in, pester him for statements, and get annoyed when he claimed that he had no memory of what had happened. He listened to their questions, though, to find how much they knew, what they'd accuse him of. Coppers always accused a man of something. But after a while they stopped coming back, and Ticky was left alone. Mr Gottfleisch never visited, of course, never got in touch – though Ticky was working for him at the time, and what had happened was pretty much a workplace accident. Not that Gottfleisch would have seen it like that. When a job went wrong you were on your own.

Ticky saw the double gates to his left. In the overgrown tangled lane the gateway had been encroached upon with greenery and it was by no means certain the gates opened at all. On the middle bar of one gate a strand of ivy shone in the sunlight. Ticky continued by at crawling speed.

After fifty yards he came to a passing space, which seemed as good a spot as anywhere to leave his Fiat.

✳

'Man that is born of a woman hath but a short time to live, and is full of misery. He cometh up and is cut down. Like a flower, he fleeth as it were a shadow, and never continueth in one stay.'

The vicar gripped his book as if he had still not learned these familiar lines. His head was raised and his eyes were screwed shut against the sun. 'In the midst of life we are in death.'

The life-restoring orb beat down feebly on the graveyard and on droplets of rainwater on the grass. Angus Fyffe undid his jacket. People shrugged their raincoats open to let in March air. The huge Gottfleisch dug the point of his striped umbrella in the turf and put his weight upon it, one white hand above the other along its handle. The point sank deeper in the earth.

'Most merciful Saviour, deliver us not into the bitter pains of eternal death.'

She could feel a breeze now, and she glanced up. In a large oak tree the leaves were stirring, dislodging raindrops on mourners at the back.

'Thou knowest, Lord, the secrets of our hearts.'

Sidonie was barely listening. As she studied the impassive faces ranged around the grave she wondered what thoughts passed through their minds. Were they thinking of Murdo? Their eyes were glazed, unfocused, as if every one of them had detached themselves mentally from this place. The vicar droned, and they stood waiting. Every one was waiting their turn to die. There was Pansy, Max and Muriel. There she was herself. Eighty-five years old.

She watched Angus in his gaping suit as he stepped forward awkwardly to scatter a handful of dry soil into the grave. She watched reality strike home. At the sound of grit rattling on the coffin he went very still. If he had had any colour he would have lost it. He stood like a tombstone by the open grave.

'We therefore commit his body to the ground: earth to earth, ashes to ashes, dust to dust: in sure and certain hope of the Resurrection to eternal life, through our Lord Jesus Christ: who shall change our vile body that it may be like unto *His* glorious body, according to the mighty working whereby he is able to subdue all things to himself.'

✳

Before Ticky clambered out of the Fiat he put on a baseball cap and sunglasses. He wore the baseball cap back to front, not to be in fashion but so the long vizor would conceal his hair colour at the back. (He didn't have much to hide at the front.) Short of donning a long false beard this was the best Ticky could come up with to disguise his wounded face. He strolled nonchalantly along the empty lane, regretting that he seemed unable to grow a beard of his own, to act as a mantle across his waxen skin. But when he had tried in hospital the beard had grown patchily, as if there were no follicles in the new skin grafts. Ticky's face had looked like the underside of a cat with furballs. So he shaved off the ginger tufts, and discovered for the first

40

time that he had less sensation in those patches where hair refused to grow.

He stood beside the overgrown garden gates.

In the lane was a country silence which wasn't quiet at all: breeze in damp bushes, a couple of birds. Far away he could hear a droning engine, perhaps a passing car – though as he listened more carefully to its earthy sound he decided it was a tractor in a distant field. Farmers never stop working.

In the centre of the double gate was a complicated metal handle which looked rusted up. Ticky tried it, and to his surprise the lever moved and the gate swung open. He pushed it further and stepped inside.

After he had closed the gate he stood listening for a full ten seconds. The country noises didn't change. Waiting motionless at the wrought iron gate, in sunglasses and baseball cap, Ticky looked as out of place as a monkey at a tea party. But he didn't care. With an insouciant air he sauntered up the curving drive to the cottage, strode manfully to the front door and rang the bell. He waited.

Always check there's no one in.

✳

So many funerals at which we stand numbed, either with boredom or with grief, in the presence of an empty husk which once held a living spirit. Its elegant new container, that wooden box with new brass handles, is a graven image paraded before us as a focus for our thoughts. That pale clean box has but a short time to live: either it will glide smoothly behind the crematorium curtain or, as in this case, be lowered gently into its pit. We watch the box and try not to imagine the corpse inside, wearing laundered clothes, a touch of make-up, its hair still growing though the flesh is cold. Our thoughts drift back to when that husk breathed, laughed and argued. When it was occupied.

I watch the box which holds Murdo's body but which cannot contain his essence. He is not here. Here is a mere gathering of people; *we* are still here. We are what matters. We are the bereaved, the sentient beings who must cope with what is left. When an old man dies, what should one feel? That death is inevitable – that, after birth, it is the second great mystery of life. All Murdo's friends are in their final years. Later today when we bid 'farewell' to each other, our words may be more accurate than we realise. Murdo is gone. We shall soon follow him.

I have stood in churchyards and crematoria. At wartime funerals we sometimes had no corpse to bid farewell to – it had been blown to

41

smithereens, had been trampled into mud, was missing, or was drowned. I have heard these funeral words so many times, and they never bring comfort. Their message is sober and realistic: we have a short time to live and are sure to die.

My father died suddenly in 1935, a lifetime ago. How many people have lived out their lifetimes since my father died? How many have been born, have come to adulthood, have raised families – yes, *raised* them, their children reaching their own adulthood – and have expired into their own graves? All in that lifetime since Daddy died. 1935. Let me think: in that year I could have been but twenty-three. We lived in peacetime. War was a faint memory from my infancy. My father was strong, indestructible, embodying all the certainties of the adult world. When I sat in church for Daddy's funeral my mourning was obliterated by a sense of outrage: how *could* this happen? How could he disappear so suddenly, my truest friend? Today one reads endlessly of dysfunctional families, but my father was like a rock – a wonderfully competent, convivial man, proud of his daughters, his wife, his country; proud of his house; proud of so many things and yet – I do believe this – never self-proud. Confident, yes, assured, but never arrogant. My father had a form of quiet decent pride which has almost vanished now; a certainty, a grasp of who he was, of how to behave, of where he belonged. People knew these things instinctively when I was young. Nowadays they turn for advice to magazines, to self-help books and psychiatrists. They have lost a basic understanding and self-knowledge. Perhaps the war destroyed it.

Before the war Britain was comfortable with itself. There was a structure and we 'knew our place' in it. Far from constricting us, it gave solidity; it helped us understand who we were. Between the tiers of society were ladders and doorways, and with diligence or good luck one could use them to change one's place. Of course a pauper seldom became a lord (or a lord a pauper, come to that) but that was a strength of the system, not a weakness. No one born a pauper can exist comfortably as a lord – they can spend the money, of course, if one assumes that a lordship inevitably brings money – but they cannot throw off their upbringing and natural behaviour to move easily in what, for them, is an alien society. To move too far from one's roots is to become an alien, and to become an alien is not a thing to crave. So much contemporary unease and resentment stems from a sense of embittered bafflement: people no longer understand who they are, where they fit or – if they are genuinely unhappy with their lot – how to change it.

One can change one's place. Murdo, for example, came from an ordinary Scottish family, and Imre Goth was penniless (several times!) yet they used their talents to help them rise. Nowadays people feel they should rise by right. My own family, I admit, was fortunate. We were moderately wealthy, we wore good clothes – and Daddy gloried in us. He would carry Mother, Naomi and I off to Ascot or the seaside (Worthing and Deauville were his favourites). He taught us to ride, shoot and fence, and occasionally he would take Naomi and I with him to his beloved clubs – not to Whites or one of those dreadful men's clubs but to gay bohemian meeting places like the Bullfrog or the Chelsea Arts. He would flaunt us there.

Oh Daddy, I hope there is no Hereafter. Desolate as I was when you died so suddenly, wretched as I have been not to keep you at my side, I remain glad that your short life was filled with exuberance and gaiety. Everything in which you took such joy and pride – your wife, daughters and splendid country – have let you down. But if there has to be a Hereafter, if after death one retains contact with this world, I hope that *your* eternity remains fixed in the pleasant days of your prime. Why not? What kind of eternal life would it be to trudge through the dull downward slide of history, rather than revisit the familiar days one loved? Let eternity, if it does exist, be spent in our happiest times.

✳

Ticky wore a pair of net gloves because he thought they would keep his hands cool. They were women's gloves, but Ticky had small hands. Knowing they were women's gloves gave him a sexy feel when he pulled them on. They seemed strong and flexible at the same time, like women's underclothes. Wearing the gloves Ticky could understand why some men liked to wear female underwear beneath their own clothes: there was something illicit and sensual about their feel against his skin.

Not that Ticky was perverted. Perish the thought. He wore gloves when he was working, and had chosen net gloves because he would be working indoors. He was pleased he had had the foresight to buy them. Sometimes when he did a house job he wore plastic kitchen gloves – bright yellow or shocking pink. Plastic ones didn't look right and left his fingers smelling sourly of rubber afterwards, but they were flexible. He could work in them. When Gottfleisch sent him to the old lady's house Ticky realised that in the unseasonably warm weather, plastic gloves would make him sweat. He tended to sweat a lot at the best of times, but net gloves were naturally air-cooled.

Another joy about a lady's gloves was the buying of them. First he had tried Marks and Spencers but they didn't have any in stock.

Ticky had gone there because the shop was large and anonymous and no one would remember what he had bought. Also they wouldn't ask him why he wanted women's gloves. But when he found that they didn't stock them he thought what the hell? What did it matter if someone noticed him buying women's gloves? The cops weren't going to dust her house afterwards and find a glove print. They wouldn't come traipsing down Lewisham High Street asking in the shops.

So Ticky had used the opportunity to try Dorothy Perkins, New Look and Principles For Women. It was good to have a legitimate reason to go into shops crammed with slips and bras and panties and soft short dresses. Since net gloves were not a common line Ticky had to visit three shops before he found one that stocked them. Each time, he had wandered around the shop with a serious expression on his face, fingering the merchandise until a salesgirl reluctantly came up and asked pointedly if she could help. Ticky hadn't enjoyed shopping so much for ages.

Here in the old lady's cottage he was undisturbed. Though he was browsing through her merchandise, he had to remember this was not a shop. Downstairs, everything had seemed so motionless – her furniture, her ornaments, the pictures on the walls, even her potted plants. Everything was dead. It was as if, without the owner in the house, all life had gone.

Ticky was not particularly experienced at breaking and entering. Anything Gottfleisch asked him to do he would make a stab at, though the fat man was not to know that burglary wasn't his line. But it didn't matter: he wasn't in the house to burgle it. Check out the contents, Gottfleisch had said, see what is valuable. Ignore her furniture and jewellery, concentrate on paintings. Not that Ticky was a judge of art. He thought El Greco was a restaurant.

Having checked through all her rooms Ticky decided that the most valuable stuff would be her furniture – heavy and old fashioned as Gottfleisch liked it, but too big to shift easily. The old lady didn't have a video or any useful stuff like that, though she did have some nifty ornaments – including a porcelain figurine of a Twenties girl balanced on one foot, wearing a skinny bathing costume, which Ticky liked. The girl looked as if she were about to take a dive. One delicate leg was cocked out behind and the little muscle at the back of her shin looked so soft he just had to touch it. He held the model in one hand and ran his gloved finger along her boyish curves. In the silence of the house he was able to fondle her. It was a privilege. He felt quite warm. He noticed that a drop of sweat had oozed out through an air-hole in his net glove onto the porcelain. Better be careful, he thought: the police could run a DNA sample off that and trace it back to him. He'd read about it. He wiped the girl against his breast and returned it to the mantelpiece. Then he stared at it one more time and pursed his lips as if to blow a kiss. He went upstairs.

Gottfleisch had told him not to pinch anything but to concentrate on paintings. Well, she had plenty on the walls, though Ticky didn't know which Gottfleisch might be interested in. There had been a couple of biggish ones down in the lounge, some in the hall, four pretty water colours here in her bedroom, none to his taste. He ran his netted hand across the counterpane on the old lady's bed. Not a single bed, he noticed, she likes her comfort. Just the right size for a spot of rough and tumble – though at her age she must sleep alone. Ticky grinned ruefully and said, 'You and me both.'

He reached inside a deep pocket for his small camera. Christ knows which of these paintings were any good. He'd just snap everything she had.

✳

The truth is that I hardly remember wartime funerals. I must have been to some, but I suppose that in those more realistic days we looked on funerals as something to be got over. We didn't dwell on them. We didn't indulge in self-pity, we fought for life. Funerals were to stiffen one's resolve. Often, instead of funerals, we attended memorial services for fallen men – brothers, lovers, so many friends – whose broken bodies had not been returned. But since the war went on for six long years, there must have been conventional funerals – the normal crop of old people reaching their natural end. Strange that one does not remember them. Life went on, death went on, yet every bereavement from those times is remembered as if due to war. When a young man died one wept for him; when an old person died, one shrugged.

Another curious thing: I can think of almost no one I knew in London killed by a bomb. Certainly I shall never forget the blitz with its attendant firebombs and devastation – those sleepless nights when bombers destroyed Coventry, Plymouth, the City of London, our East End dockyards, the Kentish coast. But to name those shabby areas makes one realise that one would not have known the people who were living there. We were not dockers. We didn't live in the East End. We survived the blitz.

So long ago, perhaps I forget. Today one can drive through Plymouth, the City of London, the Kentish coast, and nothing remains of that world war. Bomb sites – even the phrase 'bomb sites' has a legendary ring – have been erased and replaced with shopping centres and sprawling housing estates. If I were to visit one of those developments built on blasted land I might be the only person old enough to recall the war. On squares of green where children play, the parents would be too young. They would have to be over fifty – no, to really remember the second world war, over sixty years of age. What an incredible thought. Only pensioners remember the war.

We were a different breed.

My friend Tilly died in the war. How suddenly she comes to mind. I may not have thought of her for ten years, yet once… I can see her now as clearly as if I had opened a box and discovered her photograph. After all these years. My friend Tilly laughed at the war: we're only young once, she'd say, please don't be dull. And then quite early, in '41, she was killed in an automobile accident at night, driving her Lagonda without lights. That was one of those silly regulations we all obeyed, to prevent Jerry from seeing us as he flew above. So we'd be safe.

There was my mother's funeral, of course, but I couldn't go to it. Even if I had gone, I imagine that now, over fifty years later, most of my memories would have drained away. One has forgotten so much. A few sharp images emerge from the blur, there are episodes one will not forget, but all the rest might be a dream. How extraordinary it is to be the product of one's life, the last pages in a book started so long ago.

I couldn't attend my mother's funeral because by then I was in America. Did I say? It was quite impossible to come back – the sea teeming with submarines, no tickets available. A perfect excuse. Before Mother died, you see, she had stopped speaking to me – was emphatic about not doing so. I remember her shouting, 'I will not speak to you', which I thought quite amusing. She once said (again, I imagine, when she was 'not speaking' to me) that I was 'the lowest of the low' – a phrase I considered vulgar. Perhaps she was furious because I had an American boyfriend – certainly she declared several times that the Americans were interested only in sex. She said that they would *pay* for it if necessary – indeed, they almost expected to – though naturally they preferred to find an English girl foolish enough to give it them for free. She asked whether I were foolish or had I turned professional? What surprised me most was not the diatribe (routine for her) but that she returned to it next time we met. She had invented the perfect justification for her hatred of me – yes, hatred, I'm afraid – spawned in childhood when she realised that I, and not her beloved Naomi, was Daddy's favourite girl. My American boyfriend was a trivial excuse that she could use to drive me away into his arms. Having dismissed me she could concentrate on Naomi, whom the world condemned.

46

Have I told you about my American? He was like a big American meal: he looked wonderful but was absolutely without taste. Where men are concerned I have always been a slow learner, and with Mitch it took a year.

*

Ticky leafed idly through the photographs, having a whale of a time. Her Chinese cabinet – lacquered black, with fine tracery in gold paint – had twenty drawers of varying sizes behind its doors. The drawers were small, some were tiny, and they contained assorted trinkets and mementoes from the old lady's past. When Ticky opened the double doors to expose the array of ebonised drawers he hoped he would find a treasure trove. Instead he found a collection of curious oddments – a lock of hair, some faded letters, enamelled boxes, a baby's tooth. In one of the first drawers was a small jumble of old fashioned jewellery, and Ticky had fingered the pieces, unable to decide which of them were valuable. Some looked as if they should be worth something, though they could be costume jewellery, worthless. They lay tangled in the drawer as if they had been scooped up and tossed carelessly into the first drawer which came to hand. Why did she keep these in the cabinet? Sentimental value, he decided, bits handed down.

Ticky had heard that ninety per cent of stolen jewellery was junk, unsaleable, but this stuff... He shrugged and put it back.

Her photographs intrigued him – not because they were valuable: they were only trash. She had a couple of dozen, that was all, different ages, little to do with each other as far as he could tell. The oldest were muddy sepia, as if they had once been black and white but had faded. Their corners curled.

In a family group stood a tall man in a rough tweed jacket, a woman buttoned to the neck, and two pretty children, sun in their eyes. Ticky rubbed his thumb across the surface to clear the image. The little girls – they *were* girls, though you couldn't always tell in some old photographs – were blonde, their sun-bleached hair cropped crudely into pageboys. They were sisters, he could tell. He liked children.

The second brown photo showed two young women in laughing close-up, caught out of doors. Blonde hair again. One with long hair, one with short. Presumably these were the same little children, now grown up, though their resemblance to those kids was hard to find. They resembled each other, that was for sure. They wore identical open-necked shirts, and one had her arm around the other's shoulders. Both were beautiful, he thought, though they'd looked sweeter when they were kids.

One of those young women was in a third shot – was it sepia, or was it a black and white discoloured with age? She was dressed in fencing gear and carried her sieve-like mask against her breast and a long thin sword pointing at the camera. She was laughing, and looked horribly healthy – not the kind of girl Ticky liked at all. Frightening.

The last sepia was an interior shot: a man at his desk caught unawares. Light streamed in through a window to give the portrait an unreal theatrical effect. The man was handsome, dark-haired and thoughtful as he worked.

These were her oldest photographs. Ticky decided that the kiddies on the lawn had become the two young women, and that the young man might have been their brother, or…

He looked around the bedroom. Nothing masculine. If there had been a husband who had died, even years before, there ought to have been something left behind. And wouldn't his photograph be out on view? Ticky skimmed through the other snaps in his hand. Some were black and white – from the Fifties, he would guess – some coloured, a larger size. The dark-haired man did not reappear. One or two other faces recurred: three shots included the same tall erect man – first in a black and white snap with short dark hair, then in two coloured shots with greyer, longer hair. He had kept his erect stance. To Ticky none of the coloured snaps seemed interesting – middle-aged, even elderly buffers in dull places he didn't recognise. Perhaps the women in these later photographs had been the young girls in sepia brown, but he couldn't recognise them. Come to that, he wouldn't recognise the old lady who owned the house. Thinking back to his earlier search, he could remember no photos around the place. The only ones he had come across were these in the Chinese cabinet in her bedroom. Perhaps she didn't like memories on constant view.

Photographs. Ticky was here to photograph her paintings. Before returning her snaps to the ebonised drawer Ticky glanced again at the oldest ones. Mum and Dad, presumably, standing beside the two little sisters. Then the two little girls grown up. Then the swordswoman. Then the only old photograph she had kept of a handsome young man.

*

My American boyfriend was the root of it. Till then, Mother and I jolted along uneasily but civilly. She had always preferred Naomi – I was not disturbed by that; Daddy favoured me. Most families divide one child to one parent, one to the other. Mother was just more extreme. Even as a child I knew that Naomi could do no wrong – her paintings were exalted, my music ignored. She was talented, I was dull. She was so pretty, I so plain.

Daddy would have none of it. He loved both his daughters, and although he had always praised Naomi's paintings, from the first daubs on the nursery wall to the elegant watercolours professionally framed, he also encouraged my music. I had a tutor at home, and when Mother complained at the incessant scales and practice pieces, Daddy drove me to lessons at the tutor's house. He arranged my voice training. He attended every one of my modest school concerts. Though I was his favourite he was always sweet to Naomi. She didn't mind – we joked about it – but I am convinced that this was what turned Mother against me. Perhaps she was jealous. Whatever the reason she clung to my sister, no matter what she did. Later, in those dreadful days when we became separated by war, only Naomi mattered to my mother. Even when she lost contact with Naomi, Mother never thawed to the sister who remained close at hand, the one who telephoned and visited at weekends.

There was only coolness and civility – and 'poor Naomi' all the time. 'How my poor darling child has suffered.' As if I hadn't suffered! In a way, I suppose, my presence pained her, as it had when Daddy was still alive. In those happier pre-war days she would see us easy together and it would remind her of what *she* no longer had with him. I imagine that when I was a child, Daddy's particularity to me was of no consequence, but when I became a young woman on Daddy's arm – laughing, swaying, my cropped blonde hair flashing in the air – I seemed a threat. Later, deep in the war, Naomi out of reach, the very sight of me reminded her that her most beloved daughter was no longer there. Naomi was suffering.

To my own troubles in '40 and '41 Mother seemed indifferent. She was angry, certainly, but whether at me or on my behalf was never clear. Angry about me, let us say. And after those troubles she treated me like a mildly irritating servant – one she would rather be without but who could not realistically be dismissed. Then I told her about Mitch.

'An American?'

We were standing in the garden. I remember roses – dusty red English roses, heavy with faded flowers.

'Yes, he's working here—'

'A GI? My God!'

'No, not a soldier.'

'What then?'

I wasn't sure. This was before the main influx of Americans in 1942.

'He can't tell me exactly what he does – you know, 'careless talk' etcetera. He wears civilian clothes. It's mysterious, I suppose – even romantic.'

'I see nothing romantic about an American in civilian clothes. I suppose he wears uniform on Sundays?'

'He has an office job in Berkeley Square.'

'Good grief.'

My mother turned to glare disapprovingly at a drooping flower. Berkeley Square housed the American Embassy.

She swooped on a rose and snapped the stem. 'I assume he is a diplomat?'

'Not exactly.'

'He is not exactly *anything*, it appears.'

'I find it sweet that he can't tell me. You know, it adds a *frisson*.'

'I suppose he pretends he's in Intelligence? I don't approve.'

'Of Intelligence or of Americans?'

'Neither.' She had found another wilting rose. 'Have you told him about your sister?'

I shook my head.

'Or Regulation 18B?'

'Of course not.'

'Hardly surprising.' She looked me in the eye. 'You haven't reached the stage, then, of exchanging confidences?' She snapped another stem. 'Does he ask you leading questions?'

'About Naomi or about me?'

'Either.'

'Neither.'

'Then I doubt he's in Intelligence.'

She had the glint of triumph in her eye, though that was the last time she showed any hint of humour in her attitude to Mitch. In the ensuing weeks she dropped acid questions unexpectedly, and I quickly clammed up. Mitch and I had become serious about each other.

'Gonna introduce me to your mother?' he asked one day.

'You'd hate it.'

'It? You call your mother 'it'?'

'The experience. You'd hate it.'

'I'd love it – English aristocracy.'

'Are you a snob, Mitch?'

He was lying naked on my bed, and my finger was tracing a soft arc from the small of his back down across his rear. He had white haunches like a girl.

'Why are Americans built so big?'

'We eat better.'

In this indifferent post-coital state he was irresistible. He lay on his belly, trimming his fingernails with a pearl-handled nailfile.

I snorted. 'Eat better? You eat nothing but Hershey bars.'

'You eat spam.'

'Made in America!'

'For export – to dumb clucks like you.'

He grinned proudly, as if he could see his reflection in the nailfile. The room was cold – rooms were always cold in those days. My only clothing was an old silk stole – grandmother's, left to me.

'You English. What'd you live on before we came?'

'Roast beef.'

He laughed and rolled onto his back. His huge unashamed nakedness excited me.

'You're gonna love America.'

I shrugged. He was staring at me. I said, 'Oh yeah?'

He closed his eyes. 'Say that again.'

'Say what?'

'Oh yeah. No one says it like an English girl.'

I frowned. As he lay waiting, his eyes closed, he continued, 'American girls say 'Oh yeah' two times a minute. Through their bubble gum.'

'Oh yeah?'

'But you give it hidden depths – you know, your accent?'

'I don't have an accent.'

'Sexy. You English girls.'

'How many do you know?'

He opened one eye to inspect me. 'What you wearing that wrap for?'

'You Americans have no concept of grammar. It's chilly.'

He chuckled. 'Chilly! What a word. I love ya – know that?'

'You love my accent.'

'That as well.' He reached up to my stole and slipped his hand inside. When he'd found my breast he asked, 'You coming with me?'

I hesitated. 'Where?'

'America.'

'Oh.'

He was staring at me again. 'We could get married or something.'

'What sort of something?' I asked, buying time.

'Unless you want to stay here, see the war out?'

I studied him. He continued, 'It's over anyway, bar the shouting. Uncle Sam's here now.'

I snorted. He lay complacent and well-fed on my sheets. He said, 'We're gonna pull you through.'

It seemed possible. Churchill had spent years trying to drag America in, and now, finally, London's West End thronged with Mitch's compatriots – gods among the stunted English. I asked, 'Are you going back then – to America?'

He glanced away. 'I'm finished here.'

'It's only just beginning.'

'No, this is the last act. It'll all be over by summer.'

I shook my head. 'No.'

'It's finished, believe me. Germany's washed up.'

'Oh *yeah*, Mitch? Then why not stay to see the end?'

'I'm through.' He narrowed his eyes. 'You didn't answer my question.'

I watched him. He stared back. 'Was that a proposal?' I asked.

'Well, since I'm leaving…' He grinned. 'We can't go on meeting like this.'

'*Was* it a proposal?'

'Hell, babe, you want me down on my knee, plumb naked and all?'

'It'd be nice to think you meant it.'

He tapped his nailfile on his teeth. 'Sounds a good idea to me.'

As I remember, the room fell absolutely silent. Perhaps there *were* noises from the street, but I doubt either of us noticed them. We were the only people in the world. Anything we said sounded underlined. Our words echoed from the walls.

I said flatly, 'You want me to marry you?'

Our isolation in the room had entrapped us into delivering lines like actors in a play.

'Yes, babe, I'm asking you.'

'Go on, then,' I whispered.

'Go on what?'

'Oh, for Goodness sake, ask me.'

He held my eyes. 'Will you marry me?'

'In America?'

'Or England, before we go home.'

This was uncharted territory. Had he been going to ask me all the time, or was he, like me, caught with a script he had to stay with till the end? I was fond of him but not in love, yet at that time in dreary England young people entwined their lives together with extraordinary casualness. Perhaps it wasn't the war; perhaps it's what young people always have done as they stumble into adult-hood. I look about me nowadays and see penniless young couples breaking the boredom of their lives with a succession of grubby babies and I wonder why, at the peak of their young lives, they determinedly seek out the snags and burdens of parent-hood and throw freedom away.

Why did I marry Mitch – did I feel I had to marry someone? Was it really the war, or did I feel, in my early thirties, that all the eligible men had disappeared? Mitch was handsome, certainly, and virile enough in bed. He made me laugh. He came ready-charged with that gust of fresh air and openness Americans have. Those American GIs must have found us so dowdy and constrained. We had lost the gaiety of the 1930s and our lives had become dull.

Mother and I had a particularly blazing row. She refused either to meet Mitch or to participate in any way in the meagre arrangements for our wedding. But of course, every word she spat only increased my determination to marry him. Could that have been her plan all the time? No, she couldn't have been that devious. Could she? – Mitch, of course, was baffled at her attitude. He had hoped for an old-fashioned wedding in a quaint little English church, a reception later in the manor house, the squire and rustics, elderberry wine – but instead we had a registry office in Marylebone, where it was marriage by the clock, fifteen minutes a time.

Our honeymoon was spent in a creaking grey cabin in the bowels of a troopship bound for New York. All I remember are the grey metal walls around our bunk, and the grey sea. I don't remember our fellow passengers, though there must have been other faintly guilty British escaping the war. But I do remember his family. His father's face is as vivid now as if he had just this moment left the room. He was of moderate height but broad, with iron hair as streaky as a decorator's brush. He and his wife disliked me. I disliked them. Mitch's father blamed me personally, not for seducing his precious son, but for dragging America into the war.

I recall various unconnected scenes in which I was paraded before relatives, neighbours and inquisitive bystanders. I felt like a peepshow, and knowing his parents, perhaps they were charging admission: come and see the English freak – she don't dress right and she talks real funny. Half the family were convinced that America should never have gotten into this foreign war – it was my fault or Roosevelt's, and I was closer.

Then Mother's letter arrived – I remember every word, because I still have it in my bedroom cabinet. I keep it to remind me just how awful she could be. I must have trembled when I read it, and from the look of it nowadays I must have screwed it up sometime, but I didn't throw it away. I didn't burn it. I kept it so that one day I could show Naomi, to help her understand. Mother wrote that she had disinherited me – or no, let me quote her words:

'... *by your actions you have disinherited* _yourself_. *You have*

53

broken from your family, and your descendants are consequently not mine. I have arranged that when I pass away – as mothers do, as you yourself shall do one day – my possessions shall pass to my one true daughter Naomi. My lamb has had obloquies heaped on her head and has been treated with such cruelty by the world...'

There are two whole pages of this dross, into which Mother compressed all the venom she had manufactured in the past few years. But by then I was immune to her vindictiveness. I was over thirty: to be finally rid of my wretched mother signified less than that I was now stuck in America. With Mitch and his appalling family.

I cannot remember whether it was before her letter or soon after when I realised that my marriage to Mitch was nothing more than a wartime foolishness. In the blackouts of wartime London he had glowed, but on his native American soil he faded into dullness. Back in London I had imbued his embassy role with romantic mystery – I imagined him as a plain clothes agent sent ahead to prepare the ground. But now in real-life Michigan I discovered he was just a clerk. Before America had entered the war his father saw the way the wind was blowing and found his son a protected job in a minor offshoot of the State Department – a job whose main attraction was that it exempted Mitch from active service. His father told me this quite proudly – he boasted of it – during the last meal I ate in their house.

'How clever to buy your son a bolt-hole,' I responded.

'What'cha getting at?'

Seated at the dining table with a napkin stuffed in his shirt, his father looked even broader than he did normally. I continued: 'For Mitch the pen proved mightier than the sword. Certainly safer.'

I would like to pretend there followed a moment of stunned silence – but in truth, silence is something that Americans know little about. In their houses there is always a background clatter, half-heard music, a conversation between other people in the room.

'Hey, you,' his father said, pointing a fork at me, 'you're a goddam guest in my house—'

I said, 'I didn't realise I'd married a draft dodger.'

His father spluttered. Mitch said, 'I make my contribution, you better believe it.'

'They also serve who only sit and wait?'

His father rose. 'Now listen, young lady—' He plucked his napkin from his collar and tossed it manfully aside. Mitch stood up too.

I quipped, 'Don't tell me you're about to fire your first shot in anger?'

His mother said, 'You should be grateful, you know, that

America sends her sons across the sea to die for you people. Your European war.'

I smiled pleasantly. 'Mitch's only risk is he might die of boredom.'

Mitch said, 'Just because I don't wear a uniform—'

But his father screamed, 'Didn't I tell you, son? You shoulda married a decent American girl!'

I suggested: 'You could have picked one out for him.'

'I damn well coulda done, you bitch!'

'Pa! Don't you speak to my wife that way!'

Isn't that what my husband said? Oh, I don't know, perhaps he did – I can't remember now. It's more than fifty years: I can't tell you what was said. If Mitch were here – and I hope he is still alive and well somewhere – he would relate this little episode quite differently. Perhaps he'd remember his lovely English bride, snappy with anxiety far from home. Perhaps he would remember how he justified his working in an office. Perhaps he would remember the way his loving parents tried to accommodate the wayward Sidonie. Perhaps he'd remember waking up to find her gone.

But the thing is, who will ever know about it? All right, according to Gottfleisch, it has to be one thing or the other: either you take nothing – absolutely nothing, except photographs – or you take all the decent stuff you can find. Which means, as Ticky reads it, that on this occasion he is not supposed to lift anything; it's not what he's there for. Which means, coming right down to it, that if he's rootling through a Chinese cabinet which has so many drawers she can't look right through it except once a year maybe in winter when it gets dark early and the evenings stretch forever and there's not a damn thing worth watching on telly, and if, while he is opening all these drawers and finding nothing of any value, except that in one of them, in just one out of… what is it?… twenty fiddly little drawers, he finds one poxy little ring, probably not even gold, tucked away among trinkets and broken bits of chain, and if out of all the bits of rubbish that lie mouldering in the drawers it's this piece, this one interesting ring, that he'd like to take away for a souvenir, well – what the hell is he supposed to do? She's gonna miss it? Come *on*!

Ticky slipped it in his pocket.

What he liked about this ring was that it had a little skull carved on it, a realistic white and detailed skull. The ring was large – on Ticky's finger it covered practically the whole strip between his knuckle and the joint. And while fiddling to slip it on, Ticky found that the protuberant skull top twisted off to reveal a space just big

55

enough for a couple of pills. Two poppers, maybe, or four E tablets, because they were pretty tiny. Or he could put a chloral in it, come in handy to knock someone out.

At the moment, though, the compartment beneath the skull was empty.

Once he was downstairs in the old lady's lounge Ticky pondered again about Gottfleisch saying that you should either take everything or leave well alone. Best to take it, was Ticky's theory. Saved breaking in again. But the fat man had said that all he wanted was some photographs. Of paintings! Well, there were plenty cluttering the walls.

Ticky stood in the middle of her sitting room, eyeing up what she had. There was a bizarre gaudy thing, looked like a kid's drawing cut up with scissors and put back together wrong – a piece of nonsense – in pride of place. Ticky walked over, reached up and unhooked it from the wall. The thing was heavy, awkward, though of course he was reaching above his head, so the thing was bound to feel heavy. He rested the collage on the settee. Maybe it was the glass front that made it so heavy. The thing itself would weigh nothing, but the glass and four inch deep wooden frame...

Ticky puffed out his waxen cheeks. When he glanced again at her other paintings he saw that most were protected by panes of glass. If he started humping them around, the damn things might break. Perhaps it was best to do as Gottfleisch had told him – leave them on the walls and photograph them there.

Ticky picked up the collage and carried it back to the wall. He fiddled with it, trying to catch the wire on its hook. It wouldn't go, of course. Damn painting. Holding that heavy frame above his head made his shoulders ache like hell. A drop of sweat trickled in his eye.

He returned the picture to the settee and moved a wooden chair against the wall. Then he hesitated: the chair was probably antique. Ticky looked underneath, then sat on it, pressing down upon the seat. Seemed strong enough. He didn't want to clamber up on some priceless antique and shove his foot through it, smashing both the precious chair and the old lady's picture. Mr Gottfleisch would not be pleased.

But the chair seemed sound.

This time, when Ticky stood on the chair and positioned the artwork against the wall he must have got the angle right, because the picture slipped into place first time. But he let go carefully. He'd been caught like that before. Before releasing fully, he gave a tug to ensure the thing really was hooked on. It seemed stable, he thought. Gingerly, he stepped down from the chair, keeping his eyes glued to the picture. It didn't move.

He moved the chair back where he had found it.

For several seconds more, Ticky stood watching the replaced collage. He had a nagging feeling that if he turned his back the thing would fall.

Why was Gottfleisch so interested in her paintings? He'd do better with the little things – the fancy ornaments, her bits of jewellery upstairs. You can shift the little things – there's a ready market, and they find a new home within a day. But paintings: the more valuable they are, the more difficult to shift. Take that oil painting over there: it must weigh a ton. And there won't be another like it, because paintings are unique. If a punter loses, say, Van Gogh's Sunglasses, every cop in the world will know exactly what to look for. Won't need a photograph.

Which reminded him. Reaching in his pocket for the camera, Ticky decided it wasn't for him to teach Gottfleisch his job. He began taking photographs.

After a few it occurred to Ticky that he ought to have drawn the curtains first. If anyone was passing by outside and saw the flash popping indoors, it would be a giveaway. Except that no one would be passing by. Not out here: the house was isolated in its garden; the village half a mile away.

When he'd finished in the sitting room, Ticky moved out into the hall. Another two or three out here. These seem hardly worth the bother – first, because they had been relegated to the hall and second, because they were only drawings, not proper paintings. Gottfleisch had said he wanted *paintings*, so wouldn't these be a waste of film?

Ticky chewed his lip. Well, all right, one of them, that one in the most prominent position was at least in a place he could take a closer look. It hung above a dark wooden chest, conveniently placed for him to use. Replacing the camera in his pocket, Ticky climbed on the wooden chest and lifted the chalk drawing from the wall. It came off easily. Quite light. For a drawing, Ticky thought, this one really had some style. It was red chalk – he could tell that; he hadn't worked for Gottfleisch all this time and not learnt a thing – and it was a head and torso of a girl. Ballet dancer, by the look of her, resting between acts. She had her eyes closed and looked vulnerable, caught in a rare moment while she relaxed.

Ticky swivelled the picture round so he could glance at the back. There was a little label there: Boots the Chemist: £17.50.

He snorted and shook his head: it had caught him there! For a moment, he had thought this one was valuable. But the damn thing wasn't even a proper drawing, just a print. A good one though: it looked real. Showed how much *he* knew.

57

He was about to replace it on its hook when he heard something outside: an approaching car. Definitely. On the gravel. Desperately, he scrabbled against the wall with the wretched picture but found that he couldn't engage the hook. He tried again, hastily, found the hook, got the string on it, let the picture carefully down. Felt the hook loosen. Felt it come out. Kept his grip on the picture as he heard the hook slither down between the picture and the wall. It disappeared.

Ticky cursed. He jumped down from the chest, then dithered with the picture in his hands. He heard a car door slam. It was at the front of the house. He himself had come in the back.

SIX

'*Dear Mitch,*' I wrote. '*It has not worked out. For me in England you shone like a beacon; you were like Old Liberty in New York Bay.*' (I was determined, you see, to be nice to him.) '*Here in America, I don't shine out – I am resented. Your family feels my country dragged yours in to war, and that I dragged you into a hasty marriage. They may be right.*' (Again, you see, I laid no blame on him.) '*What should we do? We can drag our marriage through endless skirmishes or we can treat for peace. But no negotiations, Mitch – no conferences. The way to end this conflict is to stop and turn away. That's what I've done. Into my valise I have packed each of the few possessions I brought with me, leaving nothing to remind you of me except this note.*' (A kitsch touch perhaps, but quintessentially British, don't you think? And I'd no intention of leaving him anything else.) '*So, good-bye Mitch. Don't feel you must do the manly thing and try to follow me – it's over. Find another girl: that Myra you introduced me to – twice – she should be all right. Myra or not, it won't be difficult for you: you're tall and handsome, and all of the eligible men have gone to fight.*'

I even signed it with my love.

Leaving Mitch must have come easily – because I barely remember doing it. What I do recall more clearly, a series of images from a film, is the gloriously liberating adventure of being footloose in America, carrying only my good looks and a valise. – And my accent, of course, which brought me work. The narrow, crabbed anti-British prejudice of Mitch's family was by no means universal – I had been unlucky. Many employers leapt at the chance to rent my British accent. For several months I wandered, leaving no forwarding address. Although it was unlikely that Mitch would look for me, I didn't want to leave a trail.

Nor would I let him divorce me while the war was on. I needed a ration book and an extraordinary number of bureaucratic documents. Why America felt the need for rationing I cannot imagine, but

59

they imposed a labyrinthine one, a paper system of Dickensian complexity, with red stamps, brown ones, green and blue – each worth a different number of points. Like all complex systems it didn't work. Though counterfeit stamps were sold freely, genuine shortages came frequently and inexplicably. A town would suddenly run out of sugar for a week. Then there'd be no steak. (Whalemeat was promoted as being 'as good as beef'. In America!) One week there was even a dearth of lavatory paper. Cigarettes were often scarce. From time to time drink vanished as if Prohibition had returned. It seems unbelievable now – but perhaps America the Land of Plenty is a post-war phenomenon. The generation I knew – the one that lived through the war – had known the Hungry Thirties.

I therefore viewed war from afar. America seemed so far away; from there the European and Pacific battlefields were in another galaxy. I had been in London while bombs rained down, I had attended funerals of dear, dear friends. Yet to be in America, cut off from both the immediacy and threat of death, was worse: when I heard reports of death, they were of dead Americans. I wanted to hear – not of death, please not of death – but of the young men I had danced with, touched, held in my arms. What of them? There was no one to tell me of those I knew.

In those distant wartime days one could not leap onto an aeroplane and fly home. Sea passages were almost impossible. One couldn't even telephone. There might have been an opportunity for me to return when Mother died, but I didn't hear of it until after the funeral, and in any case, I should not have gone. By then I knew that Mother had disinherited me. I could not have stood through the eulogies at her graveside. So she died alone: Father was already dead; Naomi and I could not be there.

Not until VE Day in '45 did I finally try to buy a boat ticket home. At the time I was lightly involved with a Californian boy called Jefferson (ten years younger than me – such bliss!) who had had one foot blown off in Italy and been sent home. He did his best to hide his gloom that day. Japan had not yet surrendered, and America was still very much at war. We tried to enjoy a bottle of Californian champagne.

'Stay here,' he said. 'You've nothing to go back to.'

'Only my friends, my country.' (Yes, the words sounded pretentious, even to me.)

'Don't go.'

'I have to.'

He gazed across the surface of his wine, on through the window into evening light. 'England won't be as you remember it.'

I shrugged lightly. 'Nowhere ever is.'

He banged his glass down sharply on the table. 'I've *been* there, I've seen it. The place has been bombed flat.'

'That was Italy. I'm from London – a different part of Europe.'

'Mud and orphans. Wrecked buildings. Broken towns.'

I reached out to touch his hand. So young he was. He muttered, 'Everywhere's a mess.'

'But I must go back.'

'It'll break your heart.'

Your heart, I noticed – meaning: you'll go alone. Of course, his memories were of the battlefield where he'd been maimed, in Italy. My England would be unchanged. By that time, after two years away, I dreamt like any émigré of green and rolling hills, quiet sheltered lanes. Though I did also remember the London I had left: shattered buildings, crumbling stonework, stark gaps in many streets.

But I couldn't get a ticket. I queued five hours and then gave up. That day it seemed that every European in America was trying to book a passage home. There was chaos at the dockside and in the shipping offices. There was no hope of an international telephone call.

Jefferson, maimed foot and all, queued with me, watching Europeans scramble to get away. 'My brother's in the Philippines, defending Australia, someplace like that.'

'Oh, the Japanese will soon stop.'

'They won't.'

I remember the bleakness in his eyes. 'Your European war was civilised – I mean, they're civilised countries, right? It was a European civil war. But those Japs... Christ, I don't know what we have to do to make them stop.'

Two or three weeks later, when the war with Japan was far from done, we were driving across the huge empty continent of America to visit Jefferson's family in California. I was driving. Jefferson could drive short distances, but his prosthetic foot wasn't up to the thousand mile coast to coast run. He was reminiscing about his brother, their schooldays, the girls they'd known, long Californian days in sunshine – when he mentioned a Japanese boy from their school

'Saiichi was a Jap to look at, but he was American too, you know?'

'Were you friends?'

He grunted. On both sides of the Atlantic I'd met numerous people with a paradoxical attitude to their so-called enemy. In '39 and '40, many British thought it absurd that it was the Germans who were our enemy – we had more in common with them than with the French. So I was curious about this Japanese school friend of Jefferson's: 'What happened to him?'

61

'The hell do I know – think I kept in touch?'

I stared at the road ahead. 'In Britain we interned our aliens.'

He nodded. 'We did that too. What the hell else you supposed to do?'

I drove on for a while, before saying: 'I knew one or two of the Germans that we interned. They were among the most patriotic people I knew.'

'Sure. But to which country?'

'Britain. They'd fled from Germany.'

Jefferson wasn't comfortable with this subject but I pressed him: 'And Saiichi?'

'Christ knows. He didn't have to flee from someplace. He's lived here all his life.'

'You still interned him.'

Jefferson turned on me. 'Not me, lady.' He shrugged. 'It's what we had to do.'

'Just obeying orders?'

'Ah, nuts.'

But I could see the memory troubled him. And somewhere in that long cross-continental journey – our minds numbed, our eyes hardened from staring through the screen – an idea germinated, grew and flourished until it seemed perfectly rational. I thought it would help Jefferson come to terms with his confused feelings about the Japanese – his brother fighting them in the Philippines, his school friend Saiichi interned. Tired, stubborn (you know me, my dear, I can be stubborn), my mouth sticky and dry, I declared that I would meet Jefferson's family only if he would try to re-establish contact with Saiichi. He didn't argue with me for long. Perhaps he also thought it might turn out a good idea. Or perhaps he thought it would be impossible to find the boy – five years had then gone by. As we drove into Monterey I repeated my condition: he was to meet his parents alone, and he was to ask them where Saiichi was. Simple as that.

I hardly remember his parents at all. They were pleasant, welcoming – not at all like the grotesques in Mitch's family. And like Jefferson himself, they were worried about his brother in the Philippines. To me, the war already seemed even less real than before: thousands of miles away across endless sweeps of blue ocean.

In Monterey, on the far coast of America, I seemed as far from England as I could be. European news slipped down the headlines. Instead we had Iwo Jima, Okinawa and Saipan. There had been an air raid on Tokyo, which we all cheered as belated revenge for Pearl Harbor. (As I learnt much later, more Japanese civilians were killed in that single, pre-atom bomb night than were lost in all the air raids on Britain throughout the war.) For America, Europe was no longer the focus of their thoughts: they heard on the radio that European borders were being redrawn, that victorious armies were swilling around without a role, that there had been atrocities in something called concentration camps. But these stories fought for space behind communiqués from Eisenhower and MacArthur – ranking significantly lower than seasonal forecasts for the Californian harvest.

I remember Saiichi as a pale, exquisitely willowy young man. We met in what I at first took to be an upland farming village, largely populated with Japanese. Only afterwards did Jefferson tell me that it had been an internment camp, though the people seemed no longer under restraint. It was a drab and dusty village, like a prison without walls. Later I learnt that the village had been constructed by the Japanese themselves; that after Pearl Harbor a quarter of a million Japanese Americans (Japanese! Most had lived in America all their lives) had been uprooted from homes on the western seaboard and herded into internment camps inland. Most were eventually released, in 1944, though by then many no longer had homes to return to, their American neighbours having done their patriotic duty by ransacking them. Other families, apparently more fortunate, had returned to reasonably intact houses but had found themselves ostracised. They were the enemy and could not be tolerated, though as Japanese Americans they had no homeland to return to. They were already there.

Saiichi was waiting for us at the door to a concrete bungalow. As we approached, he stepped down the path to greet us with a smile more of gratitude than welcome. He was a beautiful boy, slim and erect, his head cocked slightly to one side and unmistakably Japanese. I remember the near-silence of the village, which lent an almost clandestine air to our meeting.

But when he spoke, he was as American as a college boy. It was Jefferson's words that surprised me: '*Okawri Gozaimazen ka.*' He said the words awkwardly, as if he'd rehearsed.

Saiichi smiled and bowed his head. Peeping sadly from beneath dark eyelashes he said, 'Oh, I'm afraid so.' He looked so sweet, my dear, I shivered. I could have fraternised with the enemy there and then.

As Jefferson introduced us, Saiichi took my hand and smiled delicately in my face: 'I've never met an English girl.'

Girl, he'd said, not woman – clever boy. I smiled. 'Let me be your first.'

When I squeezed his hand his dark eyelashes quivered. Jefferson hadn't noticed. 'Hey, Saiichi, it's great to see you. Gonna invite us in?'

But Saiichi led us instead to his back yard. There was a single orange tree, and we sat in its shade. As the two men sat and beamed at each other I said, 'Jefferson, you didn't tell me you spoke Japanese.'

'That was just a greeting; about all I know.'

I glanced at Saiichi. 'What does it mean – good morning?'

He gave a wry smile. 'It's the usual greeting among Japanese.'

'But what does it mean?'

'It means, I trust there has been no change since last we met – but I'm afraid there *has* been, Jeff.'

'Oh, hell.'

'But it's good of you to come. Really it is. Both of you.'

He was so beautiful. I think I spent the whole afternoon giving him the sort of smile that I hoped would tempt even a kamikaze pilot out of a nose-dive.

'Japanese people don't like change,' Saiichi said. 'We like time-lessness… certainty… everything in its proper place.'

'You seem more American than Japanese. – I hope you don't mind my saying that?'

'No, I *am* American. But Americans think I am Japanese!' He shrugged. 'It's difficult.'

From the back door of the bungalow appeared a teenage girl with a tray of drinks. As she lowered the tray she gave us a shy smile, but instead of introducing us Saiichi asked a quick question in Japanese. She shook her head and scurried away.

'A pretty girl,' I said.

'You think so? I am glad.'

I hated her. Saiichi smiled at me, and Jefferson frowned. Saiichi said, 'It's only orange juice – but fresh.'

Jefferson said, 'That girl—' He stared after her.

The door opened again and she reappeared with a blue china bowl of cookies. As she drew nearer, Jefferson exclaimed, 'Hitomi? For Chrissake!'

She smiled. 'How are you, Jeff?'

He started standing up. 'Hitomi! Christ, you've grown.'

Her smile showed every one of her exquisite teeth, and as Jefferson stumbled round the table to greet her I felt no jealousy at all. Saiichi said, 'My sister.'

She was not his wife. I watched benignly while an embarrassed Jefferson hugged the delightful slip of a girl. Then she said, 'Jefferson, have you hurt your foot?'

✳

I imagine that throughout the rest of Jefferson's life a casual mention of his limp brought back the war. It wasn't immediately obvious his foot was missing, that beneath his trouser leg and sock lay perforated metal, leather straps tied round his calf, the scars of war.

Hitomi trotted back to the house – not because she was embarrassed at what she'd said, but because she was only Saiichi's sister, and dwelt indoors. Jefferson, unsurprisingly, tried to have her stay but Saiichi would not call her back. He understood, he said, that this behaviour might seem typically Japanese, and indeed, had his family not spent the past five years in an almost exclusively Japanese environment, he and his sister might have grown into typically American adults – but they hadn't. Jefferson seemed uncomfortable and tried to change the subject but Saiichi was intrigued that our visit had brought out this difference. It had not occurred to him. To a Japanese girl, he said, subservience and deference were essential virtues. It was the masculine role to command. 'Perhaps I am not so American after all – though I'm not Japanese either. So what am I?'

The tiny incident cast a sombre shade to the afternoon. It had revealed topics we couldn't talk about – Jefferson's foot, Hitomi's absence – but it did lead us to address the great unmentionable: the war. According to Saiichi, the Japanese had previously regarded Britain and America as 'male' countries; Japan might not have liked us, but we were due respect. But in the years leading up to war, both Britain and America ceased to deserve that due respect, because they reverted to 'feminine' tactics of cajoling and negotiating, making threats they would not carry out. Saiichi, sipping orange juice in his back yard, tried to explain something of Japanese psychology. The Japanese were obsessed, he said, with order and control, which they expressed in everything from the rigid pruning of a bonsai tree and the regimentation of children's upbringing through to their need to resist any change forced from outside. But Saiichi found he was talking to himself; we had heard enough of war.

As the afternoon sun sank in the sky I realised it was time for me to leave Jefferson. He had done nothing wrong. I certainly did not dislike him. It was simply time for me to move on. He and I kept in touch for several years, exchanging Christmas cards, and although my story would be neater if I could say that after a couple of years he settled down and married Hitomi, I'm afraid he didn't. He took a job in a local bank, and married a nurse who hailed from Oakland.

*

And I never slept with Saiichi. In reality, neither of those outcomes was very likely: after the A-bombs on Nagasaki and Hiroshima, how could that gentle girl have married Jefferson? With those bombs Jefferson's countrymen had obliterated six hundred thousand Japanese civilians.

How could she have lain beneath such a man in bed?

We parted amicably and I worked, oh, another year and a half in the States. It became less easy to get employment – hundreds of thousands of muscular young ex-servicemen, thoroughly if inappropriately trained, were flooding back onto the job market with their invigorating can-do attitude. And did American women return to the kitchen sink? No sir. They'd found a footing in the workplace and would not readily give it up. – What a contrast to meek little England. American women had finer houses – never bombed, not even scarred – yet they wanted to spend their days outside them; British women huddled in their damaged tenements and repaired old clothes.

Yet in that jostling American crowd I had one advantage – my English accent. The jobs it found me may not have been ones my family would have approved of, but they paid in dollars every week. I was fortunate. I wasn't tied to America, of course – I could go home. But to what?

Mother was dead. She had died alone, both her daughters overseas. By that time she was no longer in contact with me, and it came as no surprise – some small disappointment, naturally – to learn that she had indeed cut me from her will. Not entirely, I should point out. Somebody had advised her that if she cut me out entirely I might have grounds to contest the will. (She must have paid for this advice, otherwise she would never have listened to it.) She left me the derisorily precise pittance of four hundred pounds (admittedly nearly a year's salary in those days). The rest of her money and estate, apart from a few ridiculously idiosyncratic charitable bequests, was left to Naomi, her favourite, golden child.

But Naomi and I did not share our mother's bile. When the legacy became known, Naomi wrote to me, care of Mitch. Her letter was returned but she made contact after several months via Neville, a mutual friend. When I finally received her letter, I wrote back that she shouldn't think I blamed her: the terms of the will were entirely Mother's doing, no more than could be expected. Naomi wrote again in 1946, from an address in Switzerland. We slowly re-established contact.

*

Zug, Zugersee, Switzerland

Sidonie darling,
Muv's legacy must definitely be <u>annulled</u> – I assume that is the term?
It was conceived in spite (as I hope you and I were not!) and it can be
<u>ignored</u> – not legally, of course, but in practice, between we two.
Graylands is our family home, and given that the place originally

belonged to Farve and that Muv simply _moved in_ with him on marriage, she ought to have understood that, if anything, she has less claim on it than you or me! (Especially you, darling, since you were always Farve's favourite.) But you know Muv!

Anyway, Sidi darling, we all know the house is supposed to pass down through the Keene generations, and although Muv might have thought that by leaving it to me she was honouring that tradition, what would I want with a large empty house? Come to that, darling, what would _either_ of us want with it? As things stand, we are neither of us exactly desperate to fill the place up with a brood of children (I hope that is not a sensitive point) and in my opinion, darling, a large draughty six-bedroomed house (counting the servants' boxy little rooms, which I suppose we can do now people are supposed not to have servants any more) is more of a _burden_ than an inheritance. So what should we do, darling – move in together like maiden aunts or sell? A blunt question, but it must be faced. All the money's wrapped up in Graylands, and selling it would raise quite a packet. I don't know about you, but I need _money_ more than bricks and grass. We had better talk about it, face to face, darling – because it _is_ a joint decision.

Thank Goodness we don't have a brother!! He'd have inherited the place and felt duty bound to fill it up with all his wretched little Keenelets. But as women, you and I can't keep Graylands in the _family_ name, whatever we do.

Where can I find you in America? You seem to roam about like a buffalo – no, strike that out: a _bad_ analogy!! Anyway, I have your Poste Restrainte address but where are you actually _living_ – in California still? Oh Sidi, won't it be wonderful to meet again? And the journey out there, I must say, really _appeals_ to me. Perhaps I'll fly! I can't imagine it – 4,000 miles, is it? I _think_ my passport will let me into America – it _is_ still valid and has a year to run. After that, of course, when it expires… Ah well, I suppose I'll have to become a Swiss! Ha! Isn't that a hoot? Can you imagine me as Heidi?

Talking of flying, darling, I don't want to _influence_ you in any way before we've talked face to face, but money raised by selling Graylands – or any sort of cash!! – would be awfully useful!

Perhaps over there in the land of greenbacks your money worries have ceased? I hope so. Here in Europe – even in safe old sheltered Switzerland – we seem dreadfully poor. Well, _I_ am, certainly! I quite envy you.

Do write back soon.

Your loving Naomi.

✳

My dear Naomi,

I love your letters; they always bring a smile. You envy me, you say, in the land of greenbacks. I am writing this from a small unheated room in a cheap brownstone hotel. I have learned to <u>darn</u> my clothes! Had America ever suffered the Blitz, then I imagine that this outdated tenement would have crumbled into dust and rubble at the first blast. No one would have mourned it. You say <u>you</u> feel poor in Switzerland? You should try Chicago. At present, (or presently, as they say here) I earn a precarious living as a glorified receptionist for a firm of highway engineers – navvies to you and me. The job should last a few more weeks.

You and I are too far apart, peering at each other from opposite sides of the Atlantic, trying to make out each other's shape. We build fantastical images from the merest speck.

It's the same with Graylands. Neither of us has seen the house for several years, and our memories of it have faded, as must our attachment to it. Yet, as you yourself say, it's our family home. To make any decision about its future without <u>being</u> there, without sensing again whatever ancestral power the house still holds, would be, I suspect, unforgivable – in that if we did sell (well, if <u>you</u> did, Naomi, for the right to sell the place is yours) then in our later years, who knows? We might bitterly regret that we had thrown away our past.

So let's meet at Graylands. I can be there in less time than it will take this letter to reach you. Nothing holds me here. As soon as you receive this note, dear, write me with a date when we can be together again.

Your loving sister,
Sidonie.

✳

I have our letters still, in my Chinese cabinet. Sundry scraps of faded writing paper. Miscellaneous fragments arbitrarily kept from an erratic correspondence. Why does one keep these defunct messages? Letters then were the commonplace communication; nowadays people post electronically, leaving no traces in the ether. Our missives were more tangible: the travel-worn envelope with its coloured stamp, perhaps from an exotic spot; the personally chosen writing paper, perhaps scented; the handwriting; a photograph or two. Some letters tied with blue. Most, of course, were discarded almost straight

68

away, but a few were hoarded in the expectation that they might one day carry a lasting sentimental value. Others were put aside to be thrown away but for some reason were scooped up and dropped into a drawer or cardboard box half full of buttons.

In an old bone-dry paper bag from Montgomery Ward I keep these few American letters, together with a BOAC ticket, an unused suitcase label and an expired passport, kept separate for some reason from my other American mementoes. I have Naomi's reply – a long, rambling and not entirely sober epistle – in which she draws an unsuccessful parallel between war-wrecked Europe and the relics of our broken family. Her words seem saturated with guilt and self mortification, as if written at dead of night. Perhaps she couldn't sleep. Part of the letter has been lost. Perhaps I threw it away because I found it painful.

To give a flavour of what remains:

...Yet since Farve died you have started blaming Muv for every-
thing. I know the silly old dear was unreasonable, darling. I know
she was partial. I know she could sometimes be a little spiteful. But
wasn't her fuss nothing more than the cluck cluck clucking of an
anxious mother hen – can't you see that? You are very like her. You
are. You always were. She would hiss and you'd spit back. You were
like circling scorpions – weren't both of you born under Scorpio?
God, that explains it. Don't you see? Won't you try? Both of you
were consumed with pride and... oh, what's the word? Complexity.
(That isn't the word but it'll do.) Farve, of course, was so gloriously
uncomplicated; anyone could see immediately where they stood with
him. His thoughts, his emotions, his feelings were written all over his
simple open face. He was easy to love – but so easy that it took little
effort to do so – while Muv was harder to love, more challenging. She
was classical Greek drama to his modern Hollywood. We must talk
about it, darling, I'll explain. I know I can convince you – but not at
Graylands, darling, not in England You know I absolutely cannot
come home.

Then follows a coy paragraph or two where she seems to mince her words, as if afraid someone else might read the letter, in which she reminds me of '*certain constraints*' put upon her for '*the reasons that you know*' which are due to '*mistakes, as others find them, that might lead to horrifying consequences*'. From that point to the end of her scrawled and blotchy letter the tone becomes quite embarrassing – and twee, like one from a Victorian grandmother – until eventually Naomi implores me once again to send her my American address, so she can come to me. Or could I not visit her in Switzerland?

✳

Poste Restrainte, Chicago

Dear Naomi,
Just the briefest line in haste. My job has folded, the rent is due, and
I'm about to leave for England! I shall arrive at Graylands on the
11th. Looking forward to seeing you there a.s.a.p. after that date.
Come quickly. Much love. Must fly! (joke)
  Your Sidonie.

✳

Though we were both nervous about returning home, for different reasons, there really was no choice. By that time Graylands was being looked after by a visiting housekeeper that neither of us had met and, for all we knew, the place had become a fully functioning boarding house. Yet when I finally did see the house again it looked so cold, desolate and forlorn. Can a house <u>know</u> when those who love it have gone away? No, that's foolish – an old lady rambling; the kind of thing Naomi would have said. The house had not been lived in, that was all.

The taxi dropped me and drove away, and I stood outside awhile in the dark mid-evening, reabsorbing the night-scented air. The cold breeze seemed familiar on my cheek. The house stood silently waiting. It was dark, unlived-in. Around me in the gloomy garden the trees and shrubberies seemed dank and overgrown. When I unlocked the door and stepped inside, the hall was cold. It smelt damp. I left my valise and prowled around the once familiar rooms before going upstairs to my old bedroom, chill and unwelcoming, where I dashed off a note for the morning's post.

✳

Graylands (Hooray!)
Come on, Naomi, everything is fine. I'm ensconced at home and
cannot wait to see you. You'll find that England is as cold, narrow-
minded and hidebound as ever, but that doesn't matter now: the war
is over. It is safe again. There's nothing to worry about any more.
Isn't that wonderful? Come over right away.
  Your loving Sidonie.

SEVEN

As she stooped closer to fit the key in the lock the old lady realised that the afternoon sun was fading. There was a cloud across the sun.

The door swung inwards into the hall. As she placed her gloves on the side table, Sidonie glanced past the flight of stairs toward the end wall. There was a bare space. On the chest below, the picture that should have hung there lay face up as if it had been placed. She was moving toward it when she heard a door close. She hesitated, then turned back to march smartly through the sitting room into the kitchen. The back door was shut. But above the handle a small pane of glass had been smashed, and shards of glass lay scattered on the floor.

Sidonie strode to the door, opened it and stepped outside. Nothing. Was that a footstep? Gliding across the path onto the soft grass she walked swiftly to the corner of the house. At the side of the house the path was gravelled. She paused a moment, watching and listening. Perhaps she should continue to the front.

She glanced behind her to the open back door. To go along the side of the house to the front would leave that kitchen door unguarded. It wasn't wise. She paused again, still listening, but the only sound now was a slight stirring as the cool breeze moved in the leaves, a first suggestion of the evening chill. Sidonie waited, undecided.

As she returned thoughtfully to the kitchen door she realised that any intruder might have run the other way – that he might even now be at the far side of the house. She could not go inside without making sure.

Keeping to the grass, she crossed to the far corner and looked along that more cluttered side of the house. Her view to the front corner was obstructed by buttressed chimneys and the lean-to log store beside the path. Plenty of places someone could hide.

'Here, Janos,' she called. 'Good boy, good dog!'

Nothing moved. She clapped her hands. Slowly she walked back to the kitchen door and called, 'Janos! Janos! Come and get your bones.'

She was watching the garden for any movement in the shrubbery. She knew the dog would not appear – it had been dead more than three years. But as she entered the kitchen she exclaimed for anyone who might hear, 'Good *dog*, Janos! Where have you been?'

She closed the door, glancing irritably at the broken pane, then she turned the key and slipped it in her pocket. Perhaps, earlier, she had forgotten to lock the door – perhaps the wind had slammed it, shattering the glass. It did not seem likely.

Fingers of dread plucked at her ribcage, and she forced herself to leave the kitchen before the fear froze her to the floor. In the sitting room she saw nothing out of place. She re-entered the hall.

The red chalk drawing lay on the chest, below the blank space where she had hung it a few days before. Its hook had gone. Sidonie touched the hole where the hook had been and found it enlarged, as if the hook might have worked free. On the wallpaper was a faint trickle of dry plaster. Perhaps the hook had been loose, and a sudden draught had come in from the open back door…

'Don't clutch at straws.'

The sound of her own voice made Sidonie realise that it was still possible she was not alone. She felt a sudden tightness in her breath.

But she mustn't allow herself to panic. She must make her leaden legs respond. She backed along the narrow hall to the foot of the stairs and in a more querulous voice than before called, 'Come on, Janos – help me look upstairs.'

As she mounted the stairs it seemed to Sidonie that their rake had become steeper. On the top landing, things looked the same. Outside the door to the rear bedroom Sidonie scolded herself: she had not brought her stick – or a kitchen knife – or any kind of weapon. She twisted the handle and pushed the door.

The spare bedroom had a lifeless air. Against the opposite wall stood a neatly made bed, its white counterpane unruffled. The very stillness of the room suggested that the room had not been entered for several days.

Across the landing was Sidonie's office. It was another bedroom, long since converted, and its few papers seemed to be in the same familiar disorder that she had left. If a thief had come in here and disturbed anything the whole pattern would have shifted. Though he would have seen at a glance that there was nothing here to steal.

Which left her bedroom.

She was about to open that final door when her eye was caught by a small mezzotint on the wall. It hung slightly crooked, as if someone might have brushed against it or lifted it from its hook and then rehung it. The print was unlike most in her collection – older,

72

Victorian, quite sentimental: a child in a night-gown, peeping from a window, an Arthur Hughes, drawn but never used for *The Princess and the Goblin*. Had someone touched it?

She straightened the picture before opening her bedroom door.

Something was wrong, she could tell immediately. At the side of her bed the damask counterpane was rumpled. There was a slight depression where someone had sat. She glanced around the room – very calmly, she thought, in the circumstances – but no one was there. Then, to soothe that one remaining irrational doubt, she went to the double-fronted wardrobe and opened it. Only her clothes. On the rail her dresses swung gently, and then stopped. Sidonie turned, glancing again at the rumpled counterpane, before she noticed the door to the Chinese cabinet. It was not quite closed. The gilt catch had always been weak and temperamental, and to engage it properly one had to fiddle with the latch.

There had been an intruder in her room.

'Wretched hell.'

A wave of exasperation swept fear aside. While she had been absent at the funeral an opportunist had broken in.

'How very brave.'

She opened the lacquered doors and glanced at the little drawers inside. She chose one at random and stared dully at the contents. Twenty-four drawers. Oh God. She sighed.

Sidonie pushed it back in place. When she went briskly to the phone downstairs she left the cabinet doors open, the black interior gaping at the room.

'I'd like to report a burglary.'

✳

While waiting for the police to come she sat on the stairs beside the phone, a shrunken old lady in outdoor clothes. The police might not arrive for hours. When they did, they would ask placatory questions but, from what she had gathered from the newspapers, they would not really expect to solve the crime. Especially if nothing appeared to have been stolen. They might dust the house for fingerprints. Presumably she would have to clean off the dust herself.

Pointless as such an exercise would be, it meant that for the present she need make no effort to tidy up. She could leave the broken glass on the kitchen floor. She could postpone the tedious checking of every cupboard and drawer. Later she would have to sort carefully through her possessions to determine what might have disappeared. The police would want a list.

God knows what they did with all these lists. One could not seriously imagine the police matching all those pathetic inventories against their occasional haul. Perhaps they entered them in a huge computer – not so much to aid the matching process as to provide statistics and 'incident analyses'. How many clerks, she wondered, sat all day at shiny desks entering figures – categorising crime instead of fighting it?

She stood up, stretched, and heard her joints creak. It seemed quite possible nothing was missing. Perhaps she had arrived home in time. Perhaps the sound of the car delivering an eighty-five year old lady had frightened the burly intruder away.

Along the hall on the Jacobean chest lay the red chalk drawing. The burglar must have lifted it down – he might have been about to slip it in his sack at the very moment he heard the car. Or he might have seen the little Boots sticker on the back. That was Murdo's idea. He had given her a number of those stickers to affix to pictures which were not obviously originals. Amateur burglars, Murdo said, wouldn't recognise an original unless the paint was wet. On water-colours and on anything behind glass the price stickers were particularly effective, though on oils or on Unity's collage they'd fool no one. Sidonie smiled at the memory. It seemed particularly apt that on the day of Murdo's funeral his little trick might have protected the drawing she had once given him, the red chalk portrait of her drawn by Imre Goth.

Murdo and Imre never met. Murdo was one of the bohemian crowd that I hung out with in the Fifties, while I knew Imre in the Thirties. Imre was almost a true Bohemian, having lived penniless in Czechoslovakia after having been exiled from Hungary. (You do know that Czechoslovakia was created from three countries, not two – the third of them being Bohemia? Even now, after the country has split apart again, little Bohemia remains a ghost. But for how long?) Imre was goodness knows what by birth – Hungarian, he claimed – an émigré certainly, without family or fortune. In our smart Thirties set, he ought to have been refused acceptance, except that his Hungarian languor and sophistication, his talent, and of course his enormous fund of continentally risqué stories brought him rights of membership. *Most* rights: though he reached the very fulcrum of café society he was far less often in people's homes. Not that foreigners were unwelcome, they simply had to strive harder to be invited in – and Imre was not the type to strive. Besides, his target *milieu*, looking back on it, was not *landed* society but artistic. He loved theatre, ballet, films. He had himself been rich – in Hungary he was well-born

74

(he claimed); in Germany, until the axe fell, he moved among the most powerful in the land. But although his beautiful manners were, frankly, as impeccable as any in society, most people here saw him only as an artist. They were blinkered.

And I am prejudiced.

Our sexual relationship lasted only a matter of weeks. I had thrown myself at him and when Imre looked down to discover a beautiful and wealthy blonde clasping at his knees he buckled gracefully. He had a room not too far from South Kensington, but the only memories I have of the room are the bed (narrow, impossible) and the permanent aroma of strong coffee.

Imre made that drawing of me on a grey London afternoon, when the only sensible place to be was in your lover's bed. I posed naked on his crumpled sheets, and to lie unprotected in Imre's room seemed more daring to me, more voluptuous, than to make love. While Imre sketched me he wore his brocade dressing gown. (He said it was against the cold, but he was a vain man in his forties who would not go naked in afternoon light.)

'I drew a similar portrait of Louise Brooks,' he said.

'You're fibbing, Imre.'

'No.' He shrugged, feigning concentration on his line. 'I did all the film stars in Berlin.'

'You are such a name dropper. All your stories are about famous people.'

'No one else is interesting. Hold still. Do not move.'

I wriggled deliberately – temptingly, I hoped. 'You're trying to shut me up.'

'I shall shut you up in a box – like Pandora.'

I shook my head. 'You never painted Louise Brooks.'

'Correct,' he said smugly. 'I drew her. Then I…' He smiled mysteriously.

'You did not.' I sat up, flaunting all my nakedness. 'I will not lie here while you fib about making love to famous film stars.'

'Lie still! Head on your hand, like before.'

'Imre—'

'If you don't lie still, I shall include your naked breasts in this drawing and exhibit you in a London gallery – in the window, for passers by.'

I moved in some alarm. 'You wouldn't—'

'Behave. I have drawn only your head and shoulders – so far.'

But I was off the bed now, moving behind him to drape my naked arm across his shoulder. The picture was quite tasteful.

'I look like a ballet dancer.'

'Mhm. I did Louise just the same.'

'Nonsense!'

'You are so very like her. Or perhaps the picture is like her. Yes, you are the same, except that Louise had dark hair.'

I squinted at the red chalk drawing. 'That doesn't look like me.'

He chuckled. 'It is a suggestion, not a likeness. You are merely my inspiration. But I promise you, that is not a drawing of Louise.'

I was still studying the sketch. 'It looks more like Naomi.'

'Of course – you are sisters.'

'You have drawn Naomi.'

'No, no.'

He grabbed my hand. At that time, Naomi and I were having one of our periodic spats. She was cross because I had stolen Imre from her two weeks before.

'Look,' he said, taking my hand closer to the red chalk surface. 'This is your hairstyle, no? These are your eyes.'

'They could be anybody's.'

'Only yours. You have – please forgive me – just the tiniest cast. There, it is most attractive. Naomi's eyes are absolutely straight.'

'You should know, Imre. You gazed into them long enough.'

Naomi had slept with Imre first, but I won him from her because, I like to think, I was more attractive to him. For several weeks, in fact, Naomi wouldn't speak to me – and she never forgave Imre. I don't know why; we shared several boyfriends. It was rather fun.

At that particular time, Imre had become something of a tradesman to society, making portraits. He painted Lady Eden and Mrs Quentin Hogg. He even painted Mother. (A wretched thing – hard colours – he didn't like her.) He painted an extraordinary eight foot portrait of Evelyn Guinness with her terrifying dog. That fiend of an animal – a schizophrenic, vicious collie misnamed Lady – lived in Evelyn's London house, the interior of which resembled a Gothic lunatic asylum. The downstairs rooms were lined with filthy black untreated wood. Upstairs rooms were bare. Half of the house was in permanent darkness, and those rooms which *were* illuminated were dimly lit with tallow candles. To make Evelyn's portrait, Imre dressed himself as a parody of Erich von Stroheim in riding coat, whip and, most important of all, leather thigh-length boots. In that house the boots were essential, because the dog, in what to Evelyn was a charming eccentricity, attacked and bit the ankles of each male visitor. Imre painted the dog in a crouching position, half concealed in shadow, a slight froth of saliva at the corners of its jaw. The implication, of course, was that the dog was rabid, but he painted it so flatteringly that Evelyn never realised. For years the portrait hung at the head of one of her enormous staircases, where it struck a qualm in the heart of every male visitor who had ever met the dog before.

Those mad nights at Evelyn's in the flickering candle light and old Spanish leather chairs typify that wonderful decade. We would talk deep into the night and fall into bed at three, rousing ourselves at eleven for the kind of heart-warming, heart-clogging breakfast I have not experienced for sixty years.

My affair with Imre survived only a little while – we were of different classes, different nationalities, different ages. I was twenty-six or so, he was forty-four. In any case, I was still engaged to Neville.

My darling Neville.

Oh, I know: you think my life was a succession of impulsive love affairs – but let me tell you this: I was engaged to Neville Stanley for two years and we have stayed close friends ever since. Our betrothal stretched far too long, and by the time we actually engaged we both soon came to realise that the flames of passion (yes, we did have those) had cooled to glowing embers – that we had, in effect, become Darby and Joan before we'd reached our wedding day. For many couples, I suppose, that would have been an ideal starting point for marriage, but we were young, life was too exciting.

Our families had known each other for ever. Simply ever. Years before, his had attended my occasional performances at musical soirees, and in the early Thirties Daddy thought Neville one of the soundest fellows he knew. Sometimes all three of us would go off together, early afternoon, for a New Party meeting.

That's right – the New Party, the British Union of Fascists. I was a member. Does that shock you? If it does, I'm sorry, but times were different, pre-war. If I'm an old biddy now, I was a spirited young filly then. And though you dutifully recoil from the word Fascist nowadays, at that time the party seemed invigorating, forward-looking – all the things that appeal so to the young.

Daddy had first gone to one of their highly public gatherings for no other reason than that he was a friend of Sir Oswald Mosley. (Oswald! It still comes hard for me to call him that; his friends called him Tom.) 'Tom Mosley,' my father declared, was 'the only person in England who spoke sense.' My father died in 1935 before people turned against the BUF, but had he lived, I'm sure he would have stayed with them. He was a right-thinking, honourable man; his principles did not come from the fashion pages of popular magazines. You, of course, will not have heard Tom Mosley speak; you were not with us in the stirring Thirties. You sit here in 1997, cosseted in consumer comforts, bored with the present election, and your image of the Thirties comes from grainy black and white films of men in caps. How drab it looks! Yet the world I remember glittered like a Hollywood musical. Life was fun and men were dashing. I know there were lots of pinched little men in caps, but they had spirit and vigour and healthy optimism – and they *doffed* their caps. Today's truculent non-working class, strutting down littered streets in garish romper suits, betray their memory. Their grandfathers knew unemployment and real poverty, they had the gritty taste of it on their lips, and they could see that Mosley had the answer. In today's cynical world of prefabricated politicians it is almost impossible to conceive that there was a time – not so long ago, in my own lifetime – when people dedicated their lives to serve their country. Mosley was one. He did not need to go into politics – he was wealthy and held a good position in society. Yet he joined the Labour Party – yes, the Labour Party, think of that: today's loutish lefties spit the word Fascist unthinkingly at anyone on the right, yet the greatest Fascist this country ever knew stepped directly from their own Labour cabinet to create the New Party, the people's party, the only party with a national plan to eradicate poverty and unemployment, and give dignity to the working man.

Could New Labour be today's New Party? Ridiculous, you cry – but *plus ca change, plus c'est la meme chose*. Funny, isn't it, that in order to win this election, New Labour has dropped any pretence of Socialism and bases its appeal on being 'new' – just as the Nazis, the National Socialists, became the least Socialist party in Europe. Socialism may attract voters but it is anathema to government. It is the dream of the wistful revolutionary.

Oh, don't mind me: I'm just rambling on. I know it's impossible to convey the way things looked – what? – sixty years ago, but people use the word Fascist now to describe bankers and millionaires. Fascism was not for people like *that*! Mosley's Fascism was exhilarating; it was the future. It would have revitalised the Empire. His foreign policy was to unite Europe and bring an end forever to the shifting, dangerous balance of power. And what happened? It took a world war, countless millions dead, before a new generation of politicians saw the sense in Mosley's ideas and created the European Community he had outlined.

I can think of few men more patriotic. A friend of Germany? Yes, he was then – along with our government, the Royal Family and the huge mass of the British people – but by '37, two years before the war, Mosley was berating our sluggish leaders, demanding rearmament *now* and air force parity with our European rivals. He could see the future. He was without cant. Sir Oswald Mosley believed unshakeably in Great Britain and her Empire.

I have become aroused, but I am not ashamed of that. Mosley was the man who could have saved this country and averted war. He could have made men proud of the British blood flowing in their veins. But at the time, in those frightened final years of the Thirties, too few men listened; they preferred the reassuring platitudes of men in suits. They believed that by doing nothing they would ensure peace.

EIGHT

'And here I am, sir,' gushed little Ticky, red-faced and flustered in his master's living room. He had told the story of his break-in and, unaccustomed to soliloquy, had embellished as he went along. Only in the final part of his narrative did he notice that Gottfleisch had remained silent.

Ticky gave an anxious grin. 'That's how it was, sir.'

Gottfleisch studied him. 'You broke a window?'

'Just a little one. At the back.'

Gottfleisch rearranged himself in the armchair. Ticky wilted.

'Did you come away with much?'

'Come... away?'

'What did you steal?'

'Nothing.' Ticky's red face was turning white.

'No little trinket?'

Ticky's throat closed. He opened his mouth twice but nothing happened. He remained as silent as a goldfish. Gottfleisch waited until eventually Ticky managed, 'Trinket?'

'Surely you didn't leave the house empty-handed?'

Ticky could only nod unconvincingly. In his trouser pocket he felt the weight of the Death's Head ring, felt it dragging against the lining, felt it bulging against his thigh. He opened his mouth again and gulped.

Gottfleisch blinked, slowly as a basilisk. 'What did you take?'

Ticky was growing red again. He shook his head.

'Let me try to guess. Perhaps, in case the old lady hadn't noticed the broken window, you stole her television?'

'No—'

'Her purse?'

'No—'

Gottfleisch closed his eyes. Ticky stared at the huge man's eyelids as if even now Gottfleisch might be watching him. The eyes clicked open. 'Was there a burglar alarm?'

80

'No.'

'No doubt there will be soon. What did you take?'

Ticky licked his lips, hesitated, tried to meet his boss's gaze, then eased his hand carefully into his pocket as if he had a rat in it that might bite.

Gottfleisch watched him bring it out. 'Costume jewellery?'

The Death's Head ring lay heavy in Ticky's palm. 'It opens up,' he said.

Since Gottfleisch did not respond, Ticky twisted off the top.

Gottfleisch seemed uninterested. 'Twentieth century; a collector's item; minority interest. What else?'

'Nothing.'

'Nothing?'

'Nothing.'

'Except the photographs, I presume? You did take those?'

'Oh yes—'

'You took nothing except photographs; left nothing except footprints?'

Ticky frowned, detecting ice in Gottfleisch's tone. When he began to blush again, it created a mottled effect across his face. Since the operation Ticky's skin did not function as it should.

'I think the photographs will come out all right, sir.'

Gottfleisch stared at him.

'I mean, I took a snap of every picture. And she had this side table downstairs, flimsy thing, looked valuable – I took a shot of that.'

'Why?'

'Well, sir, it looked the sort of thing you might be interested in. And I thought that when I go back there, it's only small, I could fetch it out.'

'Did you photograph other items of her furniture?'

'I didn't think.'

'How true.'

Ticky eyed him warily. It seemed that he hadn't got his point across. 'I mean, I concentrated on the paintings, sir. And my photographs will be like a catalogue, won't they, from an auction house? See the goods, and from the comfort of your own home—'

'Shut up.'

'Yes, sir.'

Gottfleisch sighed. 'The old woman will know someone broke in.'

'I suppose so.'

'And she'll tell the police?'

'Well—'

81

'She will. And the police will warn her we'll come back.'

Ticky looked unsure.

'Because we didn't finish the job first time,' Gottfleisch continued. 'They'll explain that in those circumstances burglars normally make a second trip.'

'That's reasonable.'

'Now Ticky, if an old lady has a collection of valuable paintings, and if a thief breaks in but doesn't take any – having been disturbed – what d'you imagine she'll do?'

Ticky hesitated. 'Hide 'em away.'

'Somewhere we can't find them?'

Ticky gulped. 'Um, from what I saw of the old lady's paintings, sir – I mean, I'm not an expert – I wouldn't say they were valuable. They didn't have spotlights on them or little nameplates.'

Gottfleisch lay his head back and closed his eyes. 'Why was I so stupid as to send *you*?'

'I don't think that's quite fair, sir—'

'You imbecile!' Gottfleisch roared. 'You've blown it, you little slug.'

As he leant forward in the armchair Ticky thought the huge man might hurl himself upon him. 'There was a time when I could rely on you, but...' Gottfleisch shook his head. 'Never again.'

'Please, sir—'

Gottfleisch glared at him. Ticky licked his lips and plunged recklessly on: 'Not for one mistake, sir. I *need* this job. No one else would... would even look at me, and... sir, I've worked for you for years.'

'Get out.'

'No, *don't*, sir – I'll do anything.'

Ticky came forward, stumbled, fell to his knees. 'Please don't send me away.'

'Leave me.'

Tears burst unexpectedly from Ticky's eyes, glistening on his remoulded cheeks like beads of candle wax. 'Just one more chance!'

Gottfleisch rose impatiently from his chair and towered above the kneeling dwarf. 'Get out.'

Still on his knees, Ticky hobbled to the walnut card table, grabbed the film cassette and waved it in the air. 'At least wait till you've developed this, sir. Look—' He tottered to his feet and scurried across. 'Here are the photographs, sir.' He pressed the cassette into Gottfleisch's hand. 'These will show you all her paintings.'

*

Sidonie Keene cast a caustic eye over the policeman while he painstakingly took fingerprints. He wore civilian clothes – a dusty suit – and in his thinning hair lay specks of dandruff. As the man stooped intently over his work she imagined flecks of dandruff floating down to join the powder he was carefully brushing onto the surfaces. She wondered if the dandruff might spoil the result.

The uniformed officer with him had removed his jacket, releasing a sharp smell of body odour into the room. Though his white shirt looked crisply laundered and there were no signs of sweat, she wondered what made him assume he had permission to take off his jacket. Both men moved easily around her house as if she had offered it for sale.

'Not much so far,' Plain Clothes said.

Body Odour shrugged. 'Even amateurs wear gloves.'

Plain Clothes smiled at her. 'I think our best bet will be that drawing.'

'I trust you don't intend to take it away with you?'

Plain Clothes began leading her from the room. 'No, no. But you say the thief took it down?'

'And I don't want any dust on it,' she warned.

In the hall he smiled reassuringly. 'It won't be permanent.'

He lifted the drawing from the wall. 'When you hung it up again last night, you didn't clean it?'

'Of course not.'

'Some people do. Their possessions have been tainted, you see, that's what they think.'

He shook out a handful of his powder.

'Be careful,' she warned.

'It'll be safe behind its glass.'

He flipped the picture over to inspect the back. 'Ah, a Boots print. Very nice.'

'It is not a Boots print.'

'It says Boots here. D'you see this sticker? They do nice prints.'

'I stuck that on to protect it.'

He tilted his head. 'Protect it?'

She was becoming irritated. 'That is a valuable drawing, an original. I put the sticker on to disguise the fact.'

He regarded her doubtfully, then lay the picture on its back and brushed powder across the glass. From the living room doorway, Body Odour coughed: 'A present, was it?'

'In a sense. You could say that.'

'Well, either it was or it wasn't.'

'Funny,' Plain Clothes said.

'What is?' They both looked at him.

'Who painted this?'

'It's a drawing.'

'All right, who drew it?'

She said, 'The artist's name was Imre Goth.'

'Never heard of him.'

The policeman asked, 'What's funny, Nigel?'

'Mm?'

'Funny. You said something was—'

'Funny, yes. It doesn't say who painted it.'

'Drew it.'

'As you prefer. The sticker just says Boots The Chemist. Normally it also tells you who painted it.'

'Drew it.'

'Originally, I mean. The original artist's name.'

Sidonie sighed. 'I told you, the sticker does not belong.'

The doorbell rang. Body Odour ignored the interruption and asked, 'Was it stuck on by someone else?'

'I have already explained,' she said, moving past him to the door.

He clung to his line of thought: 'A clue perhaps. Might the thief have stuck it on?'

Sidonie opened her front door. For a moment she stared blankly at the unexpected visitor. It was Angus, Murdo's son, wearing the same ill-fitting velvet suit he had worn the previous day at the funeral, but this time without a tie. He stared past her along the hall-way and said, 'Oh.'

'Good morning, Angus.'

He continued to stare past her, then muttered, 'Yes.'

The policeman said, 'Good morning, sir. Don't mind us. Just carry on.'

Angus drew a breath as if savouring its flavour. 'Um, something wrong?'

'I've had a break-in,' Sidonie snapped. 'Come inside.'

'Perhaps not. Um…' Angus leant forward so he could squint along the hall. 'Hey, that drawing. Isn't that the one…'

The two policemen gazed at him expectantly. 'Yes, sir?'

'Nothing.'

'Isn't that the one that what, sir?'

'Oh. It used to be in my house.'

'Really? Does this picture belong to you, sir?'

Sidonie said, 'His father borrowed it. I took it back.'

Both policemen studied Angus, who muttered, 'Um, yeah, that's right.'

84

'Well, don't worry, sir,' called the plain clothes man, lifting up the picture for them to see. 'It's safe and sound now, sir. – Oops!'

It slipped. As the heavy frame dropped like a guillotine, the man kicked and caught it on his instep, propelling it along the hall. Body Odour dived. At full stretch he caught the picture before it hit the floor.

Everybody yelled.

Sidonie scuttled forward and snatched the drawing from his hands. He rolled over to rub his knee. Plain Clothes was standing on one foot, holding his instep, while behind him, Sidonie placed the drawing on the Jacobean chest. The fingerprint man, meanwhile, hopping backwards, bumped into her, stumbled, then suddenly sat down. She snatched the Goth away just in time.

Angus said, 'Um, I'll come back later, if you don't mind.'

✳

'Is that Miss Keene?'

'Yes.'

'Excuse my phoning you. Hugo Gottfleisch. We met—'

'The art dealer?'

'Exactly. You sold me one of your sister's water-colours.'

'I have no more to sell.'

'No, no, I phoned to sympathise. It must have been quite terrible.'

'What must?'

'The burglary.'

'*Attempted* burglary. How do you know about it?'

'The newspaper. So they didn't steal anything?'

'What newspaper?'

'Local rag. I was reading the account of Murdo's funeral. I'm afraid there was just as much about your burglary.'

'Hardly a story.'

'But the callousness, my dear. To break in while you were mourning at a funeral. But it's quite common, apparently, according to the newspaper. Not that I would know.'

'I don't see why an attempted burglary is news.'

'For a local paper, my dear, an attempted jumble sale is news. And *you* are, of course, a celebrity.'

'Mr Gottfleisch, if you don't mind, I'm rather tired.'

'Do call me Hugo.'

'I've had the police here.'

'How terrible. I suppose they found no clues?'

'Of course not. They were quite clueless, as one would expect.'

'Ah, very good. Ha, ha. I assume your alarm system scared the burglars off?'

'Is that what the paper said?'

'No, I merely assumed—'

'I never read the newspapers.'

'You do have an alarm system?'

'I'm afraid I don't.'

'Security locks?'

'Mr Gottfleisch, no doubt I am a very foolish old lady, but people of my generation grew up without such things.'

'Time moves on.'

'Don't talk to me about time. I am eighty-five.'

'Miss Keene, forgive me, but you shouldn't live alone without protection.'

'What makes you think I live alone?'

'The newspaper, my dear – or were they wrong on that as well?'

'They were not wrong.'

'You see, in my profession, Miss Keene, dealing in precious things, I have become very conscious of security. If you like, I'd be happy to proffer some advice—'

'I don't wish to appear rude, Mr Gottfleisch, but nowadays I find the telephone quite tiring.'

'I understand. But allow me to repeat that offer – I would be delighted to advise you on security.'

'There is no need.'

'Well, the painful truth, Miss Keene, as the police no doubt have warned you, is that a thwarted thief tends to come back.'

'I have no intention of installing an elaborate security system—'

'It needn't be expensive.'

'That is not my point.'

'Oh, Miss Keene, I must sound like a salesman, but do please think of me as a friend.'

✳

The fact is that I have not felt comfortable with the police since 1940. Until then I hardly thought of the police at all – I had seldom heard a policeman speak, except as a comic character in a play.

When they came for me that morning (around dawn, early, their sense of drama) I had no idea why they were there. It was so sudden, so unexpected. At that time I was in my Belgravia flat, but they were absolutely adamant they could not interview me there. I had to accompany them to the police station. I was naive: when they suggested I bring a bag I asked what on earth I was supposed to pack. They said a nightgown, odds and ends. I was *wearing* my nightgown underneath my wrap! (It was dawn, and barely light.) I asked them to call back when I had dressed, in an hour or two, and the head man (there were two of them in case I should prove too great a handful for just one) sneered – he literally sneered, as if I might flee the country in the interval. In 1940? Where could one go? You must remember that in 1940 the police – no, not only the police, *all* officials: air-raid wardens, ration book clerks, even ticket-office staff at the railway station – were unbelievably officious, as if to disguise the fact that they were not making a more robust contribution to the war.

As I dressed hurriedly in my bedroom – not *that* hurriedly: I was determined to apply my make-up – I began to see the seriousness of their visit. A dawn raid, if you please, and pack your bag. I was unaware that at that very moment similar scenes were being enacted with bureaucratic bumptiousness all across the country. Thousands of innocent people were being scooped up by police and thrown in jail. Did we not know there was a war on? Well, we did now. Sitting in my bedroom at the dressing table I assumed that I was the only one, that this was one of those ludicrous blunders which one read about. My reverie was shattered by the man hammering at my bedroom door, telling me to 'get a move on'. In my own flat! I'm afraid I told him in no uncertain terms to mind his manners.

He opened the door!

'You've got two minutes.'

'How *dare* you enter my bedroom without knocking?'

'I knocked.'

'Get out.'

'I thought you'd done a bunk, see, out the window.'

'We are on the second floor.'

'You never know.'

He was more prescient than he realised. I did not know that I was one of many hauled in for questioning. I did not know I would be in jail for eleven months. I did not even know what I was charged with – and I never did know, since nobody charged me at any time. I was to be crammed in a crowded jail for eleven *months* (bring a night-gown, they had said!) before being released without apology. Quite the reverse, in fact: when finally I *was* released I received a warning that in future I must behave. Behave? I had never *not*.

In 1940 – indeed for two or three years by then – we in Britain had been bombarded with lurid stories about arrests in Germany. Over there, we were told, in that barbaric, wicked country were dawn raids, special police, imprisonment without charge – but as things transpired, was Britain so different? *Tell* me about it, as they say today. Wasn't I arrested by special police in a dawn raid? Wasn't I imprisoned without charge? Wartime emergency, I was told: special powers, Regulation 18B – under which my sentence was indeterminate, and there could be no appeal. Indeterminate: the word was deadening.

Conditions, I need hardly tell you, were appalling. In the height and heart of London's Blitz I had to leave my sweet Belgravia flat empty and unguarded (Naomi was away by then) for a narrow bunk in a prison cell. There was dirt, discomfort, execrable food. My only consolation – and I must admit that it became important to me – was that I was not jammed in with the ordinary prisoners. I was 18B. We detainees (we were not called prisoners) were thrown into any jail which had an inch of room. I was sent to Holloway. I found several faces that I recognised (though no close friends) and throughout our depressing incarceration we formed into packs and struggled to keep up our spirits.

Perhaps you thought that the renowned British pluck and humour belonged exclusively to cheerful cockneys in the Blitz? You should have been in Holloway. The Pearly Queens outside (a mythical breed, except at carnivals) suffered nightly air-raids, but so did we. And we had the additional horror of neolithic female warders. We too learnt to smile at adversity.

Let me tell you a little of how it was to be on remand – yes, remand, remember; we were not prisoners, we were never charged. Our accommodation, if anything, was worse. (Temporary, you see.) It is often said that for people of the lower orders, prison is little hardship: the food, the bedding (though surely not the sanitary arrangements) are better than they have at home. But for the middle and upper classes (who are a minority in prison) the accommodation is a shock and hard to bear.

We wore our own clothes, at least – no prison denim with stencilled arrows – and were allowed occasional parcels of things sent in. In my first week Neville sent a selection of potted foods from Harrods, but they caused such envy I had to ask him to desist. We were allowed to write no more than two letters in any week. This seemed quite ridiculous: in those days writing letters was how people communicated. In my normal life outside, hardly a day passed without my penning two or three short notes to friends or trades people. Two letters a week! Quite impossible. To circumvent this absurd restriction I selected specific friends to act as message bearers – my letters to them being crammed with points to be passed on. Our letters were censored, of course, as were our food parcels: on receipt at the prison they would be delayed for several days and rifled through. Delicacies would be stolen. Fresh food went stale.

Holloway was so crowded that everyone shared cells. I was

placed initially with a schoolteacher's wife called Mrs Donham – a scrawny, dark-haired nervous woman who didn't let a waking hour pass without muttering 'Oh dear, oh dear'. She said prayers every night. Our cell was six foot by nine, with a cold concrete floor and metal door, hard bunk beds, one hard chair (yes, one) and a small heavy table bolted to the wall. The tiny ugly room was lit by a feeble naked bulb. We had a jug and basin but of course no lavatory, simply an enamel pot with a loose lid. Our personal possessions had to squeeze onto a three cornered shelf. The bunk beds were cold. I came to discover that the whole place was cold – even in summer. Food, as you would expect, was quite uneatable – we subsisted on a diet of shrivelled boiled vegetables and weak stew accompanied by a hunk of grey bread and a blob of particularly awful margarine. Dining was communal, at long trestle tables in a cavernous hall we called Lyons Corner House. We used enamel crockery. After eating we did our own washing up – with the tiniest allowance of soap and tepid water. Slopping out the chamber pots happened once a day, though while we were out of our cells we used communal lavatories, which were foul but at least one could walk away from them.

I suppose that I must have spent the first week or two in some kind of daze – I cannot remember. I do recall that the staff's initial hostility softened over time. Perhaps they realised we had done nothing wrong. Perhaps their attitude softened after the bomb.

I imagine you've not had close-hand experience of an explosion? Night after night we lay in our tight little beds listening to aeroplanes overhead, the thuds, the thumps, the sirens. Frequently bombs fell so close that the prison walls literally shook. Can you imagine the huge stone fortress trembling like a ship at sea? I have seen my cell wall shift and felt the dust fall on my face. Eventually a bomb fell on the prison.

I had been huddled in my bed, trying to ignore the bumps and bangs of the interminable blitz outside, my thin blanket pulled across my head as if it might protect me, when a sudden crash threw me from my bed. I hit the floor. Immediate darkness as the single light went out. A terrifying sound of falling masonry. I felt a sudden chill as if the whole prison had fallen away, leaving my little cell untouched among the rubble.

In the darkness I found myself entangled on the concrete floor with the struggling Mrs Donham, who screamed and fought as if I had attacked her. I was screaming too. The whole prison seemed filled with the sound of women screaming. Some began clattering at the iron bars.

'Get away! Get off!' Mrs Donham cried.

89

I attempted to quieten her as I tried to stand.

'I've broken my elbow.'

This seemed unlikely – given the vigour with which she was pummelling me.

'What on earth has happened? Oh dear, oh dear.'

I climbed shakily to my feet. Shrieks and clamour from the other cells merged into a single howl. In the tiny darkened cell I could still see the window but when I peered through its grating I saw only murk and blackness.

'What can you see? Have the walls come down?'

Mrs Donham was invisible in the darkness. I asked, 'Why – were you hoping to run away?'

We flinched as another bomb crashed sickeningly near. I edged back to the small barred window to see outside. In the deep gloom the prison buildings were still standing, and their dark shapes blocked out my view. Only by bending to one side and peering upwards could I see a flicker of orange in the night sky.

I said, 'Let's hope they've hit the governor's office.'

'Can you see much damage?'

'Sadly not.'

'Oh dear, oh dear.'

Mrs Donham continued muttering and whimpering. At first I thought she was crying but she was only mumbling her prayers.

It wasn't for several hours that we learnt exactly what had happened. Meanwhile, as the bombing faded and the long night dribbled into day, women prisoners shouted from darkened cells, banged at the bars, and started a dozen rumours. The staff kept away.

In the grey light of early dawn I awoke once more – if I had ever been asleep – and peered again from our tiny window. Everything looked disappointingly familiar. Now that the clamour of my fellow prisoners had ceased I could hear the sounds of early morning outside: occasional vehicles, a distant voice, the clank of buckets, the scrape of spades.

We spent most of that day confined to our cells. When we were eventually let out – in small numbers to reduce the risk of riot – we learnt that the prison had indeed been hit, that the damage was sustainable, but that we were to be without electricity and running water. No lights, no heating. Lavatories blocked and unusable throughout the whole of that day and the next. One prisoner had been removed to hospital.

Monotony returned.

For most inmates, whatever their class, it was at least possible for them to count the days to their eventual release, that golden date etched into the plaster of their cell wall, the crude calendar where stick-like days could be scratched through. But for those of us on Regulation 18B such consolation did not exist: our sentences were indeterminate. By summer of 1940 we had become acclimatised – or subordinated – to the system. Hoped-for letters meandered through, a few visitors came and went. In the long boring daytime we gathered in huddled meetings to pool what information we had gleaned. We discovered that there were hundreds – literally hundreds – of us detained this way. Elsewhere, in hastily created prison camps, were thousands – seventy thousand, I later learnt – of non-British aliens similarly detained. How long would we be held? We did not know. We were incarcerated out of sight of the outside world. There seemed little demand to bring us out.

Far from it. On the subject of 'aliens' the gutter press was unanimous: intern the lot. For us in Holloway the press was even more vituperative: sterilisation, exile, death by firing squad – these were the remedies proposed by the *Express* and *Sketch* for the most patriotic women in the land. (It had been our party, after all, not the Conservatives, not the Labour Party, which was the first to call for rearmament, and whose slogans were 'Mind Britain's Business' and 'Britain Awake!')

Trapped as we were behind the high walls of our filthy prison it was tempting to believe that the raucous chants reproduced in daily newspapers represented the voice of middle England, that our countrymen *wanted* us to rot and die in jail. In the long humdrum evenings we read and reread those poisonous rags. Newspapers which two years before had supported the BUF now screamed against us and called us scum. They screamed against my friends and I. They screamed against Mrs Donham, who had never harmed a soul.

Five years earlier she had married a German Jew called Donheim, one of the last to leave that country. He was a scientist, and as such had thought himself safe. But in '37, when the German government made it clear that everyone of Jewish blood should leave, Donheim and his English wife slipped aboard a train to Holland, from where they caught a boat to England. Donheim became a schoolteacher in Plaistow, a dreary East London suburb I confess I have never visited. Early in 1939 he applied unsuccessfully to join the British Army, and in 1940 he was interned.

'But I am English. Why should I be stuck in here?' Mrs Donham wailed. 'I suppose you hate me?'

'For marrying a German? Don't be ridiculous.'

The single bulb shone balefully down. She lifted her chin. 'No, *you* hate me for leaving there. You know what Germany is doing to the Jews?'

'Putting them in jail, I imagine, as we do here.'

One day Mrs Donham showed me a letter from her interned husband. He had decorated his note with tiny cartoons of life in the prison camp where he and his fellow aliens lived dormitory style in converted barrack rooms. He had drawn men playing football, men sleeping, men in a chamber music group.

'It seems an idyllic life,' I said, glancing round our cell.

'He tries to paint a cheerful picture, but his living conditions are worse than ours. This drawing shows his dormitory in sunshine, but actually the mattresses are damp and sodden, and there's no heating. I dread to think what it will be like for him in winter.'

I noticed that in one of his sunny drawings he had included a rat perched insouciantly on a bed rail. In art, truth lies concealed.

'There are cockroaches too,' she said, her voice cracking as if she hadn't noticed the ghastly creatures in our own jail. 'Half the men in his camp have fled the terror of their own country – the purges, the sudden knock, the threat of violence to their families – and they've come to England. Yet even here—' Her voice briefly failed her. 'Even here they've heard the sudden knock. They've seen their families torn apart.'

Mrs Donham started crying. I made no move to comfort her. Sometimes it is best to let tears flow.

She said, 'We had no explanations, no trial, no accusation we could answer – just this separation and imprisonment. It's so unfair.'

'It's traditional.'

Much later, after the war when truth came out, the authorities admitted that many aliens died in those British hell-camps – some at their own hand, some wasting to death in the land that they had fled to. Meanwhile, out in the streets around Holloway Prison, were spivs, absconders and common criminals. At recruiting offices, volunteers were few. (News stories of the time showed smiling men rushing to enlist, but that was propaganda.) Yet among the seventy thousand 'aliens' such as Mrs Donham's husband – and indeed among the hundreds of Party supporters in crowded jails – almost every prisoner would have fought or worked diligently for the Britain which jailed them; an irony lost on the popular press.

By October, as cold autumnal dampness rose from the concrete floor, we heard of fellow prisoners gaining their release. It seemed that the days of pointless vindictiveness might be ending. We waited to be summoned before the governor.

It began to happen. A wardress would appear, smirking, and

suddenly one of our number would be seized – almost at random, it seemed, though we knew that it was not random – and with burning face that woman would be led away. The rest of us would wait: an interview with the governor could be for any reason. The moment our friend reappeared we could read in her face immediately whether she was to be released. If she were – oh, glorious day! – she would be mobbed by fellow prisoners, genuinely delighted for her sake. Sometimes though, the poor woman had merely been dragged off on a trumped-up charge by a malicious warden. By revealing nothing when they led her away, they could make disappointment especially agonising. Those times were hard to bear. Nevertheless, toward the last months of the year, the staff began to soften in their attitude. They could see that we were neither traitorous nor criminal – Heaven knows they saw enough women pass through who were – and they began to agree with us that we should not be there. When we had first arrived, the wardens treated us harshly, believing as they had been told, that we were scheming, dangerous fifth columnists. But as the months went by they saw the truth.

Shortly before Christmas came a flurry of seasonal releases, but I was not among them. Nor was Mrs Donham. She became depressed.

'I was so certain, and Christmas is special, isn't it?'

'Your husband is Jewish,' I pointed out. 'You don't have Christmas.'

'*I* am a Christian.'

We stared at each other blankly. She said, 'We share each other's important feast days.'

'You observe a Jewish feast?'

'Why not? – Oh, I forgot: you don't like Jews.'

'Not at all. Some of my friends—'

'Our feast days often coincide – Passover and Easter, for example.'

Though I knew she had married a Jew I had heard her every night mutter prayers to Jesus Christ. I said, 'I don't see how Jews can celebrate Christmas – it's the birth of Christ, the leader of our religion.'

She smiled: 'D'you think Jews drink the blood of Christian babies?'

What she was saying, I suppose, is that Christian and Jew shared the same fundamental beliefs and customs, the same basic law. I would say the same for Germans and Englishmen: I felt more at ease with Germans than with the majority of my countrymen. Yet when our two countries started slaughtering countless thousands of each other's people I would – despite being incarcerated by my own side – have stood with my countrymen against the common foe. Odd, isn't it, how one's loyalties are decided almost by chance, and yet one will defend those arbitrary loyalties with one's life?

Christmas in Holloway was hard for Mrs Donham. She took the continued separation from her husband badly; her spirits sunk even lower than during those dreadful weeks in summer when the *Arandora Star* had gone down. That ship, you may remember, had been carrying more than a thousand German and Italian detainees from our shores to Canada when it was sunk by a German U-boat. For over a week Mrs Donham had not known whether her husband was on board. (All the passengers had been taken from British camps, and their passage was not a matter of choice.) Once the story broke – and our newspapers gave it gleeful headline prominence – the British authorities made little effort to assuage the relatives' anxiety with speedy information. I don't know, in fact, that they ever produced a full listing of the dead. But finally a letter did arrive from Donham himself, bearing that all-important post-torpedo date.

In the run-up to Christmas, public attitudes toward us began to change. Questions were asked in the House, and the better quality newspapers queried the wisdom of imprisoning thousands of Britain's most loyal supporters. Mrs Donham's husband, like so many of them, had been driven from his old country and had chosen Britain specifically for his home. Thousands of these (often highly skilled) refugees poured into our country, desperate to lean their valuable shoulders to our creaking wheel. And we imprisoned them. Or we deported them – dumping thousands of able men in the farthermost corners of our Commonwealth, where presumably we thought they could do less harm.

Questions, as I say, were being asked, but Bureaucracy would not be moved. Mrs Donham stayed. The only Christmas present she received from the authorities was a change of cell-mate on Christmas Eve. I had long been petitioning to join my friends elsewhere in the jail, and the general Christmas move-around gave me my chance. I left Mrs Donham to the ghastly cell we had shared for seven months – one she had decorated with a pathetic Christmas display of coloured paper, stars and cheerful words – and I joined my friends on the upper floor.

It was nevertheless a dismal Christmas. The winter which followed was extremely cold. Finally, one day in April '41, there was a stir of activity on the top floor. More than half of us were marched, one by one, for a final interview with the governor. We quickly realised that on this particular day every interview meant a release – which made it hard, of course, for those not called out from their cell. The blind authorities deemed that some of my friends were still a potential danger on the streets. They had to linger on in jail. Some remained inside for years.

About the interview itself I remember little, other than that I was given no reason why I had been held so long, nor why I was now free to go. There were no explanations, no apologies, no charges laid. There was a war on, didn't I know?

Before leaving the prison I did remember to call on Mrs Donham. She had not been called for interview, and she seemed to have grown distinctly older in the past few months.

NINE

At nine o'clock when Angus Fyffe returned, Sidonie for once regretted having to turn off the television. She was amused at the second story on the News – that the increasingly desperate John Major had turned to the dragon mother who had nurtured him, that he had asked Mrs Thatcher to appeal on his behalf to the newspaper magnate Rupert Murdoch not to order his normally supportive *Sun* to ditch the Tories and back Labour instead. Thatcher was filmed after meeting the powerful Australian at Eaton Square.

But Sidonie turned the story off, poured Angus a glass of Scotch and sat opposite him so they could talk in her softly lit sitting room. In the amber light with the clock ticking they discussed his father, their words muted but distinct in the sympathetic silence of the room. Their clothes rustled when they moved. To Sidonie it seemed that Angus had only a token sadness, that she herself grieved Murdo more. He made no mention of the break-in: indeed, were it not for his having called when the police were there she would have thought him unaware of what had happened. Watching him draped uncomfortably in her armchair it occurred to her that he might have been avoiding the matter deliberately. She wondered – just for a moment – whether he might have been behind the break-in: he had *known* she would be at the funeral. He had called to see her afterwards but on encountering the police had left immediately without saying why he had come. What did Angus do with himself, she wondered, this aged hippie who had lost his tribe.

'Will you be staying down with us long?'

'No, I have to get back to town. I've been through his things and that.'

She could imagine his bony fingers picking through Murdo's clothes.

'There wasn't much, really.'

Sidonie found the thought disturbing. She asked, 'What are you doing nowadays, Angus – still studying alternative therapy?'

96

He frowned. 'That was some time ago.'

'Was it? I could see you as an alternative practitioner.'

'Well, it was a three year course – a bit long really. I'm into software now – computer programs.'

She raised an eyebrow. 'And how long a course is that?'

'Um, there isn't one really – you just sort of do it. I have this partner.'

'In which sense?'

Angus folded one leg across the other. 'It's sort of complicated to explain – well, not *complicated*…' He gazed at the ceiling for inspiration, but his face slackened as if he had seen something of interest there or as if his thoughts had drifted.

He was poor company, and Sidonie did not want to hear about his computer programs. She changed the subject: 'Did you know you have a hole in your left shoe?'

'Have I? Well, I packed in a bit of a hurry.'

'You must have brought more than one pair?'

'I've got some black ones but they're too formal – and a bit tight.' He grinned uneasily. 'I mean, I bought them for the funeral but, um, these are comfier.'

'They've certainly had some wear.'

Abruptly, Angus unfolded his long legs. 'Oh, *sorry*. I suppose it's not good manners to come visiting with a hole in your shoe?'

'Manners don't come into it, but don't you find the hole lets in the damp?'

'Some of us can't afford to buy good shoes.'

Sidonie looked askance.

Angus continued: 'You wouldn't understand that. But things have been hard for me, you know?'

There still seemed no reply worth making.

'I mean, Dad used to drop me a bit from time to time, but that'll stop now.'

'No doubt you'll benefit from his will.'

Angus snorted, then picked up his empty whisky glass and peered pointedly inside. 'There won't be much. He didn't even own the house. He rented it.'

Sidonie frowned. 'Really? I had no idea.'

'No? You were supposed to be his friend.'

For a moment they stared at each other, but Sidonie looked away.

'Oh, he wouldn't have told you, of course. He'd have been too embarrassed. He never did have money.'

She nodded. 'That's true.'

'These last few years he relied on you.'

'Not at all!'

Sidonie shifted in her chair. She wanted to stand up and move about, but that might have seemed melodramatic. She said, 'He certainly did not rely on me.'

Angus shrugged. 'That's not what *he* said.'

Sidonie stared at him with genuine surprise. 'I beg your pardon?'

'Well, he earned an income from you, didn't he?' Angus's return stare was growing bolder.

'What nonsense. Once or twice he sold a painting for me and I insisted he take a small commission, but that could not in any sense be considered an income.'

'Look, Dad had no money, right? He had no income, yet he used to sub me. D'you think I didn't wonder?'

Sidonie sat back in her chair. 'Your father may not have had a great deal of money, but he was far from destitute—'

'Exactly.'

'When you get to our age, Angus, you'll find that your outgoings reduce. He had a pension—'

'Pension!'

'And a modest income from his savings. Has it occurred to you that he might have played down exactly how much he had, simply to stop you touching him for money?'

'I like that! Anyway, he was touching *you*.'

She sighed. 'If he had asked me – *if*, because he never did – then, yes, I would have given him money. Not that I have much to give—'

'Huh! Look at this house.'

'A cottage.'

'It's worth a lot.'

'Hardly. In any case I have no intention of selling it, so whatever it might be worth is beside the point. You've got the wrong idea here, Angus. I suppose you've been sitting in your little flat, building up this fantasy, but the fact is that—'

'You were buying his silence.'

'What?'

There was a sudden moment of trembling silence. Angus said, 'I know your secret, you see? I've seen his papers.'

Sidonie took an exasperated breath.

'You didn't know that,' Angus said.

'Perhaps you'd better explain exactly what you're talking about.'

He chuckled. 'I'm his sole heir, Miss Keene. I've been alone in his house. You must've known I'd find it.'

She closed her eyes. 'Find what?'

'The reason you were paying him.'

She opened her eyes and exhaled slowly. 'What a pathetic heap you are – and from such a father. D'you know,' she continued, leaning towards him and smiling coldly, 'I often wondered whether Murdo sired you at all. I wondered whether perhaps your mother had drunk too much at a party and picked someone up, or whether she'd been raped by a desperate stranger, because it always seemed to me that you crawled out of a cuckoo's egg. All your life you've been a failure and a disappointment. Now you've concocted this fantasy – which for all I know you actually believe – and finally you have summoned up the courage to confront me with a feeble bluff. Found something? You have not found anything – if you had, you would have told me what it was. So please go back to your silly computer and...' She paused, eyes glinting as she sought for the word: 'Erase yourself from memory!' She smiled. 'You see, I know the jargon. I read the occasional article, which probably makes me as much an expert as you, Angus. You should have stuck to a career in alternative therapy – it's a bluffer's trade. After all, you have the appropriate suit. And the right shoes.'

His pale face had whitened. 'When you let yourself go, you're a tough old bitch, aren't you?'

'I'd prefer you to leave now, Angus.'

'You came out with that great diatribe because you don't believe I've really found it.'

'There's nothing to find, for Goodness sake. You're a disgrace to your father. Just go away.'

'Who's bluffing now, Miss Keene? You know damn well my Dad had evidence.'

'Angus, you may believe this twaddle but I do not. Please go away.'

'I have *proof*.'

'Goodbye.'

Angus held the pause. Slowly and deliberately, his eyes never leaving her face, he slid his hand inside his dark brown jacket and withdrew an envelope. He smiled. 'Well now, Miss Keene. What have we here?'

TEN

After a damp grey dawn the morning sun appeared. For a few minutes it was a pale disc behind heavy greyness, then the light intensified and turned the clouds a dirty yellow.

The blond chauffeur did not wear a uniform, but he leapt smartly from the Renault Espace to open the rear passenger door. Gottfleisch squeezed out, sniffed at the sparkling country air, and adjusted the red carnation in his buttonhole. Sunlight played on his pale skin.

While his chauffeur waited by the Espace the huge man approached the house alone. He rang the bell. Beneath a nearby bush a bird shuffled through the undergrowth, and in a leafy tree a blackbird sang.

After a while the front door opened.

'Miss Keene. Good day. I'm Hugo Gottfleisch.'

'Of course. Good of you to call.'

'The pleasure's mine.'

As she led him into the house his flickering eyes made a quick appraisal of the paintings in the hall. Pleasant, but not his objective.

'Do take a chair.'

She indicated a fiddle backed mahogany chair on graceful legs. Nineteenth century, Gottfleisch thought, though delicately made.

'A man of my size is safer in an armchair,' Gottfleisch chuckled. 'May I sit here?'

'Please do.'

As he sank into its sturdy upholstery he smiled again disarmingly. 'Sheraton furniture was not made for my weight. – But are you quite recovered, Miss Keene? I believe you disturbed the villain?'

'I did.'

'You didn't see him?'

'I think he feared I was a six foot bruiser. When he heard me at the door he shot off like a startled rabbit.'

'Nevertheless…'

'Next time?' she purred.

'We must take steps to prevent there being a next time. Was nothing stolen?'

Sidonie shook her head. 'One or two paintings had been moved. I must have returned home too early.'

Gottfleisch gazed at her sympathetically. 'So he came for your paintings but had to postpone taking them? I hate to say this—'

'But he will be back? Yes, the police told me that.'

'Did they offer other advice?'

'Oh, the usual platitudes: burglar alarms, better locks on the doors. Anything especially valuable should be hidden away.'

'Dull but sensible. Where had they in mind?'

She smiled. 'I really don't think I should tell you that.'

Gottfleisch laughed. 'Oh, good Lord, no. No, by George! Will you be taking their advice?'

She closed her eyes. 'I suppose I'll have to.'

'Yes.' Gottfleisch paused to peruse the pictures on her walls. 'Several delightful paintings here but – I hope you won't mind my saying – nothing of exceptional value. Perhaps the more valuable pictures are elsewhere?'

Sidonie shrugged. 'I scatter them around the house so I can see them. But no, nothing of exceptional value, as you say. My furniture's probably more valuable.'

'Perhaps.' Gottfleisch flicked his wrist impatiently at the walls. 'I'm surprised not to see any of Naomi's here. Perhaps they're in another room?'

She tossed her head. 'I have no more of my sister's paintings.'

'No?'

She stood up with surprising ease. 'Why not give me your view on the paintings I do have? I hope you'll not be disappointed.'

Gottfleisch suspected that he would be. He was struggling to rise from the comfortable armchair. 'I shall be delighted. That, after all—'

He was on his feet now. 'That is why I'm here today.'

'I thought you'd come to advise me on security? Do you *sell* security systems?'

'Good Lord, no.' He grinned expansively. 'But I understand them.'

She was moving from the room. 'These in the hall you have already seen.'

'Yes, yes, indeed.'

'There's my lovely Imre Goth.' She pointed to it. 'The burglar took that down.'

'Did he now?' Gottfleisch frowned. 'Worth a thousand perhaps. Not a lot more.'

'It is worth more to me.'

She was moving past him, back into the room they had just left. He said, 'We haven't looked upstairs.'

She hesitated. 'Oh, not today. I – another time.'

Gottfleisch glanced up towards the first floor landing. 'We should check your upstairs windows. They might need locks.'

'A burglar is unlikely to bring a ladder.'

She went back into the downstairs room, and he reluctantly followed her. 'You were jolly lucky you didn't have to face these vandals.'

'Vandals? I don't think there was more than one. We shouldn't exaggerate.'

'One or more, they will come back, you know. We'd better check upstairs.'

'Everything's a mess up there.'

Gottfleisch curbed himself. 'You're a brave woman.'

'At my age one becomes phlegmatic. I've had plenty of rocks thrown at me over the years.'

'Ah, yes.'

He held her gaze. She shrugged. 'I'm sure you know my history, Mr Gottfleisch, as indeed you must know my sister's.'

He nodded.

'Anyway, for the moment, I prefer not to let you into my bedroom.'

She smiled saucily and Gottfleisch took up the cue: 'What delicious surprises would I find there?'

'Ah, *once* upon a time...' She waved her hand vaguely at her Victorian chair. 'So you don't consider my furniture valuable?'

'It's very charming, though, you know, often one comes across the most valuable piece lying quite unnoticed somewhere around the house.'

She ignored the hint. Crossing to a small side table she rested her white fingers on its shining surface. 'I have been wealthy, Mr Gottfleisch.'

He mumbled, 'Hugo.'

'And I have been ostracised.'

He murmured sympathetically.

'I have been reviled, imprisoned, blackmailed—'

'Blackmailed too? Goodness. Well, all that was a long time ago.'

'Not really. One man tried quite recently.'

'Really?' He was only politely interested – until he saw her jaw tighten as if she had said more than she had intended.

She moved aside. Indicating almost at random a small watercolour, she said, 'That's a Walke. Rather nice, wouldn't you say?'

He barely glanced at it, watching her. 'Ethel Walker?'

'Walke. Bernard Walke.'

'But who would blackmail you, Miss Keene?'

'Oh, it doesn't matter.'

'It most certainly does.' Gottfleisch smiled at her but she shrugged him off.

'People have been trying to blackmail me for fifty years. It's quite astonishing.'

'About Naomi?'

'Yes, of course. They don't seem to realise that Naomi and I were subjected to a relentless glare of publicity. There are no secrets left.'

He murmured, 'Yet even recently, you say…'

'Childish. A mistake.'

Sympathetically, Gottfleisch touched her arm. 'I am most concerned for you. An attempted burglary. Now a blackmailer. My Goodness, I think you need a friend.'

'I am… perfectly…'

'That was insensitive of me: you have recently *lost* a friend.'

'Murdo?'

She smiled, but there was no hiding the sadness in her eyes. 'Yes, he *was* a friend.'

Gottfleisch murmured, 'If there is anything I—'

'If Murdo had known…'

Gottfleisch peered at her. He still had his hand on her thin arm. 'Whatever I can do.'

She raised her head. A tear sparkled in her eye. 'No, I—'

'Please let me help you.'

Shaking her head she said, 'Too ridiculous.'

He gently squeezed her arm. 'Anything.'

Sidonie took a breath. 'I don't suppose you've met that wearisome son of his?'

ELEVEN

Daytime. Piccadilly Circus. Traffic at a crawl. The sun casts long shadows down the faces of carved stone buildings. Taxis ease between less adept vehicles. The young boy stands out so clearly he will not last five minutes. He has a shock of soft blond hair, lean frame, clean clothes crumpled as if he slept in them last night. He may be thirteen years old – certainly he seems somewhere between twelve and fourteen. At the entrance to the Piccadilly Arcade the boy stands with assumed nonchalance, a canvas bag heavy at his side. In that canvas bag will be everything the boy possesses, everything he has brought with him. He is watching others in the dark arcade. He is wondering whether to approach somebody, or whether if he waits a while one of the other boys might acknowledge him. He seems to know that this arcade is an accepted meeting place. He stands alone, shark bait in the sea.

Ticky's practised eye tells him immediately that the boy is fresh and new. He isn't out to rent, he isn't selling anything. Not yet. Almost certainly the boy has just arrived in town and has come straight here to the centre of the universe. But he is much too beautiful. If he lingers with that telltale bag he will disappear into a darker universe. He glows against the midday sun. Even as Ticky leaves the Pick Pack Poke machine he senses that he is not the only man moving towards the golden boy. Centre of the universe. Shark bait in the sea.

In the busy street outside is a dark blue uniform. Circling. Homing in. Ticky speeds towards the unsuspecting target. 'Copper's coming. Do a runner down the tube.'

The boy glances at him doubtfully.

'Don't hang about, my friend.'

Then the boy shoots off – it makes Ticky's heart leap to watch him. His step is light. He appears to be walking although he moves at jogging speed. The cop hesitates, starts to hurry – and the boy slips down the steps of the Piccadilly tube.

By now, Ticky has shrunk back to the darker corner of the

104

arcade. If the cop has seen him warn the boy, Ticky is not the sort who can melt away. His diminutive size, his deformed face, means he can always be identified and found. Half the cops know Ticky by name in any case.

But this one has gone to the top of tube stairwell and is peering down. He has wandered round to stand by the magazine stall at the kerbside where he can look across the Circus. Beside him, the placard reads 'New Sleaze Scandal Hits The Tories'. Not another one, Ticky thinks: more kinky than a Chinese brothel – where it's always 'election' time. Ticky sniggers and the paperman scowls: the cop is bad for trade. Emboldened now, Ticky comes to the arcade entrance. But stays out of the sun.

The cop is watching other underground exits in case the kid pops up. Ticky watches too. Sure enough, across the other side of the Circus, the boy emerges outside the Criterion. He glances around – he must have picked out the cop, but he doesn't scarper. In an idle uncaring way the boy turns his back and studies posters outside the theatre. By now the cop is nipping across Regent Street, hoping to keep a view of the boy by staying above ground. But it's a long way round. Once the cop has committed himself among the traffic, the boy springs to life and shoots back downstairs.

Ticky comes onto the pavement. With the cop above ground and the kid below, Ticky trots down the Piccadilly stairs.

✳

On my first day back in London I walked the streets for several hours. It had changed and seemed a different country. I walked in horror along the Strand, through Aldwych, past the huge scar on Kingsway Corner, then into Fleet Street. Temple Church had gone. Pump Court was a pile of stones. Of Saint Clement Danes a skeleton remained. All along Fleet Street and Ludgate Hill stood wrecked and damaged buildings, and the little lanes to the side were littered with rubble and half-repaired facades. I continued numbly towards the inspiring dome of Saint Paul's, knowing that it at least had gloriously survived. But when I arrived beside that wonderful cathedral I stood aghast at its maimed north transept and demolished porch.

God had been less merciful than the world allowed: eighteen of Wren's lovely churches lay mutilated, two were completely destroyed. All Hallows, Cripplegate and sweet Saint Olave's were among many desecrated, while Austin Friars and the Old Chelsea Church had been completely burnt down. Southwark Cathedral and Saint Bartholomew were horribly damaged. Yet curiously, the secular world had been more fortunate: hardly a theatre, cinema or

105

vulgar music hall; hardly a London hotel fell. Nor did the Mansion House or the Bank of England.

When one walks the City streets today – bustling, vibrant, buttressed with walls of glass and shining steel – one has to look hard for any reminder of those stunned, drab days after the war. My return two years after it was over was still upsetting and unnerving. Whatever courage and energy Londoners had shown in wartime had been replaced with apathy and tiredness. People were weary.

On that long first day in London, as I picked my way along broken pavements and gutted buildings – wallpaper peeling in the sunlight, cast-iron fireplaces stranded ten feet up the wall, buddleia and willowherb flourishing in the bomb sites – I wondered, 'Why won't anyone clear it up? Why can't they sweep it all away?'

In America things had been different. Pessimism could find no hold. But England looked a country which had finally yielded to defeat. Conditioned to war, England could not fight the peace.

That afternoon in an attempt to revive myself, I tried what I used to do when feeling blue – went shopping in the West End. But the shops were empty. Many indeed were no longer there. Oxford Street bore terrible scars. Park Lane, Piccadilly, the Burlington Arcade: each of my favourite haunts appeared sombrely before me like a ghost. London seemed as I myself might seem to a pre-war chum meeting me today – an old and damaged lady, barely yet cruelly recognisable as that previously bright young thing. Leicester Square was patched and shabby, Langham Place was boarded up. Inside empty shops, a few white lights shone bravely. Out in the streets were joyless crowds.

Finally I caught a train – cold, cramped and dirty – which rattled from London as it took me home. I travelled First Class and found myself the only person in the compartment. When I reached the station there were no taxis. The one they telephoned took an age to come.

I remember now.

When the taxi – cold and rattling like the train – arrived at Graylands, it swept straight into the drive and dropped me at the door. Where were our magnificent wrought-iron gates? I learnt later, of course, that those gates, each bearing our family crest, had been lifted from their hinges and taken for scrap.

Graylands looked dark and neglected. As I put my key in the lock and pushed the door it never occurred to me that the house might have been requisitioned, that precious pieces of our furniture could have been grabbed like the gates for the common sacrifice. Once I had opened the door I stood appalled. The hall was bare – the carpet gone, leaving only lino. I stumbled numbly from room to room, finding relics of our furniture interspersed among unfamiliar institutional items. The parlour door had been removed. Another room, Mother's bedroom, had been divided. Two window panes were broken. The house was desperately cold. When I went to the coal-house I found it bereft of fuel. One thing that the house did have was beds a-plenty (many of which did not seem to be ours) and in a cold dank cupboard I found untidy piles of sheets and blankets. They smelt of damp.

For the next four days I slept at the village inn and spent tedious hours relocating furniture and making Graylands halfway habitable. Before the war our family had had maids and cleaners, but all that had changed. I had changed as well. In the empty house I attacked jobs that needed to be done with more vigour than my countrymen seemed capable of. In the village, for example, only one house had been bombed – but it still stood waist-high in rubble. No one went near it except village children who played among its crumbling walls. Despite the danger, nobody stopped them. Here was the birth of the post-war generation: apathetic parents, children running wild.

At Graylands I worked every daylight hour. The landlord of the inn recommended a girl to me and together we re-established order in my family home. We swept floors and scrubbed the windowsills. We cleared away rubbish. We cleaned and cleaned. In a garden outhouse I found some of our furniture which had been locked away, and the girl and I lugged every piece back to the house. She and I trundled unwanted beds down the stairs, across the dishevelled lawn and into the coach-house. I can no longer remember her name, but I don't think she uttered a single word of complaint. Out in the village, and indeed throughout the country as far as I could tell, everyone seemed infected with this new English disease of resigned weariness. Six years of long war had drained them, and in a kind of perpetual national hangover they trudged through days that were dull and lacking in purpose; saw crippled industries, worn-out roads, smashed houses – and like bleary drunks on the morning after, couldn't summon the energy to clear things up.

The bombed house in the village had stood untouched for two years by then. (The family died in it.) In the main village street, coils of barbed wire which in 1940 had been placed temporarily to deter enemy tanks stood as a rusting eyesore till 1948. Peace was a dispiriting affair.

❋

Ticky sat beside the boy in the tube train, his feet dangling six inches from the floor. The boy was talking to him. His name was Cy.

Ticky's experience of strangers was that they fell into two types: most people, who veered away from him, and the few who made a point of being nice. With those few, Ticky's plastic face worked in his favour – he was disadvantaged, so they should be kind. This golden boy, Cy, was one of the few. And he would need a friend.

When Ticky caught up with him, Cy had seemed on guard. This had been inside the tube station, which Ticky explained was notorious for zealous cops who knew that young runaways made a beeline for Piccadilly Circus – oh, had Cy just arrived? The kid didn't hesitate long. One glance at this helpful little man with his smiling, tortured face and Cy knew that he could trust him. Yes, he said, he had just arrived.

'The good news,' Ticky told him earnestly, 'is that beds are everywhere. But the bad news is that most ain't safe.'

Being a little shorter than Cy, he sat beside him on the train like a ventriloquist's dummy. 'Places like Kings Cross and Waterloo, they can be dangerous. You can sleep in shop doorways, of course – but how's your back?'

The boy sighed. 'I suppose doorsteps are uncomfortable?'

Ticky sucked noisily on his teeth. 'They're morbid. The cold comes up from the concrete like rising damp.'

He was keeping his voice down. Their compartment was one third full. A couple of passengers had thrown him a startled look, but no more than usual. To catch what he said, Cy had to lean towards him, and now and then his soft blond hair brushed against Ticky's face. Ticky liked that.

He said, 'What you need is a bed in someone's flat.'

Cy was instantly wary.

But Ticky continued: 'Except that could be *very* unsafe, couldn't it? You can't trust no one.' He sucked his teeth again.

Cy said, 'I could get a job.'

Ticky pulled a face. '*Possibly*. But they won't pay you till the end of your first week – or maybe not till the end of your first month. How're you gonna manage till then?'

'I've got a few quid with me. And I could sleep rough.'

'It's not like sleeping out for a night under the stars – not in London, my friend.'

'People do, though.'

'You can't see the stars for all the street lamps.'

Cy shrugged. 'I'll get by.'

They were pulling into a station and Ticky felt he was beginning to lose the boy, so he stood up and said, 'Come on. If you stay on this you'll end up at Kings Cross.'

'Where are we? Oh.'

There were signs all along the platform: Covent Garden. This should impress the boy, thought Ticky: lots of life up there. But since he seemed uncertain, Ticky leant towards him and threw his best line: 'I was a runaway once too, you know? They chucked me out 'cos of the way I look.'

'Did they? That's terrible.'

'Come on. The underground will get you nowhere.'

The train doors opened.

Cy said, 'I suppose this will have to do.'

✳

After a week Graylands was clean but still not warm. Coal was unavailable and I scoured the lanes and local copses for fallen wood. Fortunately, the house did have gas and electricity (by no means everybody did) but nevertheless I spent my evenings confined to one chilly room and had to retire early to my bed.

The local garage delivered Mother's car with a bill for housing it, and sold me a meagre supply of fuel in two metal cans. Since it seemed that I could exhaust the lot on one return trip to London I resolved to restrict it to emergencies and local journeys. With the car practically useless and the telephone long disconnected, I didn't bother to make contact with old friends. Throughout the war I had exchanged occasional letters with Neville and Pansy but everyone else I had let fade away. Many, of course, had *chosen* to fade away.

I hung around the lonely house, waiting for my sister.

After a week or so, she arrived.

She came suddenly, unannounced, by taxi from the station. It was late October, I think, perhaps early November, and we embraced in the freezing hall. Naomi was wrapped head to foot in what had once been a beautiful long overcoat. She wore a scarf and felt cloche hat. She seemed secretive and afraid.

'Come in, for Goodness sake. We've got a little fire.'

'We? Who's here?'

'Nobody, darling. Just you and I.'

'Does anybody know I've come?'

'I didn't till just now.'

As she followed me into the drawing room I swear she glanced over her shoulder in case anyone should be there. 'Neville knows,' she muttered. 'I suppose he's safe.'

She had contacted him on arrival in London, and he had confirmed that she might still not be safe on British soil. I pooh-poohed this while Naomi tried to warm herself at my little fire. She

109

wouldn't let me take her long overcoat. I wasn't sure whether that was because of the afternoon chill or so she'd be ready to make a run for it if she had to.

'I've been ensconced here over a week,' I said. 'Nobody's shown any interest.'

'It's different for you.'

I was sad to see that she had aged. Naomi had always had such vibrant looks but the war years had not been kind to her. Her cheeks were drawn and her eyes dark shadowed. She still wore her hair long but it no longer had the bounce it had had before. She had lost weight – yet despite all this she retained the essence of her beauty. It could be restored.

She shivered. 'Neville said I could be tried for treason. Why the hell did I come?'

'He's exaggerating.'

'You shouldn't have made me do it.'

'Do what, darling?'

I stepped closer and wrapped her in a sisterly hug. Her overcoat felt cold as snow.

She said, 'Made me come. You insisted that we meet here. I shouldn't have.'

There seemed little I could do to allay her nervousness, but by remaining silent I drove her on: 'I could be shot.'

'Naomi!'

'It's true. Look at William Joyce.'

Joyce's death was too recent to be shrugged off. – I don't have to remind you that Joyce (Lord Haw Haw, as he was known) had been executed the previous year.

'And he wasn't even British,' Naomi sobbed.

'He had a British passport.'

'Only so he could work here. Anyway, that was ages old. It had expired. He was an *American*, for Goodness sake.'

'But he did broadcast for Germany all through the war, darling. I suppose they felt they had to make an example of him.'

'They'd do the same to me.'

'You're over-dramatising, my poor sweet love.'

'That's easy to say.'

I tried in vain to reassure her. The war had been over for more than two years, and Joyce's had been an extreme case. When I tried to distract her with an admittedly depressing tour of the house and grounds, I still could not shake her. She skulked from room to room, saying she should not have come. As daylight faded, she insisted I close the curtains before lighting lamps.

110

Eventually, when we had eaten a spartan supper, I persuaded her to sit down with me and discuss the legacy. That was why she had come. It was an odd situation for us: though Mother had willed almost everything to her, Naomi couldn't easily release the money. For one thing, most of it was tied up in the house and for another, she was now resident in Switzerland. There were the most hideous regulations on foreign exchange.

'Also,' I had to inform her, 'the solicitors insist they have to see you personally.'

'Why?'

'They're solicitors. You know.'

'Why can't everything be handled through you? You're my sister. You can act for me.'

'I'm another legatee.'

'Four hundred pounds?'

Naomi was as scornful as I about Mother's spiteful bequest – and she confirmed that she and I should share the real legacy. 'It was Muv's aberration,' Naomi sneered. ('Muv' was a term she had picked up from Unity, though Mother had always detested it.) I repeated what the solicitor had told me: that the entire legacy had to be made over to Naomi, and that it was his duty to satisfy himself that it had been. After that she could dispose of it as she chose.

'Can't I *gift* it to you, Sidi?'

'No – and certainly not on my say-so. He says that, in any case, he can't pay it to you in Switzerland.'

'It's my money—'

We went round this several times. After a while, to inject some kind of cheer into that bleak wintry night, I produced a half bottle of Scotch for which I had paid a fortune on my first day in London – that famous, much castigated half bottle of Scotch.

On that dark evening, in front of a struggling, cool log fire, we drank two or three nips of Scotch – from egg cups, because I couldn't find small glasses. Naomi never took off her overcoat, though later, before we went to bed, she did open the buttons that ran down its front. I was relieved – I had begun to wonder if she was naked beneath, like a Mata Hari or an exotic whore.

She told me the story – though how much can one tell in an evening? – of her life in wartime, and I told her mine. We had the lamps turned low – in fact, I think we had turned off every one of them so we could sit illuminated by firelight. In that gentle flickering glow we could no longer see the reduced state of the drawing room. The house might have been as it had been before the war.

There followed a long, lost day. People asked me about it afterwards, but all Naomi and I did was get up late, sit around the house, wander around the damp and misty grounds. I remember Naomi taking a pair of rusty shears to attack the rose bushes. We looked for the lawn mower but it had disappeared. At some time in the afternoon I walked to the village and telephoned the solicitor. I didn't mention Naomi, but booked the appointment for myself alone. This again I would be questioned about later – why, when we were both in the house together, did I fix the appointment only for myself? The reason, of course, was that Naomi didn't want anyone to know that she was there – not even the solicitor. Especially not him. She intended us to arrive at his office together, at which point she would sign the paperwork, then disappear.

That evening we dined on an omelette and a loaf of bread. I had no ration book, but fortunately the girl who had helped me clean the house was able to procure me a dozen illicit eggs. Naomi, clad again in her long warm overcoat, cooked the omelettes with continental flair, tilting the pan over the gas flame and sprinkling the fluffy eggs with fresh new herbs she had found somewhere in the garden. We drank whisky from egg cups once again.

After supper we sat in the firelit drawing room, reminiscing and finishing the whisky. Naomi had a way of hunching forward in her chair, the little egg cup held in both hands beneath her chin as if it were a lady's hand-warmer. She would breathe its aroma and close her eyes.

The tranquil evening ended. We heard a car pull up in the drive outside – it was so silent, the still of night. We heard footsteps crunching on our gravel.

'Who on earth is that? Don't say I'm here.'

Naomi had leapt to her feet and was hissing at me from the corner. As the first knock sounded at the door, I raised a calming hand. A man's voice – unnecessarily rough – called, 'Open up! Police!' Naomi began to run.

The pounding continued as I followed her to the kitchen. She was sobbing, her long coat trailing like a heavy skirt. For one extraordinary moment she picked up a large black-handled bread knife and stared at it as if somehow the knife could save her. I must have said something, but I don't remember what. I do know that while we stared at each other in the kitchen the remorseless banging continued at our front door.

She said, 'They'll come round the back. I may just have time.'

As she moved to the door I reached out to stop her. Running away seemed hopeless. But it was late at night, we were badly shaken, and this was the hour when reason slips away. Naomi, with that stunning

112

calm one can find in adversity, whispered, 'Go to the front door and try to hold them off.'

She opened the kitchen door and gave me one last look. 'You'll be all right, Sidi. It's only me they want.'

Then she disappeared.

I suppose I should have followed. But instead I called along the hall and as I made my way slowly to the quivering front door, I called out again that I was coming. I wanted to delay them a few more moments. I rattled the door chain – it wasn't fastened, but I pretended that it was – and I asked nervously, 'Yes? Who is it?'

'Police!' they repeated for the umpteenth time.

'Police?' I responded inanely.

'Open up. Open the door, please.'

'Yes, yes, just a moment.'

I rattled the chain again, fitted the key noisily into the mortise lock, turned it, opened the door, faced the men – just as they turned away from me, shouting, 'There she goes! She's in the car!'

And I too could hear the roar of Mother's Humber, the crunch of tyres, the speeding car. I could hear my poor frightened Naomi fleeing in the dark. Even as the policemen began to run back across our drive, Naomi's headlights flared into life, and she drove out through the open gateway.

The three policemen descended on their own car like flies on meat, each wrestling with a different door, tumbling in, cursing it into life, stalling it, restarting, slewing it clumsily across our gravel, out through the gateway and along the lane.

The rest was reported in the newspapers. Naomi sped into the back lanes behind the house, lost control on a corner, spun and crashed into a field. The car turned over several times. There was no fire, no explosion, just a mangled wreck in a field of mud. The night was so dark that the police, desperate to catch up, drove straight past the point where she had left the road, continued floundering, then retraced their steps. It took quarter of an hour till they saw the gap torn through the hedge. It was over an hour before they told me.

By that time I was at the police station. They sent another car to fetch me – the extravagance! – virtually the whole of the local resources employed on this pathetic case. I was driven to the police station by a grim-faced constable who refused to say a word. I sat in the back of his uncomfortable police car wondering whether Naomi had got away – and if she had, where she might be. It hardly seemed to matter: she would be captured anyway. I fully expected to see her at the station, but she wasn't there. The search party had not returned.

113

In my first few minutes at the police station I learnt that, in any case, things had not been as serious as Naomi feared. The police had not called to arrest her.

'Quite the reverse.'

I was seated in their bleak, cream painted interview room, sipping at a ghastly cup of over-sweetened tea. Opposite was a middle-aged, pink faced bobby who spoke gently as if I were a child.

'We have to give your sister a very necessary warning – to be careful when out in public. Feelings can still run high. We want to keep the peace.'

He didn't say so, but I could tell that our wretched solicitor had considered it his patriotic duty to inform them that he thought Naomi was at the house.

I said, 'I don't expect my sister to flaunt herself in public.'

When he was called from the room I noticed that he carried a slight limp, but when shortly afterwards he returned he seemed to walk more stiffly. His face had turned a deeper pink. He seemed a kindly man – that rare thing, a kindly policeman – and he spoke so quietly I could barely hear. Yet I knew his message the moment he crept into the room.

'I'm terribly sorry. I have bad news.'

Oh, who knows what words he used? Terrible news. A tragedy. He had come to tell me she was dead.

The details – how they had found the broken hedge, the upturned car, how she was crushed behind the wheel – I know them now. But whether he told me in that interview room or whether the details emerged later I'm no longer sure. Somebody must have told me. I didn't read the newspapers. One thing I do remember is that while a policeman drove me home – yes, on that specific journey, in the back of that darkened car – I resolved not to read a single newspaper. I couldn't bear the things they'd say.

One day, sometime in the Fifties or even later, at a public library, I brought myself to look up an account of that dreadful night in the archives of the *Times*. By then, of course, the pain had died. Or was slumbering. But that day in the library as I read the mean self-righteous prose – in the *Times*, our most sober newspaper – I knew that my initial resolution had been correct. Even years later, to read those spiteful words resurrected all my anger and impotent grief. That those anonymous authors could be my countrymen seemed barely credible. About Naomi, inevitably, they had been scathing, but they had also savaged me – both for being, in their words, a traitor's acolyte, but also, more cruelly, for encouraging my sister to share the half bottle of Scotch. I had made her drunk, they said – which was why she had crashed. It seemed that some of the lower newspapers had suggested that I had plied my sister with drink deliberately, as if I'd known the police would come, as if I'd known she would dash to the car, as if I'd let her die so I could claim the inheritance. It sounds ridiculous now, but those suggestions lingered in later articles when, two weeks later, the newspapers learnt that as Naomi's only close relative, I became the sole legatee. That accursed half bottle of whisky (or one like it, since the original was removed as evidence) was photographed and splashed across the inside pages of the gutter press – the *Sketch*, my old enemy, and the *Daily Express* – and the story was carefully recapitulated in the *Times*.

Sitting in that smart, Fifties red brick library, reading the dead words of a decade before, brought back not so much the minor ferment in the press as my own long sad weeks of isolation. I had moved out of Graylands, put it up for sale, and had gratefully accepted the hospitality of my true friends Neville and Pansy. They nursed me, sheltering me for several weeks until the ranting fuss died down. I emerged once for Naomi's funeral, and faced the hyenas of the press wearing my American sunglasses and with my cropped hair defiantly set. I listened to a minister whom I had never met before as he carefully chose words for the informal address (what eulogy could he pretend for her?). I saw my sister buried and was driven away. During the service I had stood alone. Neville and Pansy had deliberately remained apart from me, so no one would realise I was at their home. Our pre-war friends largely cut the funeral. Post-war friendships had not begun.

In the seclusion of the next few weeks I read, I spent hours practising at the piano, and I took sheltered walks in damp, lonely lanes. I was convalescing. I knew that after I had had this short period of sanctuary, no one could ever hurt me again.

TWELVE

'We're becoming part of the local scenery,' Gottfleisch remarked. 'Now we know our way around.'

He lolled in the back of the Espace. Craig smiled grimly as he drove them back to the house where they had been several days before to attend the funeral reception. The village had a well-kept unlived-in look, pretty in the sun.

At Murdo's house the two men, both wearing suits, stood like estate agents at the door and rung the bell. Gottfleisch had his back to the entrance and looked out at the small garden, while Craig stared at the door as if his glare could make it melt.

When Angus opened the door they walked straight in. Craig shouldered him aside and Gottfleisch blocked the doorway. Angus bleated. They didn't answer. Gottfleisch prodded Angus in the chest and propelled him backwards into the living room. Craig was waiting and spun him round. As Angus dithered, the big man prowled about the room picking up trinkets and putting them down.

Craig began, 'Where's your son?'

Angus stammered meaninglessly.

'Your boy?'

'I – what?'

'Your boy, dopehead – where's Angus?'

'My – oh, my God.'

Gottfleisch said, 'This *is* the son. This is Angus.'

'He looks a hundred years old.'

'Dissolute lifestyle. The father's dead.'

Gottfleisch had circled to where Angus could see him. 'Good morning, Angus. Remember me?'

'Well, partly – I'm sorry, I don't—'

'We weren't introduced.'

Angus seemed to take comfort from that, but Craig asked, 'Can I hit him yet?'

Angus froze.

116

Gottfleisch said, 'In a moment. Are these your father's things?'

'That's right.' Angus nodded desperately.

Craig muttered, 'I thought he was my age.'

'Don't tell me he's too old for you?' Gottfleisch smiled.

Angus interrupted: 'Look, perhaps you could explain—'

Craig hit him. As Angus folded he heard Gottfleisch say, 'Never apologise; never explain. We're here to talk to you, dear boy.'

Through swimming eyes Angus saw Gottfleisch lift a tiny side table, glance at its underside and put it down. 'All Murdo's?' Gottfleisch asked. 'Nothing of your own? A pity. We want to break something, you see, and we'd prefer it to be yours.'

Angus glanced nervously at the mantelpiece. 'Anything.' He paused to take a breath. 'But please don't break that vase.'

Craig snorted. Gottfleisch shook his head. 'For a man of your age, Angus, that was pathetic.'

Craig asked, 'Shall I break his arm?'

'A finger should suffice.'

'How about his nose?'

'What do *you* think, Angus?' Gottfleisch asked. 'Any preference? You know, last time I was here I didn't get a chance to see around the house. I expect old Murdo had one or two nice things stashed.' He smiled coldly. 'Perhaps I should leave you two to get acquainted.' He disappeared.

Craig stared into Angus's face as if counting the pores in his sweating skin. Angus licked his lips. 'Look, can I ask—'

'Keep the fuck shut up.'

While Angus quivered in the centre of the room Craig began to prowl around as Gottfleisch had before. He spied a bowl of dead pot pourri and plunged his hand in it, scattering dried husks and petals out of the bowl.

'Sort of place you'd hide something,' he remarked. 'You a smack-head, Angus? You look it.'

Angus did not reply. He watched Craig invert the bowl and tip the contents onto the carpet. Craig said, 'Get against the wall.'

Angus seemed too stunned to move.

Craig said, 'Don't fuck with me.'

Angus stumbled across to a section of blank wall.

'Keep your back against that wall.'

Craig approached him casually, bearing the bowl as if it were filled with soup. 'Here's a trick a friend once showed me. See this bowl? – Keep your head against the wall.'

Craig frowned at Angus. 'This bowl, it's about the same size as your head with one side sliced off. Isn't it?' Craig raised the bowl head-high.

'Now, watch the bowl, Angus. I mean, study it, make yourself a part of it. You doing that? Can you feel the – what is it? – contour of the bowl? Can you imagine this bowl as if it really was your head?'

Angus kept his back pressed against the wall. His eyes were popping. He seemed mesmerised by the younger man. Suddenly Craig rammed the bowl forward to smash beside his head. Angus cried out. His knees gave way and he slithered to the floor.

Craig said, 'See? If that *had* been your head smashed against the wall, you'd be in *bits* about it, wouldn't you?'

Gottfleisch reappeared through the door, speaking as if he'd never been away: 'You fancy yourself at frightening old ladies, Angus. But you don't have my young friend's style.'

It took a moment or two for Angus to realise what Gottfleisch meant. His face trembled with surprise and fear.

Gottfleisch added, 'I have spoken to Miss Keene.'

'Oh shit.'

'Language! Stand up straight, you dreadful man.'

Gottfleisch was drawing closer. 'You won't threaten her again, will you?'

Angus shook his head. Gottfleisch pushed Craig aside. 'Perhaps you'd better give me the envelope.'

Angus swallowed. 'Envelope?'

The blow that Gottfleisch thumped into his guts carried the whole of his twenty stone. Angus crumpled instantly, and lay retching on the floor.

'Oh dear,' said Craig sarcastically. He crossed to the mantelpiece, plucked the funeral flowers from a vase, crossed back and cast the cold water on Angus's face. Angus shuddered but did not get up.

Gottfleisch repeated, 'Envelope.'

Craig pulled Angus into a sitting position against the wall, patted his shoulder, then yelled 'Envelope!' in his right ear.

Angus mumbled, 'In the desk cupboard.'

Craig patted his cheek and stood up. He went to the desk, took out a large brown envelope and asked, 'This it?'

Angus nodded.

Craig delivered it up to Gottfleisch, who glanced inside without removing the contents. 'What else do you have?'

Angus began to shake his head. He was still sitting. 'Nothing. That's all there is.'

'You wouldn't hold out on me, dear boy?'

'No.'

'That would be unwise. We're leaving now.'

As Gottfleisch wandered from the room, Craig stooped beside the groaning Angus and grabbed a handful of his wet shirt. In an exaggerated cockney accent, Craig asked, 'Can I do yer now, sir?'

He heaved Angus to his feet and immediately punched him low in the stomach where Gottfleisch had before. Angus gasped, fell sideways, and vomited on the floor. Craig kicked him, wondered whether to work him over, then stamped on his ankle and left the room.

Angus remained balled against the wall, eyes screwed tight to keep the world away. He heard the door slam, heard a car start and drive off. He didn't try to move. Though he had given up the envelope, his one consolation was that they had smashed nothing more than his father's bowl. They could have trashed the room – not that he was bothered about his father's things, but beside the bookcase stood a cardboard box full of vinyl records of the Seventies which Angus had brought down with him. They were precious. They were the remembrances of his youth. To have lost those discs would have been a mortal wound.

*

At the second squat, Ticky held back and let the boy try for himself. He suspected that if he stood well back from the doorway he would be more easily seen from inside, and one good look at his face would guarantee the door stayed firmly closed. Ticky wanted Cy to realise what he was up against. He didn't want the boy to find a home, so he stood with his heels against the kerb and scowled at the brickwork. Most of the windows were boarded up but Ticky thought he'd seen someone glancing out. In a decent world, he thought, anyone seeing this innocent young boy at the door would welcome him in, bring him off the streets out of harm's way. But times were hard now: good squats were scarcer, and those which did exist were well defended. When Cy rapped at the door a fourth time, a voice finally responded from inside: 'Bugger off.'

Cy bent down to call through the letter box. It was boarded up but he called anyway: 'I need a place. Can I sleep in the hall?'

'Sod off.'

'I've nowhere else.'

There was no answer.

'Just for tonight.'

Whoever was inside had wandered off. Ticky glanced at the upper window to make sure no one was about to empty a bucket on them to defend their fortress.

Cy looked disappointed. 'Shall we try the next place?'

Ticky pulled a face. 'There's not a string of 'em. Squatting's difficult nowadays. The government's tightened the laws.'

'New Labour's going to change all that. They'll house the homeless.'

'I bet,' said Ticky, nodding at the house. 'Mind you, these punks'll be chucked out soon. Serves the skivers right.'

As they walked away from Seven Dials he said, 'There's one other place. Five minutes' walk.'

Cy said, 'I'm hungry. Can we stop somewhere?'

'You must get used to that, my friend. We'll try this other place first. Then you'll know how you stand, won't you?'

Cy nodded glumly, following Ticky across Cambridge Circus. In Old Compton Street, Ticky noticed how the boy's eyes were drawn to the black painted windows of the strip clubs and Adults Only shops. The words and pictures left no doubt as to what lay inside.

'Nifty area to live,' Ticky remarked.

As they passed a peepshow dive, Cy veered towards the kerb, away from a large foreign looking tout lounging in the doorway. Perhaps Cy was afraid he'd be kidnapped, Ticky thought. He kept silent as he led the boy to the end of the street and through the narrow cut by Raymond's Revuebar. In Berwick Street Market the boy looked hungrily at the fruit stalls but Ticky ploughed on, leading him off into an alley at the side. Outside the club at the corner were lurid photographs and in its doorway stood an eight-foot cut-out of a freckled, fleshy woman wearing a blonde wig, sequins and a leer. Cy coloured slightly. Ticky thought the club had no chance, selling smut and sex among fruit and vegetables. That brassy cut-out was almost twice his size but she did not turn Ticky on, no sir, no way. He liked the way the boy had begun to yield himself to his leadership, was walking close to him, knocking into him as they trudged along. Cy was discovering for himself that finding a place was hard to do, that what he needed was a reliable friend. There was nothing like learning for yourself. That's when it sticks. Cy hadn't yet offered an explanation for why he had come, though it wasn't hard to guess: unhappy childhood, broken home, a final row. Perhaps the boy had walked out on an unwelcome stepfather, or perhaps he'd run away from a string of crime. Here he was now, adrift in London. And here was Ticky, trotting at his side.

The third squat was in an unlettable tenement crushed so tightly between larger buildings that it never saw the sun. Even before it had fallen derelict no one wanted to live in it. The tenement had housed a massage club, a peepshow, an import-export agency and several businesses with enigmatic nameplates by the door. At one time it had been used officially as a residential warren for London's transients. Little had changed. Its blackened brickwork foreshadowed further blackness inside. The sooty grime across the brickwork became dark lichen on interior walls.

Ticky stood patiently at Cy's shoulder while the boy waited for an answer to his knock. When he banged again, a sprinkling of mortar dust fell from the lintel. His knocking echoed slightly, as from an empty hall.

'Maybe no one's in,' said Cy uncertainly.

'They're just not answering. Mind you, the way *you* knock, you sound like a cop. Call through the letter box again.'

'There isn't one.'

Ticky rubbed his chin. 'I wonder where the postman puts their giro cheques.'

Cy stepped back from the door into the middle of the narrow alley and called up to the boarded windows: 'Hey! Anybody there? Who wants a baggie? Good stuff.'

Ticky stared at the boy in some surprise. 'Hey, keep your noise down, Angel. You didn't say you was carrying.'

'I'm just trying to get someone to answer the door.'

Ticky continued to stare at him. Christ, fourteen years old. '*Are* you carrying?'

Cy shrugged and moved closer to the boarded door. 'Three or four joints, that's all. School stuff. I can't hear anyone coming.'

'I'm surprised they're not running from the next street, the way you shouted.'

Cy grinned. 'I thought the streets of London were paved with drugs?'

'They're paved with dog shit, friend, that's all.'

Leaning his ear against the door, Cy asked, 'Where do *you* live, Ticky?'

The little man's heart leapt. 'Oh, I've got a little flat, you know.'

Cy came away from the door. 'That sounds nice.'

Ticky sniffed grandly. 'In London, you see, any kind of pad is essential. I mean, you've got to have an address. You don't have to have a smart place, like in films and TV—'

'But you *have* got one?'

'A flat? Oh yeah. Little but nice, you know – like me. Cosy.'

Ticky smiled encouragingly.

Cy said, 'I suppose there's no chance—'

The front door opened. They both spun towards it, and the sound of its opening was like a nail levered from a plank of wood. When the gap widened to about nine inches a face appeared beneath a large woollen hat. 'What d'you want?'

'I need a place,' Cy said.

'Full up.'

'Nowhere else will take me.'

'They wouldn't.'

'I won't be any trouble.'

'Huh. Don't give me that. You're a bit young, ain't yer?'

'I'm sixteen.'

'Thirteen more likely.'

'Honest. It's my birthday today—'

'Oh, isn't that marvellous? What a coincidence!'

'It's true. Look, could I use the lavatory? I'm getting desperate out here.'

The face laughed. Cy said, 'Won't take a moment.'

The man kept grinning as he shook his head. 'You certainly have all the numbers, son. How long you been in town?'

'Just today.'

The man nodded, looking Cy up and down. 'And who's um...' He stared at Ticky. 'Who are you then, mate?'

'Just a friend. I don't need a place. I'm just helping him out.'

The man wasn't sure what to make of Ticky. 'So you've got your own place, right?'

'Oh yes,' Ticky responded eagerly, thinking this would kill Cy's chance. 'I offered to let the lad stay with me but, well, he wants somewhere on his own.'

But the face said, 'He wouldn't want to stay with *you*.' He glanced back at Cy. 'Why are you on the run then, son?'

Cy paused, then mumbled, 'I had to get away, you know.'

The face sneered. 'No, I *don't* know, do I? We need better than that, son. What did you do? Cops want you?'

'No,' answered Cy matter-of-factly. 'But I'd had enough.'

'No cops? You just ran away?'

'That's right.'

'Bet your mummy and daddy will go ape-shit to get you back.'

'No chance.'

'Where *are* your mum and dad?'

Cy stared back blankly. 'I don't have any. There's just me alone.'

'What, like you weren't born, you was dug up – out of a cabbage field, is that it?'

'I'm really desperate for a pee,' Cy side-stepped pleasantly. 'Can I come in for a minute?'

'I don't think so,' the man said.

But a voice interrupted from beyond him – an older voice, behind the reinforced front door: 'Oh, let the kid come in. It's not as if he's a Jehovah's Witness.'

THIRTEEN

The bell rang again before she had finished coming downstairs. She had been in the spare bedroom searching through some boxes for a piece of jewellery she had mislaid – a German Death's Head ring which she never wore but which had associations for her. She had expected to find it in the Chinese cabinet but it was not there.

When Sidonie opened the door she found Angus Fyffe standing in the dark, staring at her in an odd appraising way. Perhaps he had come to apologise. Certainly he seemed uncertain of his welcome – as well he might, she thought. Angus hesitated on her doorstep.

Though she couldn't be bothered to continue the argument, she said, 'I am not at all sure I should invite you in.'

'No, well... I thought we ought to have... um... I don't suppose you expected to see me?'

'You were very tiresome, Angus.'

'Well, all the same... I mean...'

'Have you something you wish to tell me?'

'I'll say,' he began eagerly, clasping his hands together as if he were cold. But he seemed uncertain how to continue, and he shivered slightly in the dark.

'Don't you have a coat? Oh, for Goodness sake, come in.'

He stepped gratefully into her hallway, and in the electric light his velvet jacket glistened as if it were damp.

'Has it been raining?'

'Yes, a bit.'

She led him into the sitting room. 'Go and warm yourself by the radiator.'

'Thanks, that's cool.'

'Hardly,' she replied, her back to him. 'I switch the heating on in the evenings.' She seemed to be excusing herself to him, as if feeling the cold was a sign of age.

He said, 'Right on,' and pressed his back against the radiator, the palms of each hand against the warm metal.

123

'Would you like some coffee? It's already made.'

'Fantastic. Yeah, I'd really go for that.'

As she marched into the kitchen, Sidonie shook her head. For a man approaching forty to cling to the mumbling speech patterns and clothes of his adolescence was beyond comprehension. He was Murdo's child! She removed the coffee jug from the hot-plate and poured two coffees. She had made it in the traditional continental way – Viennese coffee, coarse ground, spooned into a jug; boiling water on the grounds, then stirred; the liquid left to infuse and settle for at least five minutes before being poured straight from the jug. It was rich and darkly aromatic. Its gritty lingering taste reminded her of a cafe in Vienna where she and her sister had liked to sit in a window seat with their newspapers.

'A biscuit?'

She was approaching Angus with a silver tray on which the biscuits were arranged in a small porcelain dish. Though they were superior to the bland confections offered in other people's homes, they were to her still not comparable to those crumblingly delicious confections served in Vienna.

'Fantastic, yeah.'

Angus was enthusiastic enough to part company from the radiator. 'I remember your biscuits now. Wow. They're great.'

'So people say. I don't make them, you know. I've told any number of people exactly where I buy them, yet when I call on them they still offer me the usual varieties.'

'Crazy.'

'As if biscuits were unobtainable outside of supermarkets. One woman did apologise to me: she said that if she'd known I was coming she would have 'got some in'. Ridiculous. Fine things should not be bought to impress one's friends, but should be enjoyed. Have you come to apologise?'

Angus spluttered on his coffee.

'Too hot?' she asked.

His face had changed colour. 'Sorry. A crumb went down the wrong way. Yes, um, wow.' He grinned in mild embarrassment.

'Better now?'

'Thanks. Yeah, since you ask... that fat man, is he a friend of yours?'

'Fat man?'

'I recognised him from the funeral.'

'Oh, Mr Gottfleisch.'

'Is that the bastard's name?'

She raised an eyebrow. Angus continued: 'I've heard Dad

124

mention him. He's a thug.'

'He's an art dealer by trade. Much the same thing, no doubt. Your father knew him.'

'You sent him round to me, didn't you?'

Sidonie studied him. 'I merely mentioned you in passing. He didn't tell me he would call.'

'He beat me up.'

She was unperturbed. 'I was distressed by your last visit, Angus. Mr Gottfleisch happened to call before I had fully recovered, and...' She stared at him boldly. 'I needed a shoulder to cry on, I'm afraid.'

'He brought his henchman and, well... they duffed me up.'

'You don't look badly hurt.'

'Jesus!'

'I wonder if you've ever seen a person who has been properly beaten up? You got off lightly, Angus.'

'Christ!'

'Though Mr Gottfleisch has unexpected talents, I see.'

'Art dealer!' Angus muttered.

'How is your own art coming along?'

'You really don't care, do you?'

'About your art? I've just asked you about it.'

'No, about the... Oh, you're something else. Well, since you ask, I'm working with this software company – Pall-it, the Designer's Friend – you heard of it?'

'Oh, computers...'

'It's a set of programs that lets you manipulate scanned images. Takes the guesswork out of artwork.'

'That's a quote from the advertisement, I take it?'

'Hm, sort of. Like, I've just been working on Olympia—'

'The exhibition hall?'

'No, the painting, Olympia – you know, Manet? – I used the program to get inside it, twist it round, see the same view from a different viewpoint. You see, we're creating a new kind of art.'

'Creating or destroying? I thought you once wanted to be a painter?'

'What, paint on canvas? That's dead, man.'

'I see. But with your technology you can do what, exactly – present an existing portrait from a different angle?'

'Yeah, a different perspective. Listen, you know how we see the naked Olympia lying on the couch with the black serving girl standing behind her? Well, how would the world look from the black girl's eyes? What if Manet had painted it from *her* perspective – what d'you think the black girl would see?'

'The back of Olympia's head, and Manet at his easel. So what?'

'This is an entirely new form of art. You know the tricky part? Not getting inside the picture and revolving it – that's easy now. The hard bit is to get the colour and texture right – I mean *really* right, so the finished product looks as if Manet painted it. Well—' He paused dramatically. 'That's the part I'm working on.'

'Trying to emulate Manet? A modest enough ambition, Angus – though when you were young I remember you believed in earth magic, and in creating things with your hands—'

'I still do.'

'You used to say that manufactured things were phoney.'

'Not phoney. I wouldn't use that word. That's Sixties shit.'

'In the Sixties people did at least believe in something—'

'Yeah – what was it? Turn on, tune in, drop out.'

'But computers, Angus? You've *sold* out.'

His face grew serious. 'Paint is dead.'

He finished the coffee and put the cup down carefully on the side table. 'I mean, I know that Dad… and your sister and all… and…'

She noticed that his hands were trembling.

He continued: 'But Dad's dead now, isn't he? And the thing is… I need some money.'

Sidonie sighed.

'I mean, yeah, I'm sorry, like – but it'd just be the same money you've been paying Dad anyway. So you can afford it, right? OK, look, I mean I know you sent those heavies round but, well, next time I'll be ready for them.'

'Ready for them? Angus, you couldn't defend yourself against *me*, let alone against Mr Gottfleisch. But please let me try to drum this into your head one final time: your father was not blackmailing me. He had nothing to blackmail me with.'

'Christ, I *showed* you—'

'An envelope with some newspaper cuttings!'

'Annotated! I mean, about your sister's death. It was all explained there, wasn't it?'

'What was?'

'She died, for Christ's sake. You inherited *everything*. I mean, you didn't have anything before – it *said* so, in the papers.'

'Never believe what you read in the newspapers.'

'Come *on*. You killed Naomi for the money. That's what the papers said.'

'It's what they hinted at. This is most distressing, Angus. I told you last time: the police were on the *scene*, they know what happened. There was never any question of my being prosecuted.'

126

'Not then, maybe – but *now*! Now, right? Yeah, you're gonna have to pay me.'

'Go away, Angus.'

'Yeah, straight to the police. I mean, I don't want to, but if you force me…'

'And you'll show them what – a handful of press cuttings? There's nothing there.'

'They're just the start. What d'you think's in the *rest* of my Dad's documents?'

'Good-bye, Angus.'

'Look, I'm not asking for anything much. – And I'm not afraid of your friend Mr Fatso Gottfleisch. No way. He won't get anything out of me, because I've taken steps.'

'Steps!' She held her fingers to her bowed forehead and seemed almost to be laughing behind her hand. 'Please *do* take steps, Angus, take steps out through the door.'

He moved towards it, watching her – and when he reached it he paused to speak: 'You paid Dad, and now you've got to pay me. It'll be like nothing has ever changed.'

'Everything has changed,' she said. 'Murdo was a fine man, but he is dead. You dishonour your father's name.'

✳

Members of every generation select one decade as the climax of their lives. For Angus it was the Seventies. He was born – when? – just before 1960, so he was too young to appreciate that decade. His own decade was featureless (as he personifies!) – continuing the soft, pot-smoking miasma of the decade before, but without its innovation and excitement. Angus was a post Sixties man. His golden decade occurred, as it does for most people, when he was between fifteen and twenty-five. Even today, in this last decade of the millennium, there is a generation who will look back to these current days as having been their golden time. That golden decade when all one has is youth itself – too little money, too many needs – when one is burdened with draining responsibilities: marriage, babies, buying a house – is the time we all look back upon as the high point of our lives! Why? Because we were young. We were vigorous and alive. We were striving to succeed.

When I remember my own golden decade I think of gay times and balls and parties – the mayfly's dance before the fire. Yet outside the warm, bright-lit glow in which I danced lay a world of poverty and excess: shopgirls saving shillings to watch movie stars; men without a job; financial empires lost; national governments overthrown;

127

idealistic young men journeying thousands of miles to the Spanish Civil War; political ideas reborn; every one of us hurtling insanely into what was then an unimaginable world war. When I catalogue those days it seems unarguable that mine was the century's most momentous decade – yet was it really? *Was* mine the paramount decade, or was it simply that I was young?

In Angus Fyffe's decade he had student demos and soft drugs while around him the flower people made love not war; but in ours we had the Jarrow Marches, the Great Depression, the Abdication and the battle of Fascism against Communism. Angus had rock concerts and Glastonbury, while I had *Parteitags* in Nuremberg and Berlin.

Does that surprise you? Did you not know that British people attended the huge Nazi rallies of the Thirties? Many of us were there. In the early Thirties – 1933 and 34 – the things happening in Germany seemed dramatic and exciting. A good number of us (a minority I agree, but one which contained many opinion makers) watched agog as that large and crippled country pulled itself up by the bootlaces – literally from the ground up – and rearranged itself, conducting an economic miracle and popular revolution before our eyes. We were young; it was our parents' generation which had imposed the monstrous Versailles Treaty upon Germany – a treaty whose sole purpose was to handicap them so ruinously that their nation never again should thrive. One does not need today's hindsight to recognise the injustice of that treaty – most thinking people saw it then. Germany was forced to suffer loss of territory, massive unemployment, hyper inflation and increasingly incompetent government, but finally, in a bold experiment, it was demonstrating the first signs of how a nation could be reborn. – If these words sound hollow now, it is with a hindsight none of us had in the early Thirties. At the time we thought we saw living proof that by political idealism and will alone a country could be redeemed and could save its soul. The transformation was being effected not by politicians and financiers in smoky rooms but by the people themselves, in streets, on farms, and in their workplaces. Can you wonder the young were inspired? Our generation was sweeping away the shackles and straightjackets which had restrained previous generations; we were turfing out doddering old leaders and self-serving institutions. We were creating the bright new world of the twentieth century. Oh, what joy it was to be young! We were the future; it would be ours.

Don't condemn too hastily. The young always create their own new gods – but see how quickly those gods tarnish. In the Forties, after the war, optimistic youth made a god of liberal Western democracy and honest politics. In the Fifties they contrasted the high-minded socialism of Bertrand Russell with the down to earth directness of Senator McCarthy – or they fell back on the new god of Rock'n'roll. In the Sixties, gods became legion: Indian mystics, American pot-heads, Bob Dylan, J F Kennedy, Martin Luther King. Poor Angus Fyffe's Seventies, naturally, could produce only second-rate and doom-laden gods: Gaia, whom you will have forgotten, sundry other ecological seers – and ESP. The god of the re-invigorated Eighties was money – nothing else: it was the single standard of that decade. Here in the Nineties, god is oneself.

In 1933, which was a *lifetime* before the war, Naomi and I holidayed in Bavaria. To do so then was in no way unusual or significant (if one had the money) other than that we were two young women on our own. We based ourselves in Munich and toured the surrounding countryside to see fairy tale castles and fine churches. I remember being particularly impressed by my first encounter with what people now call duvets – *die Federbetten* as they were known in Bavaria. To this day I recall the luxury of a Bavarian bed: sinking deep into those wonderfully soft goosedown mattresses beneath the *Steppdecken*, and floating in a nest of feathers.

We drove north from Munich with a young Count who had fallen deliriously in love with Naomi (delirious for her but frustrating for me) via Ingolstadt (where the car broke down and we spent the afternoon in the sun drinking beer and eating *Bratwurst*) and on to all the excitement at Nuremberg. Memory tells me that we caught only the last day of the four-day *Parteitag*. Earlier, the Count had been sniffy about it, dismissing it as a workers' festival, but Naomi had been determined not to miss the fun.

There were literally hundreds of thousands there – and yes, to confirm your prejudice: vast numbers of them wore party uniforms – but I found the tens of thousands of *tents* more incredible than the crowd. In huge numbers, people become simply a teeming mass, but the bivouacs, being static, were like a city sprung from the earth. Every field, every verge, practically every garden was crammed with tents. Many parts of the town and surrounding countryside were massed with impenetrable crowds. Accommodation must have been impossible but the Count knew a landowner outside Erlangen and he assured us we could sleep there. We never reached it. To travel through Nuremberg and out the other side was impossible. When the climactic day finally ended we staggered exhausted through fields of tents (and inevitably were invited into several of them!) to find our car and drive away.

I have read accounts of the annual *Parteitage* written by people who were not there, in which the huge festivals are described as military propaganda-fests. They were no more militaristic than an English torchlight tattoo: they were a vast public celebration of rediscovered nationhood. By that fourth day, of course, people were drunk, tired, out of their minds from days of carousing, but the excitement was still there – the optimism, the sense of unity and purpose. There was nothing aggressive about the festival, no ranting against other nations – quite the reverse: the prevailing mood was one of joy, that Germany had been reborn and could become the foundation for a united Europe, which in its turn could become an essential bastion between Sovietism and Americanism. United in its sovereign peoples, firm and secure, this invigorated European continent would sweep away its wretched history of petty chauvinism and civil wars, and would replace social injustices and corrupt practices to build a better world. New Europe would be led by popular and effective leaders. No more the *ancien regime*! No more secret board room deals! No more hidden puppeteers!

Yes, yes, we were young and idealistic, as the young should always be, and though our ambitious manifestos showed the naiveté of youth they became a nation's cause and creed. Those principles were voiced for us on that fourth day by the new German Chancellor, Adolf Hitler. (Were you waiting to hear his name? Of course you were.) I heard him distantly (four hundred metres distantly, in fact!) but, thanks to German electronics, I heard him clearly. By that time I could speak German tolerably well – and Hitler took care to use words which were easily understood.

When today you watch scraps of film with rasping sound tracks you think you are re-experiencing reality, but you are not. You see only shadows flickering on a wall. Every leader then – Hitler, Roosevelt, Chamberlain – now sounds feeble and dismissible. (Perhaps Churchill is an exception, but he was reciting scripts.) But listen to post-war leaders who came later – from the Fifties, Sixties or more recently – listen, for example, to J F Kennedy or Martin Luther King, or even to Mrs Thatcher and Ronald Reagan. Ask yourself: if this were the *first* time you had heard them, would you be convinced by such charlatans? No – and when you think back to when you first heard their inspiring voices, you might ask how you were ever taken in. Recordings are a pale reminder of the truth. When you look at a photograph you cannot smell the breeze.

In recordings Hitler is particularly ill-served – partly because the public address systems do not transfer pleasantly to film; partly because of the many times he has been parodied; partly (outside Germany) because people do not understand his language. Charlie

Chaplin portrayed Hitler as a jerking automaton, and the film showed an equally mechanical mob responding to his lead. Could that have been anything like reality? Do you think so? I was there. I saw and heard Hitler move the crowd. I saw him electrify and inspire.

Afterwards the Count (whose name I can no longer recall) pulled us forward, saying there was someone special he wanted us to meet. I assumed at first that he meant Hitler, but no: after a great deal of pushing and elbowing through the throng, the Count stood us before a large and clearly important man wearing, of all things, a dark green hunting costume. I took him to be a performer in the pageant, but this was to be a more auspicious meeting.

'*Herr Präsident*, may I present two English ladies who are here for the *Parteitag*? Miss Naomi Keene and Miss Sidonie Keene. Ladies, this is the President of the Reichstag, Herr Hermann Goering.'

I had heard of him, of course, though the name meant far less to me that day than it would now. Naomi said, 'We're delighted and honoured – but I'm afraid I've just lost my shoe in the crowd. I'm a bit distracted.'

'Not because you have met me, I hope?'

He was a large good looking man (if somewhat overweight, even then) but the gleam in his eyes suggested an immediate attraction towards Naomi. She, at this stage, was poised awkwardly on one foot, and she staggered forwards to clutch at his arm.

'I shall ruin my stocking if I put my foot down in this mud. I don't suppose you could be a darling and find me a chair?'

✳

Even now, it is difficult to talk rationally about that time. People have such prejudices – and whatever one says will inevitably reek of hindsight. People who were not there – people who were not even born then – assume that one must surely have had precognisance of the horrors that were to come. To attempt now to explain the concepts of fascism, for example, meets such incomprehension – such lack of a basic common language – that one might as well try to convince an American sheep farmer that socialism and communism are not the same. Fascism is, in any case, a *verboten* subject. If you open a modern dictionary or encyclopaedia you will find swear words more fully explained.

Following the *first* world war, fascism spread like a cleansing fire. That war had sprung out of rivalries which had been obstinate and obsolete; it had been perpetuated by feudal incompetence and disdain, and had finally dragged across four weary years to a climax of mutilation, death and anarchic revolution. It led to a world that could never be the same. In it a generation of young men had been cruelly depleted, and those who survived matured too soon. They saw themselves as a new breed of man. In fighting that first great war they had travelled to foreign lands, had sailed the seas, had flown the skies. They now drove motorcars, listened to radio and went to the cinema. Into their workplaces came mass production. Into their homes came electric light. These advances may not impress us now, but for that generation Science became their religion. The past was dead; people wanted to modernise. Houses of the Twenties were emptied of nineteenth century furniture. Bright young things wore smart, light clothes. Every medium in art was revolutionised: painters eschewed portraiture and became Cubists, Futurists or Suprematists; poets and dramatists scrapped descriptive prose for manifestos; cinematographers intercut and superimposed strips of moving film; musicians made discordant noise. In politics too, people sought a twentieth century muse.

These convictions were not restricted to a clique of airy intellectuals, but were shared by all progressive minds. It is impossible nowadays to recapture the excitement of that revolution. Artists today are astonishingly conventional: none can shock as Picasso or Braque shocked then by producing pictures that apparently made no sense. No music today is as 'modern' or 'experimental' as that of Stravinski, Bartok or Berg. Indeed, if a humorist today wants to refer quickly to a piece of particularly wayward modern art he will turn, like as not, to a parody of the art produced in the early decades of the twentieth century. That is as modern as art ever got. Back in that third decade, 'new' and 'modern' were the buzzwords of the age, and the new generation of politicians naturally attached themselves to the progressive theme and converted the ideas into action. ('Action' was another buzzword.)

I remember Goering telling us – not on that first day at Nuremberg, but afterwards at Karinhall: 'Out of the glories of the past come the triumphs of the future'. His belief – and in this, German fascism differed from Italian – was that it wasn't necessary to sweep the whole of the past away; one could select the best from the past and use that as a basis upon which to build. (The Italians swept everything away and have been obsessed by modernity ever since.)

He had invited us to his home at Karinhall for two reasons – neither of which he attempted to conceal: firstly, he was attracted to my infuriatingly beautiful sister, and secondly, the Count had told him we were 'high born' English ladies who knew the Mosleys and who might therefore be valuable advocates for the new German cause.

Here I sense that you recoil again: to be an advocate for the

German Reich? To act against the interests of my country? Well, I can only say that we did not look at it that way. After all, in 1933 the war lay six years into the future. Barely six *months* earlier had seen the Reichstag elections in which the Nazi party came to full power. Goering at that time was a senior member of this 'new' and 'modern' government. He was a man of 'action'. He, as the young say now, was 'cool'.

✳

On our first visit to Goering's Karinhall I didn't realise it was his own house. Built (recently, it appeared) in the style of an enormous hunting lodge – exposed wooden beams above marble walls which were themselves lined with tapestries; rambling corridors of bedrooms and staff accommodation; a private cinema; herds of unlikely animals wandering in acres of woodland beside a misty lake – it was a monument to *kitsch*. In fact, I assumed the building was a commandeered hotel.

Evidently Naomi felt the same. We had barely reached our shared room – a tactical error if Goering intended seduction – when she grabbed my arm and giggled, 'Darling, it's so Grand Hotel – and you know which actor would be ideal as Hermann?'

'John Barrymore!'

She and I had seen the film earlier that year in Leicester Square, and Hermann Goering bore a more than passing likeness to the famous screen idol. In the film, Barrymore too was past his prime but he retained enough of his previous handsomeness to make a credible suitor for the divine Garbo.

I said, 'Mr Goering seems to have the more extensive wardrobe.'

This reduced Naomi to fits of giggles on her bed, because each time we had seen the President (twice at Nuremberg, half an hour apart, and here today to greet us at his home) he had worn a different costume – and *costume* was the word: at Nuremberg he had had a Principle Boy's forest green hunting kit and a military uniform out of Gilbert and Sullivan, and to welcome us at his lodge he had appeared in a voluminous white outfit which one might have expected him to wear for an evening behind closed doors in a Turkish harem.

We ate in a colossal mock baronial hall at the largest refectory table I had seen, in the company of a dozen or so handsome young men – most of whom, annoyingly, were to disappear straight after the meal. We were left instead with a pair of silent and dull men, important but forgettable, together with Hermann and a huge blazing fire. (Naomi claimed afterwards that they didn't bother to chop logs for it, but simply felled trees and lobbed them on.)

Conversations with famous men can be disappointing, and though Goering's was far from that – he was witty and entertaining company – it was not one I need bore you with now. Except for his definition of fascism. Goering was drinking brandy (from a gigantic balloon, needless to say) when he embarked on a characteristically short monologue, which rumbled from his chest: 'The reason, *Fräuleine*, that both democracy and socialism have failed is that when individuals are left to themselves they will always please themselves. In other words, they will become barbarous and corrupt. This is human nature. But the Nation – and only the Nation, mark you, a concept everybody understands and feels – has power enough to overcome this natural drift to evil, because it brings people together in a cohesive and shared philosophy and gives them a sense of purpose. People give to the Nation so the Nation can give back to them. The more they invest in it, the richer the Nation will become – but because the people are the Nation, the richer the people become also.' He breathed inspiration from his brandy glass. 'Individuals lose themselves in the vast ocean of the Nation's soul.'

He said this on my first visit to Karinhall, and I remember that on the long – nay, interminable – journey home I could not decide conclusively what I made of him. Was he the screen idol past his prime, the vain dandy in love with his wardrobe, or was he a prescient and profound man? Later, of course, I learnt there were other ways to define him.

It was June 1934. An ornately chirographed missive invited Naomi and I to 'a special commemorative occasion' at his home in Karinhall. Since we had last met him Goering had been much in the news, descending in considerable pomp and grandeur on a number of European countries to assure them of German friendliness and support. Germany, after little more than a year of Nazi government, had become the most talked about country in Europe – occupying more pages of British newsprint than the Soviet Union under Stalin. The eyes of the world were now focused on Europe, and at the heart of Europe was the dynamic and re-emerging Reich. America, under its latest untried president, Roosevelt, had slipped off the Gold Standard into isolation while the British government was so indecisive that it meandered along for almost four years as a coalition under the unprincipled Ramsay MacDonald. That Spring, MacDonald had sanctioned air exercises over London (can you imagine the *alarm* they raised?) and not to be outdone, his rival Baldwin, one of the first British politicians to learn how to manipulate the media, made an outrageously provocative speech in which he proclaimed, 'When you think of the defence of England you no longer think of the chalk cliffs of Dover, you think of the Rhine'. I ask you: could our leading politicians have done *more* to fan the flames of fear and gloom? Wouldn't their time have been better spent in forging an alliance, or at the least, in extending friendship to this new and thriving European power? Remember, those *British* hostilities began five years before the actual war – barely a year after Hitler came to power. Yet history claims that it was only Germany who made warlike sounds.

We travelled to Karinhall by train and then by car. As we drew near the Goering estate we found the local villages draped in mourning; flags flew at half mast, dead flowers lay in the streets, shops and businesses were closed. We saw groups from the League of Maidens and Hitler Youth returning from parades. At first we thought we must have intruded on a national tragedy – the death of Hitler perhaps. (Plots were often rumoured.) But by the time we arrived at Karinhall we knew that all those villages and towns we had passed through had been asked by Goering to participate in the 'special commemorative occasion' to which we ourselves had been invited.

He was bringing home the body of his first wife. Three years before, when she had died tragically young in Sweden, Hermann had lost the one great love of his life. Her name was Karin and he had built Karinhall for her while she was alive. Now, using the enormous power at his command, he had engaged a private train to bring her body from the family tomb to be re-interred at Karinhall. Railway stations all along the route were told to array themselves in deepest mourning. The bands of uniformed youth which we had seen were but a tiny number of those who had paraded to salute the train and scatter flowers.

When we drove into the wooded grounds of Karinhall we entered a scene from Nordic myth. Around the sheltered woodland lake stood serried silent ranks of immaculate soldiers. A large military band – no, in truth an orchestra – played Wagnerian music. Mists rose from the blue waters and hung about the trees. To fanfares and throbbing drums Karin's pewter sarcophagus, carried on the shoulders of a dozen men, appeared from between dark conifers. Slowly and with beautiful formality the pallbearers took her remains across the damp grass into the granite mausoleum beside the crystal lake. Only then, as Hermann stepped forward to follow her into that hallowed place, did I see that at his side there walked the Führer.

I did not meet Hitler that day. Shortly after the impressive ceremonies had been concluded Hermann escorted him to his car. Other dignitaries, including Himmler (who at the time I would not have recognised) left shortly afterwards. For a while, Naomi and I were unsure what to do. Though some people were leaving, many others seemed in no hurry to depart. The bands played on. Many guests paid their respects inside the mausoleum but Naomi and I did not feel entitled to join them. Beside the entrance, Karin's Swedish parents stood like ushers. Though she had been dead three years, this romantic and sombre ceremony had understandably brought back their grief. Naomi and I strolled around the lake where wraiths of summer mist rose from the surface, and then we continued into the trees. The glades of conifer seemed enchanted, deep in shadow, rustling with the sounds of hidden animals.

By early evening, bonfires had been lit and roasted meat was served outside. We drifted close and made ourselves conspicuous. Young soldiers joked with us and served us food. While we warmed ourselves at the fire – smoke in our hair, classical music wafting across the lake, our group of attendant soldiers growing larger – we were approached by a striking blonde woman clad in charcoal grey.

'You are the sisters Keene? We have been neglecting you.'

She was as blonde as we were, but more substantial, with a comely, operatic figure. 'I am the *Präsident*'s private secretary. My name is Emmy Sonnemann.'

If we had been among coarse English soldiers, one or two might have sniggered: Emmy had a voluptuous gaiety that accorded aptly with the 'private secretary' she claimed to be. But these German soldiers had both breeding and good manners, and they did not react. As Emmy led us toward the house Naomi whispered to me that once again we seemed to be in no risk of an attempted seduction from our host.

*

That evening, at some point after dinner when practically all the guests had gone, we stood with Emmy and two Luftwaffe officers in the vast and rather chilly baronial hall. She was describing the tapestries, metalware and trophies hanging on the walls.

'The *Präsident* is a fine huntsman,' she declared. 'He has killed each of these animals himself, many in our grounds.'

There were deer, both with and without antlers. There were bison. There was a moose.

'Tomorrow we shall walk together,' Emmy said. 'I shall show you the menagerie.'

She told us something of her history – indeed, she chatted so freely that I thought there was almost nothing she would not discuss. She had been actress (at which Naomi gave a knowing smile) but was now married and had exchanged theatrical life for the 'high privilege' of serving the 'second most important man in all the Reich'.

I asked, 'Your husband is staying with you here at Karinhall?'

He was not.

We were standing before a vulgar painting of a female nude – not vulgar as in rude, but in technique. The subject of the work appeared to be long past thirty (we were only in our twenties then; thirty was old) and her figure was what might charitably be described as developed. Naomi was criticising the flesh tones when Goering himself appeared behind us.

'We Germans are too expressionistic for your taste, I think?'

'No, this painting is simply crude. Look, the breasts – here, you see – where perhaps the artist has lingered on them – are well done, but the thigh – here – is carelessly executed: a blob of flesh, nothing more. Look at this line – impossible.'

'You are a collector?'

'I am an artist.'

He laughed shortly. 'Ach! Always the severest critic. And what sort of artist would you be?'

'Portraits. Landscapes. In England I am quite well thought of.'

He laughed again. 'Then you shall paint my portrait – but in front of a German landscape!' He turned to the two Luftwaffe officers. 'She must paint all our portraits – yes?'

But even as they laughed politely he closed his eyes in a kind of weariness. Suddenly he seemed subdued. I wondered if he had asked the officers to stay behind simply to relieve himself of the burden of making after dinner conversation. During the meal itself he had spoken fitfully, and now it seemed he had come to see us only out of duty. As we walked around his large but random collection of paintings he alternated between silence and sudden interruptions. At one point he switched abruptly to the possibility of a closer relationship between Germany and Britain: why was our country so antagonistic to the new Reich? Was this a general attitude or was it exaggerated by the press? Was it shared uniformly between the ordinary folk and the aristocracy? He quizzed us on the important families that we might know: did we have influence? Some of the names which arose in that conversation might surprise you, and even now, after sixty years, they could embarrass the families – but as I have said before, many English people in the early Thirties welcomed what we saw in Germany. Compared to the isolation of America, the infamies of the Soviet Union and the torpidity of Britain and France, this German experiment seemed a breath of hope.

But Goering's courtesy that night seemed strained. He was presumably brooding on his dead wife. Certainly his emotions had been churned, and when he suddenly left the room I did not expect him to return. I noticed that he limped slightly. He looked tired and old.

But half an hour later he returned. His love of costume had not deserted him, and on his return he had discarded the Luftwaffe uniform for a floor-length white linen garment half way between a Roman toga and a winter nightgown. In this extraordinary gear he seemed more relaxed. He was in a new, quietened mood, and he moved a chair across to a window and sat staring into the night.

The officers glanced at each other and made their farewells. Out in the hall where we remained awkwardly, Emmy smiled at Naomi and me as apologetically as a young housewife.

'There are times when we should leave the *Präsident* alone.'

'Of course,' we murmured. 'After such a day.'

'He has also been in physical pain.'

'I noticed he was limping,' I began.

'Only sometimes,' she said hastily. 'Long ago he suffered a bullet wound in… in a personal part of his body.'

Emmy blushed, but seeing our interest, she decided it was better that she explained. Decorously she indicated the exact location with her right hand. 'He was shot in the groin. – No, it did not… It has not made him less of a man.' She was blushing still. 'But sometimes the pain flares up, and then he has to indulge in his medicine. You know…' Her voice dropped to a whisper: 'He has to take a little morphine. It has helped him since the accident.'

Naomi was agog. 'Was he wounded in the Great War?'

'He was a pilot and an air hero,' Emmy replied. 'But no, he received his wound in 1923 at the brave attempted *putsch* in Munich. Do you know of it? He was shot saving the Führer's life.'

We stared at her incredulously. We had not heard the story then.

'Those days were terrible for Germany. There was no government, really. Everything was chaos: there was anarchy in the streets, and some factories and farms had been turned into communist soviets. So of course, there had to be order – the people wanted it, the army, the National Socialists. That day was to have been the 'March on Berlin' but we were betrayed. The Governor of Bavaria – von Kahr – and the army commander, General von Lossow, had agreed to march with the National Socialists but at the last minute they changed their minds. The march went ahead anyway, but was fired upon by police and soldiers. *Präsident* Goering pushed the Führer to the ground and shielded him with his body, receiving himself the bullet aimed for our leader. On a day infamous for treachery came that one noble act.' Emmy shrugged. 'And now the Führer is the Führer, and the man who saved him is the *Präsident*. They have a special bond. It shows that our friends are important to us, and will always be remembered.'

When we returned to the dining hall Goering was still sitting at the window, lost in reverie – how much due to the emotions of the day and how much to his shot of morphine I shall never know. In his later years he became more dependent on it, but at that time he was strong and vigorous and had hardly begun to deteriorate from his peak. He sat beside the window like a Roman emperor in his camp. Naomi and I bade him goodnight and left him with his secretary.

We found it hard to sleep. We had anticipated a night of firelight and Nordic legends. We had expected to stay up through the night and to then greet the dawn across the shimmering lake. Climbing into bed and lying beneath the *Federbett* was as if we had left a final deed undone. After a while we got up again, slipped into our warm night robes and crept out of the darkened lodge into the sweetness of the summer night. As we approached the hidden lake we heard a splash and then a single girlish laugh. It seemed that the revels had not quite ended.

From where we stood inside the ring of encircling conifers we could see Emmy Sonnenheim – fully dressed – standing at the edge of the moonlit lake holding an enormous towel. Before her, in the dark still water, her master swum solemnly from end to end, his large and naked white frame cutting like an icebreaker through the lake. Emmy waited patiently as he swum up and down. Neither of them spoke. He swum stolidly, remorselessly, until he suddenly left the water and let Emmy wrap him in the towel. She dried him thoroughly and efficiently, but still neither of them spoke. It was as if his joyless swim was an act of remembrance in Karin's lake.

*

Though we rose early for breakfast the following morning, Hermann had gone. Emmy, who had, of course, no idea we had watched them at the lake, told us that he had had to leave early to make an important address at the Prussian State Council. We spent the morning with her touring the house and grounds again, now empty of people from the day before. We probably seemed cool with her at first; her role as private secretary had never been more than a polite fiction, and she was now showing us around the estate as if she were his wife. Yet she was so friendly and open that we warmed to her. She did not hide her good fortune at being plucked from a middling theatrical career to become consort to one of the most important men in Germany. At that time, Goering was the undisputed Number Two – and his popularity probably outreached Hitler's. Hermann's outrageous and flamboyant style, coupled with his warmth and impulsiveness, drew an appreciative response throughout the land. He was the people's friend.

And yet.

That lunchtime we left Karinhall and toured Germany for a few more days. Despite the extraordinary political events which were to take place that week, Naomi and I chatted more of Emmy and the awkward position the girl was in. Presumably her own marriage was at an end, but in those more constrained times divorce was not as straightforward, as automatic as today. It was then by no means unheard of for a woman to be married to one man but to live with another – it seemed more acceptable than divorce. Emmy's position was doubly uncomfortable: not only was she the unacknowledged mistress of both the man and his official residence, but the house itself was practically a shrine to his first wife. Hermann treated Emmy with considerable respect and friendliness but he made no attempt to hide the fact that he had given his heart irretrievably to his dead Karin. Emmy herself had told us, unprompted, that he still wept for her. Emmy's task, it seemed, was to console him and soothe his hurt, while living as a votary at Karin's shrine. And her role was circumscribed; the previous night, for example, she would not have dared to swim in hallowed Karin's lake.

We journeyed on. And in those gentle midsummer days as Naomi and I toured the pretty villages of rural Germany, Hermann was arranging and then executing the infamous Night of the Long Knives.

The facts are not disputed: during that week Hermann and Heinrich Himmler, with the Führer's permission, employed hundreds of SS troops around the country to put down a potential *Sturmabteilung* revolution led by Ernst Röhm. On June 30th the SS struck pre-emptively against their military rivals, and when that famous Night was over nearly a hundred plotters and unreliable SA men had been killed. Röhm himself (once Hitler's close friend, but an overt and hugely unpopular homosexual), together with General von Schleicher, Karl Ernst (SA leader in Berlin), Gustav von Kahr and many others considered dangerous to both party and state had been liquidated. Most were shot, though a few were knifed or bludgeoned to death. – But they had been playing a traitor's game: by the time Röhm was arrested, his men were already running riot in the streets of Munich. It is said that Adolf Hitler tried to spare Röhm's life, but by the time he acted, his one-time friend had been shot dead in his prison cell.

There will never be agreement on the legitimacy of that night. Many outside Germany saw it as an act of infamy, a fatal skirmish which exposed the Nazis as little more than political gangsters. Yet in Germany it was generally recognised that the putting down of an imminent coup had been a painful but necessary business, the cauterising of an infected wound. The pre-emptive strike which Goering had organised cost less than a hundred lives. If Röhm's coup had gone ahead thousands might have died and the unstable and bestial Röhm might have deposed the Führer. No amount of reasonable discussion could have dissuaded Röhm; he was committed to this showdown.

History has labelled Goering as architect of the counter-coup, though it is known and documented that Himmler and Goebbels acted beside him, and it seems indisputable that Hitler himself must have given his approval – if not for the individual killings, then certainly for the insurrection to be put down. Goering may nevertheless have been the instigator. But it seems to me supremely significant that the week of decisive action began on the very day after Karin's re-interment. Bringing his wife's body back to the home they had built together had a profound effect upon the *Präsident*. It settled the agitation in his mind, calmed him, and gave him the icy strength and resolution he needed to see the bloody business through.

FOURTEEN

The man was right: neither Ticky nor the boy Cy were Jehovah's Witnesses, though the tenement could have benefited from a missionary or two. Interior walls were the colour of sand dampened with effluent. They had once been institutional cream but had since been daubed and splattered in ways best not to think about. Several rooms housed makeshift fires, but as no room had a fireplace the smoke swirled about until it eventually gave up and stuck to the greasy walls. Central heating had been off for years. As had the gas. And electricity. Even the water was turned off: buckets stood in the lavatories bearing the message, 'Refill When Empty'. The ground floor windows were boarded. Most on the first floor were sealed as well. But as Cy and Ticky climbed higher through the gutted building, a faint trace of daylight slunk through the remaining sheets of translucent glass.

They were escorted to the second floor, as far as strangers were allowed. A large open area, in an earlier life it had been both a storeroom and small factory floor, but now was a communal sleeping area, a dossing room. No beds, no facilities. People slept here much as they might on the streets, in ancient sleeping bags or beneath bundles of rags. Cardboard boxes and piles of newspaper lay around the floor. At one end of the hall was an empty brazier, left from last winter.

'How much you carrying?' asked the man. He was big, and he spoke in a soft bass voice.

'Just a few spliffs,' answered Cy cagily. 'I wanted to come in.'

'Nothing harder? That's a shame.' The man looked down at him. 'Any crack? Pills?'

Cy shook his head. The man turned to Ticky: 'How about you – something to pay his keep?'

'Not me.'

From inside a sleeping bag someone grumbled. The big man turned wearily towards it and the grumbling ceased. Two or three others had woken up, though being midday, most of the kips were unoccupied.

The man asked Cy, 'What drugs d'you do?'

'Nothing much.'

'Grass?'

'A bit. In case it comes in useful.'

The man shook his head. He had a slight lilt to his voice, as if he might be Welsh. 'Just bluffing then, were you? I'll tell you this: what you've got with you won't buy a bed. What's your name?'

'Cy.'

'Nothing else? How old are you?'

Cy lifted his chin. 'Fifteen.'

'You don't look fifteen.'

'I soon will be – actually, it's my birthday.'

'You already used that line outside.' The big man laid a hand on his shoulder. 'Look, if the police find you here they could give us a real going over, couldn't they? You're too young to run away. Did the family kick you out?'

Cy muttered that he didn't have a family.

'Fostered were you – or from a home?'

Cy squirmed and looked uncomfortable. 'A home. But I don't want to talk about all that.'

A voice cut in from behind him: 'You've come here for an interview, old mate. So Packer's got to check you out.'

Ticky jerked round to see the newcomer, though Cy turned more casually. They saw a shaven-headed, lean built man in tee-shirt and jeans. Closer examination revealed that he was in fact wearing several tee-shirts, one on top of the other. He had hairy arms.

Packer said, 'At the moment, Cy, you're a bit too good to be true.'

The newcomer chuckled in agreement as Packer continued: 'You tell us you don't do drugs, you're not wanted by the police, nobody's after you at all. Yet here you are – if you don't me saying so – all under age, sweet and innocent. It doesn't add up.'

Cy shuffled his feet, Ticky opened his mouth, but the newcomer spoke first: 'Yeah, the trouble with being sweet and innocent... Did someone try it on with you, me old mate?'

'I can look after myself.'

'Oh yeah?' The newcomer glanced at Packer. 'What d'you think?'

'That's for me to decide,' Packer answered softly. 'Now isn't it?'

'Go ahead then.'

'Well Cy, as I say, you're a bit young, see? You wouldn't want to bed down in a room with all these dossers, would you?'

Somebody jeered from a bulging sleeping bag, and the man in tee-shirts said, 'There's a spare pitch in my room, now Dino's gone.'

'For Christ's sake, Nathan,' Packer snarled.

143

Ticky came alert.

'What's wrong?' Nathan protested. 'I just said there was a place.'

Packer ignored him. 'Look Cy, if you're really stuck, you can bed down on the floor here. It's better than the streets. Just.' He glanced at Nathan, who grinned and pulled the earring in his right ear. 'But you've got to watch out for yourself. Understand me?'

'Thanks.'

Ticky stepped forward. 'Hey Cy, can I have a word in private?'

Nathan hooted. 'Oh ho, you watch it, Cy! Your little chum's worried – wants to take you home.'

Ticky stamped his foot. 'Don't push it with me, my friend. We all know your game.'

As Nathan went for him Packer snapped, 'You two start and I'll crack your heads against the wall.'

Nathan glared at little Ticky, who purred, 'Come on, Cy, you don't know what you're getting into.'

Nathan sneered. 'I know what *you* want to get into, old mate. Don't worry, blondie, you're well rid of him.'

Cy spoke up: 'He's my friend. He helped me out.'

'Yeah, but the bill comes later, my old mate. Right, Titch?'

Ticky ignored him. 'I wouldn't stay here, Cy.'

'You ain't invited!'

Cy said, 'Don't worry, Ticky, I'll be all right.'

On the radio a commentator was summarising New Labour's manifesto, distributed that day. It sounded unlike any previous Labour manifesto in that it promised the party would support law and order, the family and sound finance; it would be a 'one nation' party in which people came together with a shared sense of purpose. Tony Blair admitted that old Labour policies had been wrong. But that had been *old* Labour, nothing to do with the bright future that he promised. New Labour would encourage trade union reform – and would place its emphasis on the individual and the spirit of enterprise. New Labour was different.

The telephone rang. To reach the phone in the hall Sidonie had to cross the entire length of the sitting room. One of these days, she thought, she would have someone install an extension. At her age, scurrying through the house was not sensible.

'Hello?'

'My dear Miss Keene. I was beginning to fear you might not be in.'

'Mr Gottfleisch?'

'Hugo. And how are we today?'

144

'We?'

'I do apologise, Miss Keene. How are *you* today?'

'I am preparing luncheon.'

'Then I'll come straight to the point. One of those coincidences really.' He paused expectantly, but she saw no reason to respond. He continued: 'A curious thing. Yes indeed. This very morning – would you believe it? – someone called to enquire about Naomi's paintings.' He paused again.

'Why is that a curious thing?'

'Because you and I were so recently discussing—'

'People do still buy her pictures, Mr Gottfleisch, and you *are* an art dealer.'

'Indeed! Well said. I should add that this enquiry came from a *serious* buyer.'

'Aren't all buyers serious?'

'If only. But with this man, I suspect we are talking a substantial sum of money.'

'Your buyer wishes to *spend* a substantial sum of money?'

'*Invest* is the better word. – Forgive me, Miss Keene, but you sound a little curt this morning. Is this not a convenient time?'

She hesitated. 'Perhaps not. I don't see how I can help you.'

'Now, that would be a shame. Naomi's paintings have become so scarce.'

'Hardly surprising. She's been dead fifty years.'

'And with poor Murdo gone, my only source has dried up.'

He left this hanging, but she switched: 'I understand you called on Murdo's son. He seemed most disturbed.'

'He hasn't bothered you again?'

'What on earth did you *do* to him, Mr Gottfleisch?'

'Not enough, it seems. I thought you might like me to – how shall we say? – dissuade him from further attempts at blackmail.'

'He claims you beat him up.'

'I, Miss Keene? I am hardly—'

'Your heavies, he called them. He says you sent the heavies in.'

'Good gracious! Quite untrue. Let me entirely frank with you, Miss Keene. My driver and I – no one else – called on Angus at his father's house. The conversation became a little heated and... well, I'm afraid the truth is that in moments of excitement we men can sometimes get a little rough!' Gottfleisch chuckled. 'But I would hardly say he was beaten up.'

'That's what I told him. I couldn't see a single bruise.'

Gottfleisch chuckled again. 'Did that disappoint you?'

'That's not what I meant.'

'But he came back to see you, you say?'

'Mhm. Quite defiant, he was.'

'Dearie me. Perhaps he *should* have been beaten up. – Oh, forgive my impetuousness, Miss Keene, but it rather seems that my gentle warning had little effect.'

She paused. 'Mr Gottfleisch, you must not feel committed on my behalf.'

✳

By the time Ticky finally arrived at Gottfleisch's house it was approaching lunchtime.

'Sorry, sir. Didn't get the message.'

'Where were you?'

'I was… Well, I was helping a friend, sir. I didn't think you'd call me – not after last time. But I'm happy to be of service.'

'Who said anything about a job?'

'Oh, no sir, but I thought—'

'Ours has been a long and reasonably worthwhile relationship, Ticky. But I dare say you're thinking of pastures new?'

'No, sir, I'd rather—'

'Have you found another job?'

'No chance.'

'I can hardly give you a reference.'

'There's nowhere I can go, Mr Gottfleisch. No one I can turn to.'

'How about this new friend you mentioned?'

'He's not that sort of friend.'

Gottfleisch studied him. 'Frankly, Ticky, the last job you handled was a total cock-up.'

'Won't happen again, sir.'

'I can't bear incompetence.'

'No, sir.'

Ticky waited hopefully, panting like a dog.

'I suppose you think you ought to be given another chance?'

'You can count on me, sir.'

'I did have one particular little job…'

'I'm ready.'

'Laughably simple.'

'Even for me, sir? Ha, ha.'

'Another break-in.'

'Right-ho.'

'Though this time you won't have to disguise the fact. I want you to trash the place. As it happens, it's in the same village where you cocked up last time.'

'Cudham Wood, sir? Well, at least I know the way. Ha, ha. Pretty place.'

'A different house. Here's the address.'

As Ticky reached for the piece of paper Gottfleisch said, 'Copy it down in your own writing. Do you have a pen?'

'Ah... um...I'll borrow this, sir.' Ticky stooped over the desk to write conscientiously. 'Copy it down, sir. Just like a spy film.'

'Copy it carefully.'

'You bet. Wouldn't want to smash up the wrong house, sir!'

'If you do, I shall suspend you by your toes from Blackfriars Bridge.'

'Yikes.' Ticky was writing. 'You'll make the blood rush to my head, sir. Ha, ha. Yes, that's finished it. I'm ready to go.'

'Listen carefully. When you arrive at that address, wait until the man who lives there has gone out.'

'So he doesn't see me? Right. Understood.'

'His name is Angus Fyffe.'

'Right. But if he's out...'

'Yes?'

'I won't need his name.'

Gottfleisch paused. His stare was cold enough to freeze Ticky's grin.

'Sorry, sir.'

'When you get there, I want you to trash the place – overturn furniture, pull out the drawers, break some ornaments – though there's no need to overdo it. It's a warning to the man who lives there.'

'Angus Pike.'

'Fyffe.'

'Right. Well, he gets off lightly. I mean, he doesn't get hurt or nothing. How will he know he hasn't just been burgled by a couple of kids?'

'Paint a warning on his wall.'

'Like 'Warning, Mind Your Head'?'

'Don't try to be funny. Paint 'This Is Your Last Warning'. Not original, but...'

'I like it. Straight to the point. Last warning about what?'

'Hm, you're right. Add the words, 'Leave Her Alone'.'

'Oh, there's a woman in it? Well, well. You want both those messages painted right across his wall?'

'Yes.'

'Any particular colour, sir?'

✳

Gottfleisch hadn't said that it had to be today, so Ticky thought he would return to the Soho squat. After he had knocked at the door twice to no effect he began calling up at the windows. He felt uncomfortable, shouting in the street.

'Cy,' he called hoarsely. 'Cy, it's me.'

Nobody answered.

'Cy! You all right?'

He beat the door again, harder this time.

What was that big guy's name? 'Packer! Open up!'

Christ, he thought, didn't they have any friends who came to call? He moved to the other side of the narrow street and glared across at the boarded windows. If there had been a stone he would have thrown it.

'Packer!'

The house seemed unoccupied. He peered at the unboarded windows to the upper floors but could see nothing behind them. He sat on the kerb. He remembered Cy suggesting that the occupants might have a special knock.

After a while the front door creaked open and to Ticky's surprise, Cy popped his head out. He nodded at Ticky but before emerging from inside he glanced each way along the alley. Ticky scrambled to his feet. 'Well, how's it going, Cy – can I come in?'

'I'm coming out.'

Cy squeezed out through the gap and the door closed immediately behind him. He began to walk away. Ticky trotted beside him and asked, 'Who was that behind the door?'

'Oh, Nathan. He came down to let me out.'

Ticky nodded: Nathan. Of course, it would be.

They were approaching the market. 'Have you eaten?'

'Uh huh.'

'Want a coffee?'

'I'm going for a job actually, Ticky.'

'You're joking. A job.' Ticky glanced at him and laughed.

Cy turned right up Berwick Street beside the market stalls. 'There's this restaurant looking for a kitchen hand. Or it was last night.'

'Kitchen hand? That's washing up.'

'I'm not picky. I have to live.'

'Yeah, but you know the types you get in restaurant kitchens? Just scum.'

Cy turned left with the assurance of a native. 'Scum floats higher than the dregs.' He grinned shyly. 'That's what Nathan says.'

'You wanna watch him—'

148

'Anyway, it's money. That's what matters.'

They were kinking through the side streets.

'I mean, I can't go home or get income support – I can't beg or busk or anything. What else can I do? Roll on New Labour, I say. Get some justice, right? Oh, here's the place.'

Chef said, 'Scrape 'em in the bin, swill here, stack this machine. It's bleedin' hot. If you've used a dishwasher at 'ome this ain't the same. Fast in, fast out, and everything's red hot. Glasses here, plates there, silver and pans down the bottom. Don't break nothin' or you'll be out. And don't nick things or I'll put you through the dishwasher with the plates. I've cooked a lobster in that machine, so just you watch it. This is your number two machine – it skins potatoes. That's not your knife. Never touch knives. Remember, kitchen knives is sharp. Hear what I'm saying? Sharp. Cut your finger off soon as winkin'. Now, there's the grills, there's the 'obs, there's the deep fat fryer. They're 'ot too, so there's the tin of acriflavine. If you get burnt, don't stop to think about it, don't yell for muvver, just slap it on. Immediate. Do it quick, you'll feel no pain. 'Esitate and you're scarred for life. Now listen: you get no sick pay, no overtime – but there's no tax neither and we don't pay your stamp. You'll work day shift, eight to four, breakfast ten thirty before the lunchtime rush. Whatever you like for breakfast – casserole, soup, yesterday's leavings – but no steak or fish till they've gone past their sell-by. Mug of tea any time you like. Don't touch the wine. Anything left in glasses goes down the sink. You're too young to drink anyway. Drinkin', thievin' and breaking glasses; spittin', fightin' or kissin' waiters – and I kick your backside out the door. Just keep your nose clean and keep my plates sparklin', and you and me will get along as sweetly as a bride and groom. Start tomorrow morning, eight o'clock.'

FIFTEEN

I have only once in my life been to the Olympic Games. It was in 1936. By then, Naomi and I had visited the new Germany several times, and on each occasion felt our batteries recharged by the electricity in the air. Everything was exciting. The very lamps in the streets burned more brightly, while those indoors gave a golden glow. (This was true, you know: British lighting had a grey-white harshness; continental lamps shone with an amber warmth.)

Berlin's huge Olympic Stadium shouted out with life and exuberance. Seated in the crowded concrete tiers we felt all the power and energy of the twentieth century – the flags, the music, the cheering crowds. Throughout new Germany was enormous pride – not only at their own athletic accomplishments but at the way the world was flocking to Berlin. Four years earlier the Games had been in Los Angeles; now Germany proved that Europe could put on a show. The stadium itself, designed by Albert Speer – a vast oval of concrete around a sunken arena – was a triumph of modernism, and the enormous swimming pool alongside took one's breath away. Outside the stadium where car parks and hot dogs stalls might lurk today were green lawns and ornamental gardens – in one of which they staged a Festival Play; an extraordinary mass pageant said to involve a ten thousand cast.

Of the sports themselves I can only remember highlights. People ran, jumped and hurled javelins. We applauded, cheered, became excited when the British competed, but were far off and distanced from the pain and sweat. Although these brilliantly modern Games were the first to be televised (how many saw those pictures, I wonder – a few hundred thousand?) we in the stadium had no gigantic live action screens such as dominate stadia today. Yet we were in touch. We might be fifty metres from the competitors, but from our perches above we could pick out every face. We felt their power, their excellence.

People have asked me since whether I did not feel undertones at those Berlin Olympics – the rising militarism, racism, the threat of war. I did not. I saw tens of thousands of ordinary people enjoying themselves. There was military *music*, certainly – brass bands and fanfares – but the outdoor strains were a far better accompaniment to healthy sport than the pop music played today, that syrupy dream-like pap which synchronises with slow motion replays on the screen. And today's TV sports programmes still use marches for their signature tunes – so why was it terrible for Berlin to sport brass bands? At that time we were unaware of the threat of war – we enjoyed ourselves in the summer sun and drenching showers.

As for racism, no, not in the sense you mean – but yes, since every nation in the world sat side by side in the same arena competing against each other in track and field, certainly we cheered our separate nations. One sat beside, walked beside, spoke to people of every religion and every hue – many of whom were from nationalities one had never encountered in one's life – and of course we were keenly interested in their differentness. In the 1930s these black, brown and yellow people were a curiosity. They didn't live in our country then. We didn't visit *their* country for our annual fortnight's holiday. If we peered at them, imagine how they in their turn, plucked from their native habitat and released into an all-white European environment, peered and gawked at us. We were as struck by the sight, sound and smell of each other as a western tourist is today in an Arab soukh.

For Americans perhaps it was different. In their fabled melting pot the world's races and colours had already – supposedly – intermingled. Their Olympics team combined black and white athletes, and when Europeans saw black athletes competing with and, on occasions, beating white competitors there was an unexpected *frisson* – even some alarm. The most successful athlete at the Games, as I expect you know, was the black American Jesse Owens. By any standards he was phenomenal: he won the hundred metres, the two hundred and the long jump. When he stepped onto the track for the sprint relay – an event which America had won at every Olympiad before – we thought he must surely be about to win his fourth Gold Medal. But he did not. His team took the Silver, and most exhilarating of all, was pipped to the Gold by none other than our own splendid British four! I was on my feet, cheering like a fishwife.

Owens was the most beautiful black man I had ever seen. (I had not seen many.) His massive shoulders burst from the straps of his flimsy singlet, his legs were long and powerful, and the effortless fluidity of his movement was captivating. When he ran, his legs seemed to power his body by a different mechanism. Not only did he run faster than the others – and in each of his Gold Medal events he outran them comfortably – but he also ran with a more perfect style.

151

Watching him run changed my perception of black athletes. I knew they were powerful and more strongly built, but until I saw Jesse Owens I imagined black men as inherently cruder and less sophisticated. Now I saw a man who commanded my attention and admiration – though my sister was less admiring: when in the long jump he fought his most tightly contested duel she cheered lustily for Luz Long, the blond German who only lost to Owens in the final leap. She complained that the black American had barely qualified for the final jump-off, and she suggested that some kind of 'fix' was going on.

Certainly it was a 'fix' that deprived Britain of a Gold in the Women's High Jump. Dear Dorothy Odam – then a mere child of sixteen, at the very start of her long, long career – tied in first place but had to be satisfied with the Silver. Naomi and I were furious (well, frankly, every British spectator was furious) and quite rightly: by today's rules Dorothy would have won the Gold. And as has been the case in so many Games, British success remained elusive. Apart from the sprint relay the only other Gold I saw Britain win was the rather comical (though no doubt agonising) 50,000 metre walk. I remember Naomi and I rising from our seats to cheer a wiry little man (what *was* his name?) entering the stadium alone at an exhausted but jaunty gait.

She and I separated for the fencing. I'm sure I watched those events alone. I was passionate about fencing then – and fit enough! – and I cheered the sabre, foil and épée, despite the fact that practically every prize was won by the Italians. (Only the French ever came near the Italians, who dominated the sport for years.)

So yes, the Games were nationalistic – as has been every Olympiad since on television. Everybody cheers furiously for their country. Perhaps the intensity of competition in Berlin seemed a little higher than in previous years (in the equestrian event three horses had to be destroyed) but nowadays when I watch the Games on TV, I see no abatement of intensity. Every athlete strives to achieve their utmost. Every competitor dedicates their life. And practically every spectator (whether present or watching TV) becomes fiercely patriotic and screams for their own country. Do we think this wrong today? No. There is a minority, of course, which hates any kind of competition, but for most of us the Olympic Games are the world's sporting climax. The Berlin games were one step on the road to where we are today.

*

'Stay a little longer and we can go straight to the *Parteitag*.'

Unity clasped our hands as if we would need persuading. The

exhilaration of the previous week was upon us and Berlin seemed an enchanted city.

'A little longer?' Naomi echoed. '*Natürlich*, darling, this is the only place to be.'

'Berlin is *wunderbar*,' I cried.

'Party time and *Parteitag*.'

One cringes now. But we were in our twenties, sparkling eyes and glowing cheeks, enthusiastic, naive. Do you blame us for wanting fun?

'We'll drive down through Leipzig,' Unity declared. 'And then via the Reichenbach Falls – it's elementary, my dear! Then Bayreuth – it'll take days, absolutely days!'

'*Wunderbar*,' we sighed.

Unity was more Naomi's friend than mine. Naomi loved the wildness in her, her determined disregard for convention. But while Naomi loved town and the Bright Young Things, I had already developed a preference for the country. She and Unity would whoop it up in Bloomsbury while I preferred the peaceful riverside at Swinbrook.

In Germany too, whiling away the days until the *Parteitag*, we tussled amicably over where to go. Fortunately there were four of us, so I was not always the odd one out. Erich, one of Unity's boyfriends, was driving us (or was meant to be – because although it was his car we all took turns with it, racing through little lanes and villages like spoilt children with a brand new toy) and we tended to fall into two pairs, rather than let one of us – myself inevitably – become the gooseberry.

Again, people have asked me since whether the signs of war were not inescapable. We saw pretty villages, and if perhaps there *were* too many flags they seemed mere bunting; if too many uniforms they did at least mean men in work. Those little villages showed none of the surly poverty of rural villages in other countries, and the larger towns bustled with commerce and reconstruction. I remember driving on a brand new autobahn – an incredible experience: a long wide empty highway with gangs of workers adding finishing touches as we swept by. England had millions out of work, while here active men were taken off the demeaning dole and set to useful toil. Were the Germans wrong? Is it better that a man gets up late and lounges around street corners than that he works constructively outdoors? Germany had autobahns in the 1930s; Britain had no motorway till the 1960s.

On one of those autobahns – no, it was another road, under reconstruction, near a copse of fir trees, I remember now – we had to stop because of an incident on the road. At its heart was a sight you can see in England even today: a gypsy encampment beside the road – and as with all gypsies in real life, they and their conveyances were tawdry and not at all romantic. Open carts, half covered wagons whose dirty canvas flapped in the wind, dishevelled horses, mangy dogs, filthy adults and snot-faced children standing in the mud. Soldiers or perhaps police (I am not sure: there were so many types of uniform then) were clearing these people from their horse-drawn wagons and herding them together. Sundry onlookers stood a little way off watching the action with quiet satisfaction. Heaven knows where they had come from – we seemed miles from anywhere. The police – no, SA, I remember now: brown shirts and those distinctive crossover belts – began loading the gypsies onto lorries, raising a small cheer from the onlookers as they did so. That disturbed me (yes, yes, I know you think me a hardhearted old biddy) and as we waited in Erich's large open-topped tourer like guests in the royal box, I said so.

'Local people will be glad to be rid of them,' Erich replied – and leaping from the car he began a shouted conversation with one of the onlookers.

'You see,' he said, turning back to us. 'These vagrants steal from the land, and they don't work. Their children pick pockets and attack local children.'

'I heard what the man said.'

Erich still sometimes thought he had to translate for us.

'Oh, you are upset, of course. It is not a good sight for a young woman's eyes.'

Naomi laughed. 'She's not squeamish, Erich.'

The last of the gypsies were climbing into the lorries. Some children were crying and an old woman stumbled and hurt her knee, but the small crowd remained delighted.

I muttered, 'Look how those people laugh at them.'

'It is with relief,' Erich explained. 'How would *you* like thieves at the bottom of your garden? They are parasites, those people.'

The tailgate of a lorry was raised and slammed shut. As the vehicles trundled away the crowd shouted and cheered. Someone called, 'Let's clear this trash away!' But as they converged on the encampment, SA men blocked their path.

'There now,' murmured Erich. 'Everything is in order. The local people will not be allowed to make their bonfire.' He nodded in satisfaction.

'Well, I'm cold,' remarked Unity. 'Can't we drive on?'

I relate this scene because, with hindsight, should it not have given us some kind of warning? It certainly seems so now – if you select this one incident and examine it on its own. Yet it was the only incident of that kind which I remember from that holiday and I suppose we gave little thought to what might happen to those we saw taken away. If we had asked someone, no doubt we would have been told that they were to be rehabilitated or expelled. Rehabilitation, we knew, meant work camps – but if people who had never done an honest day's work in their lives were sent off to a work camp for a while, did that seem unreasonable? A work camp, after all, was better than a dark prison cell. Expulsion, the other alternative, simply removed outsiders from German land.

Today such an attitude seems frightening, but consider: Germany was still clawing its way back from defeat, from grinding poverty, from rampant inflation and from all the terrible human consequences of a collapsed economy. In that daily battle everyone had to play their part. There was no room for shirkers. By the middle Thirties, thank Heaven (or thank Hitler, for he did seem the architect) life was visibly on the mend. People could feel it; they did not need to read promises from economists in the newspapers: people had jobs, shops were well stocked, good times were here again. No one was complacent: in the memory of every living adult lay the long desperate years before. This blessed but fragile recovery could not be jeopardised by people who refused to pull their weight. Germany was a team now; there was no room for anyone not committed to the side. There was no room for parasites, whether they be rich: landlords, bankers, moneylenders; or poor: unemployed, idle, malcontent. The team certainly could not afford to harbour those who might work actively against it – communists, for example – nor could it afford expensive passengers, such as the incurably insane or severely handicapped. Foreigners *could* be tolerated, provided they made a positive contribution to the side, but many foreigners simply scrounged like gypsies or exploited like Jews.

Do those words startle you? Perhaps. But I am recalling the thoughts of sixty years ago, and for Jews today the world has crawled humbly through five decades of apology, atonement and contrition. Images of what would eventually be found in the camps blur every account. The unspeakable nature of those reports – I don't deny the horror of those final days – suggests a barbarity so inhuman as to be past any attempt at understanding. Yet these were the acts of man on man. They must be understood. Not to do so is to fail to learn.

In the 1930s the world was as hostile to Jewry as it has always been. In many languages the word Jew was a casual insult: Jews were miserly and untrustworthy; they kept to themselves and indulged in secret unnatural practices.

155

For Jews and gypsies there was no place in Germany. Other countries might take a more liberal view – so why not let those other countries house them? If people all over the world kept insisting how clever and valuable the Jews were, wouldn't they welcome such paragons into their own countries?

Some Jews left and some would not. What was Germany to do? Unwanted citizens could not be put on a boat and cast out to sea – and despite what was eventually to happen, there was no clamour before the war to throw them in jail. They were not criminals. They simply were not wanted. Some *were* imprisoned – as were far more Germans (communists and the like), but the main policy, perhaps the only practicable policy, was to discourage Jews from hanging on. But people are obstinate. Most Jews would not leave. The government's response was to increase pressure. Laws were introduced prohibiting Jews from certain professions. A year later, since this law yielded only limited results, a Citizenship Act was passed and intermarriages became forbidden. By the time Berlin welcomed the world for the Olympiad there was open hostility to Jews throughout the land. Had they not been told over and over again they were not wanted – why wouldn't they go? Openly anti-Semitic journals were sold in the streets – though I noticed that during the Olympiad season the red cabinets displaying *Der Stürmer* around Berlin were taken down. To help people shop correctly, Jewish shops and businesses had a yellow star painted outside – though Jews themselves were not imprisoned in any numbers until the depth of war in 1941 when their loyalty could no longer be relied upon.

Looking back, it is of course possible to see each step leading inexorably towards what became known as the final solution, but at the time each step was simply another notch in the ratchet of persuasion. Jews were unwanted throughout Europe. Poland, for example, had suggested that Jews be given their own land in Madagascar. (Think: we could have had the Madagascan Liberation Organisation instead of the PLO!) Anti-Semitic political parties in France (yes, an Allied country) swelled to several *million* members. Italy passed anti-Semitic laws. Britain was more covert, though would later fire on ships of Jewish refugees, and our navy would hove to to watch Jewish children drown.

What might it be like to know the future? But we didn't. We were aware only of our exciting present. We saw a prototypal twentieth century country which could mark the future shape of Europe. It was progress – now.

*

156

Fame relies on distance for its mystique. When we met Goering next time he seemed shorter and distinctly fatter. His striking Barrymore looks were fading. During a *Parteitag* he could strut and fill the stage but between acts he looked deflated and tired.

Naomi whispered that men too often achieved greatness when past their prime. I said that when she painted him she should try to reveal what lay below the surface, but she asked gloomily, 'What would I find?'

He had commissioned a portrait in that airy offhand way of his, where you didn't know whether he might not remember, or worse, he might not forget. That year we met several luminaries of the establishment – but not Hitler; only Unity had done that. We did meet Goebbels – briefly: a shake of the hand, a joke, and he was gone – and we met the SS leaders Himmler and Heydrich.

This was at a *Parteitag*, when we were in the Diplomatic Tent – not the largest marquee in the field but the most expensively furnished, with leather hunting chairs, fur rugs, Gobelin tapestries and fine silverware. It was such an exclusive tent that not even Unity could have gained us access – but the *Präsident* swept us in to show us off.

Heydrich, a cold but alert man, acknowledged Goering's beaming introduction with: 'Three girls at once, Hermann? Your appetite grows more prodigious every year.'

'Allow me to introduce,' Goering responded, 'the niece of Mr Winston Churchill.'

Unity was not quite Churchill's niece, but she didn't quibble.

Heydrich asked, 'Do I know such a man?'

He looked down his large beaked nose, teasing Goering, I assume – though in '36 Winston was still in the wilderness. Hermann played what at the time was a stronger card: 'She is also sister in law to Sir Oswald Mosley.'

Heydrich inclined his head. 'Almost too well connected.'

'Reinhard is never satisfied,' Hermann chuckled. 'This is Miss Naomi Keene, the beautiful English girl who will paint my portrait.'

'Another portrait?' purred Heydrich.

'And her sister Sidonie Keene.'

Heydrich smiled at me. 'Only 'her sister'? Can Hermann think of nothing more to boast of you?'

'She plays the piano,' Naomi said. 'And she sings a bit.'

I said, 'Not in company.'

'A pity,' Heydrich said. 'There is quite an audience outside this tent.'

We met his boss who, as I remember, spent the short period of our conversation polishing his spectacles. They were round, metal

framed, inexpensive looking – the kind which after the war epitomised cheap NHS glasses. They seemed so fragile, and Himmler
polished them so earnestly they seemed sure to break.

'You find the air outside invigorating?' he asked, huffing on his
spectacles. (We were standing by the entrance.) 'Out there are ten
thousand tents. In one of them—' still huffing on his spectacles— 'at
this very moment a new German child is being conceived. Even as I
speak, the woman's seed is being fertilised. What d'you think of
that?'

We could think of no sensible reply, so Himmler continued: 'Tell
me, out of all those tents you see, which one do you think it is, eh?
Can you tell me that?' He was using his handkerchief to bring an even
finer polish to his warm glasses. 'Somewhere out there,' he said.
'Imagine it.'

'Well,' said Unity, breaking what could have been an embarrassing pause, 'in nine months' time you can send a note round to all the
hospitals, and have the girl identify herself.'

'There will be hundreds of them!' he roared. 'Thousands! Each
Parteitag is a great aid to fertility. Every year we see a great surge in
the birth statistics the following July. Study those tents, my girls.'

As he left, smiling to himself and still cleaning those spectacles, I
wondered whether he had registered us at all. Much later I asked
Unity how short sighted he really was.

'Himmler has peculiar vision,' she said.

We were drinking chocolate in a cafe in Munich. Unity had
chosen it because she knew that Hitler sometimes lunched there, and
she hoped she might be noticed. 'That is the Führer's table,' she whispered. 'There at the back. But you were asking about Heini.' (She
meant Himmler.) 'He is a wild man. He believes the most extraordinary things.'

'For instance?'

'Reincarnation, he believes in that. Also in folk medicines and
numerology – and he eats wild plants.'

Naomi looked bored. 'Oh Unity, people make up such ridiculous
rumours—'

'I have seen him in the morning half-light, stripped to his underclothes in the garden, making his salute to the golden dawn.'

'In his underclothes?' I exclaimed. We all giggled. 'It sounds like
Herr Goering.' And we told her about the time we had seen
Hermann's midnight swim at Karinhall.

'With Emmy?' she asked. 'You know he has married her now?'

'No!'

'Truly.'

She assured us that Hermann really had married the blonde ex-actress who had been his secretary. 'I expect she will be good for him.'

We pulled wry faces and finished our chocolate.

'Herr Deutelmoser!' Unity called. 'More chocolate, if you please.'

'*Fur die Unity? Ja, ja.*'

'Do they know you here?'

She shrugged. 'It is my regular. Listen. That Heini, a few months back... when? Yes, summer solstice, near Verden, he conducted a ceremony for the SS. But with ten thousand worshippers!'

'What kind of ceremony – d'you mean like Druids? How wonderful!'

We had to stifle our amusement while Herr Deutelmoser approached.

'*Heisse Schocolade, bitte.*'

'*Danke.*'

'The thing is,' Unity continued, 'and you mustn't laugh, but Heini believes that the Germans – well no, *all* Aryans actually – are descended from giants.'

Naomi exploded into her chocolate.

'He does! He believes it. All Aryans are descended from a race of giants that comes from... oh, I don't know, somewhere near Greece.'

'Greek giants?' Tears ran down Naomi's face.

'You're making it up.'

'No, he believes that he himself is reincarnated—'

Naomi spluttered again. 'From Achilles?'

'He *is* a heel,' I said.

Unity waited for us to subside. 'And he says men and women should make love in *cemeteries*.'

'Oh, for Goodness sake!'

'It's true.'

'Disgusting.'

'Bizarre certainly.'

I leant forward. 'I hope this isn't from first hand experience, Unity?'

'Ugh, he's a nonentity. No! But let me tell you why he does it -'

'I don't want to know!' laughed Naomi. 'In a cemetery?'

'I'll tell you why Herr Himmler believes this—'

Naomi snorted. 'He thinks he's a vampire?'

'He's too small,' I said.

'So are vampire bats.'

Unity smiled. 'He believes that when you make love in a cemetery—'

'Oh, really!'

159

'Any child conceived will inherit the spirit of the dead heroes buried there.'

I groaned disbelievingly.

'Heroes?' Naomi scoffed. 'How many cemeteries have heroes buried in them?'

Unity nodded. 'Didn't I say? It has to be a Nordic cemetery with lots of war graves.'

Naomi and I shook our heads. I stirred my cup. 'Some friends you have, Unity.'

'Oh, he's quite boffo,' she agreed lightly. 'But rather fun.'

When I think of Himmler now, I remember the way he scrupulously polished his spectacles – those unflattering frames. They were the kind of glasses the school swot wore and yet from time to time they have become inexplicably fashionable. They came back recently, in fact, and an Italian design house – Armani, I think – offered them at over two hundred pounds a pair. In the Sixties they were *de rigeur*. John Lennon wore them – they were his trademark. And Heini, like Lennon, had a dry mocking humour, believed in mysticism, and had a cruel sarcastic tongue. His jibes were funny, unless you were the butt of them. I can imagine Himmler, like Lennon, hiding behind those deliberately unflattering glasses, lying in bed for a week and inviting journalists to a hotel bedroom to report his solemn prognostications on the future of mankind. He had – I'm perfectly serious – the same charisma that John Lennon had.

These men were stars – yes, I do mean the Nazi leaders. You may find it hard to accept, my dear, but you have been conditioned by a lifetime of propaganda. Every word you use to describe them is prompted by continual propaganda: you use the words inhuman, diabolical, gangster, despot, beast. But simplistic invective conceals a less convenient truth.

They and their millions of followers cannot be depersonalised. They were as human as us. If they had not been – if they had been anthropomorphised from the vilest beast, if they had been aliens, if they could in any way have *not* been human – then, and only then, could we dismiss them. They would have no message for us today. But they – I mean the leaders and the millions who were led willingly – were human, of the same flesh, with the same strengths and weaknesses, the same faults and virtues as every person alive today. So we cannot disassociate ourselves by demonising these men. We cannot blame everything that happened on the errant behaviour of a few deviant monsters. They were mortal men who did these things – human beings like you or me. Unless we understand this, we have learnt nothing, and will eventually make the same mistakes again.

SIXTEEN

Ticky beamed with pride as he stroked the door of his ancient green Fiat. Cy frowned. 'Is that yours?'

'It's a goer.'

'You can't use your own car to do a job.'

Ticky's face fell.

'We'll have to steal one.'

'Right.' Ticky nodded thoughtfully. 'I'll see what I can do.'

'Leave it to me.'

Ticky squinted at the blond boy. 'Have you nicked a car before?'

Cy shrugged. 'It isn't hard.'

Ticky grinned feebly. 'I brought mine here special. Have to drive it back again now. Oh, well. Hop in.'

As Ticky began to manoeuvre the car along the tight alleyway he said, 'We can pick another one up down Deptford.'

'Something decent,' Cy muttered. He was watching Ticky's driving. 'From a multi storey.'

Ticky was inching into Brewer Street. He heaved on the wheel, and as he pulled the car round the corner he gave a scuff and a scrape to a car parked opposite. But he didn't notice. 'Have to buy two tickets – one for each car.'

'Choose a prepaid place, with machines.'

'I'll still have to buy a ticket for this one, won't I?'

'Aren't they paying you to do this job?'

Ticky took the next corner erratically. He muttered, 'We might be gone for several hours.'

'So park outside.'

Ticky braked suddenly and hooted at a large man carrying a box across the street. The man scowled at the little car. Then, seeing the diminutive size of the two occupants, he came round to Ticky's door.

Cy said, 'Go for it.'

Ticky put his foot down.

*

161

As Cy led him around the gloomy multi storey appraising cars, Ticky thought he was looking for one with keys. Cy scoffed. 'No one leaves the keys unless they want the car nicked.'

Ticky nodded knowingly. 'That one's nice.'

'Diesel,' Cy said. 'Slow starter. There's one'll do.'

He had seen people at the far end of the row of cars, so he knelt to tie his shoe. 'Keep walking,' he muttered.

Ticky hesitated but strolled on. When he reached the end of the floor he glanced back and found Cy gone. The couple were in their car now and it was coughing into life. Rather than walk back towards them, which might look peculiar, Ticky walked up the concrete slope to the next level and waited till he heard them drive away. Descending to the original floor he saw Cy standing between two cars, fiddling at a door. By the time Ticky reached him, Cy had worked his wire into the window slot and was twisting it inside. Ticky heard a clunk as the door unlocked. Cy retrieved the wire and grinned.

'It would have been quicker to smash the glass, but there's no point freezing on the journey.'

He sat inside and tugged at the wires beneath the steering column. He had to lean further in so he could see to make the connection. Then the car fired. Cy emerged, leaving one leg inside to work the accelerator.

He said, 'You'd better drive, Ticky. A kid like me might attract attention.'

✳

A mile outside Cudham Wood, Ticky narrowly missed a woman cyclist in a lane. Fortunately, she had been riding towards them, so she didn't follow into the village and create a scene.

Cy said, 'Perhaps you should have let me drive.'

'Just watch the map.'

Cy smiled softly, looking for the left turn. 'That's it.'

'That's what?'

'Where you turn left.'

Ticky turned the car clumsily and asked, 'How far?'

'Half a mile it says on here.'

At the next bend the car was brushed by overhanging branches.

'It sure ain't a motorway,' Ticky said.

'Somewhere on the right.'

'This one?'

'That's a field.'

They found the gateway to the cottage beyond a small copse. Ticky misjudged the turn, stopped, reversed and tried again.

He said, 'I wouldn't buy one of these useless motors.'

The driveway bent away from the cottage before swinging back, which let them park the car out of sight. Ticky glanced at Cy. 'How do we switch it off without a key?'

'Hang on.'

Cy leant across his lap and disconnected a wire. Ticky would have seen which one if he hadn't been gazing at Cy's blond head as it bobbed above his thighs. Cy sat up and said, 'Go and try his bell.'

'Oh yeah.' Ticky licked his lips. 'Make sure the guy is out.'

They approached Angus's house carefully and rang the bell. It didn't seem to ring, so Cy knocked. Because there wasn't a rapper he used his fist.

He said, 'Better try round the back.'

At the rear of the house they found a casement window propped open on its metal bar.

Ticky said, 'That's helpful. Who's going in?'

'I will.'

Ticky laced his fingers for Cy to put his foot into. As the boy squirmed through the open window Ticky placed a helpful hand on his bottom, and remained with his hand poised in the empty air, staring after him as Cy dropped inside. Perhaps the risk made Ticky excited, because when Cy opened the kitchen door Ticky seemed out of breath.

Cy checked: 'We're just to make a mess of the place, is that it?'

'And leave the message. Yeah, that's all.'

'Might as well start here in the kitchen.'

Cy grinned, and in one joyful movement swept all the crockery from the draining board. He laughed aloud. Ticky ran to a cupboard and began pulling jars and packets onto the floor.

Cy called, 'Come on.'

They ran from the kitchen into the living room. Ticky went to the mantelpiece and began smashing ornaments. Cy snatched a picture off the wall. He broke it against a side table, and when the table toppled, Cy stamped down on it, breaking a strut between its dark legs. He stamped again but the little table seemed quite strong. He had ruined the picture. When he glanced across the room he saw Ticky lift the music centre and hurl it to the floor, then jump on it with both feet. It crunched and splintered. Cy joined to attack the wooden record cabinet, and laughed with scorn. 'Look at this vinyl! Out of the ark.'

The records tumbled and slithered across the floor and Ticky grabbed at some, tearing covers and bending disks.

'Flippy floppy,' sneered Cy, following suit.

They were cackling like goblins when the man yelled, 'What the hell's going on?'

They hardly heard at first. He was shouting: 'Bloody well leave that alone!'

He was tall, long-haired, wearing pyjamas mid-afternoon. He started towards them, but in those pyjamas he didn't look threatening. He raised his fist and shouted again, then hesitated. But when Ticky dashed at him the man lashed out surprisingly fast and knocked him across the room. Ticky fell groaning, stunned, and the boy waited for the man to make his next move. As he came closer the boy did not flinch. The man reached out confidently, and in one smooth movement Cy pulled out a kitchen knife and thrust it in his heart.

✳

'Sit in the armchair. Settle down.'

Cy wouldn't let Ticky do a thing. Twice, as Cy started tidying the room, Ticky stood up and Cy snarled at him to sit back down. 'We have to clean the place, make it look as if no one was here.'

'Yeah, but Angel—' Ticky was on his feet.

'Sit down. Leave this to me. Wait there while I see if the kettle's boiled.'

Ticky waited uncomfortably. He heard the kettle clank, heard water pouring, and before he saw the boy return, smelt coffee freshly made. Coffee, he thought – now?

'Drink this. Then I've a job for you.'

Ticky sat with his cup of scalding instant coffee, his feet too short to touch the floor. He watched the boy sweep pieces of broken china and replace damaged records. He watched him use a handkerchief to clean the surfaces. He watched him say, 'Pity we bust his stereo.'

'And the picture.'

'That doesn't matter – I threw it in the bin. Perhaps they won't notice the stereo.'

Ticky muttered glumly, 'This is a waste of time.'

'It'll be OK. Just as well we didn't have time to paint the message.'

'Angel, this is getting nowhere—'

'Nothing can be linked to us. Or to your boss.'

Ticky blew on his coffee. Cy said matter-of-factly, 'We'll have to move the guy – make it look like he disappeared.'

'What, done a runner?'

'Yes.'

'Why would he do that?'

'Everyone's got something they want to run from. Ready to do something useful?'

'Um—'

'Wet a cloth and clean the blood up off of the floor.'

'It won't work, Angel—'

'Why d'you call me that?'

Ticky licked his lips nervously. 'We can't get rid of every scrap of blood. Forensics are bound to find something.'

Cy stared at him. 'Why should there be forensics? The guy just disappeared. We'll carry him away, that's all.'

✳

Cy had brought a blanket from upstairs. Together they lifted Angus and dropped his body onto it. Ticky said, 'Those pyjamas are covered in blood.'

'So?'

'Well, if we leave him wearing 'em they could be a clue to his identity – you know, eventually, when the cops find him, they check the label, trace where he bought 'em—'

'Why should the cops find him?'

'We should put the pyjamas in his washing machine, on automatic. Then when the cops arrive, there's no sign of him – only his clean jim-jams in the washer—'

'Get hold of this.'

Cy showed Ticky how to take the blanket by two corners and wrap the body inside. Ticky wittered on: 'Look, there's more blood on that loose rug. We might be able to squeeze it in his washing machine—'

'We'll take it with us. Lose it somewhere.'

'With the body?'

'Perhaps. Decide on the way.'

They lifted the bundle and struggled with it to the car. Angus was six foot one. Cy wasn't tall and Ticky was shorter. As they forced the awkward parcel into the car Ticky kept glancing at Cy's impassive face. The boy pushed at the body determinedly to cram it in. Then he turned to Ticky: 'Get that carpet with the bloodstains.'

Without a word Ticky trotted to the house. Cy was in command.

SEVENTEEN

Snow had fallen again in the night. When I opened the shutters to the blue morning sky a shower of white fell like dry bread crumbs from the ledge above. Sharp mountains across the valley seemed so close it would be only a short walk to reach them. Crags glistened in the dazzling light.

The view suited the exhilaration I felt at awakening in the private retreat of the most talked about man in the world. In the crystal silence any occasional sounds had the same clarity as the view. Two servants crossed the yard, smacking their hands together as they chuckled at the cold. The woman was Frau Mittelstrasser, the housekeeper who had welcomed us on our first night. The man could have been anyone, perhaps a chauffeur.

Turning back into my prettily furnished room – warm, despite being decorated in pale blue – I collected my handbag from the double bed. Those Bavarian *Federbetten*!

When I reached the dining room I found several people already at breakfast. Naomi was there – she was an early riser and had been out that morning to paint the colours of dawn sun upon the snow – but of Hitler and Goering there was no sign. Unity, of course, was still in bed. We ate continental style – rye bread and biscuits, cold meat and cheese, coffee and cocoa, but with the addition of tea for the English guests. Hitler was a late riser and Goering seemed to follow suit. The house was quiet. I remember statues, dull paintings, and sombre furniture in the halls. The Berghof felt like a museum. Outside was a winter garden in which snow-crusted seats stood among blobs of frozen shrubbery. Out in that quiet garden one was seldom alone; Hitler had banned smoking inside his dwelling, and since almost everybody smoked, there was an ever-changing huddle of addicts outside. Beside the terrace a charming cluster of temporary offices had been built to resemble rustic extensions, and beyond the stone parapet was a magnificent vista of mountains and hills. Salzburg was a toy town in the distance.

166

We stayed three days, I think, perhaps four. It was January, 1939. Each morning started with a long, quiet and peaceful time in which all the main celebrities remained off stage. Naomi went skiing with Albrecht, her doctor friend – or she painted snowscapes – Unity and Janos remained in bed and I walked outside. One of the maids had found me some fabulous boots, and wearing those and a huge fur coat I would tramp along pathways cut in the snow. Up there the air was pure iced oxygen, the sky bright blue, and the freezing air stung one's face to a tingling red and left one oddly warm. It was an exotic tonic, but I couldn't take much of it – an hour at most.

One morning as I stamped back up to the Berghof garden I realised I was being filmed. From a plateau above, a fur clad woman with an 8mm cine camera on a sturdy tripod was tracking our progress up the hill. (I had been walking with a young man called Werner Warsonke.) Though completely hidden in heavy furs the dogs gave the woman away; Eva's black terriers accompanied her everywhere.

Werner called, 'Are we allowed to wave or shall we pretend we haven't seen you?'

'Do both – then I can cut out what I don't like.'

Eva Braun was crazy about photography. In daylight hours I seldom saw her without a camera – the cine, a Leica or her chunky Hasselblad. No one else was permitted to take photographs – Hitler was sensitive about them, believing (with some justification) that he was never flattered by the camera, especially unposed. 'Cameras jeer at me,' he said. Often in daytime he would wear a peaked cap and sunglasses against the snow, and Eva would stalk him for the one moment she could snap his face. But that day she was taking land-scapes.

She said, 'Do you know the two most difficult things to photo-graph? Water and snow. When I photograph in a snowy landscape – like you two, walking up this hill – I get only dark smudges in a sea of white. Yet look at this view. I want it. I want to hold it for ever on my film.'

Outside the Berghof the land dropped away through snow-laden forests and sparkling streams into the lovely Berchtesgaden valley. Beyond were mountains – the Unterberg, the Watzmann, the Steinernes Meer. Everywhere was white, untrodden, spotless.

Eva loved the mountains. Wrapped in furs, wearing enviable high boots, she would stride across the snow, laughing in the sun. When she came indoors she brought fresh air with her. She was blonde and pretty, always well dressed, elegant and informal. Why Hitler didn't marry her I can't understand – she was the perfect wife. Perhaps he feared that if he did marry, the German people might think he had become domesticated, enfeebled like Samson after Delilah cut his hair. Yet he loved Eva. They were at ease together and often teased each other. (No one else teased Hitler!) He niggled good-humouredly about her lovely dresses and complained that by eating so little she would waste away. She scoffed at him for knowing nothing of the latest books and films.

'Oh yes, your films,' he said. 'Shadows on the screen, and preening actors pretending at reality. Music drowning out their conversations, as if it were an opera!'

We were eating dinner, the second night I think, in a rectangular pine-panelled dining room. Not every seat was occupied. We ate off Rosenthal china and drank from heavy crystal goblets. Hitler sat between Eva Braun and Unity.

Eva said, 'Films combine music, story and photography. It is the greatest modern art.'

He said, 'Simply a way to tell a story.'

I sat beside Werner. Naomi and Albrecht sat opposite each other – and spoke to no one else.

Eva laughed. 'You do like films really. I have seen them make you laugh and cry.'

'Laugh perhaps, but you have never seen me cry. A man does not cry at shadows on the wall.'

Eva smiled and looked away. Though not abashed, she knew the limits beyond which she should not go.

Hitler turned to Unity: 'Are you also an admirer of the cinema?'

She shrugged. 'It will kill the theatre – if that matters, which I doubt. Nowadays, instead of squinting at actors who shout at us from the far end of a theatre, we can stare up their nostrils while they whisper in our ear.'

'You find that attractive?'

'It depends on the actor.'

Hitler smiled. 'Eva says I am censorious, but your point sometimes worries me. Is it right for thousands of young girls to sit in darkened halls and fall in love with a complete stranger? Is it healthy, do you think?'

'In the theatre, men have always gazed at chorus girls. At least in the cinema we girls can see the men properly in close up.'

'But the men are painted. They wear women's make-up.'

Goering interrupted – yes, he was there, with his new wife Emmy. He said, 'Some men see chorus girls in close up too – but not till after the show, you understand!'

He laughed, but Emmy did not join in the banter. Since marrying

168

Hermann she had grown larger, more maternal, more impressive. But on this point, Naomi for once broke her silent dualogue with Albrecht opposite her. She was further along the table, beyond Hitler and between Janos and Hermann: 'In Berlin we were invited to the UFA studios where a film was being made—'

'A history film,' yawned Unity. 'Very educational.'

'And the set was even cruder than in a theatre – rough wood, poor quality painting, abrupt endings where the set ended off camera. And the make-up was simply daubed across the actors' faces. Costumes were held together with pins. Yet when the film is finished the effect will be absolutely lifelike.'

Unity continued: 'They said the paintwork was left shoddy and unfinished deliberately because it photographs more believably.' She laughed. 'The actors use wooden swords, and the clang of metal is added afterwards.'

Hermann interrupted: 'Illusion becomes reality. It is safer that way. With wooden swords our delicate actors do not get hurt. Did Joey show you round?' (He meant Joseph Goebbels.) 'He enjoys showing ladies around his studios.'

'He did not,' Unity replied. 'And he doesn't show *ladies* round. He prefers chorus girls, I hear.'

This raised a slight snigger because Goebbels, now grandly entitled Minister of Popular Enlightenment and Propaganda, was not popular with his colleagues – and where actresses were concerned he had a sordid reputation, as I'm sure you know.

But Hitler admonished Unity: 'You mustn't believe everything you hear of Doctor Goebbels. People envy him because he works in films and publishing, but they forget the magnificent work he does for his country.'

Hermann grinned. 'He works day and night – especially night!'

'That is rumour,' Hitler snapped.

I suspect Goering was the only man in Germany who would have dared continue. 'Oh, there is seldom smoke without fire, I think. Seriously, how does that stunted cripple net such a trawl of chorus girls? It is no wonder people envy him. Such a wonderful job!'

Hitler closed the conversation. 'Since you mention his deformity, I will point out that ninety-nine cripples out of a hundred would use their club foot as an excuse to sit back and seek our sympathy. But not Goebbels. He has overcome his disability and risen to one of the most important jobs in the Reich. I consider him an example to malingerers everywhere.'

Everyone fell silent – except the irrepressible Hermann. 'Truly that is inspiring,' he said. 'He should make a film about it.'

※

Throughout our stay Hitler usually had Unity sit beside him. He was flattered by her admiration for him, and was genuinely fond of her – but there was nothing more between them. She never slept with him. (I only make this point because the allegation has been made by the press and self-appointed biographers who, like most biographers nowadays, consider the sex lives of their subjects the most interesting part of their story.) I spent several days with them, and I would have known. During our stay, Unity was pleasurably occupied with Janos and in any case, Eva was with Hitler – not only at the Berghof but in Berlin and everywhere he went, accompanying him as securely as any wife would her own husband. The Allied media sneered at Eva, calling her his mistress (a dark slur then) but they had been together since 1933. She was the only woman in his life – no other woman has ever been suggested, despite many fruitless searches. When we met them at the Berghof their relationship was five years old, and though none of us could know it at the time, Eva would remain with him till the end.

But in our trips to Germany it was clear that Hitler did not lack female admirers and it is to his credit that he did not take advantage. Despite what you have heard of him – what you think you know of him – he was a fundamentally decent man: neat, clean, with a pale skin which Eva told me burned quickly in sunshine, especially in the mountains. He was of medium height and his hair – which photographed so atrociously, like a wallpaper brush slapped across his forehead – was in fact exceptionally fine and always neatly brushed. He had dark blue eyes and though you will not want to believe it, they were compelling and romantic.

Unity? Yes, she admired him. And he saw *her* as a useful ally (one of many) among British aristocracy. On our first evening he boasted, 'Your king himself' (he meant Edward) 'stayed here last winter, in this very house.'

He liked women, and was genuinely at ease with them – though this doesn't accord with what you know of him from propaganda. You 'know' he was a loathsome little man – ugly, incompetent and ultimately insane. Have you never wondered how such a man rose from penniless obscurity to become leader of his country, and transformed a wrecked Germany into a modern and successful state? Like all war leaders, Hitler made terrible mistakes and committed horrendous atrocities. I don't deny that. Nor do I deny that what was done to the Jews was unforgivable, nor even that eventually his quest to rebuild Europe failed. I deny neither his failings nor his accomplishments. He had a dream which failed. But how close he came. How close.

✳

That January at the Berghof, though ostensibly we were relaxing, suspense was in the air. Hitler and Goering seldom discussed strategy at their dinner table – yet both there and at the fireside later, ideas and hypotheses were floated before their English guests. Unity (that dear excitable girl) was almost too enthusiastic, leaning eagerly across the table, eyes ablaze, urging further conquest – that was the word she used: conquest! '*Eroberung!* A cleansing sword to reclaim Europe!'

Goering laughed but Hitler beamed. 'At your birth your parents named you aptly – Unity *Valkyrie* Mitford – what a wonderful name: it suggests bold and heroic acts. You know the Valkyrie greets fallen heroes on the battlefield?'

'Of course.'

'I can imagine you riding on your flying horse with your fiery spear and your blonde hair streaming.'

'Why not?' She held a goblet of wine – red wine, she drank only red. 'Your own heroic acts have already recaptured the Rhineland and the Saar, as well as Austria and the Sudetenland. You must ride on.'

'Oh, the Saar voted to join us,' Hitler laughed. 'We did not have to recapture it.'

Hermann raised his glass: 'Over ninety per cent voted to rejoin.'

'And Austria welcomed us most cordially.'

Hermann agreed: 'Their Chancellor invited us in by telephone!'

Hitler's voice dropped to the throaty whisper he often used at home: 'It was the Rhineland that posed the greatest threat. Back in '36 – when was it, Hermann?'

'March.'

'I'll tell you something: when our troops crossed the bridges they were supported by ten armed planes – just ten! That was all Hermann could afford!'

Goering spluttered indignantly but Hitler laughed him off: 'I told my soldiers not to shoot if confronted by the French, because we weren't strong enough to win.'

Hermann said, 'We may have had only ten planes *armed*, but we flew two squadrons. I sent them up, scattered them about, then landed them a dozen at a time and changed their markings. Each time they flew they looked like a fresh wave of aircraft.'

Hitler reached for his glass of *Fachingerwasse*. 'If the spineless French had taken any action we would have been forced to turn back. But they did not, and now they never will. Destiny is on our side.'

Goering was staring at me across the table. 'Have you noticed? Every woman at our table tonight has a head of blonde – look: you three English, Eva, my wife: all blonde. Perhaps you are all Valkyries.'

Emmy was the only one with a figure normally associated with Valkyries; the buxom secretary had become a voluptuous *Hausfrau*. Hermann was bloated too, almost unrecognisable from the beautiful Barrymore he had once been. Little remained of the tragic hero who had created Karinhall. (Or perhaps too much remained: he was a mountain of flesh!)

'A Valkyrie does not always wear a helmet,' Hermann said solemnly. 'In time of peace she dresses as a swan and flies gracefully above the forests searching for a lonely lake or woodland pool. A passer by may see a swan and not realise she is enchanted. Sometimes however, when the Valkyrie is certain she is alone, she sheds her plumage of soft snowy white and swims in the pool in human form. Imagine stumbling across a pool at night and glimpsing a maiden swimming naked in the cold dark water, her coat of feathers lying on the bank. Do you know her secret?' I remember his eyes focused on mine. 'If a man steals that soft white plumage she can never escape him and must do his will.'

He continued to stare at me – yet I don't believe it was me he saw.

Heinrich Himmler took up the story. Oh, I'm sorry, I'd forgotten he was there. But he was a self-effacing man, able to sit silent and unnoticed, blinking owlishly behind his glasses while watching what was going on. Having attracted our attention, he removed his round spectacles, huffed on them and smiled.

'When Brynhild was surprised by King Agnar – you know the story of the *Nibelung*? Not the opera, of course; Wagner concocted that from a miscellany of tales—'

'He made it up?' Hitler asked, surprised.

'Everyone knows that.'

'I have sat through it so many times – almost as many as *Die Meistersinger*.'

'At least that's shorter,' Goering observed.

'You know, I once told someone it was my favourite opera,' Hitler confessed. 'Foolishly – because now wherever I go they serenade me with the wretched *Die Meistersinger*. I hear it everywhere.'

'It's a good job you didn't say you liked *The Ring*,' Goering chuckled. 'It's four times as long.'

172

'Exactly. *Meistersinger* was my favourite Wagner opera, but actually I prefer the Merry Widow.'

'Who wouldn't?' Hermann joked. 'Every man likes a merry widow!'

'In the original Nordic epic,' Himmler cut in primly, 'Agnar demands that Brynhild give him victory over Hjalmgunnar. But Hjalmgunnar is the protégé of Odin—'

'Who was?' interrupted Naomi.

Himmler looked at her in some surprise. He replaced his glasses, blinked twice and explained: 'Odin is the most senior Teutonic god.'

'Also called Wotan,' Albrecht murmured helpfully.

'Odin rules Valhalla. He is the God of Thunder. When you hear skies rumble on a stormy night it is the gallop of horses bearing phantoms of dead warriors. Their troop is the Furious Army and at its head rides Odin, god of intelligence and war.'

'Intelligence, war and thunder?' murmured Naomi. 'How industrious.'

Himmler paused. Candlelight glinted on his spectacles.

Naomi prompted him: 'But Odin had a protégé?'

'Many, including Sigmund, father of Siegfried—'

'I've seen this at Bayreuth,' Goering interrupted.

Hitler laughed. 'No, you slept through it, Hermann – I heard you snoring!'

Himmler permitted himself a short dry smile. 'Odin was angry and vowed to punish Brynhild – but because she was a goddess and could not be killed, he stabbed her with a magic thorn. She fell into an enchanted sleep.'

'Oh, that old story,' began Naomi.

Himmler didn't stop. 'Odin imprisoned the sleeping Brynhild in a hut and surrounded it with a ring of flame.'

Goering said, 'I remember that from the opera—'

'A different story,' Himmler snapped. 'A concoction, a corruption of the Teutonic myth. Listen. Brynhild was divested of her supernatural powers and became mortal woman. And the only man who could win her as his bride was the one who dared ride through the wall of flames—'

'Can't see why he'd bother,' Naomi said, 'if she was only going to become mortal.'

'I *do* remember,' Hermann insisted. 'This is the climax of the opera.'

'No. Wagner stole his best scenes from the sacred epic. Put it out of your head. Finally such a man appeared, and his name was Siegfried—'

'Exactly like the opera—'

'In the fairy story—' Naomi began.

Himmler persisted: 'After this, Odin sacrificed himself for the world—'

'Ah, no,' Hitler corrected him. 'Not for the world. You are wrong there, Heini. He sacrificed himself to rebuild his inner strength.'

Himmler waited politely in case the Führer wanted to continue, but when he didn't, said, 'There are some acts of mysticism a human cannot judge. Godlike behaviour cannot always be understood. But tell me, do the English ladies know the next part of the story?'

It was a shrewd line, guaranteeing him the right to speak on. He licked his lips. 'Odin impaled himself on his own spear.'

'To each his own,' murmured Naomi.

'He consecrated himself to himself, you see? Then he tied himself to a tree.'

'Was he still a god?' Naomi asked. 'Just wondering.'

'By this act, Odin learnt how to achieve rejuvenation. He wounded himself with that spear and for nine long days hung from the branches of an ash tree. Eventually he saw before him some magic runes.'

'Had they been there all the time?' Naomi teased. 'Or was he hallucinating?'

'The runes were *revealed* to him. By their power Odin was released and could drop to the ground restored to vigour and youth. This was his resurrection. It was magnificent. What we learn from this story is that by pain and self-sacrifice we can approach immortality. Death is a state of glory from which we shall return.'

Suddenly, Unity stirred herself to reach across the table for some more red wine. 'If we're going to tell fairy stories I vote we do it in front of the fire.'

*

I don't remember Himmler joining us in the living room – perhaps he went off to march naked in the snow. The living room was as warm and comfortable as one would want in a mountain chalet. It was furnished with large sofas and low chairs. Subdued lighting came from a number of candles and one large standard lamp. Hitler sat in what was presumably his accustomed place to the right of the splendid fire and Eva sat – or almost lay – beside him in a huge armchair, her feet resting on a stool. That night, she wore a heavy silk dress with a wide bell skirt and a short bolero jacket. Beside her on the floor lay her two black terriers. I heard Hitler whispering in her ear, asking if he could bring his own dog in.

She shrugged. 'You know our dogs do not get on. But I'll send mine outside if you really want me to.'

'No, *Liebchen*, I don't want that. Perhaps later on?'

'Yes, later. Drink your tea.'

Although this conversation was whispered it was not completely hidden from us. In the Berghof, Hitler was content to be the family man. – Incidentally, that tea which Eva mentioned was a frightful cumin flavoured drink he took for his digestion. He suffered from stomach ache quite frequently (twice in our short stay at the Berghof) and stuck to a particularly plain and unappetising vegetarian diet which seemed to comprise soup, fruit, gruel and mashed linseed. Whether the diet was because of the stomach ache or *caused* it is debatable. But the rest of us could eat whatever we liked, and there was plenty of alcohol, though not for him. That evening, I remember, we were drinking *Bowle*, a punch of champagne and Sauternes with fruit which had been popular at the Berlin Olympiad in '36 and which had finally made it to Bavaria. We ate apple strudel, one of the few sensible foods Hitler could eat.

We sat in deep chairs and sofas arranged around the fire: Hitler by Eva, Unity with Janos, Hermann dozing in a huge armchair with Emmy at his side. Werner and I sat in a small two-seater; Naomi and Albrecht sat some distance away. In that low-lit room, the logs shifting in the whispering fire, Hitler sounded us out about British attitudes.

'I see your newspapers only in translation. I have spoken to your silly Chamberlain – I might as well have spoken to his furled umbrella – but *you* must tell me what the people think.'

'The man in the street?'

'No, the men with power. In every country real decisions are made by a chosen handful. How else could it be? A nation cannot vote on everything. So tell me, Germany and Russia – which do the British see as their enemy?'

'I should have thought that was obvious.'

'I am not so sure. Which countries are your closest friends?'

'America and our colonies.'

'But in Europe?'

'I really think our closest friend is Germany.'

Goering chuckled, his eyes still closed. 'Who else would matter – Italy, France, the Netherlands? Britain and Germany are the only powerful countries.'

Hitler said, 'In future, either it will be Germany and Britain against Communist Russia, or it will be Germany and Russia against yourselves.'

'You don't think Britain might side with Russia?' I suggested lightly.

Unity laughed. 'America would never allow it. – What a ghastly thought!'

Hitler raised a placatory hand. 'We already know the views of *die Unity*, but how does the rest of Britain stand? Take Czechoslovakia, for example—'

'You already have,' quipped Unity.

He smiled. 'It was not a real country, but one manufactured from bits of old Bohemia. And now that the Sudetenland has returned to Germany, what of the rest? The Czechs do not like the Slovaks, and the rump of the country will one day fall apart. Last September I would have invaded to save their nation – yes, I tell you frankly – but Hermann persuaded me to talk to Mr Chamberlain.'

'And I was right,' said Goering cheerfully – always happy to stand up to Hitler. 'To invade meant war – and our people weren't ready for it. I saw their faces at the march-past in Berlin. They watched fearfully because they didn't want their sons to die.'

Hitler frowned at me, then glanced across at Naomi, murmuring with Albrecht and paying little attention. He smiled briefly, apologetically, and to my surprise he invited me to sing. When we had first arrived, Hermann had introduced Naomi and I as 'the talented aristocratic sisters' (which I thought more than a little flattering) and Hitler must have decided it was now time for me to demonstrate my skills. I thought quickly.

'I will play *Der Erlkönig*,' I said, rising.

'Ah, Schubert,' exclaimed Emmy Goering. (It might have been the only time that night she spoke.) 'I am very fond of Schubert.'

I smiled apologetically. 'I'm afraid this is the other version, by Carl Loewe.'

'Is Loewe German?' Hitler asked.

'Yes, and it is still Goethe's ballad, of course.'

'Oh, I know the poem,' he said lightly. 'We had to learn it by heart at school.'

'Then you must not mock my accent.'

Though I spoke German fluently I could not quite pass as a native. Naomi by then was almost faultless.

I sat down at the piano to play. It is, of course, a wonderfully ghostly song, ideal for a darkened room by firelight. The Loewe melody, though admittedly easier than the fiendish Schubert, is genuinely effective, alternately rushing and hesitating, capturing the growing terror of the lone rider in dark woods at night, pursued by the spirit of evil. In the last verse my voice fell to a whisper as I – the rider – realised that the *Erlkönig* had caught up with me and now held me in his arms. That last timorous sigh of horror seemed to echo in the silent room.

Fortunately, it is a song that can have no encore. It brought a pall of contemplation around the fire. Our conversation was desultory, leaving gaps no one thought they had to fill. The fire was low now, well past midnight, and in his fireside seat Hitler was in semi-darkness; but I could feel his eyes flickering between we sisters as he spoke.

'Poland is another pretend country, designed by committee, a folly of compromise. You know Josef Beck?'

Of course, we assented, we were aware of Josef Beck. He was Poland's rabble-rousing insatiable Foreign Minister, a dark haired, beak-nosed dangerous man.

'Beck wants his country to be the leading force in middle Europe, a bastion between Russia and ourselves. A few weeks ago we had his ambassador, Lipski, here. We suggested a sensible compromise, merely that the city of Danzig be returned to us – it is no loss to them; it does not belong to them; the Poles even ship from Gdynia now, not from Danzig, as their port. The only other thing we asked was a road and rail link across the Polish corridor to rejoin the two halves of Prussia. That is reasonable, is it not? We would allow Poland to maintain their corridor – this excrescence – across our land. All we asked was a transport route across theirs, but Lipski refused. He said his people would not allow it. His people! Who are they? A mix of Germans, Ukrainians, Lithuanians, Russians, Czechs and of course Jews – one third of whom, incidentally, live like parasites on government relief. Nothing new there, eh, Hermann! This mess is the Polish 'nation'. And it is on their behalf that the jumped-up Beck – he may be a Jew, you know, he looks Jewish – that Beck dares to oppose me. To oppose *us*.'

No one said anything. This was not a speech one could interrupt. Hitler threw his hands wide and smiled. (I thought it a curiously Semitic gesture, but I held my tongue.) He said, 'So what does Beck want, d'you think – does he want war?'

Silence continued.

'Well, I think he does, you know. He has a high opinion of his Polish armies but – Hermann, tell our friends what we know about Beck's armies.'

'Hmm?' Hermann roused himself from a state of drowse.

'Beck's armies. The Polish threat. What does it comprise?'

'Cavalry,' Hermann grunted. 'Men on horses facing up to tanks. Attractive uniforms, though.'

Hitler bent forward, and his head emerged from the shadows. 'Beck believes that you British and the French will back him. He wants a treaty. He wants your support to help Poland – yes, Poland! – become the third power in Europe. He is an ambitious man.'

Unity shrugged.. 'He has nothing to offer in return.'

Hitler nodded, watching her gravely.

I cleared my throat. 'What if Beck continues to be obdurate – will you seize Danzig and return it to the Reich?'

He smiled. 'I don't need to. The people there are German. They will rise spontaneously.'

'Are you sure?'

Goering laughed. 'It can be arranged.'

'And after Danzig,' I asked cautiously, 'the rest of the Polish corridor?'

Hitler shrugged. 'I want nothing more. We will then have all our lands back.'

His dark blue eyes held mine. They were impenetrable.

Unity said, 'Well, I say you should take it. Make an end to the whole boring business. I mean, who else cares, really?'

'What will England do?'

Unity laughed disdainfully. 'What on earth *should* we do? Nothing. Everyone agrees that Danzig is German, really. Everyone knows the corridor was a mistake. Why should we care about a rotten strip of land?' She laughed again. 'And some boring old agreement from years ago.'

Naomi said, 'Too ridiculous, darling, simply too ridiculous.'

She laughed too. I can hear them now: Naomi and Unity laughing in the candlelight by Hitler's fire.

✳

That final morning I awoke late, into a stillness and lack of light. Silence was not unusual in the mornings – both Hitler and Goering arose late, and apart from occasional clunks from servants around the house there were few other noises to disturb the air. The mountain retreat was far from habitation, so the Berghof mornings were undisturbed.

When I sat up in bed I must have moved the *Federbett*. Werner stirred and asked the time. I told him. He seemed surprised it was so late. But the previous night we had crawled into bed at nearly two and, being young, had not gone straight to sleep but had exhausted ourselves still more. My thighs ached, and my mouth felt sticky and mildly acrid from hours of woodsmoke in the living room. Werner grunted and turned away.

I stepped out of bed, reached for my dressing gown, but then left it where it lay. In this mountain residence one felt a careless closeness with uncluttered nature. Each bedroom looked out onto a mountain vista, and the first sight each day was of awesome peaks, dark green conifers against the snow and sparkling blue sky.

I walked naked across the room and in one flamboyant gesture threw open the curtains to expose the view. But there was nothing. The view was gone. In its place was a thick grey mountain mist, impenetrable, unmoving. A dense, cold, opaque jelly had set around the Berghof. If I pushed open the window, I thought, it would meet resistance from the fog. I peered through the glass but could not make out a single shape – nothing of the garden, the stone walls and out-houses, the snow-laden trees; nothing of the valley or mountains that lay beyond; nothing of that awe-inspiring sky.

I had expected the morning sun to warm me as it had every day till then, but instead I felt cold, shabby and disappointed. I collected my dressing gown and put it on.

Werner said, 'No sun today, *Liebchen*?'

I shivered. 'Winter has come.'

Book Two

Damnant quod non intelligunt

EIGHTEEN

She recognised the sound but couldn't place it: heavy cleaver on wooden block. Meat in a butcher's shop. Crunch of bone, squelch of flesh, thunk of wood. But she and Paul were walking in a forest, nine o'clock at night, and the wide pathway curved before them green and damp beneath a moon-filled sky. Trees hung darkly on either side.

Paul paused. She felt his hand quiver and stop. They glanced at each other and Paul frowned: whoever was making the sound was round the curve ahead.

Cool air clung at her ankles.

When Paul glanced at her she shook her head, and with a sideways nod indicated they should turn back. He smiled absently. On the cold mossy ground she stepped away from him, but he held her hand more tightly and raised his other to signal silence. In the growing gloom she couldn't read his face.

Laura tugged his hand but he did not react. The sound stopped. As they waited motionless on the wooded path it seemed to her that every tree was waiting with them. A subdued sigh came from the leaves.

She heard the clang of metal against stone. Before she could say anything, she heard a new sound – the chop of spade on forest floor. She heard a grunt. Laura's voice was barely audible: 'Let's go back.'

But Paul had moved ahead of her, was peering through the tangled trees to see around the bend. She pulled at him. 'I don't like it.'

He let go her hand. Incredulously she watched Paul walk forward, as if drawn by some mad male imperative which drew him on a dare towards the sound. Her feet seemed to sink into cold ground. When she reached toward his back she was like a sapling rooted in mud, one thin branch extended, shivering in the air.

No choice. She couldn't stay like this; neither could she turn back and go to the car. She had to follow him.

She scurried along the mossy path. The only sound was someone digging. She caught Paul at the sharp curve of the path where cold grey gloom lurked between the trees.

The digging stopped. So did they. The unseen man cursed, threw his spade to the ground and muttered words they could not catch. Laura reached for Paul's hand but when she laced her fingers in his, Paul's hand was cold as stone. Perhaps he would change his mind. As they hesitated on the silent path she stretched up to whisper in his ear, 'I'm frightened. Please take me home.'

Then came that sound again, that sickening crunch they had heard earlier, the butcher's cleaver – but closer now. Each blow accompanied by a grunt.

'No,' she whispered. 'We must go back.'

The sound seemed to pull Paul forward. He walked steadily along the dim moonlit path, round where the curve bent back on itself, and Laura followed as if in a dream. They were in an s-bend. Moonlight illuminated the shadowed path and the chopping sound grew louder. Whoever was there was not chopping wood. The sound was muffled, dampened. The snake bend straightened, then they saw him.

Ticky glanced up as they came in sight. Who the hell were they? Unsure whether to stay or run, he leapt out and wielded the axe. The girl stepped back and fell.

Ticky shrieked, 'Get out! Get out if you know what's good for you.'

But they wouldn't move. Oh Christ, Ticky thought – where the hell was Cy? 'Go away!' he yelled.

The damn idiot man ignored his girl sitting in the mud – and started inching forward! The girl screamed at him. Ticky raised his axe. The man was close now – looked tough – Christ! Ticky turned to run.

Beside the stump lay the dirty pillow case, inside which was the dead man's head. Oh Jesus, they'd see his body – he couldn't let the fools do that. Ticky stood by the stump and raised the axe again. He might have to throw it. He'd do it too.

'Move back,' he spat.

If that idiot took one step further he'd see the body and that would be that. Ticky would have to kill him. And the woman. Christ, once you start.

'Back!'

He had to stop him. The man was hesitating. A single step could mean his death.

Now the bonehead was backing off. Ticky snarled, 'Further. Go past the girl.'

He wouldn't, of course, but Ticky didn't care. All that mattered was they kept away from the tree stump and hole. Ticky grabbed the pillow case, swung it across his shoulder and felt the skull thump at his back.

The stupid woman was still in the mud. 'Get up,' he called.

As she struggled to her feet Ticky determined to keep the upper hand. 'Can you walk – you? Try your ankle. Walk away – back where you came.'

He saw the woman tugging at her boyfriend. Heard her: 'Come on! Please.'

Yeah, she was pretty – and pretty terrified. Ticky imagined his axe thumping into her. 'That's right – *please*,' he jeered.

They were edging away. No, Ticky thought, chop the boyfriend, leave the female standing there. Then ask her – want to save your life? That would be good, he thought. Here in the woods, tell her to take her clothes off. Lay her on the ground—

A piece of wood hurtled from the trees. It was Cy. About time the kid appeared.

Ticky called, 'See? There's more of us. You're surrounded now.'

Another branch flew out. But missed.

Ticky yelled at them, 'Start running!'

Then – would you believe it? – Cy *howled* at them from the dark: screamed like a banshee. Ticky grinned. This was getting good. Maybe he *should* use his axe and chop the guy. Put the girl on the ground, then he and Cy could take turns with her. It was probably Cy's first time.

But they were moving off. Ticky grabbed his spade, tucked it beneath his arm – and it tangled with the pillow case. He swore, raised the spade to chuck it – but no, he had to take everything. Leave nothing. Except those lumps of meat.

The stupid couple had stopped again. Didn't they want to get away?

'Keep going,' he yelled. 'Round the corner.'

Cy howled again.

Ticky saw the man having second thoughts. He was at the bend in the path, sizing him up. Ticky glared at him. If the guy made a rush, could Ticky be sure to get him with the axe? The man was big. If he threw the axe and missed, or if the bastard knocked it aside...

Ticky scuttled off among the trees. For a moment he thought the man was following, but presumably the guy had realised it would not be wise to blunder through the trees in the pitch dark after someone waiting with an axe. But if he stayed out there he'd find the body.

Ticky stood stock still. He couldn't see into the clearing but could picture the scene: the guy and his girlfriend creeping hand in hand towards the tree stump.

Beside the stump was an uncovered grave, most of a body dumped inside. If they saw it they were bound to call the cops.

Someone touched his arm. He jumped like a rabbit on barbed wire.

'Ssh!'

He dropped the bag.

Cy whispered, 'Let's get going.'

Ticky muttered, 'They'll find the body.'

'Someone has to. You only dug a few inches.'

'The ground was—'

'If we stay we'll have to kill them.'

Ticky paused. It sounded real, the way Cy said it.

'I know, but—'

'Got a taste for it? Done one, might as well do more?'

Ticky didn't answer.

Cy said, 'That's how life goes – you take one step and everything changes. Take another, things change again. Once you've started you can't go back.'

✳

In the interview room the harsh light bounced off painted walls. The grey metal table was ugly and brutally designed. The chairs were functional but uncomfortable. A tape recorder hummed.

Kerrigan had taken off his jacket. Not that it made him seem less formal.

'There's the two of you in the woods, late at night. Why's that? Somewhere quiet for a bit of sex, was it? – Don't give me that look.'

'We were walking.'

'That's romantic. In the dark.'

Laura flared up. 'How dare you! We're here as witnesses. We're not criminals.'

'I'll be frank with you,' Kerrigan said. He leant across the table, smiled pleasantly and released a burst of shirtsleeve odour. 'Your story seems rather strange to me. Two people, late at night, no reason to be in the woods, discover a freshly slaughtered man. I mean, not just dead – he's naked, half chopped up. Really done for. And you say he was done in by someone else – a dwarf, for Goodness sake!'

'He looked like a dwarf,' exclaimed Laura. 'Perhaps it was a child wearing a mask.'

'Look,' Kerrigan said. 'I know kids are devils nowadays, but come on! A kid murders and dismembers a grown man in the woods late at night?'

'It was evening,' Laura said.

'Dark, was it?'

'Not when we saw him.'

'Saw *them*,' Paul corrected.

'Oh, it's a *gang* of school kids now?'

'Two,' said Paul.

'Both wearing masks?'

'We never saw the other one. It was dark.'

'Exactly.' Kerrigan beamed. 'That's what I said. Dark. You were in the woods, wandering in the dark.' He scratched his stubble. 'Why?'

Laura closed her eyes. 'We went for a walk.'

'In the dark?'

'It wasn't when we started.'

'Yet when you got to the middle of the wood it *was* dark? *That* wasn't too bright. Ha, ha.' It was not a cheerful laugh.

Paul said, 'It's a pleasant evening.'

Kerrigan looked at his watch.

Paul said, 'It *was*.'

Kerrigan took a deep breath. 'Till you happened to stumble across a dwarf?'

Paul snapped, 'I never said it was a dwarf.'

'*She* did.'

'He was small,' explained Paul. 'Probably a child.'

Laura said, 'He hardly sounded like a child.'

Kerrigan rapped on the desk. 'It would be nice if you two agreed on your story. Who was the man you were burying?'

'We weren't—'

'Look, there's two of you, right? We've established that. You're lovers—'

'We—'

'You're out late at night in a dark lonely wood – just the pair of you and this naked dead man. Just been murdered. I mean, his body wasn't even stiff. Did that make it easier to cut him up?'

'For God's sake!'

'And there's a freshly dug grave with the bits in. Where's his head?'

When they didn't answer, Kerrigan said, 'A body, a grave, a dark lonely wood. Two lovers. Now, what am I to make of that?'

Paul's voice was level: 'Let me ask *you* a question, if I may. If we *had* been burying someone, and if this man *had* been – I don't know – the third person in a lover's triangle—'

'Your words, sir, not mine.'

'If we were burying him, as you say, alone in the dark, why would we stop half way through and come to you?'

187

Kerrigan's face remained blank. 'This person, then, the one you claim that you saw running away—'

'More than one.'

'A whole gang of dwarves in the woods? Amazing. – All right, all right, a bunch of kids, out in the night.'

'Just two.'

'You saw them?'

'Saw one. Heard another.'

'So these kids will have seen you?'

'One kid threw a piece of wood at us. The other threatened us with an axe. Yes, I think we can say they saw us.'

'There's your answer.' Kerrigan folded his arms. 'You were in a nice lonely spot, well ahead with burying the body, when this kid – or these kids – turned up half way through. Oh, dear. I expect you chased him – am I right?'

Paul jerked his head angrily. Laura refused to speak.

'But in the woods you couldn't catch him – surprising how nippy kids can be. And you thought to yourself, what will the perisher do? He'll go home, tell his parents, and they'll stay up half the night. Eventually, when they decide their boy's not lying, why, they'll get on the phone to the Old Bill. – In the morning, perhaps. Certainly not for a while. So you thought, I know, let's switch it – let's nip in and tell the police ourselves.'

Paul stared at him incredulously. 'Why?'

'So we'll hear your version first. Then when the kid finally gets in touch, we'll think the kid did it – because after all, you did tell us you found him chopping up the body – or perhaps neither of you done it: you both happened to turn up at the same time and mistook what you found. Someone *else* had just run off. Is that what we're supposed to think?'

Laura shook her head and Paul asked, 'Why on earth would we bother? Why wouldn't we just disappear?'

Kerrigan smiled in triumph. 'You saw the kid run to the road. Right? He'd have to run straight past your car. Right? So he could have taken the number. He'd be able to place you both right there.'

✳

As the morning light improved, the police widened their search. They already had the body – or most of it – but not the head. And they were missing one hand. In the first check of the surrounding woods they had accumulated a number of clues – scraps of paper, match boxes, cigarette ends, a drinks can, two used condoms, a dead biro and a twenty pence coin. There were plenty of footprints – or realistically, smears – in the mud. And at the side of the road were numerous tyre prints of uncertain age.

By the time the dogs arrived, so had the first reporters. Until ten o'clock the police had concentrated more on keeping them away than on searching for clues, but after that they organised a thorough trawl. Word from the station was that given the freshness of the corpse, the missing pieces might be close by. None of that was released to the press.

Officially.

But policemen talk. As they picked their way between the trees they speculated about what they might find, and in the quiet country air their voices carried. Two journalists disappeared to see if they could circumnavigate the wood and slip in the other side.

When Sammy Hahn arrived he immediately made for the incident car. 'Who's in charge, lads?'

Sammy, by dint of expensive coat, discreet approach and reassuring manner – plus a calling card from BBC Television News (false) – quickly charmed himself into the back seat of the inspector's car.

'Yes, a body has been found.'

'Looking for another?'

'No comment.'

'Might that be a yes?'

'I said no comment.'

'Of course. Don't worry. It's just that I don't want to misquote you on the telly.'

'Well, this is off the record, you understand?'

'Absolutely. Maybe we can get you an appearance on the lunchtime News, in between all that election twaddle. Perhaps an interview for the Six o'clock? That be all right?'

'One thing I can tell you, Mr Hahn: this is an official murder investigation in which, so far, two people—'

'Men? Local men?'

'A man and a woman are helping with enquiries.'

Sammy sighed happily. 'A woman. That's good.'

'We have reason to believe that a third, as yet unidentified person, possibly a child, may be a witness.'

Sammy waited but nothing further came. 'Will there be an appeal for the child to come forward?'

'Not at this time.'

'The Six o'clock News will be best if it's a child.'

'The child may not exist and may not have seen the actual murder. But if he did see anything, of course, we shall want him to contact us immediately.'

'A boy,' confirmed Sammy. 'Are you going to set up a confiden-
tial number?'

'That might be wise.'

'How old's this child?'

The inspector sucked his cheeks. 'I don't know there is one.'

'How would you like me to put the story out?'

✳

For Ticky it was an increasingly anxious day. Because he didn't know
what to say to Gottfleisch he had not rung him, and had stayed out of
his flat, away from the phone. Around lunchtime he went to the
squat but they told him Cy was out. At work, they said – but how
likely was that? Without much hope, Ticky went to the restaurant,
knocked at the kitchen door and was refused admittance. A man
dressed in kitchen whites gave him a black look and told him to
scram.

Ticky wandered off to kill time in a dingy video store off Old
Compton Street where they showed Dutch movies. The main one
was a film inside a film in which a scrawny blonde armed with a
video camera wandered around Utrecht sneaking shots of unsuspecting couples. In a series of unlikely scenes, obliging couples copu-
lated in shop doorways, a deserted church and on a late-night tram
journey. Finally in a chilly park, a curvaceous black girl suddenly
noticed she was being filmed – but instead of reacting angrily, she
chose to perform even more lewdly for the blonde with the camera.
In a stunningly awful performance she leered across her boyfriend's
shoulder, unzipped his fly and manoeuvred him around to stand in
profile. On the damp green grass she sunk to her knees. The man
stared stoically into the distance and pretended not to know he was
on Candid Camera. Even when the photographer closed in, he stood
as static as the *Mannequin Pis*. Perhaps he'd done it so often it had
made him blind.

By this time, the camera was so close it was practically bouncing
off his naked thigh, till in a jerky pull-shot the man pretended to
realise it was there. Since the film had now abandoned any semblance
of reality, he took over the camera while the two women sported.
Then an unseen hand commandeered the camera to let all three stag-
ger through an ungainly triple-decker. Who was holding the camera
now? Must have been the park keeper.

Ticky left the video show feeling sorely dissatisfied. He'd got a
bigger thrill from *Pocahuntas*. He wandered off to eat a cheese roll in
a pub, then went to kick pigeons in Soho Square. After a while, he
strolled down to the Piccadilly Arcade, glanced furtively at a couple

190

of rent boys, and stood on his own to play the Tic Tac machine. Standing in the darkness looking out at the sun reminded him of the time he had first seen Cy there, blond and innocent.

He trudged along Coventry Street into Leicester Square.

The trouble with hanging around town was that he couldn't hear a radio to check the news. He bought a Standard, found nothing in it apart from election guff, but was not reassured: this edition was printed two or three hours ago. The pub had had a TV but it had been on too softly, and as far as Ticky could tell hadn't covered the story. Would there be a story at all? Maybe the couple had their own little secret and had kept their noses clean. Ticky wouldn't go to the police voluntarily about *anything*. He looked in the paper for the football results but Charlton hadn't played.

He was avoiding Mr Gottfleisch. How could he explain? Blowing a job was one thing, but to let Cy kill the guy! Perhaps it was unavoidable. Once the guy caught them trashing his things they'd had to stop him, because if he'd called the cops it would have been the end of everything. What was it Cy said about you take one step and you can't go back?

Cy should not have pulled the knife – but equally, the guy should not have picked a fight. What was he thinking of? He was just as responsible for what happened as they were. Afterwards, once the prat was dead, the rest was just a matter of tidying up. It would have cleaned up nice and sweet if it hadn't been for that prying couple. What were they doing in the woods at night? Ticky could guess. After all, he had just seen a video about courting couples out on their own. Bet your life those two were courting, because they sure as hell weren't married. Not to each other. Would a married couple leave a warm front room to go for a roll in the chilly woods? Perhaps they would in Utrecht.

Not that marriage was a state of which Ticky had experience. He didn't know how a couple on an evening stroll might feel if they came across an impromptu burial. Though that couple had certainly been persistent.

God knows.

Since they probably weren't married and had a secret to hide (why else were they in the wood?) they might not have phoned the law. Why get involved? Cy said he was positive they would not. He said that he and Ticky should go back to the uncovered grave and fill it in. Whatever happened, he said, the cops were not going to come in the next ten minutes, so they had plenty of time either to cover the bits up or to scoop them in the blanket and carry them away. But Ticky couldn't face it. His nerve had gone. He had blathered on

191

about road blocks and though Cy had laughed, Ticky had insisted they drove home. Thinking about it now, he wondered if Cy had not been right.

The kid seemed able to see most things straight.

✳

It was not until four o'clock that the boy came out of the restaurant. Ticky suggested a coffee or a Big Mac but Cy had been indoors too long. He said he didn't want to go straight to the squat, because the place depressed him. Ticky asked if anyone had annoyed him. 'You know – that what's his name?'

'Nathan? Oh, I can handle him.'

Ticky led him to the comparative quiet of Saint Anne's church-yard. Outside in the Soho streets the day was closing – street market winding down, first of the office workers going home, tourists fading. In the shrubby square a few winos sat around. They called across for change but without conviction. Mottled pigeons strutted on stone flags.

When Cy flopped onto the empty bench his young body sagged. It had been a hard day. Ticky was aware of his pale face drained of blood, the faint shadows below the eyes: this afternoon Cy looked vulnerable and innocent.

'About that knife then, Cy – you get rid of it?'

'I put it back.'

'In the kitchen?'

'I only borrowed it.'

Ticky chose his words: 'You want to be careful with knives.'

Cy shrugged. 'Tell that to the man we killed.'

'You should keep away from knives, that's all.

Three sides of the churchyard were walled in by buildings. Leaves on the bushes were new-grown but sticky with grime. Several park benches were occupied by people that no one in their right mind would sit next to, yet the yard provided tranquillity among the narrow London streets.

Cy reached into his trouser pocket and brought out something which at first sight looked like a piece of bone. He held it in his lap and glanced around the churchyard.

'Anyway, this is easier to carry around.'

Ticky was puzzled till Cy flicked the catch. In a flash of steel, the lethal blade shot out, making no greater sound than a barber's scissors, just one snip.

Cy used both hands as he carefully closed it. 'It's a six inch blade.'

'Where the hell did you get that?'

Cy flicked it open again, then shut. 'It was you said I ought to have protection.'

He cradled the switchblade in his lap.

Ticky licked his lips before asking, 'Where did you say you got it?'

Cy shrugged. 'Oh, I've had it a while,' was all he would say.

NINETEEN

I haven't told you why Naomi remained in Germany. It wasn't for any political reason, but because of Albrecht. He was a successful and rising doctor – not especially Nordic, but dark, tall and good-looking. Frightfully polite. At the Berghof he taught Naomi to ski properly. He was comfortably off, well-born, discreetly knowledgeable about art – and he was musical. One evening, I remember, he and I sang with Winifred Wagner. (I'm name dropping again!) She came with her four children – Wieland, Wolf, Friedelind and Verena.

How odd the things that one recalls. To me the Wagner grandchildren were more glamorous than their hosts. I don't think they stayed the night, and we sang – Albrecht, the Wagner family and I – at the piano in the living room. What did we sing? Oh, I forget now, but not Richard Wagner. Schubert perhaps, and Richard Strauss. Old folksongs certainly, and German carols. Naomi's Albrecht had such a fine tenor voice. – My God, it returns to me now: his sweet voice through all these years.

No wonder she was crazy for the German doctor.

Reader, she married him. – Summer '39, quietly in Munich. Mother didn't come. But I was there – my last time in Germany till after the war. We had hoped the Führer himself would come, but by then it had become too difficult. He was so busy. I remember thinking a few weeks later that it was as well he stayed away. The wedding caused enough fuss with our friends and family; imagine how much worse it would have been if *he* had come. There might have been photographs in the papers.

Naomi and Albrecht honeymooned in Slovenia – does it still exist? At the time, Slovenia was a popular resort for southern Germans, but Naomi may have been the only Englishwoman there. She wrote to rave about the magical landscape, a forgotten world from picture books, with tiny gabled buildings, narrow streets, lights in the branches of darkling trees, the sound of hooves against cobble

194

stones. She sent a postcard – or was it a photograph? She may have painted while she was there, but nothing survives.

Albrecht, then, was the reason she remained in Germany throughout the war. Why was she condemned – should she have left her husband and denounced him as her enemy? In their first year of marriage?

On the third of September when war was declared, Naomi and Albrecht were in Dusseldorf. For less than a week had there seemed any serious chance of war, though rumours had rumbled about it for years. Now, after months of negotiation, Germany had retaken Danzig. Neither Britain nor France cared about Poland: they wanted to subdue the upstart Germany. Poland was irrelevant, both then and six years later when the war ended and Poland was gifted, lock, stock and barrel to the Soviet Union. We didn't fight for Poland: that war, like all European wars, was about the balance of power.

In Dusseldorf, Naomi was aghast at the news and took to her bed. In Munich, a day's drive away, Unity saw her world collapse. She couldn't believe that common sense would not prevail. On the morning of September third, Unity sat alone and waited for a last-minute compromise. It was a pleasant day. In the Munich parks a breeze ruffled the leaves, but not enough to make them fall. At eleven o'clock that morning – noon there – the ultimatum expired.

It was in one of those green and leafy parks, in the Englischer Garten near the river Isar, that Unity took her last stroll on Bavarian soil. At a little distance stood two German policemen, instructed to keep an eye on her because *Die Unity* was a valued friend of the Führer. In that sweet and open park, Unity opened her handbag and produced a little pistol. Before they could stop her she had shot herself in the head.

They rushed across to her, lifted her from the grass – blood running from her head – and carried her to a clinic. They believed she was dead. But in fact, although the bullet had lodged in her brain it did not kill Unity immediately. She lay in the clinic for several weeks. The war gathered pace, yet every week the clinic received anxious telephone calls from Adolf Hitler. Late in October Unity returned to consciousness. Within days he was at her side. But she was gravely ill.

Naturally she received every attention. She was obviously frail and Hitler was desperately concerned. He arranged for Janos to contact her parents in England and he provided my sister with a car to make it easier for her to visit Unity. In December Hitler asked Unity to consider seriously what she wanted to do: she was welcome to stay in Germany but if, given her condition, she preferred to rejoin her family, that also could be arranged. Unity chose England.

We had now been ten weeks at war. For another two weeks Unity stayed to recuperate in the German clinic, until Hitler arranged a special ambulance train to carry her across the border into neutral Switzerland. She went with her own doctor and nurse, and of course with dear Janos. They arrived in Switzerland on Christmas Eve.

Janos stayed in Berne until her parents arrived, and was waiting at the station to take them to the hospital. They found her extraordinarily frail and in permanent pain. Her skin had yellowed, she had lost a lot of weight, and by then she had developed a hard-eyed, absent look. After three more days she was removed to an ambulance carriage on another train and sent home with her family via France. Janos waved goodbye to them from the platform and they never saw each other again.

✳

Naomi did not return to Dusseldorf. The war was intensifying and Albrecht phoned to tell her he had been posted to a hospital in Hamburg. She went there.

They were strange exciting days in Germany in the early months of war, with spectacular victories – Poland buckled inside ten days, France collapsed in six short weeks. Norway, relying on help promised from Britain, was overrun – the British forces having arrived too late. Britain herself was hastily assembling her own defences while Germany, ever victorious, went on to conquer northern Europe. Yet at the same time, German civilians felt they were in a phoney war. It was still possible to travel by train. Naomi could write to us via Switzerland – she even phoned me once by some circuitous route from Hamburg to the Surrey countryside. Such things were difficult but could be done – though soon, of course, it was to become very different. For Naomi, Britain was a lost, unreachable island off the coast of Europe. Her loyalties were split as painfully as Unity's had been, but Naomi had a husband and hence a home in Germany. She loved both countries but Albrecht was there. Albrecht could not have left even had he wanted to, so she stayed with him. In 1942 she produced a baby son.

✳

'Got him!'

The constable flashed a triumphant smile. He was waving a sheet of paper like a toy flag. 'Body in the woods, sir. Got a name. One Angus Fyffe, thirty-seven years old.'

Kerrigan nodded and sipped his milky coffee. 'Someone come forward?'

'No.' The constable paused. 'Got him by his fingerprints.'

'Never! The boy's got form?'

'Nothing recent.'

'Spit it out, man.'

'Six years back we had him for possession. On two counts.'

'Intent to supply?'

The constable shook his head. 'Probation and a fine.'

'Nothing much, then.'

'Enough to put him on computer.'

'So he's a druggie. Well, well. Any needle scars?'

The constable laughed. 'He was nothing but scars, wasn't he, sir? He was joints of meat.'

'Ah, yes.'

'Except his head, of course. I reckon they took that home and boiled it down to make a broth.'

'They?'

'Well.' The constable shrugged. 'I don't mean our pair of love-birds, sir. But according to their story they saw more than one, you know, running away.'

'They saw fucking dwarfs, man! Those lovebirds must have been sampling our man's drugs!'

'The dwarfs were kids, sir.'

Kerrigan sniffed his coffee, hesitated, then decided against drinking any more. Sensible decision. 'Kids!' He poured the dregs into the waste basket. 'Chopping up bodies? Burying them in the wood? No.' He crushed the cup.

'Kids nowadays, sir – you know how they are.'

'This body – what was its name?'

'Angus Fyffe. Single, thirty-seven. Well, he was single *then*, sir. When we last nicked him he was thirty-one.'

'Six years ago.'

'In London. That's his last known address.'

Kerrigan snorted. 'It still could be. No drug addict would live round here.'

'Don't count on it. Though we don't know he was an addict.'

'Probably a dealer.'

'One offence, sir.'

'But on two counts. He's thirty-seven. He was thirty then. What does that tell you?'

'Lifetime of use?'

'Exactly. So he's a dealer, isn't he? Don't give me any bollocks about 'recreational use'. Not when he's thirty-seven.'

'You either grow out of it or become a part of it.'

'He hadn't grown out of it when he was thirty. So what've we

197

got? A London drug dealer, chopped into bits and buried in the forest.'

'Except his head, which is conveniently mislaid.'

'Well, even if we had it, it wouldn't have told us anything. Ha, ha. – You're allowed to laugh, you know: it wouldn't have *told* us anything! They should've chopped his fingers off as well.'

'Nearly did, sir. One hand went missing with the head.'

'The head and hand.'

'Sounds like a pub.'

*

After the war, in the late 1940s, I lived like a nun – or like a leper perhaps, isolated from the world that lay about me. My sister's death was not lamented. In the cold and dreary post-war years she was dismissed by most people as a traitor. I shared her shame. At first, after the funeral, I locked myself away – not a complete recluse, but a very private person.

A few months later I left Britain and went abroad. One says that easily today, but in 1947 I had to claw my way through a morass of obstructive bureaucracy. I crossed the Channel on a boat that was so ancient and uncomfortable I wondered why it had not been sacrificed in the war. I took a succession of trains. In Switzerland, so sane, so civilised, but so expensive, I found Naomi's flat and cleared her things. Because of the awful currency regulations I had arrived there virtually penniless, without enough money for a decent meal. On my first day I had to trudge around to sell her furniture. I bundled her clothes and gave them away. Sell or starve.

Were you expecting me to tell you that I found a hoard of Naomi's paintings? Only a few. I crated them up with other personal mementoes and had them shipped slowly home. Several of her local views – melancholy water-colours, tastefully done – I sold to a gallery in Lucerne and I used that money to finance my own slow journey back through ravaged Europe. I would have lingered longer on the journey but the wreckage and poverty was too unutterably sad. In northern Italy the mountain villages seemed as hard and cheerless as the surrounding stone. French farms were desolate and overgrown. I did spend two days in Germany but was chased away by the appalling damage, hollow-eyed people and the pallor of defeat.

I returned to England penniless again, even more introverted and alone. There seemed no country where I belonged. But in this cold island, emptied of family and friends, I did at least have money and a house – not a home, you notice, just a shabby and draughty house. My new-found money had descended to me reluctantly. Father left it all to Mother, who spent freely before bequeathing what was left to my big sister. Only Naomi's tragic death brought anything to me. The legacy had dwindled by then, but was enough.

It was accessible, though, only in Britain. If I went abroad I would be subject to the same absurd currency restrictions as any other would-be travellers. I had to stay at home.

✳

One cold Autumn morning I went to see Unity. By now she had been a permanent invalid for years and on the morning I saw her she was wrapped in blankets in a wheelchair, placed outside on what should have been a sunny terrace. Her eyes were dark and her cheeks drawn in. Her hair looked terrible.

Though we talked for a while it was the kind of forced conversation one might have had with an aged relative in a nursing home. Unity found it hard to concentrate. Occasionally she winced with pain, but whether that pain was physical or mental I cannot say. She spoke slowly, inconsistently, and seemed confused about who I was or why I was there.

After an hour I fled to the station for an earlier train. I never saw her again. A few months later that sad girl died.

✳

I sold the family house and bought this one, worked on the neglected garden and became middle-aged. In the next few empty years I occasionally went to London, made desultory attempts to contact old friends, and at the Colony Room I met Murdo.

In 1953, I remember, I invited him to watch the Coronation on my television. In those days few of us had the box, but I liked it: I lived alone and it broke the boredom. Perhaps that was the first time Murdo visited my house – it doesn't matter now. You will probably guess that I have always been a royalist and somehow, justifiably I think, I saw Elizabeth's coronation as heralding a new and forward-looking era. Two years earlier I had visited the Festival of Britain, but to me a bleakly transformed site beside the Thames only emphasised Britain's meanness and lack of vision. I thought that perhaps a new queen and Elizabethan age might finally blow away the dust of war and encourage the nation forward. Murdo and I became very drunk.

By the middle Fifties I had shed my agoraphobic tendencies, had settled in to this house, and had become accustomed to the sedate life of the village. Hardly anyone knew me and I made no particular attempts to know them. I began to travel more freely. I bought another car.

Politics no longer interested me. The horrors of war had been put aside. Old friends from the wild and wonderful Thirties were replaced with acquaintances who, if less exciting, were less demanding. Everything at that time *was* unexciting. Britain was not the country I had been brought up in – though it did seem to be gaining a brisk modernity which I found not unattractive. Time enough had passed, I thought, for me to return to Germany.

✻

Here indeed was a different country, with vigour and drive, a sparkle in the air. I was delighted to find landmarks that I recognised, even if they had been reassembled from rubble after the war. It was a delight also to hear the language again – like hearing a favourite old record I had not heard for years. Yet among these comforting reminders I was also aware of Germany renewed. Gone were the uniforms, slogans and propaganda posters. Gone was the destitution caused by war. Instead, after a single decade, I found an easygoing affluence. Compared to Britain the shops were better stocked, people better dressed. You may protest that Germans always have been harder working, but in the 1950s they seemed to work with greater cheerfulness than before the war. Everyone seemed smart, clean and proud of their blossoming country. I visited Hamburg and found, in impressive contrast to grubby London, that the wartime wounds had almost disappeared. Though Hamburg had been bombed more comprehensively than any British city, its centre was already rebuilt, its port and docks were thriving, the city shone with glass.

Not only had Hamburg been flattened in the blitz, but it had lost its main source of income. Before the war vast quantities of goods flowed daily down the Elbe into Hamburg's docks for onward despatch across the Baltic, but now that East Germany was behind the iron curtain, the trade was lost. Where a British city would have thrown up its hands in self-pity and succumbed, Hamburg reset its sights and established itself as the main northern gateway in and out of West Germany.

One or two of my English friends, when I told them I was going there, had sneered and warned me 'not to talk about the war', yet in Germany I found that hardly anyone seemed to remember it. They were not interested; their eyes were on the future. The nightmare of the past had faded in the healing sunlight. Death and agony had been sluiced with the Elbe mud down to the sea. Where in London I saw bomb sites, rubble, and grey people trudging through their lives, here in Hamburg I saw only energy and reconstruction. Shopping in the *Platze* was more exhilarating than in Bond Street. Department stores made ours look like shabby warehouses.

Because these northern towns had cheered me I caught a train (spotless naturally) down south to Munich to seek out old friends from before the war. Many, including the famous ones, were dead but some of my friends were not only alive but back at their old pre-war addresses. It was a curious testament to the German love of stability that even where large areas of an old city had been destroyed and rebuilt (as certainly was the case in Munich) the streets were restored and numbered just as they had been before. Families 'returned' into completely new versions of their earlier addresses. Several years after their homes had been destroyed, women would emerge from new front doors of recreated houses and greet the same neighbours they had known before.

It was at his old address that I met Werner Warsonke.

Curious, isn't it, when you meet a lover from earlier years? No *frisson*, no spark, no reawakening of desire. You ask yourself: did I once sleep with this man and feel him moving warm inside me? Nevertheless, you can return to a shadow of that old familiarity: no passion but the same old ease. You have become as *dis*passionate as you once were at three in the morning, all passion spent, the night before you stretching long. With languid curiosity you note the new lines in his face, the new sheen to his skin, his thinner hair. Any tension you may have felt before this meeting – that knot of dread and timidity – has gone. You feel comfortable.

'Come in. This is wonderful You look just the same.'

'No, I've changed, I know.'

'Just a little, perhaps.'

Werner seemed shorter, a bright little man, about forty years old. His apartment, like so many German flats, was surprisingly spacious. It was on two floors.

'This is Ingrid, my wife.'

The dark-haired neat woman eyed me more intently than Werner had, but she smiled pleasantly as she held out her hand. 'I have made English tea for you.'

The flat was decorated along clean spartan lines. Cakes were arranged on a low table. I saw a child's photo, though the boy himself was nowhere to be seen.

Werner asked, 'You are on holiday?'

'Revisiting.'

'Do you often come here to Germany?'

'This is my first time since the war. Almost the first.'

Werner nodded. 'Our own holidays are spent here in Germany.'

'Perhaps in two years time,' said Ingrid, 'we will visit Italy.'

Her voice softened when she spoke, as if she had longed to go

201

abroad for several years. Foreign travel was a luxury at that time, though to go from Germany to Italy would require only a car. At that time few people had motor cars.

'Will you take your tea with lemon or with milk?'

As she poured into beautiful pre-war porcelain cups Werner and I exchanged a reminiscent smile. He was like an old schoolfriend.

'You will have some cake, please?'

I took a piece, barely glancing at it, but as soon as I bit into the sweet almond pastry I gasped, instantly transported to the fine *Konditoren* of the Thirties.

'*Linzertorte*,' I breathed. 'I haven't tasted this since…'

My eyes dampened as the memories flooded back. They both smiled at me.

'Yes,' Werner said. 'It has been too long.'

He looked away. I took a second bite of the cake, and shuddered. At that moment, had we been alone, I would have gone to bed with him.

Ingrid said, 'Life is good now. You know, Werner is an electronics engineer? In fact, he runs the factory.'

'Do you own it?' I asked, my mouth tasting of almonds.

Werner smiled. 'I am only the manager. I am a better engineer than manager.'

They seemed proud of his status – as manager of a factory that made radios. Here was the man I had made love to in Hitler's Berghof, yet he was content now in a factory!

'I have a present for you,' he announced when I left.

He gave me a small radio, a product of their factory, their latest line. At the time the gift did not seem significant: I could see that it was a small intricately made radio in a transparent perspex case. It was battery powered and had, for the Fifties, delicately lightweight earphones.

'Like a crystal set,' I said.

Werner smiled. 'It is a transistor radio.'

It was tiny, the size of two cigarette cartons, and until I was back in England I did not realise how unusual it was. In Britain neither I nor the general public had heard of transistors, though presumably our electronics companies had. I can remember no transistorised products in the shops. I must have been one of the few people in England to own such an innovative item – developed and made in defeated Germany.

I liked that radio, but the fact that one had to listen to it through earphones meant that on my return I put it away in a drawer. Only now, looking back, do I see that even in the mid-Fifties Germany was overtaking us on the racing track to recovery. We were unaware of it at the time. We were unaware a decade later, cock-a-hoop as ringleaders of the swinging Sixties. We would have shrugged: we didn't care. Until that time the ordinary Englishman dismissed Germany as the defeated enemy from the war, as a convenient and faintly ridiculous villain. Perhaps in the laid-back, aimless Seventies we may have begun to realise that mighty Germany was leaving us behind. We would have resented them, as we often had before. Germany continued to stride ahead while we grumbled and went on strike.

For me, that transistor radio was one of the telling moments of the Fifties. And in the Sixties I remember another similarly pivotal moment, this time on television – no, not the death of JFK, not the landing on the moon – but another of those quietly undramatic moments that sneaks up and glides past as it drops a time-bomb at your door.

This was a moment for me alone. I was watching TV before going to bed – alone, I'm afraid: in the swinging Sixties I normally slept alone. (God, if I had realised what lay ahead of me: thirty years of sleeping alone.) There was an arts programme at the time called Late Night Line-up. The twin presenters, Tony Bilbow and Joan Bakewell, were wonderfully companionable members of Sixties intelligentsia (if a trifle left-wing for me) and they had sufficient relaxed grace for one to welcome their TV images into one's home. They were discussing fashion in art (as one did endlessly in the Sixties) contrasting the drippy but enduring Bloomsbury set to their unfashionable contemporaries such as Unit One (abstract and unapproachable), and Bilbow was contrasting pacifist war poets such as Roy Fuller with the politically unacceptable Ezra Pound, and Walton and Britten against Arthur Bliss, when suddenly, among shots of Thirties paintings, appeared one of Naomi's: a dark interior of the Osteria Bavaria, in which sharply delineated diners sat at separate tables. That painting, I heard with surprise, had recently fetched a high price at auction – not an astonishingly large sum (indeed, low by today's standards) but high for a painter with no reputation. But from what Bilbow was saying on the programme, Naomi did have a reputation – in what he described as a minor but specialist genre.

I watched in astonishment, since as far as I knew, Naomi had never before been credited with a reputation – certainly not as an artist to be mentioned on television – and the rather different reputation she had once had was surely forgotten. She had, after all, been dead at least fifteen years. They mentioned her name casually, tossing it lightly in the air as a name the cognoscenti would recognise, and Joan commented that the price was an indication of the fact that

Naomi Keene had become collectable.

'Within her genre,' Bilbow purred.

'Hardly a genre,' Bakewell laughed. 'She was practically unique. Very few of her paintings still exist.'

'Though there may be a few undiscovered ones.'

'To add to the excitement! Of course, what makes this particular one desirable is that one of the diners is Albert Speer.'

'Yes, she did the Hitler portrait—'

'But these intimate, informal studies are more desirable.'

'Certainly more fashionable. But would *you* buy one, Joan?'

Bakewell laughed. 'They're excellently done, but I wouldn't want to put a Nazi on my wall, whether he was at work or play.'

'But that's precisely what we find fascinating about Keene's work – the personal glimpses behind the scenes – the unpublic image.'

'I'd rather have one of her landscapes.'

'They're not fashionable.'

'At least I might be able to afford one. But you're right, Tony: Miss Keene is collected mainly for these revealing portraits, as an artist inside Hitler's cabal.'

'Accomplished.'

'A competent colourist.'

They made no digs at her 'fascist leanings', nor did they resurrect old reports about her tragic death. I was grateful for their tact and was pleased – not to say astonished – that after so long, Naomi's paintings had become appreciated as works of art. At the time I didn't see the consequences. Significant moments, as I have said, happen unexpectedly, and often their true significance does not reveal itself immediately. I heard the compliments – indeed, I basked in them – but I skipped past the fact that Naomi had become collectable. People were buying Naomi's work.

TWENTY

Given the circumstances, Ticky thought it better he wore a tie. He had put off the interview for more than a day – having taken that long to drum up courage and get in touch. To appear in person before Gottfleisch and admit the job had gone wrong he would need a tie, he'd have to look smart. He would need all the help he could get.

'You were supposed to deliver a warning, Ticky.'

The little man shrugged helplessly. No point trying to say something smart. He was standing in his boss's sitting room – Ticky rooted to the carpet, Gottfleisch pacing round.

Ticky tried: 'He interrupted me. Started a fight.'

'I told you to make sure he wasn't in.'

Ticky had rehearsed his story and had decided he'd better not mention Cy. He was in deep enough already. 'I thought he was out.'

'You stabbed him?'

Ticky gulped. 'Yeah.' The knot in his tie had begun to tighten.

Gottfleisch came closer. Ticky trembled. 'You stabbed him, Insect – where?' He jabbed Ticky in the chest. 'Here?' He jabbed lower down.

Ticky opened his mouth.

'Or here?'

At the third jab Ticky gasped for breath.

Gottfleisch spun on his heel and strode away, leaving Ticky like a schoolkid with the stomach cramps. He wasn't sure which would incite Gottfleisch more – to show the pain or take it like a man. He didn't want to awaken the big man's appetite.

'Did you leave any fingerprints?'

'No, of course not, sir, I—'

'There's no 'of course' about it, cretin. Did you paint my message on the wall?'

'No, I thought—'

'Good. Did you leave anything behind?'

'No—'

205

'Not even the body?'

'Well.'

Ticky knew that Gottfleisch was staring at him. 'Well... you know—'

'The body?'

'I drove away with it, sir, into the woods.'

'You mindless pathetic numbskull!' Gottfleisch exploded. 'Haven't you heard the News?'

Ticky felt his innards melt. He closed his eyes. 'They've found the body?' he asked hopelessly.

Gottfleisch pronounced each word as precisely as a run of hammer blows: 'Let me get this right. You drove off and buried the body in the woods?'

'I thought—'

'The headline is 'Gruesome Remains Found In Woodlands'. That was Fyffe?'

Ticky nodded.

'The police don't know his name yet – or they're not releasing it. How did they find his body so quickly – didn't you bury him deep enough?'

'Oh, it was about...' Ticky used his hands to indicate a possible depth. He wished he'd managed to hear the bulletin.

'Did anyone see you?'

Ticky didn't know what to say. Had the couple who'd seen him been on the News? Had they reported it or not?

'I don't think so,' he said cagily, his eyes wide.

But Gottfleisch was no longer watching him. He was frowning as he thought. 'How did you get Fyffe to the woods?'

'Well, in the car, sir.'

'In that Fiat of yours – isn't it too small?'

Ticky dared not mention the larger car Cy had stolen. 'No, sir.'

'They said that the body had been chopped up. Is that true?'

Ticky whispered, 'Yes.'

'Did you cut it up to fit in the car?'

'No.' Ticky's voice had almost disappeared. He wished *he* could. 'I took a chopper along to the woods with me.'

Gottfleisch shook his head. 'What were you thinking of?'

'I wanted to hide the body.'

Gottfleisch gave an incredulous stare. 'You remember why I sent you and what I said?'

'Yes, sir.'

'Yes, sir. But you didn't check he wasn't in. You wandered in, banged around, and let him catch you. Then you killed him.' The big

206

man's voice began to rise. 'Then you crammed his body in your stupid car – his body dripping with tell-tale blood—'

'Oh, no, sir—'

'No *what*, sir – no, the body wasn't bleeding?'

'No.' Ticky licked his lips. 'I mean, it wasn't my car, sir. I forgot. I stole one—'

'You're lying!'

Gottfleisch grabbed a handful of Ticky's shirt. 'Don't lie to me!' He shook him angrily, then pushed him away across the room. 'You used your own car to transport the body—'

'No, I stole it—'

'For God's sake! Why do you lie to me?'

Ticky tried to loosen his tie. 'I don't know. I mean—'

'Have you ever lied to me before?'

'No, sir!'

'How do I know?'

The big man's voice dropped several semi-tones. He sounded like a judge. 'When someone works for me our relationship must be based on trust. If you break that trust you break our relationship.'

'Oh no, sir—'

'I cannot rely on you.'

'You can. You can, sir.'

'And what makes it worse, Ticky, is that I had given you a second chance.'

'Please sir, this job is all I have.'

'You betrayed me—'

'No sir, not betrayed!'

Gottfleisch gazed at him mournfully and asked, 'How much damage have you done?'

Ticky shook his head.

'What shall I do with you?'

Ticky felt his flesh go cold. 'Sir, please don't…'

Gottfleisch let the pause hang. 'Don't do what?'

'Don't…' Ticky took a breath. 'Don't fire me, sir. I'll do anything to put things right.'

Gottfleisch whispered, 'It's too late.'

✳

'Police have released more details in the case of the headless man in Cudham Wood. He has now been identified as Angus Wilkie Fyffe, a thirty-seven year old man from London. Unconfirmed reports suggest that it may have been a drug-related killing, and although police are unable to comment at this stage, a spokesman has said within the last hour that the viciousness of the killing could have been an attempt to make the corpse unrecognisable. The head is still missing, as is one hand. It is possible that the killer or killers were disturbed before they could sever the other hand. The spokesman went on to say that although the general public does not appear to be in immediate danger, people should remain vigilant. Anyone with evidence, no matter how slight, should contact the police in confidence.'

The newsreader gave out a phone number.

✳

'Want any more?'

Craig turned off the radio. He stood beside Gottfleisch's specially adapted bath where the enormous man, already pink as a half-cooked lobster, lay camouflaged by foam and steam.

'More hot water, my dear boy.'

'Be careful you don't melt.'

'It does wonders for my complexion.'

When Craig reached over to turn on the hot, Gottfleisch bent his knees and created waves. Craig was wearing only tee-shirt and slacks but felt as clammy in the steamy bathroom as in a sauna. He said, 'I wouldn't have thought little Ticky would be up to it.'

'Hidden depths.'

'Say that again. Stabbed the fucker.'

'Language!'

Craig was gasping for air in all that steam. 'How'd he drag him out to the car? He's such a runt.'

'Mhm.' Gottfleisch closed his eyes and sank slightly.

'Shall I turn the water off?'

'Another moment. Quite delicious.'

'It'll go over the rim.'

Gottfleisch was sinking lower in the hot water.

Craig said, 'I'm turning it off – you'll flood the bathroom. Will the cops nail him for it?'

'Can't tell.'

Craig turned off the water. 'If they did, would he name you?'

Gottfleisch appeared to be half asleep. 'It might not matter. The old lady knows we leant on Fyffe. She might think we went back and leant too hard.'

'Would *she* talk?'

'I doubt it – she'd become involved. If she asks me, I'll take the police line, that it must be drugs related.'

'Think she'll swallow that?'

Gottfleisch shifted into a sitting position, water slurping wildly against his flesh. 'Time for my back, I think.'

Craig picked up the loofah and sweet smelling soap, saying, 'You'd better talk to her. You can't just wait and see what happens.' He began lathering the soap.

Gottfleisch purred with pleasure before he spoke. 'Yes, I'll speak to her.'

'Soon.'

'Mhm. Use your nails, dear boy – that's right, just there.'

'You could phone her – it'd be quicker.'

'I will, I will. Oh yes, that's nice. Just a little more. Yes, I'd like an excuse to go down again – so I can see her paintings for myself. Sending Ticky was a mistake.'

'He wouldn't know a painting from a photograph.'

'Use the loofah now, dear boy. That's better. Aah. You know, I suspect she still has a little hoard. Every now and then, one of her sister's paintings comes onto the market.'

'She letting them out?'

'Somebody is.'

'Shall I do your chest?'

'I can reach that. How about my legs?'

As Gottfleisch subsided into a prone position, a gallon of water sploshed out of the bath. Craig stepped forward, leant across, lifted a massive leg and rested it on the side.

Gottfleisch said, 'The theory is that her paintings appear rarely because people are ashamed to admit they have one – you know, Hitler, and all that jazz – but I don't subscribe to that.'

'Not when they've gone up in price.'

'Money conquers shame.'

He watched Craig smearing his leg with soap. 'If the old lady has any left I want to find them.'

'Is that likely after all this time?'

'They're an investment. If she cashes one every two or three years, she can live like a queen.'

Craig cocked an eyebrow. 'Queen, eh? Gets her chauffeur to scrub her in the bath?'

But he wasn't quick enough: Gottfleisch grabbed his arm. 'Want to join me?'

Craig laughed. 'No, don't, I'm fully dressed.'

'*Half* dressed.' Gottfleisch moved his other hand across. 'You're not even wearing underclothes.'

Craig gave a little gasp. 'Hey, gently now.'

'I think we'll take these off.'

Gottfleisch released a button, unzipped the fly. 'The old lady is very old. She won't last much longer.'

Craig was exposed now, rude and strong. Gottfleisch pulled at the slacks to let them fall.

'I'm not coming in there,' Craig said. 'It's too full – and hot.'

But Gottfleisch stroked him. 'Where's your sense of adventure, you lovely boy?'

TWENTY-ONE

In the year of Jubilee, 1977, came the day Murdo arrived at my house with one of Naomi's paintings. He had been asked to vet it and to act as agent for its sale. By then her work was better known – but only among a small, if wealthy, set of collectors particularly interested in this byway of Nazi art. The problem Murdo had was to secure a satisfactory price. This, he pointed out, is an everyday problem for dealers when an artist commands high prices but has limited appeal. There may be only three or four people world-wide prepared to purchase, yet the vendor has to create the impression there are plenty of rival bidders eager to buy. Neither vendor nor potential purchaser wants the price to fall – the vendor to protect his commission, the collector to protect the market value of what he already owns. Even if no one wants or can afford the latest piece it must not sell below its mark. In cases like these, galleries often settle for a dummy sale, where they and a buyer – sometimes 'Anonymous' – pretend a deal. They announce an apparently satisfactory price, photographs appear of men shaking hands, but the work in question remains unsold. It disappears to languish till an upturn.

Murdo was on twelve and a half per cent. It was odd for me to be sitting in my living room – on a cloudy day, I remember: the summer of '77 cool after the blistering drought of the previous year – while Murdo, squatting on my carpet, opened a large and crumpled carrier bag to reveal a water-colour in a dingy frame. It was the Goering portrait – do you know the one? – a smiling Hermann wearing one of those fantastical fancy dress costumes he affected: a white silk blouse in Renaissance style with bulging sleeves, a pale yellow jerkin, a green cravat, a ruby ring. Naomi had made the painting in 1939. But you'll know the portrait, of course – it's famous now. In real life that costume would have appeared gaudy (I've seen him wear one similar) but in Naomi's portrait the colours are muted and limited to a soft quiet palette. – How different from Imre Goth's, which became harder and more brittle as war approached.

211

'It's unquestionably by Naomi.'

'You're certain, Sidi?'

'I've seen it before. And there's her signature.'

I pointed to the bottom right-hand corner where part of a stylised monogram peeped from beneath the frame. Murdo nodded uncertainly, and said, 'It's half hidden – not quite the same as on the ones you have.'

'I know the painting, Murdo, I saw it done. You must strip off that ghastly Fifties frame – it clips the edges.'

Murdo tilted the painting against the light. 'Yes, a better frame would improve the price. Should it be modern or contemporary?'

'Modern. You're not convinced, are you, about its provenance?'

'Your verdict is what matters.'

'Who's the owner?'

Murdo smiled evasively. 'Apparently he bought it thirty years ago – paid nothing for it, I dare say. This is an exciting piece, you know, Sidi – not catalogued, no one aware of its existence. An unknown Naomi Keene. Goering, for Goodness sake!'

I smiled ruefully as I gazed at it. 'It could so easily have been destroyed. Many were. How d'you like it, Murdo?'

'It's beautifully done.' He grinned mischievously. 'Which will increase the value. She had a lovely line. Economical. But frankly, it's the subject that's important – together with the fact that *she* painted it.'

'In 1939.'

'It's almost unique.'

Murdo bent his head and caught my eye. 'If this fetches the price I'll be asking, all her others will shoot up in value.'

'I have none of Herr Goering.'

'They'll *all* be more desirable. This will set a new standard and drag everything else up with it. Will you mind?'

'Why on earth should I? I'll be delighted to see Naomi's paintings get the respect that they deserve.'

In 1977 that was my attitude. And now, twenty years later, I believe that particular portrait has been sold twice again. Back in '77 when Murdo sold it, the Nazi collectors' market was more discreet, and the painting didn't fetch anything like what it would today – but I don't complain. By agreeing to publicly confirm its provenance I earned two and a half per cent – and since the painting fetched slightly more than Murdo had hoped, it was most welcome.

I bought a case of Trittenheimer.

*

212

Sammy Hahn smiled pleasantly, a businessman's smile. It felt chilly in the country pub and he had left his coat on, the collar warm behind his neck. He placed two pints upon the table as he sat down.

'I hope this is as good as you made out.'

Duncan Devonshire took his pint. 'I think so.'

Sammy raised his glass. 'Cheers.'

'Your very good health.'

Sammy glanced disinterestedly around the empty bar. It was early evening and the amber wall-lights made the room look cold.

Devonshire said, 'The position in a nutshell is that my client gave me an envelope—'

'Client?'

'To be opened only in the eventuality of his death.'

Sammy smiled and reached into his coat pocket. 'Mind if I record this? Quicker than a notebook.' He slid a pocket tape-recorder onto the pub table and turned it on.

'No recording. Definitely not.'

'OK. It's just my old memory fading, you know? But if you don't want it…'

Sammy chuckled disarmingly and slipped the machine back in his pocket.

Devonshire looked at him, cold-eyed. 'Could I see that turned off, please?'

Sammy looked askance and reached into his pocket, surreptitiously flicking off the switch as he produced the recorder for inspection. 'See? It was already off.'

When he returned it to his pocket he turned it on again.

Devonshire said, 'It seems rather dramatic, doesn't it, that kind of letter? People seldom write them, you know. And when they do, it places their solicitor in something of a quandary.' He took a sip of beer, while Sammy watched and smiled encouragingly. 'What should one do with it?' continued Devonshire. 'Though it was addressed to me, it was really an open letter, you might say. By its nature.'

Sammy looked at his watch.

Devonshire said, 'I had to decide what line I should pursue – what my client would have preferred of me.'

He paused again, and Sammy decided to speed the tale along: 'Your client being Angus Fyffe?'

'Uh-huh.'

'Whose letter named a particular person?'

'It did.'

'Who might have killed him?'

'I leave such inferences to you.'

213

Sammy smiled at the careful solicitor. 'Of course. – But why me, Duncan, why not the police?'

'Aren't you interested?'

Sammy leant across to touch his wrist. 'Of course I am. I just wondered why you're doing this.'

'My client would have wanted me to.'

'Mr Fyffe being... the kind of person who was not well-disposed to the police?'

'I did not say that. My client—'

'Angus Fyffe,' said Sammy helpfully.

'Would have wanted his story to be given proper publicity. If I tell the police, it might be hushed up.'

'Now, why would they do that? Are we talking a public figure here?'

'I'm afraid not.'

Sammy's face fell. Devonshire said, 'If the police can't prove a case – and you know how the DPP always want the odds stacked in their favour – if they can't prove a case categorically, the case can just disappear.'

'I see. So what you have is something unprovable – which you want my paper to print? That would be libel, wouldn't it?'

'Not necessarily.' Devonshire reached for his beer but changed his mind. 'Not if you simply print the contents of the letter without comment.'

'No comment – in *my* paper?' Sammy chuckled. 'OK, let's take a look at it.'

'First we should agree the terms.'

Devonshire raised his beer deliberately.

'Oh, you want paying then, Duncan?'

Devonshire gave a dry look across his glass. 'This is a big story. Sell a lot of copies.'

'And I thought you were just doing the best thing for your client.' Sammy shook his head. 'Anyway, the election's already added fifteen percent to the circulation. This is a very small story. Won't add much more.'

'Nonsense.'

'And my paper never buys sight unseen.'

'Doesn't it? Well, thanks for the drink then, Sammy.'

Sammy's voice stayed level and calm. 'Don't gulp your beer – you'll get the burps. What you've given me so far is not exactly a prize-winner, Duncan. What have you got? A doubtful letter from a local drug dealer who got the chop.' Sammy grinned. 'Literally.'

'An innocent man has been murdered – a man who stumbled on an amazing secret.'

214

Sammy waited, hoping to draw him out, but when it became clear that Devonshire would not move beyond that teaser, he carried on: 'And the secret is in the letter?'

Devonshire nodded.

'Is that a yes?'

Devonshire's brow flickered, as if for a moment he had remembered Sammy's tape recorder – which he had seen turned off. He said, 'The letter gives explicit details.'

Sammy nodded. 'Which suggests your client was trying a little blackmail which didn't come off?'

'He doesn't say that.'

'Well, he wouldn't, would he? So, we have a secret – a *government* secret?'

'No.'

'Major public figure?'

'No – though it is a public name.'

'But no election link?' Sammy gave a droll look. 'Well, is it a name my readers might recognise?'

'Some of your readers.'

'A minor public figure.' Sammy shrugged.

'She's not minor in her field.'

'Oh, there's a woman in it? Sex, drugs and murder, eh? A love letter from beyond the grave.'

'Not a love letter.'

'Though you could say Angus lost his head for her! A possible headline. Well, we could be interested, Duncan – but you'll have to tell me a bit more.'

∗

Ticky slouched along Rupert Street munching a hamburger he couldn't taste. Though it was a summer evening he still felt cold. The Big Mac was tepid, and to Ticky the white pappy bread was indistinguishable from the paper napkin it was wrapped in. He was chewing paper with the bread but was unaware of it. Everything tasted of tomato sauce.

As he cut through the alley by the Revuebar he didn't even glance at the pictures on the wall. If his hamburger had been wrapped in a sequinned g-string he wouldn't have been aroused. He had lost his job.

Somewhere among the debris of the vanished street market Ticky dropped the remains of his Big Mac meal. He stared at the pavement five yards ahead, breathed through his mouth, and every few paces he shook his head as if trying to solve a problem in differential calculus.

215

He arrived at the squat and knocked at the door.

Nothing happened.

Ticky took off his shoe and began beating insistently at the door, one beat per second. The dull mechanical rhythm told those inside he wouldn't go away. A window opened three floors above.

'If you don't stop that fucking noise I'll drop a bucket of piss on you.'

Ticky didn't have to look up. He knew who it would be.

'I thought we told you to stay away.'

Ticky glanced up at the shaven head. 'I want Cy.'

'He's out.'

'I want to see him.'

'Listen, runt.' Nathan leant a little further out the window. 'I know what you want him for, and so does he. You haven't a hope, so just piss off.'

'Tell him I'm here.'

Nathan spat a thick gob which landed splat on the concrete.

Ticky said, 'Come down here and try that.' His maimed face was blotchy with rage.

Nathan sneered, but the little tyke looked so determined that Nathan stayed upstairs. When he withdrew his head, Ticky shouted, 'Cy!'

'I told you he's out,' came Nathan's voice.

'Cy!' called Ticky again, but nothing happened.

'Cy!

Ticky banged at the door.

'Cy!'

✳

But the boy *was* out, a few hundred yards away. He had decided to quit the restaurant job. Now he had found his feet he reckoned there were easier ways to earn a living.

He walked into the Piccadilly Arcade and wandered casually between the video games and slot machines. He had a little money, but would have to be careful if it were to last longer than a pound spent on the Lottery. To while away some time Cy leant against a Storm Force Paratroop machine and began to file his nails. He was dressed in tight faded jeans, cream tee-shirt and mock leather jerkin. Although the tee-shirt appeared clean it had a one-inch hole off-centre against his chest. Through the hole you could see his pale skin.

The boy who approached was about two years older and a little heavier. 'What you doin' here?'

'Waiting.'

'For what?'

'For you to go away.'

The boy looked at Cy – slender, clean and innocent – and prodded him in the chest.

'Don't fuck with me, boy.'

Cy glanced beyond him to the taller dark-haired youth watching them. 'I suppose he's with you?'

'Yeah.'

Cy gave the ghost of a smile. 'Two's company, three's a crowd?'

'That's right.'

'One of you'll have to go, then.'

The boy prodded him again. 'Clever bastard, eh?'

'If you touch me again,' Cy said reasonably, 'I'll snap your finger off.'

The boy snorted. 'You need a lesson,' he said.

Cy indicated to his left. 'You're ignoring a customer.'

Several machines away stood a portly man in a jacket which was too young for him. As the boy briefly eyed him up, his dark-haired companion wandered across to the man and asked coyly, 'Excuse me, sir, you wouldn't happen to have a pound coin?'

'I might.'

'I'd be awfully grateful.'

As the man slipped his hand into his pocket he was looking past the dark-haired boy toward Cy and the heavier lad at the Storm Force Paratroop machine. He shouldered gently past the dark-haired boy and asked, 'Having an argument?'

Heavy Boy moistened his lip. 'Lover's tiff.'

'I see.' The man hesitated. 'Are you two an item, or do you come separately?'

'Oo!' The boy hooted. 'Who's the cheeky one? – I might be interested, but *he's* not for sale.'

'That's a shame.' The man turned to Cy and smiled encouragingly. 'Won't you change your mind?'

∗

Out in the bustling street the light was fading. The dirty pink of evening was shoved aside by electric glare: shop windows, theatres, neon advertising.

The man said, 'We could catch a cab to my place.'

'Sounds dodgy,' muttered Cy. 'I don't know you, do I?'

'I'm perfectly trustworthy. Honestly. What's your name?'

'David,' Cy replied.

'Oh, hi, David. I suppose you'd better call me Jonathan.'

Though the man smiled at him, he was also watching up and down the street. He was thirty-eight, while the boy was—

'How old are you, David?'

'Twelve.'

The man gasped.

'No, fourteen. Or twelve. I don't know – which would you like?'

The man smiled nervously. As far as he could tell, no one was watching them. 'Let's get a cab.'

'I'm a bit frightened, to tell the truth. I mean, I'm only twelve, aren't I?'

'You needn't be frightened.'

'I know a place nearby where I'd feel safer.'

The man's eyes narrowed suspiciously. 'What kind of place?'

✳

He gave Cy a coin to go in first, then after half a minute he followed. Cy was waiting by the cubicles. The man knew that from time to time the police clamped down on the notorious Gents in Piccadilly Underground. Some years back the authorities had cleaned the tiles and installed a coin-operated turnstile, but these measures were no antidote to vice. Smackheads still thought it a cheap haven to jack up, and a number of homosexuals hung around because they liked the tang of the place. The Piccadilly toilets had always appealed to closet queens.

Cy slipped inside the end cubicle and held the door open so that Jonathan, or whatever his real name was, could follow him in. In the narrow space they faced each other, and after a moment's hesitation Jonathan clasped his David to his breast. He nuzzled the boy's lovely blond hair, tried to work down to his lips, but found the boy was bending his face away.

'How's this?' Cy asked.

He placed his hand on the inside of the man's thigh. Jonathan sighed. Cy was stroking, teasingly, just below his genitals. The man took Cy's face in his hands and tried to lift it, just as Cy's soft fingers moved higher, cupped him, and gently squeezed, pulsing slowly like a heartbeat.

Jonathan moaned.

Cy unzipped his fly.

When Cy had unfastened Jonathan's belt and slid his trousers down to his knees the boy began to disentangle him from his underpants. By now Jonathan was so racked with pleasure that he had to support himself with one hand flat against the partition screen. His other hand stroked Cy's blond hair.

218

Cy had freed him now.

The man felt the cool air waft across his testicles, felt Cy take hold of it, felt something cold lie against his skin.

Cy whispered, 'Make a sound and I'll cut it off.'

He leant back so the man could see the viciously sharp knife, then waited for him to shudder and jerk away. Instantly, Cy twitched the point of the knife and made a tiny cut.

The man's hands flew down.

'No,' Cy snapped. The knife twitched again. 'Don't make a move.'

The man shivered as if he had just reached climax. He looked at his hands poised beside Cy's head, thought about it, then raised his hands chest high.

'Where's your money?' Cy asked quietly.

'What?'

'Where's your wallet?'

'Oh, Christ.'

'Don't stand there feeling sorry for yourself. Which pocket is it in?'

'Oh, shit.'

Cy kept the point of the knife pressed between the man's scrotum and his rapidly shrinking penis while feeling with his other hand in the crumpled trousers. He pulled out the wallet and slipped it in his jacket.

'Hands up,' he said.

'What?'

'Put your fucking hands up higher.'

'But—'

'Up!'

The man raised his hands and Cy stood to face him. The knife was stabbing painfully in Jonathan's groin, making the tears come smarting to his eyes. Cy rifled though his jacket pockets. Jonathan didn't care now. To hell with the money. Just get that knife away from his cock.

Cy pressed against him and the knife moved again, widening the cut. The man whimpered. Cy tugged at his wristwatch.

Suddenly Cy ducked again to the floor. Each time he moved, the knife stabbed painfully. The boy – what was he doing? – was pulling off his shoes. He was rolling Jonathan's trousers all the way down. He was—

'No! Please don't take my trousers. Please—'

'Whisper! Keep your voice down.'

'Don't take them, David, please don't. How will I get home?'

'This is to keep you here – that's the point.'

'I'll stay. I promise. Just leave my trousers, please.'

Cy had removed them now. He stood facing him, that knife jabbing his tender groin.

'Which d'you want – your trousers or your wallet?'

'My trousers.'

'Times like this, you find out what's important to you – isn't that right?'

When Cy smiled at him, Jonathan almost smiled back. If it hadn't been for the pain he might have done – at the indignity, the absurdity, the exquisite shame.

Cy left him.

Jonathan stood in the lavatory cubicle, the open door flapping in the air. He had his trousers bundled in his arms and an ache between his legs. He pulled the door shut.

No point chasing the boy. By the time he'd put his trousers on, the boy would have disappeared. He couldn't accuse a – what did he say? – a twelve year old of robbing him. He would have to explain how it came about.

At least he was still intact. Even if he didn't have his tube fare home.

TWENTY-TWO

Naomi was hardly an overnight success. For a decade and a half after her death she seemed totally forgotten, both as a person and as an artist – difficult as that may be to believe nowadays. In the Sixties her name reappeared and one or two of her paintings exchanged hands for modest sums. In the Seventies prices improved – but sales remained occasional. It wasn't till the Eighties that her prices peaked. High prices were, of course, symptomatic of that decade. People paid absurd prices for *anything* – tangles of rusty iron were presented as modern sculpture and they sold for hundreds of thousands of pounds. Share prices boomed. One-room flats in London's dockland fetched £300,000. Mediocre wine at auction went for thousands of pounds a case. Champagne so precious that no one dared drink it was traded like gold. It was an insane, South Sea Bubble decade. Vast quantities of newly printed bank notes fluttered like confetti to celebrate the marriage of City brokers to the lower middle class. Inflation soared. People rushed to invest in commodities – among which art, antiques and collectibles became products, vendible merchandise, convertible stock. As the tide raced, Naomi's paintings rode like surfriders on its crest. – No, I exaggerate: she did not sparkle, fashion's star, but was swept along in the current. Indeed, the general populace never sung her fame – she was desirable to the connoisseur. At any one time, even at her peak, I don't believe the market for Naomi's work ever exceeded a few dozen patrons, each of whom, in their determination to acquire one of her rare and controversial paintings, would battle for the prize, outbidding each other at auctions – carefully managed, had they but known it – driving up the value of both the piece on sale and her other paintings sold previously.

For these fanatical collectors Naomi was almost uniquely attractive: genuinely talented (no one disputes that), decoratively contentious – and dead. Relatively few of her works ever surfaced, but because they had been dispersed by war there was always the possibility that another would turn up. Occasional discoveries *were*

221

made, and they added glamour and excitement. She was a collector's dream.

It was a characteristic frenzy of the Eighties, and she was not the only artist affected. One who epitomised that era – do you remember? – was that American who painted replicas of hundred dollar bills; they were not counterfeits, he insisted, but works of art. He would pay with his lithographed banknotes in restaurants and stores, saying they were worth whatever value the receiver cared to place on them – a truth for all art. He turned money into art. Naomi was one of those who, like Jeff Koons and Le Cicciolina – or like Damien Hirst and Claes Oldenburg – turned fame (or infamy) into art. And being dead, she could be libelled, vilified, re-invented. She could be whatever you said she was. Her value was whatever you were prepared to pay.

In the Eighties, as in this present decade, most people had not even been born in the Second World War, and certainly did not feel a part of it. In the orgy of nostalgia which drained the wallets of '80s middle class *arrivistes* the 1930s became another collectable decade. Eighties people with too much money in their purses flocked to antique *markets* (the very thought!) to buy their mother's discarded junk. Wealthier buyers distanced themselves from the scrum and chose property and art. In those heady days one of Naomi's water-colours finally topped £100,000. – Such a sum, for a quiet painting done in a single afternoon fifty years before! Today, in the more sober Nineties her paintings struggle to reach £100,000 – but they do still sell. Previously undiscovered paintings still emerge. And of course, if someone did have a tiny hoard of them, and if that someone were to gradually – very gradually – release them, then I suppose that person could live on the money the paintings fetched – not fabulously, not flamboyantly, but agreeably, as from a long-term investment yielding up its dividend.

But I don't have such a hoard. Believe me.

✳

At the height of the frenzy, in Summer '87, when media mentions of Naomi's paintings concentrated less on their artistic qualities than on the prices realised or the delicious sinfulness of her fascism, I too became their target. There was no reason I should answer for my sister's notoriety. I did not like the attention, I did not want it. So I disappeared.

I went first to Germany, where talk – two years too early – was that the Berlin Wall might finally come down, then on to Switzerland, which had lost its charm. I returned quietly to England

and spent several weeks holidaying in the north, discovering magnificent countryside and quiet haunted towns in which it was surprisingly easy to become anonymous again. Twice I read a story in the arts pages, and once I caught a snippet on TV – laced with ancient family photographs and library shots of Naomi's paintings – in which I was portrayed as a strangely poignant, even Garboesque enigma: it was journalism, of course, pure rubbish. I was the sister, last of the line, the one of whom nothing much was known. Someone had found a photo of me in a wide-brimmed hat, and that much-used shot (you know the one?) became the emblem of my deliberate anonymity.

These occasional stories were sustained less by popular interest in Naomi's life than by astonishment at the prices her pictures fetched. But they were filler stories; they would not last. And in October that year, when twin hurricanes swept the country – the meteorological storm which uprooted woodlands, and more worryingly, the metaphorical storm which ravaged the stock market – money crashed, and the Keene saga stopped. There could have been a story, had anyone reported it, in that the price of Naomi's paintings halved overnight. (Murdo was negotiating a sale at the time. We wept together.) But we were no longer news.

The papers occupied themselves with a wealth of juicier stories: false dawns in the stock market; the Berlin wall; Germany reunified; the collapse of the Evil Empire; Tory schisms over Europe; government scandal, ubiquitous sleaze, the bitter Balkan war. Suddenly Germany found herself undisputed leader of the economic community of Europe. One could not help remembering the Thirties and the clearly stated aims of fascism: for a united and federal Europe in which national governments would willingly be subsumed, in which co-operating countries would allow themselves to be pulled along by the most able – seen then, like now, as Germany. Today that proud country *heads* a federal and united Europe. It sets the rules. If there is an afterlife, and if in it Adolf Hitler maintains any interest in the petty doings of this small world, he must surely smile.

*

They went in at dawn. A large police van, black and angular, blocked the narrow street while a squad of heavies broke in the back. The squatter's amateurism showed. They had barricaded the front of the house effectively, nailing up windows and strengthening the door with bolts and chains, but the back, overlooking a small disused yard, was only lightly protected. The police were streaming up the stairs before the inmates awoke.

223

Most were trapped in the large dormitory on the second floor. Three men – half-awake and half-dressed – tried to fight the police, while others burrowed beneath ragged bedding trying to hide. An advance guard of police stormed through the building, rooting out smaller groups upstairs.

That was when the operation had a glitch. The house was filled with shouts and cries, and the few remaining squatters upstairs were scurrying from room to room looking to escape, when two police-men burst into a washroom to find an ill-clad man crouched on the window sill, half in, half out.

'Don't come any closer,' he yelled in vain.

As they rushed at the man he jumped. There was only one direction he could go, and he took it, three floors straight down. One of the policemen leaned through the window to see the body huddled and still.

He eased his head back through the window and turned to his colleague: 'Don't look good.'

'Think of the paperwork.'

'Right.' The policeman shut the window. 'I wonder which window he fell out of.'

'*Jumped* out of. Jumped's easiest – his own free will.'

'No one saw him.'

'Must have been an accident. Let's go.'

＊

At the station before being booked in, the squatters were searched for drugs – but by then anything incriminating had been dropped or abandoned at the squat. On the floor of the police van lay the contents of a bag of resin and two wraps, split open and trodden into the dirt across the floor. There was also a syringe in a tin. As the squatters tumbled from the van someone kicked the tin beneath the bench, where with luck it might not be found immediately. A little guy called Malcolm had been carrying coke, and he'd sniffed the lot on the short journey. As they stumbled across the yard his eyes popped like a bat released in daylight.

Cy felt apprehensive. He had dropped his knives and roaches at the squat, but he couldn't hide his age. Of all the residents he was the youngest. He could pretend to be fifteen at the most, but he'd still be a minor, whatever he said. While other squatters would be released, he would be handed over to Social Services. They would want a positive identification, and if he refused to help he would be kept inside. The irony was that some of his companions might have appreciated a few days inside, to get a decent sleep. They might even have liked the food.

'What's your name, son?'

He wouldn't say 'David' again, that was for sure – not that Jonathan would have reported him.

'Tom,' he answered irritably. To hell with them. Fascist bastards.

'Tom what?'

'Phelan.'

'Age?'

Fascist scum.

✳

He had to wait for hours until they came, and what made the waiting interminable was that the police decided that because of his youth he could not be kept in the same holding cell as the others – despite having been living with them at the squat. He was put in a small room on his own. It wasn't a cell, they said, though it had barred windows and a locked door.

After a while a uniformed man came in. He appeared sympathetic and tried to coax Cy into answering simple questions, but Cy would not cooperate. The police were irrelevant to him. The Social Services would be here soon.

When the policeman left the cell, Cy noticed that the door locked automatically as it closed. He pursed his lips. When the Young Offender people came, they would interview him here behind a locked door.

After another hour he heard a noise along the corridor that sounded like his visitors. Quickly he unzipped his fly and urinated against the wall. Footsteps approached but walked past his cell. They were not for him. It didn't matter, he thought: the effect would be the same.

When the Young Offender team finally turned up – a man and a woman, easy meat – his locked room smelt like a neglected urinal. The pair turned in disgust to the uniformed officer, who turned in annoyance to the blond boy.

Who said, 'I have a problem with my bladder.'

'Why didn't you—'

'I knocked on the door but no one came.'

✳

In the interview room Cy was as good as gold. He enjoyed himself inventing a sad background for poor Tom Phelan and he answered their questions politely and imaginatively. After a few minutes the policeman left, and in the next few minutes a cosy bond grew between the Social Workers and the subdued boy. Eventually they asked if he would like a cup of tea.

'Yes please, Miss.'

When the woman went to fetch it she left the man to keep an eye on him. The boy noticed that when she went out, the door to the interview room remained unlocked. After a few seconds he said, 'Oh, she won't put milk in it, will she? I'm allergic to milk.'

'Allergic?'

'I can't drink tea if she puts milk in it. Shall I—'

He stood up helpfully.

But the man said, 'No, I'll tell her. You wait here.'

The man looked stern. He was not going to be caught that easily! He popped his head out and looked along the corridor. 'Jill?' he called. He hardly noticed Cy drift behind him to the door.

Jill was out of sight.

The man stepped further into the corridor. Because he was still on duty he kept a firm hand on the wooden pillar to the doorframe. 'Jill?' he called once more.

It was several seconds before he realised the boy was gone.

TWENTY-THREE

'Well, Mr Gottfleisch, this is an extraordinary business.'

'It most certainly is.'

He was at his most avuncular. Seated in Sidonie's comfortable front room in a large armchair, a glass of sherry in his hand, Gottfleisch was relaxed. He could take his time.

She said, 'I'm only glad his father didn't live to see it.'

'You and Murdo were very close.'

'Close?'

'He lived nearby.'

'Close in that sense, yes.'

Gottfleisch eyed her blandly across his *copita*. 'Murdo acted as your agent.'

She put down her glass. 'About Angus,' she prompted.

'Dreadful business. Though he did try to blackmail you.'

She sat erect. 'And then, by coincidence, he was killed.'

Gottfleisch sighed sadly as he drained his *fino* sherry. 'Most pleasant,' he said.

She sat watching him.

He asked, 'Presumably no one else knows that Angus tried to blackmail you?'

'No.'

'Jolly good.'

'Neither does anyone else know, Mr Gottfleisch, that *you* tried to warn him off.'

'Well, I hardly—'

'Twice.'

He paused. 'I beg your pardon?'

'I assume I am correct?'

'What exactly are you saying, Miss Keene?'

She smiled politely, a duellist on guard. 'It seems to me at least conceivable that you called on Angus a second time to reinforce your warning, but that on this occasion there was… some kind of altercation.'

227

'Surely you don't believe that? Look at me, Miss Keene – a man of *my* girth!'

She held his gaze but did not return his smile. 'You have a muscular young driver, and I'm sure you have other... assistants.'

Gottfleisch shook his head. 'Miss Keene, I know we are alone, but this is an outrageous accusation.'

'Let me make myself quite clear. Angus Fyffe was a scrounging little wastrel. I loved his father – not in the biblical sense; the word has been coarsened nowadays – and for Murdo's sake, therefore, I was pleasant to his pathetic son. Angus tried to blackmail me – on spurious grounds – and to be frank, I do not regret his passing. Will you have more sherry, by the way? Please help yourself.'

'A-a-ah.'

Gottfleisch managed to extend this word to three long syllables, then added, 'My Goodness,' as he began to push himself from the chair. 'As I understand what you are implying, Miss Keene—'

'Sidonie. You may call me Sidonie.'

'Most kind.' He was on his feet now. 'And you must call me Hugo.'

He waddled to the side table and twisted the stopper from the decanter. 'Can I offer you—'

She extended her glass. 'Of course.'

'Yes indeed, most excellent sherry. It has a whiff of salt – from an Atlantic breeze,' he extemporised.

When he had refilled their glasses he continued, 'Forgive me if I seem a tad obtuse, but are you saying that you think it possible – I put it no higher than that – *possible* that I might have conspired in the unfortunate death of Angus Fyffe?'

'Probable, I think.'

He raised his brow theatrically. 'And yet you consent to see me again?'

By now he had returned to his armchair and he stood beside it, gazing down at her.

She sipped her sherry and said, 'I don't know why Angus died, but if his death was in any way brought about by you—' Gottfleisch stretched himself ominously to full height but she continued: 'I should then reach one of two conclusions: either it was an accident – since after all, you had no reason to want him dead – or you killed him on my behalf, an act of friendship, as it were.'

She smiled up at him.

'Friendship,' he remarked, and drank some sherry.

She said, 'Perhaps, Hugo—' and as she spoke his name for the first time she stressed it. 'Perhaps, Hugo, you might respond to my hypotheses?'

228

'I actually came to discuss something different.'

Gottfleisch drained his glass, and remained standing. 'I was wondering whether I might glance at your sister's paintings?'

'Hugo, won't you please sit down? Though before you do...' She raised her empty glass.

'Of course.'

He returned to the decanter and recharged their glasses. Sidonie waited till he was walking back to his chair before saying, 'I *used* to have a few of Naomi's paintings – as you know: I sold a couple to you.'

'One. You sold me only one.'

'Really?' She looked genuinely surprised, but carried on: 'Well, I have none left now. I am not a rich woman, Hugo.'

Gottfleisch glanced around the room.

'I'm sure you know, Hugo, that over the years my dear friend Murdo managed to find some of my sister's paintings.'

Gottfleisch watched her carefully but chose not to speak.

She said, 'I was able to authenticate their provenance.'

'Who better?'

'We had an amicable business relationship.'

'I'm pleased to hear it. And how d'you think Murdo... came into possession of the paintings?'

'I didn't like to ask. I understand that dealers don't.'

Gottfleisch smiled.

She added, 'At no time was the ownership of any of them challenged.'

'Which suggests that Murdo may have been acting for the owner?'

'For all I know, the paintings might have been *his*.'

Gottfleisch thought that hardly worth responding to. He drank some sherry and murmured, 'Sidonie, we are quite alone, you know. I can be most discreet.'

She smiled, appeared to yawn, then drank another mouthful from her glass. 'Let me make a small admission, Mr Gottfleisch—'

'Hugo.'

'When a previously unknown painting by a recognised artist appears, there can be doubts about its authenticity. Though Naomi is recognised, she has not been greatly studied. There has never been a decent exhibition, for example, of her work.' Sidonie smiled. 'People won't loan the paintings.'

Gottfleisch nodded. He knew when not to interrupt.

'None of her works are in museums or standard catalogues. Many were lost in the war. Of the few that have turned up, there was bound to be some question of their provenance. I could help... give them that.'

Gottfleisch picked up his glass but found it empty. Realising she had paused he tilted his empty glass toward her and murmured, '*Give* them provenance? Might some... not have been genuine?'

Sidonie glanced into her own sherry glass and found that it too was empty. She raised it pointedly. Gottfleisch began again to extricate himself from the chair,

'I will confess to you, Hugo, that Murdo did, on a couple of occasions, bring paintings which I could not truthfully guarantee. One was an obvious fake, but the other... I could not be sure. – Thank you.' Gottfleisch was refilling her glass. 'And he did bring me another which was almost certainly Naomi's but... wasn't up to standard. So I called it false.'

'Oh, bravo!'

Gottfleisch had overfilled his own glass, and he changed hands so he could lick the sherry from his fingers. 'Spoken like a true art dealer! How many paintings do you have left?'

'I told you. None.'

Gottfleisch grinned. He had hoped to catch her.

She said, 'Murdo used to find them for me.'

Gottfleisch lurched back to his chair. 'Useful man,' he commented, sitting down heavily. 'But now your source has dried up?'

'One can never tell.'

She waved her long-stemmed sherry glass. 'Actually, I lied.' He smiled. 'I do have one last painting, but it is not for sale. It's a portrait of Gwen John.'

'From Naomi's early period, I assume – pre-war. May I see it?'

Again she waved her glass. 'Oh, it must be somewhere upstairs.'

'Allow me to fetch it.'

Gottfleisch began to rise from his chair.

'It is not for sale. Sit down, Hugo, please. – Unless you want to fetch us another drink!'

She giggled. Gottfleisch flopped back against the cushions. He felt distinctly dizzy. He said, 'Shame it's the early period. Look, my dear Sidonie, if by some curious chance, another of Naomi's paintings – from the later period—'

'The German period?'

'Precisely. If... um... should somehow fall into your hands from... ah...wherever they are held... would you consider a relationship with me?'

'A business relationship?'

230

'Of course! I didn't mean to imply—'

'What a pity. Clearly I've lost my once famed allure.'

The old lady leered at him. Gottfleisch was startled, and answered hurriedly, 'Not at all, Miss Keene, no, no. It's more that... ah... that *I* may have lost the ability!'

He patted his huge stomach. As he smiled blearily across the room he thought for a moment that the lined parchment of her face had composed itself into total stillness. A faint smile fluttered on her lips. Behind that mask she held the remains of great beauty and the timeless mystery of woman.

TWENTY-FOUR

It was a day for unlikely news stories. First, with little over a week until Election Day, a startling new ICM poll showed Labour's lead collapsing to a mere five percent – despite Gallup sticking to its earlier forecast of around twenty percent. Bulletins began with five minutes of feverish and hypothetical voting analysis before the more mundane news:

'In an extraordinary development on the Cudham Wood murder enquiry, tomorrow's newspapers will carry a letter purportedly written by the victim, Mr Angus Fyffe, shortly before his death. In the letter Mr Fyffe claims that his life was in danger because of what he knew about an alleged murder fifty years ago. Our reporter Martin Taylor has the details.'

'Yes, according to the letter, Mr Fyffe had evidence that the artist Naomi Keene, reportedly killed in a car crash fifty years ago, was in fact murdered by her sister for financial gain. The sister, Miss Sidonie Keen, had been cut from their mother's will and the entire estate had been left to Naomi. Mr Fyffe's letter alleges that in 1947 Sidonie Keene murdered her sister and faked the car crash to gain the inheritance. The letter further states that when Mr Fyffe discovered this he feared that his own life would be in danger. The bizarre story is given a further twist by the fact that Sidonie Keene, accused of plotting the death of thirty-seven year old Angus Fyffe, is now a woman of eighty-five.'

'Martin, her dead sister *Naomi* Keene was a controversial figure?'

'Yes, in the Thirties she was a member of Sir Oswald Mosley's British Union Party, she was a friend of Hitler, and after marrying a German officer she spent the war years in Germany. After her death her paintings, often including members of Hitler's notorious entourage, became highly collectable – and they still fetch high prices.'

'But Sidonie Keene is still alive?'

'Apparently so, yes. But in an early reaction to the letter the police have stressed that they have no evidence to link Miss Keene with Mr

Fyffe's recent death. They have a copy of the letter, they say, and they regret its precipitate release.'

*

Sidonie insisted that the officers sit down. She was not prepared to have them loom over her and she herself did not wish to stand. She had a headache. She placed the sergeant in an armchair and the raw-faced constable on a fine writing chair which looked barely strong enough to bear his weight. The constable looked timid enough to sit delicately, but the sergeant did not

He said, 'You are aware of the contents of this letter?'

'I heard it discussed on the wireless this morning. It sounded quite preposterous, as I trust you agree?'

'Preposterous, ma'am?'

'You agree?'

'*We* ask the questions – as they say in Germany.'

'Do they really?'

'I understand you were acquainted with the deceased?'

'Which one? The newspapers seem equally interested in both Mr Fyffe and my poor dead sister.'

'Mr Fyffe.'

'Which Mr Fyffe? Mr Fyffe *senior* is also, as you would put it, recently deceased. He was a dear friend. His son was not.'

'But you were acquainted with Mr Angus Fyffe?'

'Certainly. When I first met Angus Fyffe he was wearing – let me see – a terry towelling nappy, in which he looked as ugly or charming as any baby can in his first weeks on earth. But I dare say you're more interested in what he was wearing last time we met?'

Kerrigan stared at her. 'The last time you saw him he was stark naked, wasn't he, and covered with blood?'

Sidonie returned his stare scornfully. 'Oh, you agree with the newspapers – you think I did it? I'm flattered.'

He frowned. 'Flattered?'

'How do you imagine I did this dreadful deed – did I overcome him in a fight or mug him with an axe?'

Kerrigan glared at her. The constable suggested, 'You could have attacked him in his sleep.'

'A credit to the Yard,' Sidonie purred. 'Mr Fyffe was where, exactly – satiated in my bed after a bout of sex?'

Kerrigan leant forward. 'We know where Mr Fyffe was murdered. In his letter the charge against you – one of his charges – is that you would arrange to have him killed. Apparently, you had sent a gang of men around already.'

'Ah yes, my band of brigands. You believed that?'

'Why would Mr Fyffe be afraid of you?'

'He wouldn't.'

'You've read the letter.'

'No, *you've* read the letter. I've heard excerpts.'

'He knew your secret, Miss Keene.'

They stared at each other as if willing the other to speak – a game the sergeant often played. Eventually Sidonie said, 'You believe I murdered my sister?'

Kerrigan remained silent.

She continued, 'You have read the original file, I assume – or has somebody lost it?'

'Miss Keene, a file on a fifty year old accident enquiry is not something I keep on my desk.'

She nodded. 'The file is long closed.'

He sniffed. 'You came into your sister's inheritance, though, as the letter said?'

Sidonie glanced at the constable perched on the fine wooden chair, watching seriously, like a child at a parent's quarrel. Then she turned back to the sergeant: 'The police chased after my sister's car. She panicked. She drove too fast, then crashed into a field and died. From the scene of the accident, the police went straight to the house and broke the news to me. Tell me, what exactly is your charge?'

✳

After they had left I felt empty and numb. When I first heard the news story on the wireless I was astonished, shocked. All those old, disproved allegations and innuendoes. All the bile which came so easily to journalists I had never met. Did they really believe their odious conjectures, or was it grist to the mill of increased sales? Have journalists any sympathy for the living, breathing, feeling people they expose? – Because be that person guilty or innocent, public or private, they are exposed: their photograph printed on the page; a brief, inaccurate biography; their private pain revealed. Subjects of such stories have their unique and complex lives reduced to cruel distorted epitaphs: Man-Hating Feminist; Fun-Loving Housewife; Gay Vicar; Kiss'n'Tell Girl; Hitler's Pawn.

In 1940 I was the Traitorous Toff. Well, a toff I may have been, but I was never traitorous. In the late 1930s we in the BUP were the loudest patriots, clamouring for Britain to re-arm. Mosley and Sir Winston Churchill – who at the time was another lone and ignored voice – were in complete agreement. Traitors? Never. We *railed* against Britain's lazy unpreparedness – in which lamentable condition our country would, at the very worst moment, declare war on militarily stronger Germany over a border quarrel not worth dispute. Poland was an excuse: when the war was over we sold the Poles immediately into communist enslavement. We sold Czechoslovakia also – and when that artificial country regained independence fifty years later it promptly broke apart – as Hitler always said it would.

Perhaps you think the war was fought to save the Jews? No, Britain neither fought for them nor helped them when she'd won – indeed, ask any Jewish activist, and they will tell you how we British shelled their refugee ships and sunk them in the sea. We were no help to Jews before, during or after the war. In 1940 thousands of Jews here were imprisoned, like me, as untrustworthy aliens. In fact, most of the 'aliens' that Britain jailed were Jews.

Germany too imprisoned undesirables. By the late 1930s the Jews were enemies of the state – they were, after all, the mainspring of the communist party. Nevertheless, Germany imprisoned Jews later in the war than Britain imprisoned theirs. (Britain exported thousands to Canada and Australia.) In Germany it became impossible to release these potential traitors onto the streets. The country was being bombed and starved into surrender. The whole world was ranged against her. Conditions were unimaginable. Is it surprising that after four years of grinding war, some of her citizens – the most hardened, the prison guards – asked themselves whether these unwanted prisoners had the *right* to be housed and fed at the nation's expense?

What they did was inexcusable. But imagine, can you, the resentment smouldering in a jailer's heart on the day he hears that last night a city dear to him – Hamburg, say, or Munich, Cologne or Dresden – has been blitzed so hard that in that one single night tens of thousands – yes, *tens* of thousands of civilians have been killed. Women and children. Grandparents. Tens of thousands dead. Imagine his feelings when he takes a hot cooked lunch in to his prisoners, the bombers' friends.

We can't imagine how those jailers felt. But we do know that a German jailer was little different from a Russian, Japanese or Chinese jailer. Or, since the war, to an African, Indian or Yugoslavian. He was little different to any conscript under duress.

If there had been no war these atrocities would not have happened. Millions of Jews would not have died. Nor would soldiers have been shot. Nor civilians bombed. None was killed as a consequence of Nazism – nor indeed of fascism, communism, royalism, republicanism, or any other ism. They were killed by war.

Do I feel angry? Not after all this time. I feel sorrow, sympathy and regret. Such deep regret.

235

TWENTY-FIVE

Ticky fluttered around his grotty flat, trying to make it more acceptable for Cy. The boy had turned up unexpectedly that evening, saying only that the squat had been closed down and that he had nowhere else to go. Ticky told him not to worry, he was welcome here. He was, of course, delighted to see Cy in his flat, and while the boy slurped a cup of packet soup, he scurried round like a doting parent.

Ticky smiled. 'Dirty night out.'

'It smells in here,' Cy muttered. 'Is there a gas leak?'

'No way. I don't have gas. Don't like it.'

'Gas is better than electric.'

'It's dangerous. Don't like naked flames.' Ticky chuckled mirthlessly. 'Well, I wouldn't, would I?'

Cy remembered. 'After what happened? I forgot.'

Ticky nodded. 'Get caught in a fire once, you don't forget. Believe me.'

'At a circus, wasn't it?'

'Fairground,' replied Ticky absently. He sank slowly to his haunches and caught Cy's gaze. 'I didn't always look this way.'

Cy waited. Ticky said, 'I used to be good-looking – well, reasonable, you know? You wouldn't think it now.'

The waxen patches across his face and the displaced hairline obliterated whoever Ticky might have been before. He seemed in permanent disguise.

Cy said, 'You were always small, though?'

Ticky sniffed. 'Well, I didn't melt down like a candle.'

'I meant—'

'But the best things come in tiny packages. I used to be real neat.'

He began to rise, but Cy stopped him: 'Was it a *big* fire?'

Ticky thought a moment. 'Yes and no. Not the whole fairground, just one trailer. But that trailer went up like a bonfire.'

'And you were trapped inside?'

'A little kid was. Belonged to one of... to one of the women work-

236

ing there.' Ticky shrugged. 'But she wasn't around. Someone had to get the child out. So I went in.'

Cy seemed impressed. 'Even though the place was...'

'On fire, yeah. Oh, it was burning strong. Yeah. I couldn't just leave the kid in there to die though, could I?' He grinned as he extemporised. 'Bleedin' hero, me.'

'And did the... did the kid...'

'Oh, the kid survived. She was out the trailer before I was.'

'How come?'

Ticky cocked his head. 'I pushed her out the window, didn't I? The trouble was that opening the window let the wind come in. Fanned the flames. Anyway, I got out eventually.'

Cy was staring at him. 'The fire burned your face?'

'Yeah. Lost my hair too. And my girl.'

'The little girl?'

'Her mother. Before the fire, well, you know, we had something.' Ticky shrugged. He liked this story.

'But you saved her daughter. Wasn't the woman grateful?'

'Well, grateful's not the same, is it? She didn't say, 'Well, thank you very much – come and get your oats.' Look at the state of me.' Ticky chuckled. 'I mean, would you?'

'That's terrible.'

Ticky stood up. 'Some people never look below the surface. – I'll get another pillow for the bed.'

As he wandered casually across the room, Cy said, 'Hey, wait a minute – where am I sleeping?'

Ticky attempted a sickly grin. 'Oh, it's big enough, my bed. We'll be all right.'

'I can sleep on the settee.'

'Have you tried even *sitting* on that thing? It sags like a busted shopping bag.'

'It'll do for me.'

Ticky blinked twice, but he knew he shouldn't push the boy. The important thing was to keep him in the flat tonight. He said, 'Hang on.'

Reaching beneath his shambolic bed he pulled out an ugly green plastic squab. 'Welcome to the spare bed.'

Cy drank the last dregs of his packet soup while Ticky unfolded the lump of green plastic and affixed a foot pump. He began treading to inflate it. It seemed painfully hard work. Perhaps there was a hole in the mattress, Cy thought – he wouldn't be surprised. He watched Ticky gamely pumping, trying not to pant. When the little man had the airbed half inflated to a faintly comic flaccid state which released

237

a cloying smell of old stale rubber, he stopped to ask Cy if he wanted more to eat.

The boy didn't, but he felt Ticky deserved a rest. 'Got any bread?'

'Money?'

'Bread to eat.'

'No, it went off. Had to throw it out the window. Bet it poisoned the pigeons.'

They smiled at each other. Ticky said, 'I've got a box of cake.'

'That'll do.' Cy laughed. 'Let me eat cake!' He laughed again unaccountably, and Ticky frowned as he fetched it from the kitchen. The boy was still laughing when Ticky brought the cake and ripped off the cellophane.

Cy read from the package: 'Chocolate *Yule* Log. – Jesus, Ticky, when's the Sell By?' He turned the packet over. 'January 31st. It's April now.'

'Happy Christmas.'

'Well, at least it's January *this* year. Where'd you get this – in a street market?'

'It's Christmas cake – lasts for ages. Everyone knows that'

'But it's chocolate cake.'

'Christmas. Says on the box.'

Cy grinned and shook his head, turning the package over as if it were an unopened present. 'You've had this since Christmas?'

Ticky shrugged. 'Well, you know, I didn't have… what's it?… an occasion to open it. – Still, we've got an occasion now.'

Cy tore open the inner wrapper and removed the lightweight plastic tray. He sniffed the cake and prodded it. 'Just like Mother used to make.'

'You have *got* a mother, then?'

'Somewhere.'

Cy stared at the cake. Ticky sat down and handed Cy a bread knife, which the boy used to slice off the end of the chocolate log. He nibbled it. 'Mm. Not too bad.'

'Don't eat it all yourself.'

Cy cut a second slice. 'Yeah, I've got a mother. Sure. She drinks.'

'Oh.' Ticky munched and swallowed. 'Got a Dad as well?'

'Yup.'

Cy cut off another slice of cake. It was his turn to tell a story. 'He used to have a paper shop. Went down the swannee. So he had to sell at a loss – I mean a real loss.'

'A proper businessman.'

'The privileged class,' Cy continued wistfully. 'Oh yeah. He was out of work, heavily in debt. We sold the flat – well, we had to, it was above the shop. Then they said we couldn't have a council house.'

'Long waiting list?'

'We didn't qualify. Ex-property owners, see? So even though we were homeless, the council couldn't rent us anything. Regulations. They had to put us in Bed and Breakfast.' He cut off more cake. 'Mum's drinking got more obvious. Still. Happy Families, eh?'

Ticky finished his slice. '*My* family kicked me out when I was about your age.'

But Cy wasn't listening. He picked pieces off the chocolate cake as he developed his story: 'We were in this real dump of an area. Bloody awful school, and of course I bunked off and got in trouble – you know? Mum and Dad stuck in this rotten room – Mum half sozzled, Dad ranting on about blacks and Asians – and I grew up. I had no choice.'

'Did you run away?'

'I walked away – but not from that place. The Social said my parents couldn't control me, so they pulled me out and put me in so-called 'secure accommodation'. You know what that means.'

'Prison.'

'Not at my age, Ticky. Secure accommodation means you get banged up with a load of other hard cases. Shoved in through the one-way door. I hate the lot of them – fascist bastards.'

He continued picking morosely at the half-eaten cake with Ticky's bread knife. Ticky said chirpily, 'So one day you just nipped out the window?'

'More or less. But now I'm out, what can I do? I can't work, I can't rent somewhere, and I can't go back. Zugzwang.'

'Eh?'

'You don't play chess then, Ticky?'

'Christ, no.'

'Zugzwang is the next worse thing to checkmate. You're trapped. Whatever move you make, things can only get worse.'

*

After Cy had finished the cake, after Ticky had put on some music, after they had settled down to the long slow evening, Cy picked up the dress ring he'd noticed on the table. 'What's this?'

'Oh, that's… that was my Grandad's, you know? You like it?' It was the Death's Head ring Ticky found at Sidonie's. 'Try it on.'

Cy slipped it on his finger. 'You can keep it,' Ticky said.

'But if it was in your family?'

'No, I'd like you to have it. Wear it for me.'

Ticky was staring at him as if he had given an engagement ring.

Cy said, 'It'd make a neat knuckleduster.'

Ticky chuckled nervously, watching the boy adjust the ring on his finger. He asked casually, 'Want to try a popper?'

'What sort?'

'Angel's Wing.'

'Never heard of it.'

'Well, it's an upper. You know: you can fly higher on an angel's wing. Ha, ha.'

Ticky laughed softly and produced from his pocket a small medicine bottle. He unscrewed the top.

'Oh, amyl nitrate,' Cy said flatly.

'Well—'

'I know that stuff. I don't want it.'

Ticky chewed his lip. If the boy knew what it was he'd probably tried it. And if he'd tried it… Ticky looked at him. A key effect of amyl nitrate is to relax muscles; gays use the drug to relax the sphincter. From what Ticky had learned, it was particularly useful on young or inexperienced boys – and it worked for girls also, he'd been told, though he'd not managed to test that for himself. Ticky had had this bottle for several months – even longer than the Yule Log – and was longing to use it again. He said, 'You've tried it, then?'

'Thanks, but no thanks.'

'Come on, Cy, it's good. Helps pass the time.'

Cy looked at him and said, 'I don't mind grass, if you've got any. I left mine at the squat.'

'This does the same but more so.'

Cy picked up the bread knife, flashed it in the light and ran his fingernail along its serrated edge. 'I'm all right as I am,' he said. He ran his thumb along the blade. Though it left a line on his skin it didn't cut the surface. Cy jabbed the point of the blade lightly against the ball of his thumb. Again it didn't pierce the surface.

'Not very sharp,' he said.

'It's a bread knife.'

Cy looked at him absently. 'Ticky,' he said. 'In the morning – d'you shave with a cut-throat razor?'

Ticky shook his head.

'Pity.'

Cy glanced at the airbed. 'Have you got a sleeping bag to go on that?'

'I've got some blankets.'

'They'll do.'

Later that night when Cy crawled beneath the blankets he took the bread knife with him.

TWENTY-SIX

When the police spokesman rose to his feet it was to the morning ritual of journalists clearing their throats. Some of the older ones used short-hand notepads, others raised pocket tape-recorders, but the privileged broadcasters took their direct feed from microphones cluttered on his desk. He unravelled his statement as if he'd never seen foolscap before. In the rows of wooden chairs before him, less than half were occupied.

'Enquiries are continuing into the murder of Mr Angus Fyffe, and several leads are being followed.'

He paused to cough, grimace, and cough again.

'Following the release of a letter purportedly written by Mr Fyffe, there has been speculation – I might say clear *suggestion* in some quarters—'

He glanced into the room to see how this extemporisation had gone down.

' – that the person named in the letter, a Miss Sidonie Keene, is suspected of having carried out Mr Fyffe's murder. This has naturally caused her some distress. We wish to make it clear that the aforesaid Miss Sidonie Keene, an elderly lady of eighty-five, could not possibly have carried out this particularly brutal murder herself.'

He was in his stride now, and could pause for effect.

'We wish to further state that, following the testimony of two independent eyewitnesses, we now wish to interview a male person of small stature – possibly a child – or possibly two children – who was or were in the Cudham Woods on the evening of the crime.'

He looked up from his sheet of paper, found the television camera, and gazed solemnly into it. His confidence growing, he referred to his prepared statement less and less.

'This person, or these persons, will almost certainly have had blood on his, her or—' He smiled learnedly. ' – *their* clothing. We are therefore appealing to anyone – including friends or members of his, her or their family – anyone in fact who has information about a small or young person – or young persons – out late last night – and especially, of course, any person or persons who came home with unexplained blood on his or her – their clothing – to contact the police immediately. This they may do in complete confidence.'

He glanced down at his sheet of paper but seemed unable to find his place. He looked up earnestly.

'Someone must know who this person or these persons is – are – and we urge them, for the sake of that person or persons themself – themselves – as well as for the public at large, to contact the police in confidence on the following number.' He looked down again. 'On the following numbers.'

✳

Cy had left shortly after breakfast and it was now mid-afternoon. Ticky had waited in the flat, then tidied up. He made both his bed and Cy's, tucking in the blankets on the inflated mattress. Making the boy's bed gave Ticky genuine pleasure. He pushed his arm right down inside, beneath the blankets where Cy had slept. He put his face under them and tried to inhale Cy's fragrance, but smelt nothing but rubber. He did notice, though, that the bread knife Cy had taken to bed with him was no longer there. Later, Ticky checked the kitchenette. It wasn't there either.

For their lunch Ticky had opened a can of spaghetti hoops, but Cy did not come back. Ticky waited but eventually, around two, he heated half the contents of the can and ate them alone. Afterwards, since there was nothing else for him to do, he washed his plate and cutlery.

When Cy finally did turn up he brought a gust of fresh air with him. He had a wild sparkle in his eye which warned Ticky immediately that the boy might be moving on. Ticky asked if he had eaten lunch and when he admitted that he hadn't, clucked at him like a mother hen. While Ticky heated the remaining spaghetti hoops Cy announced that he had found somewhere else to live. Ticky didn't reply but later Cy complained that he fussed round him like his mother before she turned to drink.

✳

The new squat was to the east of Tottenham Court Road, half a mile from the previous squat in an area of scruffy offices and small hotels. Ticky accompanied his young friend, carrying a bag of shopping from the local street market as if he were valet to the boy. Most of Cy's possessions had been abandoned at the police station, so they had bought cheap socks and underclothes, two tee-shirts and a blue acrylic sweater which had had the maker's label scissored out. Cy had let Ticky choose the socks and underclothes while he drifted off among other stalls. When the boy reappeared looking pleased with himself Ticky knew he had lifted something, but they didn't talk about it.

'This is the place.'

They stood in front of a low Sixties office block soon to be pulled down. The windows were boarded and the concrete facing was pitted and stained. At the side was an alley to the back, where they found a metal single door intended originally as a fire escape. Beside the door was a half brick which Cy used to rap rhythmically – two, two and five – Come Out, Come Out, Whoever You Are. Then he stood away from the door so he could be seen, advising Ticky to wait out of sight close by the wall.

After a while the back door was unbolted, and they were let inside the dark interior.

'Not that little turd,' was Nathan's welcome.

Ticky glared up at his shaven-headed rival. 'I'm with my friend.'

'You ain't staying.'

'I wouldn't want to.'

They trudged up the dimly-lit, dusty concrete stairs to the second floor. What light there was came from back windows where the boards had been removed.

'Not as cosy as the last place,' Nathan admitted. 'But when we get some stuff in, it won't look bad.'

Left-over rubble lay along the corridors. Internal partition walls had been removed. Towards the front of the building, still boarded, the feeble light grew gloomier. Everywhere they walked held a smell of plaster dust and mould.

Nathan said, 'They only used this place for storage, so it's sort of lacking in facilities. But the water's on.'

Ticky whispered, 'You can't stay in this dump, Cy.'

Nathan said, 'It'll be nice to have a West End address.'

Ticky snorted. 'Where's the bedrooms?'

Nathan laughed. 'Bedrooms? La-di-dah!'

'Yeah, but where are they?'

Nathan peered at him through the gloom. 'What's it to you?'

Cy touched Ticky's arm. 'I'll be all right, Ticky.'

'Dead right,' Nathan agreed. 'If you stay with *us* you will. Come on.'

From above they heard clunks and voices. When they reached the top floor they found a man and a woman carrying boxes from room to room. The partition walls were still in place.

Cy asked, 'Where's Packer?'

'Must've found somewhere else.'

Ticky said, 'This is it then – just those two and you?'

'We'll soon fill up.'

Cy rubbed his hands together, more against the chill than to show enthusiasm. 'Want me to do something?'

Nathan pursed his lips. 'You could hunt up some food.'

'OK.'

Cy glanced at his wrist but his watch had been abandoned at the police station.

'Just gone seven,' Ticky muttered.

'Try Leather Lane,' Nathan suggested. 'There should be bits left over from the market.'

Ticky sneered. 'Mouldy cabbages and squashed tomatoes.'

Nathan snapped, 'You get right up my nose, you know that? You want the boy to kip at your place, don't you? Well, he'll be safe here and he'll have a damn sight better time. Am I right, Cy?'

Cy shrugged.

Nathan placed a friendly hand upon his shoulder. 'Say goodbye to your little friend, then we'll get something to eat.'

Ticky rose to his full four feet ten. 'Let me take you out for a meal, Cy.'

❋

As they strolled in the twilight down Charing Cross Road – the bright shop windows, crowded pavements, busy traffic, and smells of cheap foreign cooking wafting through the air – Ticky said, 'When you're down to scraps left behind at street markets, you know you've really hit rock bottom. That's what I reckon.'

'Yeah, and it's too late anyway.'

'Dead right. Nathan don't know what he's talking about. Berwick Street's the best market.'

'And closer.'

They were crossing Cambridge Circus, thronging with theatregoers and late shoppers, office workers in and out of pubs, young girls hardly older than Cy, when Ticky asked, 'You fancy Chinese? I know a cheap one.'

'Sounds neat. Better than a hamburger.'

'We can cut through China Town. It's on the other side.'

They strolled through Newman Court into the garish glitter of the Chinese ghetto. Restaurants varied from dank and steamy cafes to smart forbidding palaces. Among the hundreds of Chinese were even more Caucasian visitors.

244

Ticky said they were almost there.

*

Ticky's chosen dank steamy cafe had a notice outside proclaiming that it sold the cheapest Chinese food in London, which wasn't the most appealing advertisement. He and Cy sat at a counter around the wall and ate crispy rolls and spicy chop suey. After that, they wandered on to the White Horse in Rupert Street. When Cy asked for a Coke, Ticky surreptitiously slipped a vodka in it. They had two more drinks and Ticky began to feel relaxed.

When they came out into the darkness, Cy said he'd like to wander back through China Town. Crowds had lightened now, with people ensconced inside theatres, pubs and restaurants. Cy seemed happier too. The hot food had given him a lift, as perhaps had the three vodkas he had drunk without realising. He began laughing at Chinese shops, at gaudy arches across the streets, at Chinese lettering, at busy restaurants with shrivelled poultry hanging in the windows, at passers by.

'Let's smash a window,' he suggested. 'Some fancy restaurant.'

Ticky tried to hurry him along.

'Hey Ticks, where does that go – a Chinese brothel?'

Cy pointed to an unmarked door, opening onto uncarpeted stairs. Inside the narrow doorway was a small sign stuck to the wall in hand-written Chinese, done with a green felt tip pen. 'I bet that means prostitutes,' Cy declared.

'No, it'll be a Chinese club or some sort of Chinky meeting place. Come away.'

'Hang on.'

A light had begun dancing in Cy's eyes. 'Let's creep up and listen. See what's there.'

'No way!'

As Ticky reached towards him the boy slipped inside. He ran softly up the stairs, leaving Ticky peering though the door. He took a breath before he followed.

On the first landing, lit by a dim red bulb, he found Cy listening at a closed green door. Chinese voices came from inside. Ticky plucked at Cy's jacket and the boy grinned at him. Ticky tugged again.

To his relief Cy stepped back from the door. Then the boy reached into his pocket, pulled out a handkerchief and used it to muffle his hand while he stretched above Ticky to remove the red lamp bulb from the wall. He chuckled in the gloom.

'Ouch!' he cried suddenly. 'That's hot.'

245

He dropped it on the floor. As the bulb smashed he laughed again. Shouts came from inside the room. Cy knocked against Ticky and began running down the stairs. Before either could reach the bottom, the door opened and angry men appeared. Cy and Ticky shot outside and along the lane. They nipped round a corner and leant against the wall to catch their breath.

Suddenly a Chinese man appeared. He was so close he almost grabbed them, and as they darted along the alley they heard others arrive. Ticky and Cy ran to the corner, sprinted round, and pelted down the street. Passers by watched in amazement. Cy laughed aloud. But the Chinese men kept coming.

Ticky and Cy were running fast, but the gang behind weren't giving up. In Shaftesbury Avenue Cy took one look at the traffic and plunged across. Ticky yelped and darted after him. A van hooted. A taxi swerved. On the opposite pavement Ticky glanced back to see several Chinese men starting to cross.

He and Cy darted up Frith Street, swerved into Dean, cut through to Wardour Street and took a left. They were back now in the vicinity of Cy's first squat but they kept running, taking every corner till it seemed certain they had got away.

They leant against a wall, both out of breath.

'You're a nutcase.'

'Don't call me that.'

Ticky gasped for breath. 'It was stupid.'

'Fun, though, wasn't it?'

'Bloody dangerous.'

'Yeah! They'd have skewered us like two kebabs.'

They paused a moment to pant.

Ticky said, 'Chinese don't eat kebabs. They eat chop suey.'

'Chop, chop, chop.'

Ticky smiled for the first time.

Cy said, 'You're right though. We shouldn't mess about with Chinese. Next time we'll pick someone easier.'

Ticky stopped smiling.

In their separate houses later that evening Sidonie and Gottfleisch sat down to watch *The Late Show* on TV. It promised to be an oasis of calm in the shifting dunes of political analysis. Labour's lead was now back to twenty-four percent; it would be a 'Labour Landslide', people said. Sidonie, in dressing gown and nightwear, had settled into her armchair with a mug of cocoa and a Balkan Sobranie in a tortoiseshell holder. Gottfleisch, in his Greenwich sitting room, was fully dressed – but as a concession to the late hour had allowed himself a mug of hot milk (no flavouring, except honey), a handful of biscuits and a piece of cake. Anything more would spoil his diet.

Before them on their TV screens the presenter, Sarah Dunant, wore a Schiaparelli-style silk dress – black, slinky and reminiscent of the Thirties – while Brian Sewell remained rooted in the Nineties in mauve Ralph Lauren shirt, loose cream jacket and soft dark slacks. Jane Strachey wore a white trouser suit and suntan, and had the athletic languor of a big-game hunter home from the shoot.

Sarah smiled eagerly at the camera and gave a brief and pithy introduction. She recapped the dead man's accusatory letter which had brought about today's police rebuttal, then moved on to a prepared résumé of the Keene sisters' life. For what Sarah called 'the Keenes' flirtation with fascism' the programme interposed a clip of footage from a 1930s Mosley convention at which, said Sarah, both sisters had been prominent.

Sidonie could not recall the particular meeting and thought it unlikely the BBC had acquired a delegate list, but it was good to see Tom Mosley again, so slim, so young. Meanwhile in Greenwich, Gottfleisch scowled to see Jane Strachey, who at the beginning of her career had worked for him in his gallery. She had learnt her trade well, before moving on.

'For many years,' Sarah Dunant said, 'Naomi Keene was an artist in disgrace – never mentioned, her paintings never seen – until finally, in the 1950s, they began to reappear.'

BRIAN SEWELL

I think you underestimate the period of her isolation. Her paintings remained untouchable till the early Sixties.

CUT BRIEFLY TO STRACHEY

STRACHEY

(to Sarah Dunant) Bear in mind which of her paintings reappeared first.
Strachey pauses expectantly until Dunant prompts.

TRIPLE SHOT – THE THREE AROUND THE TABLE:

DUNANT

And those were?

STRACHEY

Minor works. General views around the Berghof – a cafe interior.

SEWELL

The Goering portrait.

STRACHEY

That was the *only* significant work. The more desirable pieces – the portraits, half portraits – didn't turn up till later.

DUNANT

Why is this significant?

STRACHEY

Nothing valuable appeared till there was a market—

SEWELL

Oh, please!

CAMERA CLOSES ON SEWELL AS HE CONTINUES:

SEWELL

When an artist's work has little value, few pieces appear in auction rooms. Those with a greater potential value are held back. – I hate to reduce art to a monetary scale, but it's how the business works.

CUTAWAY TO STRACHEY NODDING AS SEWELL SPEAKS:

SEWELL

Prices remained flat until the Goering portrait, which gave the first intimation that she might have both merit and commercial value. The Goering, with an exquisite spot of carmine colouring on his cheek—

DUNANT

—Because Goering did wear make-up—

THE CAMERA STAYS ON SEWELL

SEWELL

But in life, would he have worn it so flamboyantly? Was it really make-up, do you think, or could the *Reichspräsident* have been excited by the proximity of a beautiful – not to say adoring – English girl?

STRACHEY

Or is the painting fake?

CUT TO STRACHEY'S QUIZZICAL EXPRESSION. THEN COME BACK TO SEWELL AS HE GETS INTO HIS STRIDE.

SEWELL

Jane, I know you want to make this point – it's a drum you have beaten for several years – but the Goering portrait has been in the public domain since the Sixties—

STRACHEY

Hardly the *public* domain—

INTERCUT BETWEEN STRACHEY AND SEWELL:

SEWELL

Everything about the painting says it is right. It is of the period—

STRACHEY

Naturally!

SEWELL

It is in her style. It is on the right cartridge paper – authenticated pre-war paper. The watercolour, the actual pigment, is *sixty* years old.

STRACHEY

Allegedly.

SEWELL

It has been tested.

STRACHEY

Not by me.

DUNANT

(cuts across them) Let's be clear here.

CAMERA ON DUNANT, AS CHAIRPERSON

DUNANT

Jane, you're convinced that some or all of the Keene paintings are fake while Brian, you are content with them?

CUT TO SEWELL

SEWELL

As is any diligent and established critic—

CUTAWAY TO STRACHEY'S AMUSEMENT AS SEWELL CONTINUES:

SEWELL

—because the line and application of colour is quintessentially Naomi Keene.

CAMERA RETURNS TO SEWELL

SEWELL

Let me say this. Our educated intuition encourages us to accept these works as undeniably authentic. But beyond this, cold scientific analysis *confirms* our intuition. Jane Strachey claims *her* analysis to be coldly scientific but *(he smiles at her)* she has always been a maverick. She makes her living by mounting bold assaults upon orthodox and established views.

DUNANT

Jane?

CAMERA FLICKS TO STRACHEY, BUT RETURNS TO SEWELL

249

SEWELL

(Continues regardless) She makes good television, and I would be the last to deny her the right to make a living, but please don't confuse her provocative allegations with profundity. Jane Strachey is to art *criticism* what Rolf Harris is to art.

DUNANT

(smiles indulgently) Jane?

STRACHEY

Thank you.

CLOSE IN SLOWLY ON STRACHEY

STRACHEY

Back before the Flood, Sarah – before the Sewell overflowed – you asked whether I considered every Keene work to be fake. Of course not. Highly unlikely. She was an artist, we know that. She was in Germany, we know *that*. She met Hitler. As an artist, then, some of her paintings must have survived. Perhaps some of her German works do exist. But curiously, no saleable work was discovered, or even heard of, till the late Sixties.

CONTINUE IN ONE-SHOTS

SEWELL

The Goering was known and highly 'saleable', as you call it, before then. So were at least two studies of Adolf Hitler.

STRACHEY

The Hitlers have little value—

SEWELL

Oh, come!

STRACHEY

Check the sale results. He's too famous. Hitler has been painted *thousands* of times.

SEWELL

Less often than one might think.

DUNANT

(to Strachey) Don't you accept the Hitler paintings as genuine?

STRACHEY

I accept nothing that I am forbidden to examine.

SEWELL

Forbidden! *(He laughs)*

STRACHEY

Put one in my hands. Allow me to assess it properly.

SEWELL

(Demonstrates his point with an elegant finger) She wants to prick it with her hypodermic needle, Sarah. She wants to X-ray it! But the pictures have already been assessed. There is no challenge to their authenticity.

CUT TO DUNANT

DUNANT

Let me interrupt you here. As I see it, Jane, you accept that *some* of her paintings are genuine—

RETURN TO STRACHEY

STRACHEY

Not necessarily. She was a minor artist, working before the Second World War. She died in 1946—

SEWELL

Forty-seven.

STRACHEY

She had no studio of unsold works. She lived through the war in Germany – precariously – so it is quite likely that no original Keene survives.

RETURN TO ONE-SHOTS

SEWELL

How absurd! We have some of her pre-war paintings – the portrait of Duncan Grant, for example – with unimpeachable provenance.

STRACHEY

But the German ones—

SEWELL

Continue the line. They are executed by the same hand, sometimes on the same batch of paper. There is absolutely no question about this.

STRACHEY

There *is* a question about the intimate, behind-the-scenes portraits of Hitler, Goering, Goebbels and the gang. The Eva Braun, for example, with that *gramophone*, is far too good to be true. Her Master's Voice, indeed! And so many of Keene's German paintings have the same fortuitous quality – oh look, this one just happens to have Hitler in the corner, while this—

SEWELL

(throwing one arm wide) That is precisely why she painted them. Good Lord, it was 1939 – she knew who these people were. They were the glitterati of the age. And she was able to catch them not in

251

formal studio portraits but in charmingly informal vignettes.

CUT TO DUNANT GLANCING AT HER NOTES

DUNANT

What about her landscapes?

BACK TO ONE-SHOTS

STRACHEY

Uninteresting. Competent. Well executed, nothing more. Some of *those* may be genuine, but they're not valuable.

SEWELL

You think any valuable Keene must be fake? Only the landscapes – which you call dross – can be authentic? For you, Miss Strachey, authenticity is to be gauged by price, rather than price being a function of their authenticity?

STRACHEY

(turning to Dunant) Of course, Brian knows nothing about landscape.

SEWELL

(outraged) I hardly—

STRACHEY

(still talking to Dunant) It's well known. Brian is a clot on the landscape! *This reduces Dunant to giggles, and she is unable to continue for several seconds.*

SEWELL

(huffily) You were on safer ground when you dismissed everything as a fake. If you admit that the Keene landscapes, which you dislike, are genuine, and if the more interesting *portraits* are by the same hand…

STRACHEY

(who has been shaking her head at Sewell's words)   I don't accept your premise – and I don't *dislike* her landscapes. I simply point out that they're not commercial.

SEWELL

(leaning back in his chair) But you are wrong. The two Hamburg studies, for instance – shell-shocked civilians shuddering in awful stillness after a night of dreadful bombing – are quite magnificent: a sombre fusion, if such a thing were possible, of Paul Nash and Otto Dix.

CUT TO A TRIPLE SHOT, AND HOLD FOR THE NEXT EXCHANGE

STRACHEY

The Hamburgs are certainly different from her other work – more deeply felt, perhaps. But that, of course, makes one ask whether she painted them.

252

SEWELL

Of course she did – but in 1943, not '38 and '39 – a lifetime apart. Four years of war and the Hamburg blitz would transform the output of any artist.

STRACHEY

So you admit they're different?

SEWELL

Jane, you're overlooking a more interesting story—

CUT TO DUNANT AS SHE INTERRUPTS

DUNANT

Today's story? That Naomi's sister could have murdered her? – Allegedly!

CUT TO SEWELL

SEWELL

No, no, that is simply another illustration of the old Fleet Street maxim that the more ludicrous the story the more prominence it gains. No, the real story lies in the way that over the years these undoubtedly genuine paintings have dribbled onto the market, as if someone were releasing them from their hoard.

CONTINUE IN ONE-SHOTS

STRACHEY

Or was forging them—

SEWELL

Far too slowly, Jane, far too slowly. Forgers work quickly, for a quick profit.

DUNANT

Might someone really have a hoard?

BACK TO THE TRIPLE SHOT

SEWELL

Jane tells us that Naomi Keene had no studio of unsold works. But do we know that? Keene must have had a studio originally, so what became of it? After the war, she did return to England – albeit briefly.

STRACHEY

Tragically. She died here.

SEWELL

Indeed. She died suddenly – as we have been reminded. So Naomi would have been unable to go back to her studio in Europe – a studio to which somebody somewhere must have had the key.

253

STRACHEY

Brian, are you seriously suggesting that somebody – her lover, perhaps? – has sat on the paintings all these years? Well, really!

RETURN TO A ONE-SHOT OF SEWELL

SEWELL

Nobody sat on the paintings, Jane. Look at their history. Since the end of the 1950s they have slowly been *released*. Fortuitously for whoever *was* sitting on them, their value has progressively increased.

CLOSE IN ON DUNANT AS SHE SPEAKS

DUNANT

Well, we seem to have a number of potential suspects here. Naomi Keene was living in Switzerland – but with whom? Was there a land-lord? A cleaner? Who cleared out the flat after her death? We know she had been married—

STRACHEY

Notoriously—

DUNANT

And though her husband was dead, what of the various other members of his family? Did she take a new lover – several lovers? Did she have an agent?

SEWELL

(laughs) Not in 1947!

RETURN TO ONE-SHOTS AS THEY SPEAK

STRACHEY

(shrugs) The list of suspects seems endless.

SEWELL

Half the population of Europe – any one of whom could have acquired her work.

DUNANT

(leaning forward) If someone did hold the key, then when they reopened the door to Naomi Keene's studio, it must have been like re-entering Tutenkhamen's tomb.

SEWELL

It would not have seemed so at the time. Keene was merely a talented but unsuccessful artist.

STRACHEY

This is pointless conjecture. Keene was a wartime refugee, a hunted traitor. She did not have a studio.

SEWELL

She must have had one *sometime* – if not in Switzerland, then in Germany. Or perhaps in England. As I say, the list of potential suspects extends to half the population of Europe!

Gottfleisch had heard enough. Half the population of Europe was not on *his* list of potential suspects. It was perfectly clear to him who had garnered the paintings – and who had been releasing them slowly ever since – as an annuity, as it were. The only thing Gottfleisch didn't know was where she was hoarding them.

TWENTY-SEVEN

Nathan had rigged up a couple of oil lamps from jam jars, paraffin and string, but no one had much confidence in them. Someone had loosened boards in the windows at the front, and that let some light in from a streetlamp. There were several candles.

After a surprisingly short while Cy found that not only had he grown used to the lack of light but he preferred it. Deep areas of dense shadow concealed the shabby dereliction of the building and the scattered pools of light were like dim nebulae in a void. He and the three others sat close together in the glow of two candles and an oil lamp, their faces lit from below, their shadows wavering about them. From time to time one or other would cup their hands beside a flame. They had been smoking skunk, which made Cy's head spin.

After the Chinese meal he wasn't hungry, and the effect of the three vodkas he didn't know he'd had, combined with wooziness caused by skunk, made him weary and ready for bed. The fitful conversation in the candlelight seemed as if it would last all night.

He stood up carefully but couldn't avoid a whoosh of giddiness. Over by the door stood a single candle in a cup, and as he headed towards it he felt curiously detached, free-floating, like an asteroid in space – a manned craft heading for dock.

Behind him, Nathan clambered to his feet. 'I'll bring the lamp out.'

'I'll be all right.'

'You'll need it in the passageway.'

'No, I can see.'

The back hall was lit after a fashion by a small high window onto the night, but the room Cy had chosen was very dark. He stood just inside the door until he could see enough to pick his way across to the flattened cardboard boxes by the wall. When Ticky had seen the boxes he had urged Cy to spend another night in his flat or to let him return later with a couple of blankets. Nathan had encouraged the boy to send him away.

As Cy sat down to take off his shoes he decided he should not have let himself be swayed. He had swopped a night in Ticky's flat for a bed of cardboard.

From outside came the city's melody – engine noise and brakes, occasional sirens, rare voices, the faint beat of music far away. As he wriggled between stiff sheets of cardboard the sound of slithering boards was like someone breathing in his ear. He was cold and uncomfortable. Whenever he tried to adjust his bedding, the unyielding sheets began to slide apart. He saw why experienced dossers preferred a large box to snuggle into.

He wasn't getting warmer. He didn't think he'd sleep.

✳

Flames flickered around him but gave out no heat. Wreckage of the building lay across his chest and when he flailed against the fallen panels he thought the tenement was collapsing in the dark. He tried to sit and found to his surprise that he could move easily. Then he realised that the flames were Nathan's oil lamp, that the walls were sheets of cardboard, that the voice was Nathan's voice.

'It's all right. Don't worry.'

Cy stared at Nathan's silhouette against the light. The man's hand was beneath the cardboard, resting on his leg.

'I was just checking you were awake.'

Cy reached down and moved his hand.

'Don't worry,' Nathan repeated. 'Ain't you cold in there?'

'I was asleep.'

'Well, I'm bloody cold. Mind, the other two have got each other. So they're not cold.'

'G'night.'

Nathan shifted some cardboard. 'What're you sleeping on?' He began to feel around in the gloom. 'Can't be comfortable.' His hand slipped beneath the boards again and found Cy's chest. 'Ain't you got no polythene in there? You'll freeze to death.'

Cy tried to move Nathan's hand but this time the man kept it there, saying, 'I got some polythene next door. Want me to bring some?'

'Don't need it.'

Cy tugged at his hand but Nathan only moved it lower down, flat against his belly, and asked, 'Want another smoke?'

'No.'

'Help you sleep.'

'Look, I'll see you in the morning, Nathan, all right?'

'Don't be like that. Everyone needs a friend in London.'

Nathan moved closer and put his other arm around Cy's shoulder. They were now almost embracing. Cy shrugged away from him. 'Get off. I don't do that.'

'Hey, hey.'

Nathan removed his arm, but only to lay his fingers against Cy's cheek. His other hand remained against Cy's stomach. Cy took a firmer hold and pulled his hand aside, but Nathan swung his leg across and straddled him. Sheets of cardboard slithered away. One piece remained between them.

Cy said, 'Fuck off, Nathan.'

But the man used both hands to hold Cy down. 'Grow up, kid. This ain't home, you know, safe in your bed. If you wanna live this way, then live it.'

Cy gave a sudden heave, but Nathan was too strong for him. In the faint light of his oil lamp on the floor he looked like a ghoul at Hallowe'en.

'Come on, kid, it's not something awful. You'll like it. Ever tried?'

Cy braced his feet on the floor and bucked, but couldn't throw the man off. Nathan rocked like a bronco rider but sat secure. He leant closer to Cy and grinned.

'Time for a bit of rumpty-tumpty. You got a hard-on yet?'

Shifting his grip, Nathan used his right forearm to hold Cy down and reached behind with his left, shifting the cardboard and feeling along the outside of Cy's clothes to find his crotch.

But Cy had an arm free now. He began groping beneath the cardboard, his body squirming beneath Nathan's weight. Nathan started tugging at Cy's zip, but from his position above he couldn't shift it, so he moved sideways, freeing Cy just as the boy's hand found the knife he had stolen from the street market. He stabbed up and across and plunged it in Nathan's side. It didn't take a moment. Nathan grunted but felt little pain till the boy pulled the knife out. Then he gasped. As Cy sat up, Nathan slowly began to sag. In the fluttering oil light they sat facing each other like lovers on dishevelled sheets. Cy could see no blood through Nathan's clothes. There should be blood, he thought.

When Nathan slumped towards him Cy stabbed again. Nathan tried feebly to push him away, and with the weight of the man against him, Cy found it harder to extract the knife. He had to heave on it, and as it came free Nathan gave a little yelp. He was slipping sideways. Cy stabbed again but the blade bumped against his breastbone and would not go in. Cy grabbed his collar and stared into Nathan's face. The man was alive, and he gaped back, horrified. Cy rammed the knife into his throat. A series of spasms contorted Nathan's face and he made a gargling noise. As he toppled backwards he clutched

258

the boy and they sprawled to the floor beside the oil lamp. Nathan's arms flailed towards the dangerous flame. Cy tugged him away. He could still hear that gargling noise, and in the faint light he could see a new expression in Nathan's eyes – desperate, imploring; a look that seared into his brain. Nathan had begun to vomit blood. Cy was poised with the knife and Nathan stared at him, begging silently for his life. Those wounded eyes, beseeching him. That sickening thrill, the sense of power. Cy punched the knife in Nathan's eye.

Cy had blood on his hands and along his forearms. He was up to his elbows in blood and gore. But he continued to stab the man, eradicating his final plea with the knife. As Cy stabbed he sobbed, and his sobbing turned to savage laughter. Again and again he stabbed, pummelling the corpse. Dark blood slurped like oil from a punctured can.

Eventually Cy tired. He dried the blade on Nathan's trousers and tried to wipe off the blood, sticky on his hands. He would have to wash. A deadened calm settled on his shoulders. In the glimmering room the silence throbbed. Controlling his breath, he listened for the other couple along the hall. Nothing. He heard a car slip by.

Then he heard a cry. For a moment he thought Nathan had sobbed – one final gasp – but it wasn't Nathan. The noise came from outside. He heard it again. A grunt of breath. Then he realised it was the other couple making love. The woman cried out and tried to stifle it. The man was grunting as if in pain.

Cy picked up the oil lamp and searched around his makeshift bed for any possessions he should put in his bag. He found only the knife and his pair of shoes, which he pulled on. The sound of the other couple had regularised, but the man didn't seem to be enjoying himself. He sounded as if he were hauling a load up an interminable hill.

When Cy looked at the body it was a piece of meat. He felt inside Nathan's pockets and took out an ancient wallet and the tin of skunk. He used Nathan's handkerchief to wipe more blood from his hands but then gave up and dropped the dirtied rag onto the body; a single flower onto a grave. He collected his bag and Nathan's oil lamp and moved cautiously into the passageway. The noise of the other two was unchanged. The man was still grunting, while she came back with intermittent yelps.

By the light of the feeble oil lamp Cy began to pick his way downstairs to the lavatory, where he made a partially successful attempt to clean his clothes. He mustn't take too long, because at some point the other couple would surely reach a climax. Not that they were likely to get out of bed. They'd be too exhausted. Cy shook his head; sex was disgusting.

He let the tap run quietly. Soon he was soaking wet but at least the blood looked less obvious. He should be safe now in the streets. It was after midnight: to walk to Ticky's might take an hour. The little man could be relied upon to put him up and should know where to find an all-night launderette.

✳

'Sorry, Ticky, did I wake you up?'

'Yeah, but… Christ, I didn't know who it was.'

'Going to let me in?'

Once they were inside his flat Ticky grinned awkwardly: 'Did they throw you out?'

'I left.'

Ticky didn't appear to notice anything unusual about the way Cy looked – perhaps his clothes had finally dried – yet he seemed distracted, as if there were some other person in the flat that he didn't want the boy to see. Cy said, 'You look edgy, Ticks. Something wrong?'

'Everything's fine,' said Ticky unconvincingly. 'All tickety-boo. Are *you* all right?'

'No problem.'

Ticky frowned at him. 'Well, why've you come here – did someone try something?'

'I got fed up. What is it, Ticks, don't you want me here?'

'It isn't that.'

Ticky sat down, then immediately stood up. 'I'm worried, if you must know.'

'About me?'

'It's Mr Gottfleisch – you know, my boss? When you rang the door I thought it might have been him.'

'Oh yeah?' Cy wasn't really interested in Ticky's problems.

'He was the one who sent us on that job.'

Cy remembered. 'Oh, when we killed the guy. I forgot.' He smiled, realising that the memory of the earlier killing had been eclipsed. 'What does *he* want?'

Ticky looked anxious. 'He wants to talk to me – first thing in the morning.'

'So what?'

'Well, after the… after the cock-up, he kicked me out. Said he never wanted to talk to me again.'

Cy was tired. 'OK, so he changed his mind. Where's the blow-up mattress?'

Ticky knelt down to fetch it from beneath his bed. 'Gottfleisch doesn't change his mind. He's got in for me.'

Cy sat down. His legs were aching. 'Then don't go. Christ, Tick, you don't know how much I missed that stupid mattress.'

'Really?'

For one brief moment Ticky's cares appeared to lift. 'So you're not going back to that grotty squat?'

'No, I thought I might stay here for a bit.'

'Great.'

'If that's all right?'

'Of course it is.'

Ticky began pumping up the airbed. He looked more cheerful – no longer a spectre from the uncharted depths of one o'clock dreams. But Cy thought he had better get things straight: 'No dodgy stuff, Ticky. Don't try it on.'

Ticky grinned and reddened slightly – or perhaps he just looked that way from pumping the airbed. 'Oh, come on, leave it out! I mean, would I? I'm your mate.'

Cy gazed at him solemnly. 'Just don't. All right?'

'Sure, sure. You're fine with me. Safe as houses.'

He continued pumping. Cy could see Ticky's thoughts returning to the worries on his mind, so he asked, 'Do you *have* to see this Gottfleisch?'

'Oh, yes.'

'Just don't turn up.'

Ticky gave him a withering look. The kid didn't understand.

Cy asked, 'Want me to come with you?'

'Not wise.'

'Well, I was with you, wasn't I? In a way I started it.'

'All the more reason. No, don't be daft. Don't tangle with Gottfleisch, Cy.'

The boy shrugged. It seemed to him that Ticky was over-dramatising his boss's reaction. It was true that they had killed the guy, but they had got away with it – there was nothing to link the crime to them. It was just as well Ticky knew nothing about this latest mishap – that would *really* spook him out. Though again, Cy thought, there was nothing to link the crime to them. All they had to do was keep out of Soho for a bit. Keep their heads down in Deptford, in Ticky's flat.

The little man had stopped pumping, but was breathing heavily. 'There you are, Cy – all pumped up. Tight and bouncy as a young girl's backside. You should be comfortable on that.'

'Thanks, Ticky. I'll sleep like a baby tonight.'

TWENTY-EIGHT

Age had finally caught up with him. Well past forty, Gottfleisch could no longer manage close work without spectacles. At first he had been self-conscious in them, as if they were – as if? – because they were a sign of his growing older, his muscles easing into middle age. After a week he found it uncomfortable to read without the glasses, which had moved quickly from being an aid to his deteriorating eyesight to becoming an indispensable comfort, a welcome friend. Now he would sit at his large Victorian partner's desk – drawers and cupboards on either side to let the partners sit face to face – and would peruse his documents with the brisk efficiency of a corporate chairman. Or a corpulent chairman – but brisk, certainly.

He was studying a set of itemised insurance inventories provided by his occasional colleague Turmold, when Craig showed little Ticky in. The runt had clearly made an effort, Gottfleisch noted: he was wearing clean clothes and his most ingratiating manner. He goggled at his boss – either in fear of his summons or because he had not seen him wearing spectacles before.

'Where have you been?' Gottfleisch barked.

Ticky seemed puzzled. 'Oh, was I supposed to be here, sir? I thought—'

'Yesterday. I sent Craig for you.'

'I must have popped out. Good morning, sir.'

Gottfleisch glared at him. 'Morning?'

'Yes sir, it is, sir. Things are looking up.'

Ticky's desperate attempt to restore their old familiarity brought his blotched face out in sweat. He blundered on: 'Looking up, sir. Oh, yes. I reckon this election is all crap.'

'What?'

'Labour will never get in. No way.'

Gottfleisch groaned, removed his spectacles and rubbed his eyes.

'No sir, I mean, it's like the last time, isn't it? Like, five years ago they reckoned the Tories would get whipped. But come the day, well, that's when they stuffed 'em, wasn't it?'

Gottfleisch eyed him.

Ticky said, 'Which is good news, isn't it? People *say* they'll vote Labour but when it comes down to it, well, Labour always sticks the taxes up. People don't like it.'

'You never *pay* taxes.'

'No sir, but if I did. You take it from me, sir – Labour won't win. You'll be all right.'

Gottfleisch leant forward. 'Because I vote Conservative?'

Ticky looked nonplussed. 'Yes, of course, sir – you're rich.'

Gottfleisch sighed. 'Cast your mind back, if you'll be so kind, Ticky, to your abortive attempt to case the Keene household.'

Ticky seemed disconcerted. 'The old lady?'

Gottfleisch realised that the odious little slug thought he'd been called back about the Fyffe murder. 'The old lady. You recall what I sent you for?'

Ticky was turning to a different page in his memory. 'The old lady's house,' he said cagily. He hadn't prepared for this.

'You took your camera.'

'To photograph her pictures, sir.' He remembered that.

'And to look for anywhere the old lady might have kept a small hoard.'

'That's right, sir. Yes. But she came back before I finished. Mind, I'd done all the rooms by then. I think.'

'When I called on her I wasn't allowed to go upstairs.'

'Oh, I did, sir. I saw all the bedrooms, sir.'

'The roof? The attic?'

Ticky looked nervous. 'Did she have an attic, sir?'

'You tell me.'

'Oh, right. No, she didn't.'

'Did you look?'

'Um, yes, sir.'

'Are you sure?'

Ticky was cautious. 'Well, I couldn't finish the job, sir. She came back. Did she tell you she had an attic?'

'I ask the questions, Ticky.'

'Quite right, sir. Yes, you do.'

'You have nothing to smile about, Ticky. You screw everything up. On your next job you *killed* someone.' Gottfleisch tapped the desk with his spectacles. 'Fortunately the police don't seem to have got far on that investigation.'

'Oh, good, sir.'

'But it made Miss Keene a household name.'

263

Ticky winced.

'I want to know exactly what you saw in her house, because somewhere – are you paying attention? – somewhere she has a hiding place. It could be a large safe or even a locked room.'

He put his glasses down on the desk and stared at Ticky, who declared, 'I didn't see one, sir.'

'No attic?'

Ticky looked uncomfortable at Gottfleisch's persistence. 'I don't think so, sir.'

'A cellar?'

Ticky licked his lips as he thought back. 'No. No, there wasn't a cellar.'

'A room you didn't get into?'

'Oh, no.'

'A large rug or tapestry on the wall – one that might have concealed a door?'

'No, definitely not. I'd have moved it.'

'A door hidden behind a wardrobe?'

Ticky was shaking his head. 'There were a couple of sheds outside the house. One had logs in. And there was some sort of what-do-you-call-it in the back garden… um… like a bandstand.'

'Gazebo?'

Ticky looked blank. 'A summerhouse, kind of.'

'She wouldn't keep paintings in a summerhouse.'

'They'd get damp.'

'Exactly. The house, then: here's a sheet of paper. I want you to draw me a plan – room by room from memory.'

'Drawing's not my strong suit, sir.'

'Do it.'

Ticky stooped obediently towards the huge wooden desk, and began his crude drawing like a standing clerk in a Victorian shipping office. Gottfleisch watched the upside down, emergent artwork. He put his spectacles back on but it didn't make the drawing clearer. Ticky didn't seem satisfied either. He frowned critically. 'I could go back and look again.'

'And what would you do for me this time – kill Miss Keene?'

'Oh, no sir.' Ticky did his best to look insulted. 'I don't always cock things up.'

'No. There was a time when I could rely on you. I'll send Craig.'

'No, sir, this is *my* job. I'll do it properly this time.'

'You will not.'

'Please, sir, give me a chance to… make up.'

'No.' Gottfleisch took the sheet of paper. 'Well, you're no artist.'

Ticky grinned. 'I don't know, sir – I reckon I'm a dead ringer for Toulouse Lautrec. You remember Toulouse? One loo upstairs, one... out the back.' The joke died on Ticky's lips. 'No, but seriously, sir – I want to put things right.'

'No.'

'I know I screwed up, sir, but we go back a long way, you and me, and I'll do it right this time, sir, not a doubt.'

'Craig will go.'

Ticky hung his head and thought a moment. 'Mind, the cops are interested in her now, sir, so it will be risky. I mean, if Craig gets caught – which he might, sir, being he's just a driver—'

'Chauffeur.'

'He'd be linked straight back to you, sir. Being your... well...'
Gottfleisch waited.

'Chauffeur. Yes, I mean, if it was me, sir, and I got caught – which I wouldn't, being as... being as I'm professional, well, I couldn't, could I? No.'

'Couldn't what?'

'Be linked to you, sir. I mean, I don't drive you around the place. And if I was caught, sir...'

'Yes?'

'I wouldn't blab.'

'No.'

'I've always been loyal, sir, you know that.'

Gottfleisch studied him. Ticky had a point. And he *had* put on clean clothes.

For a late night programme it made quite an impact, don't you think? By claiming that Naomi's paintings were fakes, the wretched Strachey woman created an instant ripple in the market – according to the wireless today. On Kaleidoscope they said that owners had been contacting dealers all day for reassurance. And despite my leaving the receiver off the hook, two dealers managed to get through to me to ask whether I could refute her claims. Why should I help them? I suppose I'll have to. When a buyer pays a huge sum for a Naomi Keene it is she herself he is buying – not only her talent but her mystique and cachet. When a buyer acquires an original Keene he does so partly because that framed sheet of coloured paper was touched by the artist, but also because it was handled – even treasured – by someone famous. It has always been so. For many years collectors tussled to buy Queen Victoria's slipper, Napoleon's wallpaper, Marilyn Monroe's skirt. Ordinary people at auctions pay high prices for everyday items from stately homes or palaces. Wealthier patrons – equally insecure and uncertain in their tastes – pay absurd sums for Jacqueline Kennedy Onassis's cutlery or for the discarded costume jewellery of Mrs Wallace Simpson.

Much as I might wish collectors bought Naomi's paintings for their artistic merit alone, I know their commercial value is enhanced – no, transformed – by their association with some of the most powerful figures of the twentieth century. But last night the Strachey woman tried to rip that association asunder, saying that although the paintings have some artistic merit they do not have a definite link with Hitler's private world.

She is wrong. But how to prove it?

Naomi's paintings, like those of many artists, have swung in and out of fashion several times. Paintings lie dormant, begin to rise, escalate when too many collectors chase too few pieces, then collapse to more realistic levels as the false peaks fail. If one could be bothered to chart their mean values over the last twenty years, one might produce a graph very much like that of the Share Price Index. Both graphs would be erratic; tracing unpredictable trends in a complex market, driven by gamblers' moods. But would such a graph give a true representation of an artist's worth?

For a dead artist, perhaps. After all, once an artist is dead, what is there to say, other than what she is now 'worth'? Her work is done, her output complete; she herself gains nothing from today's opinions. All that remains are the works themselves and our present evaluation of them. The monetary value of Naomi's paintings will continue to fluctuate, as for any artist, according to quite arbitrary whims. Following Strachey's attack, Naomi's stock may briefly fall – though with continued media coverage it may as easily rise. Who knows? To find out, one would have to test the market – to release a newly discovered painting, perhaps. It would be the ultimate test. How much would the painting make?

If – I am supposing here – if someone did have such a painting, previously undiscovered, then that person would want to put it on the market just at the point Naomi's value surged. Collectors, after all, are investors – they apply investors' rules. They know about surges in value, the dangers of buying too early or too late. They know that sometimes a price may have been talked up, and that it may be wise to hold back and let someone else take the risk. But at the same time they know that a sudden interest can herald the start of a new dramatic surge, and that to miss buying now might be to place future opportunities beyond reach.

Naomi's next sale, then, must be carefully managed and timed. Don't you agree?

266

*

'Sidonie? Hugo Gottfleisch here.'

'Hugo.'

'It has been impossible to get hold of you. I imagine you're plagued by journalists?'

'And dealers.'

'Ouch. I suppose you feel trapped in the house?'

'I have been walking in the woods, out of earshot of the telephone.'

'Sidonie, could I... could I take you away from all this? Could I invite you to dinner?'

'My Goodness.'

'Tomorrow night, say? Here in Greenwich, perhaps.'

'Well, I'm not sure—'

'I know it's short notice—'

'To be honest, Hugo, I seem to have caught a slight chill. From walking in the woods, I suppose.'

'Don't worry about getting here. I could send a car.'

'I can still drive. I am not that old.'

'Excellent. You could stay here at my house.'

'I don't think so.'

'My house is cavernous. Three spare bedrooms, all warm and dry!'

'I am flattered at your invitation, Hugo – though I do have this chill.'

'Please. I can promise you some excellent sherry.'

'Sherry, Hugo? I don't come *that* cheaply.'

'Champagne?'

'That's better. Oh, I don't know... A night out might be rather fun.'

TWENTY-NINE

It wasn't often Ticky sang a song, as you'd have guessed from the tuneless drone he emitted, but he sang today. Things were looking up; back to normal.

> *'Ha, ha, ha. Hee, hee, hee.*
> *Little Brown Jug, don't I love thee?'*

For several years he had served Gottfleisch loyally. He had been as reliable and discreet as a solicitor. Anything told him was not betrayed.

> *'Little Brown Jug don't I love thee?'*

Even Ticky realised that part of the reason he could be trusted was that he never had anyone to tell. Few people talked with him, so Ticky was never trapped into warm cosy conversations which might lull him into sharing confidences.

> *'My wife and I live all alone*
> *In a little old flat we call our own.'*

The first friend he had had for ages was the teenage Cy.

> *'She loves whisky and I love rum.*
> *Between the sheets we have lots of fun.'*

Cy was waiting for him in the flat and seemed genuinely interested in what Gottfleisch had had to say. He wouldn't be fobbed off. What had Gottfleisch wanted? Had he threatened him? Ticky's attempts at vagueness got him nowhere. Keeping secrets was easier when no one asked questions.

'Was Gottfleisch going on about that Fyffe bloke again?'

'Not really.'

'But a bit?'

'Sort of. D'you want a cup of tea?'

'About something else?'

'I had biscuits somewhere.'

'Does he want you to do something?'

'I'll put the kettle on.'

'Have you got to burgle someplace?'

'I could swear I had some biscuits.'

Ticky emptied the kettle and refilled with fresh.

> *'I'll feed my sheep on finest hay*
> *And hee, hee, hee ten times a day.'*

Cy clicked his tongue. 'I mean, we did him together, didn't we? I've a right to know.'

'It wasn't anything to do with that. Did you eat those biscuits?'

'What *was* it about?'

Ticky paused. 'It was on a "need to know" basis.'

'A what?'

'It means you only tell someone who needs to know.'

'*I* need to know.'

'It was about something completely different.'

'Like what?'

Ticky ostentatiously checked the kettle, still far from boiling. He put two tea bags in the pot. 'They were chocolate biscuits, and all.'

'This job – can I come with you?'

'What job?'

'For Christ's sake, Ticky! Is it a break-in?'

'No.'

'It is.'

'It isn't.'

'I'm on for that.'

'You're not.'

'Ticky—'

'I shouldn't have taken you with me last time.'

Cy began fiddling with his Death's Head Ring. 'It was *my* fault, I suppose?'

'You could say that.'

'It wasn't my fault that bloke came bursting in. You said the place was empty.'

'The kettle's boiling.'

'Please let me come.'

Ticky strode into the kitchen. 'There are some things that a man just has to do. On his own.'

'You're not a fucking cowboy, Ticky. Why d'you have to be on your own?'

'Because I do.'

'Why?'

'Because Mr Gottfleisch says so.'

'Why?'

Ticky jerked the kettle and spilt boiling water on his hand.

The following morning Sidonie woke to find that she did have a chill. Presumably it was from the strain of recent days, she thought, exacerbated by her long stroll through the woods. She prepared some beef tea, though being made from a stock cube it wouldn't be the same. Last year, she remembered, stock cubes had disappeared from the shops because of a renewed scare about mad cow's disease. At the time she had laughed with Murdo: 'If I caught mad cow's disease, how would we tell?'

Neither the beef tea nor the aspirins at lunchtime shifted the chill. At her age to travel up to town, stay up late and sleep in an unfamiliar bed was not advisable. She had better postpone. Hugo would understand. He wouldn't mind.

✳

But he did mind. He had briefed Ticky to do the house while she was away – that was the point of the invitation. Her cold was an unexpected nuisance. He'd have to change the plan.

When he phoned Ticky there was no reply.

✳

Ticky already regretted bringing Cy along. The boy had persuaded him he could help steal a car, and Ticky remembered Gottfleisch's wrath when he thought Ticky had used his own car last time. Ticky dithered, and Cy pounced. What kind of car did he want? A fast one.

The boy brought him a Mondeo.

Ticky sniffed. 'That's boring.'

'Boring's what we need.'

Ticky wouldn't let him drive. Cy punctuated the journey with parodies of childhood songs, getting back at Ticky for 'Little Brown Jug', and Ticky became increasingly irritable. In Croydon he snapped at Cy to stop singing. The boy's flippant attitude did not bode well.

They drove in silence down the A233.

When they found her house Ticky cruised slowly past, stopped in a lay-by, turned and drifted back. He parked at the side of the lane, ten yards from her gate, in the shadow of a tree.

'You should park in her drive,' Cy suggested. 'We'll be off the road.'

'We're not parking in her front garden. It's a give-away.'

'It's not a give-away out here?'

Ticky looked along the lane. There was another hour until dark.

'She's left a light on,' he said. 'Upstairs.'

'And the downstairs hall. Trying to fool the burglars.'

Ticky removed the ignition key. 'She don't fool us.'

They got out of the car and walked to the gate. From a nearby tree a blackbird squawked incessantly. A small bird sang. They peered through the gate. As Ticky opened it the birds continued to sing.

When they approached the house the blackbird flew from the tree, screeching as it went. Ticky studied the front of the house but led Cy round the side. He touched Cy's arm.

'Remember,' he whispered. 'Professionals get in without breaking windows or anything. So no one knows they've been.'

'Then they walk out with the video? And still no one knows?'

'We're not taking anything.'

'We'll have to do a window,' Cy responded. 'There won't be a door open.'

'Ssh.'

'Why're you whispering? You said she wasn't in.'

Ticky whispered, 'Professionals do it silently.'

'Unless you pay extra.' Cy was examining the windows. 'None of these look easy. Is there a downstairs lavvy?'

'I think so, round the other side.'

'People don't lock their lavvy windows.'

As they walked along the back of the house they tried the kitchen door but it was locked. The glass had been replaced. Ticky was more chipper now: the ground floor was empty. He didn't want a disturbance like at the Fyffe house. – Disturbance? It made him shiver to think about it! They rounded the final corner and saw that the little lavatory window was ajar. Things were improving by the minute.

Cy asked, 'Who's going in?'

'You're the youngest.'

'You're the littlest.'

Ticky looked almost hurt. But he brightened and said, 'All right. 'Cos I know the way round inside.'

The boy helped him up and Ticky opened the window to its full extent. He straddled the sill and clambered inside. He was excited now. To walk illicitly along silent halls into dormant rooms where the only sound might be the clock ticking was a rare thrill. He couldn't deny it. There were people in the straight world who didn't know what this felt like.

In the kitchen the only sound was the hum of the refrigerator. He opened the garden door and Cy entered. 'Here we go, Ticks.'

'Ssh.'

'The house is empty, isn't it?'

'You never know who's walking by outside.'

Ticky reached into his pocket and drew out his grubby sketch plan of the layout, on which Gottfleisch had marked possible hiding places for the hoard.

'Best to start upstairs.'

They strolled through the empty lounge into the front hall and began up the thickly carpeted stairs. On the top landing a floorboard creaked. From one of the rooms came the sound of another clock.

The spare bedroom at the rear of the landing had a sloping roof. Gottfleisch had suggested there might be a cupboard in the dead space where the roof slanted, but that wall looked blank. It was papered. Ticky felt along the surface but found no cracks.

'Nothing here.'

Cy said, 'No built-in cupboards. It's really old fashioned.'

Back on the landing Cy pointed to a trap door in the ceiling. Ticky groaned. 'An attic. Would you believe it?'

Although the hall ceiling was low the trap was out of reach. Cy glanced into the bathroom. 'There's a chair in here but it's got a cane seat. You'd have to tread carefully.'

'The chair's too low anyway. We need a ladder.'

'Stand on my shoulders.'

'I'm not a bleedin' circus star,' Ticky muttered, but he slipped out of his shoes while Cy squatted down.

Cy braced his hands on his knees and Ticky placed one foot then the other on his back. Though the boy was squatting, Ticky felt precarious. He crouched nervously on Cy's shoulders, then placed his hands on Cy's head and balanced, knees bent, as Cy stood up. Once the boy was upright Ticky let go of his head and began to stand. All he had to do to steady himself was keep one hand on the wall.

Fully erect, Ticky pushed the trapdoor. It was loose. He pushed again, and as the trap moved it loosened a small shower of dirt and dust. Ticky pushed again, and the trap toppled back into the dark roof space.

'What are you doing?' came a voice.

Ticky froze. He glanced down to see an old lady in her dressing gown. *An old lady?* She held some kind of cane, an officer's swagger stick, and she jabbed Cy with it hard in the stomach. He gave a gasp and crumpled. Ticky wobbled, began to fall, and clutched desperately to the trap.

'Don't move!' she snapped.

Ticky dangled from the ceiling. Below him, Cy was getting up – but the old lady swished at him with her cane and clouted him round the head. Cy howled with pain.

272

She glared at Ticky. 'Come down.'

He couldn't hold on much longer but he didn't want to let go.

'Who *are* you?' she demanded

Ticky's arms hurt.

'You, boy! Stand up and face the wall.'

She turned to Ticky. 'Drop down.'

Ticky shook his head. His arms were hot with pain.

She raised her stick to him – and Cy suddenly rolled sideways, leapt to his feet and shouted, 'You old bitch!'

Ticky saw the knife Cy had stolen in the market. He yelled, 'No!' and fell to the floor. The old lady swung her cane at him to hold him back, but the boy was advancing – his knife extended. 'Drop that stick, you bitch.'

For a moment it seemed she might. Like a school mistress she slapped the cane against her palm. She twisted, pulled, and in one movement separated the cane in two. It was a swordstick! Ticky cringed. When she flicked her wrist a thin blade glittered.

Cy held his ground.

The woman spoke: 'Drop that knife or I'll whip your eye out.'

Cy grinned, and Ticky gaped at them. Though the woman looked as old as the Surrey hills she held her sword like a rapier. The boy did not move.

Ticky said, 'Let's get out of here. Come *on*!'

'No.'

Ticky's muscles were dissolving. But he couldn't leave this foolish boy to be skewered on her sword. He said, 'Just run. She'll never catch us.'

'She won't use that.'

Ticky grabbed him, and as they struggled the old lady stayed on guard. She was balanced. She did not look old. Ticky shouted at her, 'Back off and we'll go away.'

She said, 'Drop the knife.'

Ticky kept his hold on Cy. 'You better not use that sword, missus. You'll get done for murder.'

'I should care.'

She raised the blade.

Ticky dived at her, striking below the knees, and she fell instantly, suddenly frail. Ticky clambered across her, tugging the swordstick from her hand. Behind him, Cy screamed, 'I'll cut the bitch!'

As Ticky rose from the old lady, the swordstick trailing from his hand, he felt astonishingly dominant. 'Listen to me for once. Act professional.'

Cy stared at him.

Ticky turned to the old lady, cumbersomely rising from the floor: 'You don't want to get hurt, do you? Tell us where your safe is.'

'My safe?' she queried tremulously.

'Where the things are hidden.'

She was on her feet now, shaken but unbroken. 'I don't have a safe.'

'Where d'you hide your paintings?'

'My what?'

'Them paintings they was talking about on TV. Where've you hidden them?'

She shook her head. 'That wretched programme.'

Cy interrupted from behind: 'Listen, bitch, I'll cut your face open. Where are the fucking paintings?'

'There aren't any.'

'They were on the telly.'

She sniffed. 'You don't look the type to watch an arts programme.'

'Don't tell *me* what type I am! Just tell us.'

She shrugged. Cy stepped closer. 'I'll cut you.'

Ticky grasped Cy's arm. 'For Christ's sake.'

The old lady seemed to suddenly give up. Her head drooped. 'If I let you have my paintings, will you go?'

'Where are the sodding things?'

'All about you.' Wearily, she pointed at the paintings on the wall. 'I never bother to lock them up. I... I like to look at them.'

Cy glanced at one and touched it. But Ticky snapped, 'Don't give us that! This is just the ordinary stuff. Where—'

The telephone rang. Downstairs.

For several seconds no one moved. When the old lady tried to step forward Ticky stopped her, saying, 'Stand still.' He felt much stronger with her sword. A little pirate chief.

She said calmly, 'That'll be the police.'

'Belt up.'

The phone kept ringing. She said, 'After the publicity from the TV programme they keep an eye on me. They'll be phoning to say they're on their way.'

The phone didn't stop. She moved again. 'They have to check that I'm all right.'

As she came forward Ticky put out his hand. He felt her empty breast against his palm. 'I said shut up.'

The phone stopped. Its ringing echo hummed through the house.

Cy snarled, 'Let's get on with it.'

Ticky pointed the sword at him. 'Put your knife away.'

Cy stared.

274

Ticky said, 'I'm in charge now. Put it away.'

Cy hesitated but obeyed. He said, 'Did you get a look inside the roof?'

'Too dark. But you couldn't squeeze a big picture through that trap.'

Cy stared at the woman and sneered. '*You* couldn't climb up there anyway.'

She didn't answer. Cy turned away. 'I'll do the bedrooms. Look after the bitch.'

The boy marched into the main bedroom. Ticky and Sidonie followed, and watched the boy peering behind her furniture. He opened a closet and said, 'Nothing but old clothes. This could take for ever.'

'She won't run away.'

Cy put his hand in his pocket. 'I can stop her doing that.'

Ticky said, 'Give over. I'll tie her up.'

'Stick the sword in her,' Cy laughed.

'Check the other bedroom.'

Once Cy had left the room Ticky rummaged in the woman's dressing table drawers and found her tights. 'At the drop of a hat he'd stick his knife in you.'

'I'd say you had three minutes till the police arrive.'

'Bollocks.'

'Get out while you can.'

'See this sword?' He waved it threateningly. 'Maybe I should use it, like he said.'

She stared back, unmoved. The boy returned. 'Bugger all in that room.'

'Let's look downstairs.'

Cy went first, followed by the old lady. Ticky hesitated a moment with her swordstick, then he threw it on her bed. Best to keep it away from Cy.

Downstairs, while Cy crashed around looking for her hiding place, Ticky began tying the old woman up. He sat her in a dining chair and lashed each wrist to a chair leg. Then he tied her ankles together and anchored them to the chair.

Cy wandered back in. 'No sign of these sodding pictures – unless they *are* those on the walls.'

'The boss said she'd have them hidden. – Don't say his name.'

Cy grinned knowingly. 'Why not? Aren't you going to kill her, then?'

'Professionals never use real names. Look, the paintings must be somewhere – he wouldn't have sent us else. Let me take a peep.'

'I'll sit with the old lady.'

Ticky hesitated. 'No fear. Those sheds outside – take a look in them.'

As Cy went out, Ticky noticed for the first time that the light was fading. He glanced around her sitting room, then wandered off to the other room across the hall. More cupboards and drawers, none of them large enough to take a hoard – unless…

He climbed on a chair and with some difficulty lifted a large painting from the wall. But there was no wall-safe behind it. Where the painting had hung was only a rectangle of faded wallpaper. He left the picture on the floor and returned to the old woman, trussed up.

'You got a cellar?'

She stared at him blankly.

'Maybe you've got a safe in the floor.'

He watched her face for a reaction. Some hope: she was as expressionless as a lizard. He went back across the hall to the other room. In the centre of its wooden floor was a dark coloured rug, held down by the heavy table. Ticky wandered round the rug, lifting its edges to peer underneath. Without shifting the table he could expose most of the floor. This seemed promising, he thought – no cellar, but a concealed trap door. Perhaps that door would lead down to the cellar. Old houses often had trap doors – he had seen such things in films. Yes, he warmed to this idea. After all, Gottfleisch had seemed convinced she had the pictures in the house, and he'd also said they would be hidden. A secret trap door was something no one would have thought of – Gottfleisch hadn't, nor had Cy. What a terror that boy was! A beautiful kid but streetwise, a razor in a sheath. Having the boy sleeping in his flat had been exquisite agony. He had heard Cy breathing in the night, had sensed his naked boyishness beneath the blankets – Ticky's own blankets, in Ticky's room. It would have been so achingly easy to slip out of bed and into Cy's, to snuggle down with him. – Not that Ticky was perverted, but he couldn't help it if yes, he loved the boy. And surely the fact that Cy had come to live with him must mean that Cy liked him a little too?

There wasn't a trap door.

Ticky meandered along the hall, past the lavatory, to open the wooden chest by the end wall. Old lady's clutter. That red chalk drawing had been replaced above, but it was only a Boots' print anyway.

Back in the living room, Cy had not returned. Ticky approached the old lady and asked, 'All right, are you then, dear?'

From the straight-backed chair she glared at him.

276

When Ticky placed his hand on her shrivelled breast her face didn't flicker. He squeezed. 'Not much there,' he said, and moved away.

He was at the entrance to the kitchen when the back door burst open and Cy dashed in. 'I've found the buggers! They're in that summerhouse out the back.'

'Are you sure they're—'

But Cy rushed past him to confront the old lady in her chair. 'You stuck up old bitch, I've found your pictures. I've found them, you fucking Nazi scum.'

He reached in his jerkin and pulled out his knife. 'You fucking fascist pig.'

But she ignored the knife. She was staring at his hand – at the Death's Head ring on his middle finger – as he shouted, 'Those fucking Nazis *skinned* their prisoners – didn't they?'

Ticky grabbed his arm. But Cy pulled away. 'Bitch, you thought you'd hidden them.'

Ticky shouted, 'Stop it, Angel. For Christ's sake calm down.'

'I'll cut a swastika on your face. How'd you like that?'

Ticky kept his hold and stammered, 'You saw them in the shed?'

'The fancy summerhouse. It's got two rooms. One is full of lawn-mowers and stuff, but the other's where she—'

The door bell rang.

The woman drew breath to scream as Ticky slammed his hand across her mouth. They waited, and the door bell rang again. She began struggling, rattling her chair, and Ticky had to use his other hand to press her down. He hissed, 'Shut up or I'll set the boy on you.'

He glanced at Cy, poised, listening. From outside the house they heard a shoe scrape against the step. Cy whispered, 'I think they're going.'

There was a sound which might have been someone moving off. Anything. A scuff on gravel. Cy put his knife away. 'Could be the cops she said about.'

'Quiet. Wait.'

The woman began to struggle again. Cy muttered, 'D'you think they've gone or not? I'd better look.'

'Don't them 'em see you.'

Cy nipped across to the window and squinted into the growing gloom. Moving back, he said, 'Can't see no one.'

'Hang on a bit.'

'I won't let the cops get me. They'll send me back.'

Cy slipped across the room to the kitchen, but at the door he

collided with a large man coming in. The boy dipped for his knife –
but a heavy thump knocked him slithering across the floor. The man
was fast. His boot crunched down onto Cy's wrist and he stooped for
the hunting knife. Leaving Cy on the kitchen floor, the man rushed
on into the living room. Sidonie was tied to the chair. Ticky quivered
at her side. The huge man bore down on him.

Ticky spluttered, 'No, sir, I can explain—'

'Shut up!'

The same sweeping blow that had toppled Cy sent Ticky reeling
across the room. As Gottfleisch bent to untie Sidonie he heard the boy
shout from the kitchen, 'Right, you fascist pig! You fucking Nazi!'

Ticky tried to speak.

'Stay there,' barked Gottfleisch. He was trying to free the tangled
tights, but the fabric had shrunk into dense knots of nylon. So he
took the knife to them. 'Did they hurt you, Sidonie?'

'I'm all right, Hugo. How did you—'

'That boy who ran out—'

'He's just a hooligan, that's all.'

Gottfleisch glanced at Ticky. 'Where'd he go?'

'I don't know. Outside, sir. There's a summerhouse. He may
have...'

Gottfleisch repeated, 'Summerhouse?'

Sidonie said, 'I need a handkerchief.'

Gottfleisch plucked one from his breast pocket. 'What was that
about Nazis, Sidonie?'

'Oh.' She wiped her nose. 'He saw some paintings out there.'

'Naomi's?'

She nodded. Gottfleisch shot a glance back to the kitchen. He
frowned. 'Wait here.'

Gottfleisch stalked across and out into the kitchen. Ticky drifted
after him. Sidonie was so stiff she could hardly rise from the chair.

At the kitchen door Gottfleisch stared across the darkening
garden. In the summerhouse the lamps were on. He could see someone – obviously the boy – moving inside.

'He'll ruin them,' muttered Gottfleisch.

As he stepped forward the boy also emerged – backwards from
the summerhouse onto the deck, stooping as he came. Gottfleisch
hesitated. Then he saw that the boy was carrying a petrol can which
he was emptying onto the floor. 'Stop that!' roared Gottfleisch as he
charged onto the lawn.

The boy shouted, 'Fahrenheit 451!' and disappeared inside.

Ticky ran after Gottfleisch. They heard the boy call, 'This is what
the Nazis did to the stupid Jews!'

278

There came a muffled whoosh, a shout, a blaze of orange from within. Gottfleisch checked his stride, but Ticky rushed past him. He had almost reached the summerhouse when a flash of flame burst from the door. Ticky tottered. Gottfleisch stopped aghast. Then he saw little Ticky dash forward again, crying, 'No, my Angel, no!' Ticky ran in through the door.

Gottfleisch edged forward, his hand raised against the heat. Flames filled the window. Smoke spewed into the night. Using both hands to shield his eyes Gottfleisch inched nearer the open door. He heard a yell but couldn't see who had made it. He saw the flames, the garden furniture, and for one awful moment, a glimpse of Ticky staggering inside, his hands pressed against his face as he reeled through the blazing interior, calling something that Gottfleisch couldn't hear.

And for one moment as the smoke clouds shifted, Gottfleisch saw a painting on an easel – a Keene for sure – a last Naomi Keene consumed in flames.

Gottfleisch stumbled closer – despite the heat and acrid fumes – one hand outstretched towards the flames. But there was too much heat, too much scalding light. The wooden walls were now ablaze. Through running eyes Gottfleisch tried to peer inside, but there was only a riot of flaming red, yellow and gold. He could no longer see into the summerhouse. Nor could he see behind it, where a tiny figure leapt from a blazing window onto scorched earth.

The policeman said, 'Clearly the boy started the fire deliberately. But he used *your* petrol, so his action may not have been premeditated.'

'As if it mattered,' Sidonie sighed.

'You have a petrol lawnmower,' the policeman pointed out.

They were in her living room. Sidonie sat in her armchair, an additional blanket across her knees. The policeman wandered about the room. Gottfleisch busied himself making cups of tea and wished he had taken the opportunity to talk to her properly before anyone else arrived.

The policeman smiled reassuringly. 'Two of them, you say? And did their motive appear – if you'll excuse me – political, in any way?'

'Political?'

'Well, nothing was stolen, ma'am, and you did mention that the younger man was carrying on about fascist pigs and Nazis.'

'I'm not sure what he said.' Sidonie regretted she had mentioned this at all.

The policeman jiggled his pencil between his teeth. 'As you know, ma'am, there have been stories about you in the papers mentioning Nazis and… well, I believe, when you were young, you and your sister were, shall we say, sympathisers?'

He did not seem comfortable with this line of questioning: she was the victim, after all. Gottfleisch intervened. 'Miss Keene's sister lived in Germany during the Second World War, but that was a very long time ago.'

'Yes sir, but they've dug up the story again, haven't they? All of it, including… her unfortunate death. And, of course, the death of Mr Fyffe. Did these intruders mention Mr Fyffe at all – might they have been friends of his?'

'No.'

'Did they shout slogans of any kind?'

'No.'

The policeman looked at her. She added, 'I think 'fascist' was just a meaningless swearword. Young people today… I shouldn't have mentioned it.'

'Not at all, ma'am. The most insignificant details can sometimes turn out to be…'

'Significant? No, these were just would-be thieves.'

'You're probably right, ma'am. Though whatever their motive, it went horribly wrong for them.'

The fire engine had left ten minutes before, but two men were still raking through the ashes in her back garden. Gottfleisch looked out at them through the back window.

The policeman asked, 'Mr Godfrey – sorry, Mr Gott*fleisch*, sir – it was very fortunate that you arrived when you did.'

'Indeed.'

The policeman prompted him: 'Any reason for that at all?'

'We are friends, Miss Keene and I. She has a chill. I came to sympathise.'

The policeman digested this and wrote something in his note-book. When he looked up, he saw both Miss Keene and Mr Gottfleisch sipping their tea. He decided to wait for one of them to speak.

Gottfleisch put down his cup. 'Hooligans, by the look of it.'

The policeman nodded but didn't speak.

Gottfleisch added, 'Or the Anti-Nazi League, as you say.'

'I didn't mention that organisation specifically, sir.'

'No.' Gottfleisch glanced slyly into his cup. 'Point taken though.'

'Miss Keene, you will need to recall what you kept in the shed. It will help, you see, with the insurance.'

'You mean my summerhouse. It was not a shed.'

'Oh, quite. Fine building. Big. Might it be, then, that the summer-house – the building – was more valuable than its contents?'

'Undoubtedly.'

Gottfleisch looked away.

'So there was nothing especially valuable inside?'

'Well, there was *one* thing.'

Both men watched her expectantly.

'My lawnmower cost over a thousand pounds.'

✳

When one gives evidence of any kind one tells only a version of the truth – a sanitised, self-flattering version – to hide our guilt about what is being investigated. We may say we didn't witness the event at all, or we may say that we saw it more clearly than we did. We all have our little secrets, and we continually add to them. I told the policeman there was nothing valuable in my summerhouse – except the lawnmower! That was the truth, but not the whole truth.

I had lost little I could claim on my insurance. The paintings, of course, could not be insured. In the summerhouse there were what – five? – yes, five Naomi Keenes. On a good day, in exceptional conditions, they might have raised half a million pounds. No, I see you frown, no, not half a million. Not as much as that. Yet at what is called 'insurance value' – the maximum one might have to pay to replace the irreplaceable – one could put the paintings at a hundred thousand each. A determined buyer, you know, would pay that much.

Are you surprised I am so sanguine? Let me explain. First, I am too old to worry about what is irretrievably lost. (I lived through the war, remember, so this comes easily to me. I lost many precious things, and no amount of grieving can bring them back.) Secondly, in the last twenty years Naomi's paintings have brought sufficient income to leave me comfortably off. The fire destroyed only some additional income for the future, and for me the future is not something I need save up for. If I *am* spared to live a little longer, then who knows? Perhaps one or two more paintings may be discovered. It's possible.

Perhaps the world has enough paintings already. It is the *subjects* of Naomi's portraits – that tiny band who rescued and then sacrificed their Fatherland – who, after sixty years, need Naomi. Their official portraits are stiff and formal. Their photographs are worse – sludgy black and white shots from the Thirties. Statesmen and politicians at that time, unlike film stars, did not use studio photographers and retouch artists. They were caught unposed, in the harshest light. Men of that era appear to us as old, stodgy and unwashed. Even the golden men of the cinema seem unappetising now. From those dreary mono-chrome mementoes, how can the present generation see the attrac-tion of Himmler in his glasses, Goering in his bell-tent coat, Adolf with his uncapturable moustache? Only Naomi can reveal their personalities. But I knew them too, Hugo, I knew them well. I see them still in her soft water colours. Naomi's paintings rebut the familiar demonic images and show that these men were *not* phan-toms from Hell. We should not exclude them from the human race as if they were some kind of unique aberration. If you had met them, Hugo – and I do mean *met* them, not merely listened at some huge rally – you would have found them charming, entertaining and yes, likeable fellows with whom to spend a jolly evening.

You may cock your eyebrow – but are not villains often the most fun? I'll wager that you would have been (in more than one sense) enchanted by them – not only because you are such an old scoundrel yourself! Those men transformed their country – oh, here she goes, you say, banging on again – but try, just for a moment, to imagine how it felt to be an ordinary German between the wars. Their once proud race had been reduced to penury, to hyper-inflation, to massive unemployment and discontent. Within four short years – yes, Hitler in his manifesto said 'Give me just four years', that was all he needed – within four years he rebuilt Germany and blew new life into empty lungs. The crippled country stood up and ran.

I admit that people didn't notice *how* he succeeded, but only noticed that he had. But his success was *not* achieved through trick-ery. – Oh yes, it was, you say. But if it was, if success could be bought so easily, wouldn't every politician pursue that path? Nor was his success achieved through fear, as people claim. You can bully a nation into obedience but you cannot bully it into optimism and achievement. The unwelcome truth, Hugo, is that Hitler and his notorious cabal *inspired* their people. I know there was a price to pay – a terrible price – but by then the Germans were running so fast they could not stop.

Think of the early years, the first half of the 1930s; think of the triumphant regeneration and ask yourself, what did those Nazi lead-ers *do* that others were not able to do before? The country had tried left wing, right wing, centralist governments, and each had piled calamity onto calamity. Why did Hitler succeed? Was it really because he was the devil in disguise?

Yes – say the countries that defeated him. After the war, when the full horror of the camps was known, who could stand up to say, wait, there is another story, things were not as straightforward as they may seem?

Nobody dared.

Nobody dared tell Poland it was their country that carried out the first massacre of the war. On the very first day, the Poles massacred several thousand German civilians – several *thousand* – simply because they were living peacefully in the northern territories that had been taken from Germany some years before. The Poles massacred them – yes, I use the word – *massacred*: women raped, husbands slaughtered, babies smashed against the wall. Do people remember this, Hugo? It is recorded.

Nobody dared tell America that they fought the so-called war of racial purity with white and black soldiers segregated into separate regiments. America interned a quarter of a million Japanese-American civilians and subjected them to ferocious racial bigotry, stole their houses, destroyed their businesses.

Nobody dared tell England they slammed seventy thousand aliens into concentration camps. None had a trial. None had committed any crime. But because they were not of true British stock those people were crammed into rat-infested prisons. (Most of them were Jews.) In 1940, England knew she was losing the war – she had been driven out of Scandinavia, she had fled Dunkirk. At night the Luftwaffe destroyed British towns. You cried out for someone to do the same to Germany – to 'give it back with knobs on' as newspapers said. In the Battle of Britain you played your final card.

—And against the odds, you won.

But what if you had not? What if, as the whole world expected, you had lost that airborne battle; what then? As weary, war-torn Britain sank further into the unimaginable mire of death and near starvation; as every British family suffered with at least one family member dead; as every city and town saw its buildings bombed with impunity; as every week brought desolate news of 'glorious' retreats, of reversals, of territory lost, of ships sunk and men captured, of ever tighter food rationing, of a lowered age for military conscription, of gloom, misery and death – how would you feel, Hugo? With interminable months dragging on into another year; with your children visibly malnourished, your doctors increasingly burdened, your medicines no longer available; with another ship sunk and another thousand British servicemen lost at sea – how would you feel about the seventy thousand alien prisoners sitting out the war in safe British camps; eating British food and being kept in good health with scarce British medicine?

Imagine holding a wretched child in your arms, Hugo – in your house, perhaps, if it were still standing – imagine weighing its life against the lives of those prisoners. Wouldn't you say, 'My child comes first'? In other words, the prisoners come second. We British are half starved, you would have said, we are shabbily dressed, sick and appallingly housed: let the prisoners come second. They are aliens, our enemy.

And if at this desperate time Churchill had stopped pampering the aliens, had stopped lavishing on them your food, medicine and clothes; and if those precious commodities then became a little more available in the shops, wouldn't you have praised Churchill's wise move? You wouldn't notice *how* he had succeeded, you would only notice that he had.

Let me ask one final question. Among your miserable citizens, who would be the ones running the camps? Who would be the warders, what kind of people? Wouldn't they, like all warders, have been brutalised by their experiences; wouldn't they have detested their surly prisoners and told you that only by discipline could order be maintained? Remember, you have told the warders that prisoners must come second to your citizens. How would they translate your command?

Let the prisoners eat less. Let them be more densely housed. If prisoners fall ill, let them die. These words seem hard, but remember: your people are sick, they live in towns pummelled into the ground. And by this time the warders are brutalised – small numbers of tired men, herding prisoners in droves. The more prisoners that die, the more the burden will be eased. It will even ease the burden for the prisoners' companions – so let a prisoner die for fellow prisoners; the sick have a duty to die.

Ah, you recoil, Hugo. But you had these camps in England: seventy thousand aliens, plus fifty thousand other criminals, plus Goodness knows how many prisoners of war. Your civilised reaction today, Hugo – a luxury of peacetime – is to recoil from my pitiless words. But what would you have said in wartime?

No one learns anything from war. One side wins, another loses, life goes on – but both sides remain convinced that right was on their side. That is why many wars are refought a few decades later. Perhaps the Second World War was unique: because of the Holocaust and its attendant, hugely publicised notoriety, the defeated Germans could not persist in the belief that they had been right. Succeeding generations have been browbeaten by that notoriety. The war, we're told, was all the fault of the beastly Germans. Yet they had a legitimate cause. You may not agree with it, but their case should be heard. If we are to learn anything from that dreadful war we should face the facts. After fifty years, Hugo, it is time to blow away the myths.

THIRTY

It was fairly late but the pubs had not started turning out, and London streets were relatively empty. Cy meant to abandon the Mondeo in the outskirts but had changed his mind and continued on towards the centre. It was a risk, of course – not because the car was stolen and some cop might recognise the plates but because, whatever he thought of his abilities, Cy looked too young to drive a car. But he gambled that as long as he drove steadily and unobtrusively he would be safe. There was no reason he should be stopped. He wanted to keep the car until he was within walking distance of the West End, because outside the car he would be vulnerable. Out on the streets he would stand out, a young kid late at night. He was fourteen and a half, and looked it. He wondered what it would be like to be eighteen, a real grown man. For that he would have to wait three and half years – a quarter of his lifetime, though it felt like *half* a lifetime- three and a half years: could he survive that long?

Maybe he shouldn't return to the West End. They wouldn't let him back into the squat and – oh Christ, he'd forgotten Nathan. The blood and mess. What had happened about that? When he and Ticky had done the Fyffe guy it made headline news, but about Nathan there had not been a word. But Cy hadn't been listening to the radio.

He'd go to Waterloo. Around the station in the arches were plenty of places he could sleep – the arches attracted vagrants and winos of every kind: outdoor dormitories where the homeless huddled for security. Police turned a blind eye. Homeless people had to bed down somewhere and if they created nomadic camps where no one lived, that suited everyone.

Or he could sleep inside the car – which would be warmer, although even with locked doors it would not be safe. He was tempted to head for Ticky's, but…

Cy couldn't understand why Ticky had followed him into the blazing summerhouse – hadn't he realised Cy would get out? Christ, Cy hadn't torched the place to kill himself. No way. He could not

285

make Ticky out. Plunging after him into the flames was suicidal, and Ticky had been paranoid about fire. He had told Cy that story about the fairground where he'd rescued the child but had been caught himself in the fire. At the time, Cy had neither believed nor disbelieved it. But nor had he believed that Ticky would follow him into the summerhouse. And when he did follow he had not believed the little man would not get out. It was the sort of thing Cy didn't want to think about. He had heard Ticky scream. Even now, he could see Ticky's waxen face melting in the flames. Poor little sod. No one liked him, that was the trouble, he had had no friends. And yet in the end, despite what people thought of him, he had laid down his life in friendship. Cy shook his head. Well, he wouldn't forget him. A guy like that would be an inspiration in later life.

Perhaps among the dossers at Waterloo he'd find someone new to hang around with, someone who might turn out to be half the friend Ticky had been. But no, anyone around that place was more likely to make trouble for him. Cy was mature enough now to gauge how people were. Ticky had been OK. But he was gone. He was history. For every Ticky there would be a hundred Nathans. Cy slipped his hand into his pocket and closed his fingers around the handle to his knife. He wasn't worried. He was a big boy now.

Suddenly he became aware of lights flashing behind him. He knew instantly they were police. He thumped the steering wheel. How had the bastards got onto him so fast? He accelerated. He was in a stolen car: they must have seen him, thought something wrong, and radioed through to the national computer. That was incredible. He shook his head. What had he done wrong? It wasn't fair.

Well, if they wanted a game, he would show these fascists how to play. He rounded a corner, surged hard away, shot down the centre of the wide empty road. Behind him the police car closed the gap. It's lights were flashing. The siren started. This was more *like* it!

Cy pressed forward, foot to the floor. He sensed the police driver pull out, come alongside, glance in at Cy, then effortlessly slip past to block his path. Which was what Cy had expected him to do.

Once the police car was in front Cy made an exhilarating hand-brake turn. The Mondeo reared like a startled donkey, almost burst a tyre, and while the world spun crazily the metal chassis grated on the tarmac.

But by the time the cops had squealed to a halt, Cy's Mondeo had swivelled a hundred and eighty degrees and started away. Cy was so excited that he slammed into fifth gear instead of third and lost a second or two. But while the cops were still executing their three point turn, Cy shot ahead, took the first left, and squeezed into a narrow lane.

He took two rights to double back. Shit! A cul-de-sac. No – he could see an alley on the left. Cy snatched at the wheel and hit the brake, and the Mondeo wallowed sideways and hit the corner. It jumped out of gear but didn't stall. Cy found first and slammed the Mondeo forward, parting from the wall with a shrill shriek of scraping metal.

As he increased speed he heard the car dragging chromium along the ground. Cy braked, slewed at right angles and leapt out. He started running down the alley and had reached the corner when the cop car appeared behind. They had taken the corner at speed – they saw his car too late – and rammed it. Quite a smash. Cy shouted with joy as he ran out of the alley. He was free. On top of the world. Better than Ecstasy.

He heard a shout, glanced behind, tried in vain to increase his speed. The cop hurtling after him was six foot three. He was a black guy, and he could sprint like Linford Christie.

THIRTY-ONE

Gottfleisch leant back from the dining table. 'You've lived alone too long, my dear – this torrent of words...' He smiled easily, relaxed. 'I haven't enjoyed a chat so much in years.'

'A chat?'

'Oh Sidonie, I live an intellectually impoverished life. We must talk more often.'

'As long as I don't mention the war?'

Gottfleisch smiled.

She inhaled the fragrance of the wine. The low light in the room softened the web of lines across her face and emphasised the bone structure beneath. She had an ageless quality.

'I remember the *first* Great War, the war they said would end all wars. We really believed it, Hugo, for a time. Yet such carnage. Such loss. We expected a glorious adventure. Wars often begin that way, don't they, with optimism and enthusiasm? When the First World War broke out, men everywhere rushed to enlist. Imagine it! Well, they must have learned their lesson, because in the Second World War, they enlisted warily.'

She twirled her glass slowly, staring into the residue of the wine without drinking it.

'In 1914, I remember being driven by my father to the recruiting office to see him enlist. A family outing. Many families went with their brave young men. Mothers and children waited outside flag-draped town halls while their heroic men went in to enlist.'

'Weren't you frightened for them, going off to war?'

'War was glamorous. And my father was one of the first men to enlist. While he was inside the Town Hall I stood on the steps with a bunch of ribbons in my hand, giving one to each young man as he came out. We all laughed about it. Such naive days.'

'Your mother laughed?'

'Oh, perhaps she was tearful underneath – but to me, a little child, Mother seemed to laugh with everyone else.'

'How did your sister feel?'

'Oh, she was… I don't know.'

'She was too young?' Gottfleisch held her gaze. 'In 1914, my dear, your sister Naomi was four years old and you were only two. I'm surprised you remember it so well.'

'Perhaps it was a little later than 1914 – but it remains an indelible memory, an incredible day.'

'Indeed. One that Naomi might remember.'

Gottfleisch wiped his finger around his plate and smiled. 'Earlier this evening, before that wretched boy set your summerhouse alight, I noticed a painting on an easel.'

'Naomi's, yes.'

He licked a crumb from his finger. 'Last time we met, you invited me to call you Sidonie. What should I call you now?'

'I'm sorry, I don't—'

'In 1914 you were two years old, yet you remember it as if you had been four. Now, though you cannot paint, you have a painting on your easel. In your studio.'

'So I could examine it.'

'That won't do,' he said. 'But I see now why you are the only source of Naomi's paintings.'

'I'm not the only source—'

'The true source. Don't worry, my dear, I shan't surrender you to justice!'

She paused before asking wearily, 'What on earth do you mean?'

'It wouldn't be in my interest, after all.'

Gottfleisch smiled.

She said, 'This is a preposterous suggestion.'

'Let's not pretend.'

She inhaled slowly as if she might be about to explain, but in the end did not.

Gottfleisch prompted: 'I imagine it was your sister who died in the crash?'

'That's right,' she replied eagerly. 'Naomi was so very scared. She tried to escape and drove too fast—'

'You are Naomi, aren't you?'

'Of course not.'

'Come, come, it isn't a crime to impersonate your sister – is it, Naomi? After all, your sister Sidonie returned from America almost penniless while you, Naomi, were the legitimate inheritor. At least, I assume that part of your story was true?'

'All of it was true.'

He smiled conspiratorially. In the subdued light Gottfleisch

289

looked almost as old as she. With a wave of the hand she admitted, 'Most of it was true.'

She moved her wine glass to the centre of the table as if, where it was, someone might accidentally knock it over. 'I was the beneficiary.'

She gazed at him across the table. 'Oh, you may be right. Perhaps I don't have to continue this impersonation – except that after fifty years it's easier to continue than to stop.'

She gave a continental shrug. 'When I told you that... that Naomi was frightened to come home, I was telling the truth. She was – I was terrified, weak with fear. It may seem irrational to you now, but then, in 1947, with the world still shuddering from war, I was a traitor in my own land. Let me make this clear: traitors were being executed. You remember Lord Haw-Haw – William Joyce, the American, not even British, whose only crime was to broadcast propaganda from Germany, the country he believed in? After the war he was captured. He had a mockery of a trial, then the British hanged him – just for what he'd said. Well, Hugo, whatever you think of William Joyce (and most British listeners laughed at him) he was surely entitled to his opinion? He wasn't British, so why should he fight on the British side? He killed no one. Under what kind of justice could Joyce be hanged? Only the justice of civilised victors. Meanwhile in Germany they held the Nuremberg trials – and executed another clutch of people. Please Hugo, remember who I was: a fascist, a Nazi sympathiser, a friend of Hitler and his gang, the mother of a German baby—'

'Mother?'

'Oh.' She sighed and closed her eyes. 'There are things I haven't told you. But the baby stayed in Germany. I returned alone.'

Gottfleisch moved to a safer subject: 'But you were wealthy. Your parents' money had become yours.'

'What was left of it. That was why... That was why Sidi wanted to talk to me, of course. The money was here in England, where neither of us could get at it. I was living in Switzerland – if you could call it living, I was very poor. I needed my inheritance. Sidi got in touch with me, saying that to release the money we must both come back.'

Her face crumpled as if the late hour was taking its toll. Gottfleisch gently prompted: 'And you met her at your old family home?'

She nodded. 'Refill my glass, please, Hugo. There's a dear.'

✳

Let me tell you what really happened. Sidi and I had re-established contact. The tales I told you of America were true – only they were true for her and not for me. She married Mitch etcetera and sat out the war there, but afterwards she didn't rush back to England's battered shore. Why should she? England was in tatters; she was better off in America. But she realised that we would have to come home to claim the inheritance – *my* inheritance, yes, it was mine: that part of the tale was true. Mother had always favoured me, but I wasn't grateful. Instead, I was profoundly uncomfortable: guilty to have been preferred. But as Sidi said, there was no point in letting the money rot. So I agreed we should return, though I insisted it be in the strictest secrecy. I cannot stress too strongly how frightened I was of my countrymen. They had imprisoned Sidi in 1940 (yes, that was Sidi; it wasn't me) and despite never finding anything that they could charge her with they kept her in jail for almost a year. What would they do to *me*?

I slunk back home.

When I arrived at the house, Sidi was already there. She had been back several days and had brought all her possessions and clothes back from America. She intended to stay. From the start Sidi seemed cold to me – not wanting to be beholden for the money, I supposed. But I behaved as if nothing were wrong, as if I hadn't noticed, as if we were loving sisters again. And slowly Sidi thawed. Conversation began to flow. I learnt of her American experiences, little realising how soon I would adopt them for my own.

On the second evening she remained on edge. We ate a dreary meal – and drank that whisky. There was no fuel to light the fire and the house was freezing. Our conversation became strained. The minutes ticked by so slowly that time itself seemed stiff with cold.

Then came that ring at the front door. In fact, the only thing substantially different to what I told you earlier is what happened next. But it is getting late now, and it's time to tell the truth.

I heard the doorbell and sat petrified. It sounds melodramatic, I suppose, but that night I felt the noose around my neck. I didn't move when Sidi got up to answer the door.

Did she go to it? I am no longer sure. What I do remember is that rough male voice: 'Open up. Police.'

I seemed to have lost the will to resist. I could not move. To have survived the war and now to be captured in my own home! I felt completely drained.

We must flee, my sister said. I nodded dumbly. She took my hand and pulled me from the chair. Perhaps she slapped me – I don't know, but some kind of strength began to return. I felt hope again. Until they laid hands on me I would have a chance.

The doorbell rang again. But by then Sidi and I had run out through the back and were slipping through the courtyard towards her car – actually, it was Mother's car, which had been laid up on bricks in our garage; Sidi had been using it.

So the two of us – not Sidi alone, or Naomi as I told you earlier – jumped in and roared away. I saw the policemen waiting at the front and somehow the sight of their faces in the night made me realise there could be no escape. I turned to Sidi but she shrugged me off, her face distorted with delight. She was enjoying this. I was astonished. I remember thinking that America must have wrought some change in her: she was playing Cops and Robbers as if in a film. Then, as we hurtled through dark narrow lanes she glanced across at me and in an unreal voice cried out, 'We mustn't let them catch you, darling. They'll claim that by running away you are acknowledging your guilt.'

As she turned away I saw a smile flit across her face. I cried, 'You *want* them to catch me, don't you? You phoned them. That's why they came.'

Sidi laughed aloud – and began to reduce speed. I imagined the police behind us in the narrow lanes. 'Mother's little darling,' she said.

I screamed, 'Please go faster!'

But Sidi laughed again and slowed a little more. We were going no faster now than on an evening drive. She said – and I remember exactly her final words: 'When they hang you, darling, I'll be so sad – as next of kin.'

And I grabbed her, punching, scratching at her face. She let go of the wheel – and in one seamless moment the car jolted and shot off the road. It smacked against a tree, spun sideways – headlamps spraying through the dark – then rocked over and crashed. I remember sudden blackness, headlamps gone. I remember realising that the car was lying on its side, and that I was crumpled across Sidonie. As I clambered from the mangled car I trod on her, and I hardly noticed that she didn't move. My only thought was to get out. I stood in blackness beside the car. It was a huge dark mass, wheels towards me, and though the engine had stopped running, something inside still hissed. The metal creaked like a kettle about to boil.

I don't remember worrying that it might catch fire – I'm not sure cars do, except in films. Then, in that odd calmness which can descend, I reached inside towards my sister. Even as I touched her I realised that her head had become wedged between the door pillar and a piece of engine which had burst through the dash. The steering wheel had come away. I didn't touch my sister again. I had touched enough dead people in the war.

The air was cold. It was horribly dark. I stood motionless as a ghost and watched a car's headlamps flow along the lane. I knew it was the police car passing by.

I occasionally wonder how long I waited in that field. Given the cold, it was probably no more than a few seconds. But I didn't panic, I didn't run. It was as if I wasn't really there. This wasn't me. This wasn't England. This wasn't the car... which had...

I drifted away. That is exactly what I did – I drifted through the darkness across empty fields. I was still in the field when I heard the police car stop and groan into reverse. I glanced across my shoulder and saw its headlamps filtering back between the roadside trees. But I continued walking. I didn't run. I walked like a sleepwalker across wet fields. I remember the black, damp and chilly night. I remember hearing policemen shout – but they were shouting at each other, not at me.

In the house I cleaned my shoes, then went upstairs to change. When the police finally came to the door – and they did take an extraordinarily long time – I had dressed as Sidi and I gave Sidonie as my name. Apart from Sidi's American clothes, the only other attempt I made to disguise myself was to pin up my hair to hide its length. The following day I cut it as short as hers had been. I continued to wear my sister's clothes.

I told the police – tearfully, rather incoherently – that Naomi had physically prevented me from opening the door to them, and that she had driven off in my car. I let them break the terrible news to me before I allowed myself to become distraught.

Later, I insisted on a quiet and private funeral. Soon afterwards I left for Switzerland, travelling under Sidi's name, of course, but reverting to my own for a time in Zurich. After a while, I tried to get to Germany, but in the Forties it was too complicated – and in my case could have been dangerous. So I stayed in Switzerland several years, returning home in 1952.

THIRTY-TWO

'I claim my right to silence.'

In the harshly lit police station these were the only words that Cy had uttered. He said them twice – first, when cautioned by the Duty Officer, then again in the bleak interview room when a sergeant replaced the DO. Cy knew better than to speak. The sergeant emphasised the caution: Cy had the *right* to remain silent, but…

Cy said nothing more.

When the sergeant left they switched to a woman officer. She seemed sympathetic, going so far as to roll her eyes behind the sergeant's back as he left. A bit obvious, Cy thought: Mrs Nice Guy. She told him she wasn't concerned about the joy-riding offence, she'd just take his details and fill in the form. He did not react. She asked name, address, previous address, was there anything he'd like to tell her about his parents? He stayed shtum.

'You'll need a solicitor, young man.'

As she tidied her uncompleted papers her smile became less friendly. 'Is there any particular solicitor we should call?'

He shook his head.

'Anyone you've used before?'

He did not reply.

'Then you can have the duty one,' she said. 'Though it may be an hour or so till he comes in. What name shall I tell him?'

Cy looked away.

*

The smell of bacon and fried tomatoes. The crunch of toast. As Gottfleisch poured tea into her Limoges breakfast cup he beamed like a chef.

'Start the day with a proper breakfast,' he declared. 'Then you won't be nibbling through the day. Take it from one who knows.'

'I can't normally be bothered.'

'A great mistake. I should have thought that someone of your generation—'

294

She shrugged, and began spreading butter on her toast. The pretty plate matched her breakfast cup and the butter knife with its mellowing bone handle was pleasingly old-fashioned. 'It's nice to be waited on for once.'

'The least I could do, in return for a bed.'

Gottfleisch helped himself to some sugar lumps, then stirred his tea and licked the spoon. 'All these years, and you've not stopped painting.'

'Let's not go back to that.'

'But I'm interested – naturally. I was wondering as I lay in bed: nowadays you turn out – what? – one fresh painting a year?'

'Fresh is hardly the word I'd use. My paints are ancient, and I have a tablet of pre-war cartridge paper. It's rather tedious, if you must know – painting from memory, not allowing my style to develop in any way. I was freer in the Fifties, when no one was interested in what I did.'

'Because Sidonie couldn't paint?'

'In those days I travelled back and forth to Switzerland. I had a flat in Zurich – in the centre, which is far more bohemian than you might think. I dabbled in pop art and symbolic wall-hangings. Can you believe it? Ha!'

Her face lit up.

He asked, 'What happened to them?'

'Oh, they were Fifties trash. Everyone was churning the stuff out, but no one bought it.'

She chuckled as she drank her tea, then took a dainty bite of toast. Gottfleisch cut another slice of bread. He'd let her reminisce.

'All our output was derivative, you see? In the Sixties things became healthier – we had no interest in the past. We lived for the day, like grasshoppers. But even those laughable Sixties paintings I destroyed. It was *my* choice, do you see? If I didn't want it I destroyed it.'

Gottfleisch was spooning out more marmalade. 'Were all your original paintings destroyed in the war?'

'Practically all. There were one or two in England which survived. But everything I had in Germany... paintings... far more important things...'

'You had the baby.'

She looked down, and Gottfleisch waited. He wouldn't spread his marmalade until she spoke.

'Little Klaus,' she whispered. 'How very German!'

She glanced up with a smile of pain. 'He survived the blitzes with me in Hamburg. Oh, that sounds nothing to you now, nothing.

England had blitzes. We've heard so much about the gallant cockneys in the Blitz. Well, in Germany, every city, one after the other, was flattened to the ground. In Hamburg, where I lived with little Klaus and my husband Albrecht, the first real blitz came in July '43. It was dreadful – the noise, the shaking ground. We rushed to communal air raid shelters in the streets. They were well designed, those shelters, with benches down each side, but when the bombs fell there was standing room only. Indeed, some people were locked out. They would rush from street to street but of course, if you were out of your area, and people did not know you... Well, we were lucky. Because of Klaus I was usually allowed to sit.'

She paused to finish her cup of tea. Gottfleisch wondered whether he would appear insensitive if he cut more bread.

'One could not sleep through such a barrage. On the first morning when we emerged, we saw a number of buildings clearly damaged, but things didn't seem too bad. Then the authorities began counting bodies. In Hamburg, in that one night, we learned that fifteen hundred people had been killed.'

She lifted the lid of the teapot and peered inside.

'Fifteen hundred Hamburg citizens in a single night. That day everyone was sombre. We did not know, of course, how very *few* fifteen hundred was. Soon there came a night when we had forty-eight thousand deaths – in Hamburg, on a single night! Can you imagine it – forty-eight *thousand*? Of course you can't. In that single night's bombing, Hamburg suffered more deaths than London did in the entire war. They say it was the night Germany lost the war. It certainly felt that way to us, but during the blitzes Hamburg alone lost more civilians than the whole of Britain did in the war. Imagine it. We had two months of incessant bombing. Large parts of the city were completely destroyed. American airplanes dropped phosphorous bombs which caused more fires than could be put out. The streets became so hot the tarmac melted. Some of the houses had been built of wood, but *any* house hit by phosphorous burned to the ground. They burned all day. As you picked your way along a street a burning building might collapse beside you. The sound of tumbling walls, the blast of heat... The very streets seemed to catch alight. Blazing branches fell from the trees. Even when not under attack, the city was continually smouldering. Everything became coated with soot – the streets, the walls, our clothes, the food we ate. Soot got everywhere. By August there were so many dead we had to burn their corpses. The city reeked of smoke. You couldn't tell whether the smell was from burning buildings or burning flesh. At the peak of the blitz, permanent black clouds of smoke hung over the city and, as if anything could increase the gloom, it rained incessantly for days and days. One of the many direct hits was on the redbrick prison – fancy that: since the prisoners could not get out, they roasted and suffocated in their cells. Rough justice, was it not? By then, of course, we had no phones, no electricity – certainly no mail or newspapers – no public services of any kind. Because of the breakdown in electricity none of the cold storage plants could work; meat was rotting in the warehouses, so they threw open the stores to the starving public. By that time – oh, this was still 1943, you know: only two more years of war to go – by that time the whole city had been overrun by rats – hordes of huge terrifying rats up from the sewers. Ugh, I can still see them.'

Gottfleisch nodded glumly. 'Did you remain in Hamburg throughout the war?'

Albrecht wanted us to move somewhere safer, but there was nowhere safer one could go. Every town of any size was being flattened. And since Albrecht worked in the Hamburg suburbs at Rendsburg we couldn't leave – not until the following year, when suddenly *I* had to leave. By then, in 1944, Albrecht had been transferred from the Rendsburg camp to a more dangerous posting behind the Western front, where his medical skills would be more useful. Klaus and I were camping out in the concrete garage next to what had been our house. One day in the previous December, you see, we had come up from shelter to find our own house had been bombed. It was rubble, our possessions smashed. My paintings, of course, were destroyed, but all I thought about were our warm winter clothes and the few pathetic Christmas presents I had bought for little Klaus. When we searched the rubble for bits and pieces I found the Christmas tree. It was large and easy to spot, but the presents were lost – most of our things were lost. Every day I picked through the gritty rubble, shifting planks and masonry with my bare hands to retrieve odds and ends from underneath. Any clothes that I pulled out looked like a tramp's discarded rags. But one day I found a cup, I remember, one unbroken china cup.

I kept it with me for months.

Living in a garage was not unusual in Hamburg. As the lovely buildings crashed to the ground the dispossessed families sought any shelter that remained. They lived in cellars, in reassembled garden sheds – and in concrete garages, which were strongly made. Unless a garage received a direct hit it would remain standing even when the house next to it collapsed. Houses which did survive became like guest houses, each spare room offered to neighbours or homeless friends. Hamburg developed a great spirit of community, as they say.

Until 1944. Then a law was passed – they were always passing laws – forbidding anyone other than a true German to share the communal air-raid shelters. By 1944 I had lived in Germany so long I thought I *was* German. Admittedly, since the raids first started, the shelters had excluded... some people, but I had always been welcomed in. Some of the neighbours knew that I was English – or English-born – but being married to Albrecht gave me German citizenship. Now the warden apologised: the law was the law. My friends protested: *die Engländerin* was one of them. But it was no use. What could I do? My house was gone, my husband away at war, and now in the desperate conditions Hamburg had sunk to, we could no longer be protected.

I managed to contact Albrecht and I pleaded with him to find a way to help us. A few days later I was visited by a man and woman from the National Socialist Party Welfare Association, the German social services. Since I was no longer able to provide a home for Klaus, they said, he must be handed over to my husband's family. I could not believe what they were saying. But it was imperative, they said, not only for the sake of Klaus but because of the 'world political situation'. Once bureaucrats hide behind their jargon you have no redress.

I would not let him go. They insisted. I became hysterical but nevertheless they took the boy away. He was barely two years old. I spent the next day frantically trying to get a railway ticket to Cologne where Albrecht's family lived. Tickets were unobtainable. Every railway station in Hamburg was jammed with people. I tried to squirm onto a train but unbelievably in all that chaos, the tickets were still scrupulously inspected.

I called at the offices of the Welfare Association. They were polite but firm. There was nothing they could do. Eventually a stone-built woman in her early fifties waved in front of me a slim dossier of correspondence about Klaus. A dossier on my little boy – it was unbelievable! She wouldn't let me read the file, but I noticed there was even a telegram from the Western front.

✳

It must have been another week till the Gestapo came. In those few empty days I had ceased to be a German. My close neighbours were sympathetic but others who knew me less well began to mutter about this *Engländerin* who seemed to be causing so much trouble. I went back to the Welfare Association. I telegrammed Albrecht. In the night-time air-raids – less frequent now but still as terrifying – I cowered above ground in my concrete garage.

When the Gestapo came they were polite but cool. – Today we hear the word Gestapo and think of jackbooted thugs, but I found them much like police anywhere. They wanted to assure me, they said, that my son was being well looked after. However, my own status – as an Englishwoman no longer living with my husband, no longer caring for my son – had become irregular. Would I care to accompany them to their offices?

*

I never saw the garage again. I spent the next ten months in a succession of jails and camps. (In my sister's story and mine, here's a curious coincidence: at the beginning of the war she spent ten months interned as an undesirable: I spent ten at the end treated the same way.) I was technically a German, I had not committed a crime, and I still had friends – supposedly – in the highest places. So I don't claim my treatment was typical – though I can assure you that not every Gestapo prisoner was strung up by their wrists.

I was allowed to write letters, and I wrote not only to Albrecht but to Hermann Goering and to Hitler himself. My guards seemed to find this unremarkable. They seemed used to their prisoners writing to the German high command. Perhaps they found it easier to give us writing materials, to gravely take the letters away, but then to never send them on. The Bundespost was barely functioning. Why burden it with the prisoners' plaintive pleadings to the Führer?

Whatever the case, no one replied.

We were 'Special Prisoners'. In the course of the next ten months I came to discover that there were several hundred of us – either important foreigners or the unconvicted relatives of the Reich's political enemies. No one was quite sure what to do with us. We were not to be placed with common prisoners, we were not to be harshly treated, but neither were we to be pampered or left unguarded. For much of the time we suspected that we might be being stored as potential bargaining counters – hostages, as it were, against the imminent defeat. By then, you see, every German knew the war was lost, but they couldn't admit it.

Throughout that final winter of 1944 into '45 we Special Prisoners were herded from camp to camp in an appalling succession of broken buses and derelict trains. Sometimes we rode in carriages so rickety they seemed to have been left over from the nineteenth century; sometimes we rode in open cattle trucks. By that stage in the war this was how most people travelled by train through Germany –

such excruciating conditions were not reserved for prisoners. Troops travelled this way as a matter of course. A few days *before* my imprisonment I was one of thousands of civilians trying to clamber aboard similar open trains at Hamburg station.

Usually we were incarcerated in camps – there were over a thousand camps in Germany – but occasionally in the confusion of transfer we would spend a night or two in an evacuated hotel. Once, I remember, we spent several days in an abandoned spa resort half way up a mountainside. But usually we were in camps. Being Special Prisoners we were given special quarters – equally grim huts, no doubt, but less crowded, and fenced off from the long-term inmates. We were always cold, but we were used to that by then. By Spring we were moved more frequently. As the invading armies of Britain, Russia and America seeped further into Germany, as the first camps began to be liberated, our group of valuable prisoners was shifted and protected like a chessboard king, out of the reach of advancing troops.

We were not insensible to the fate of less privileged prisoners – though I dare say you consider me insensitive. No, we saw them through the fences. Occasionally we would call across to them through the wire, but they seldom responded, and I'm afraid the whole business was so dispiriting and – frankly – pointless that we made little effort to establish a real bond. Our position was bleak; theirs was worse; nothing was to be gained from tainting ourselves with them. At such times one clings to the little advantages one has.

Soon, in the last agonising months of war, the meagre allocation of food ran out and our keepers became visibly desperate. They feared for their lives. The Allied guns were within hearing distance, and we seemed to be being moved on every week. Usually we left before the soldiers got too close, though sometimes the camp seemed within a single day of being liberated. Those days were the worse. We were never certain what happened behind us in the camps we left. Were the emaciated inmates abandoned, or was it possible they had been executed? It was a terrible thought. But by then, few of us expected to survive till peace. The attitude of our guards had changed – some became more callous, some wheedled with us to incur favour. But we had no purpose any more. Our guards didn't know what to do with us – they waited every day for a clarifying order from some higher authority, but nothing came. It seemed we had been forgotten – as we almost certainly had: by then we were a trifling detail. We felt that even if we did survive till liberation we would not walk out of the camp unless we could be of immediate value to our guards. But what value did we have? The worst of the guards jeered at us and jabbed more freely with their rifles. Several Special Prisoners died. Every day we heard the approaching Allied troops, and we estimated their distance by the loudness of their barrage. They were ten short miles away. Then five.

Suddenly came the anti-climax. As the Allies advanced on us at speed – three miles, then two, then less than a single tantalising mile – our fearsome jailers, the once mighty SS, slipped into civilian clothes and scuttled away. They hadn't time to shoot us. We no longer mattered.

After a few strange minutes we walked tentatively out of the camp. It was the most uncanny feeling. There was nobody to stop us. There was nobody outside. We could hear the monstrous pounding of Allied guns – sudden silences, then pounding again – but we could see absolutely nobody. Having summoned the courage to walk from the camp we stood like children, unsure what to do next. The only danger seemed to be from our liberators' shells.

We joined hands and walked slowly towards the guns.

✳

I spent three months trying to relocate my family. The Germany I had known no longer existed. Everywhere was chaos. There was no transport system and in order to get anywhere, one walked. Wherever one went there were people walking – stumbling would be a better word. Hollow-eyed, gaunt, disbelieving crowds of the dispossessed. Towns and cities in ruins. Troops in jeeps from whom one could sometimes cadge a lift. Rumours. Horror stories – the teeming rats had finally brought the plague; there was cholera; don't go near the Russian Zone. The black market was rife.

After two weeks I reached Cologne and contacted Albrecht's family. It was a painful meeting. They agreed to talk to me only because I was British and they thought that therefore they had no choice. Despite my ragged clothes and unkempt state (I looked like everyone else in Germany) they regarded me as from the victorious side. Grudgingly they told me that their son Albrecht was dead. He had been killed the previous year. They had not been given the exact date of his death but it seemed suspiciously close to the day on which I had been approached by the Welfare Association. No, little Klaus was not with his grandparents in Cologne. No, he was not with other members of his family.

I tried to contact the Association but it seemed to have been disbanded. Then began my long trawl around desolate offices in which weary clerks tried to piece together the shredded remnants of the nation's family life. I learnt that Klaus had been fostered. It was explained to me that although this might seem harsh it was in fact perfectly logical: the little boy's father had been killed and his mother was locked in a prison cell. He had therefore been moved into a healthy environment with a foster family. Foster families were carefully chosen and vetted by the Fatherland to ensure that they would nurture the children and help them grow into conscientious citizens. But the clerk was unable to tell me where the foster family lived.

I demanded to see the clerk's superior. It was not possible. I created a ruckus and was ejected onto the street. I went back the next day. And the next. After several days I was given the address of the Foster Bureau.

When I found the relevant office it had been newly painted and had fresh glass in its metal window panes. The man who dealt with me was elderly, with an old man's patience. He and his redecorated office had an air of calm and order which reminded me of Germany before the war. He apologised that he was unable to offer me coffee.

In July 1944, the elderly man explained, his predecessor had chosen a suitable foster family for young infant Klaus. To help him settle easily the child had been placed with a family in his home town of Hamburg. Where shortly afterwards he had been killed in a blitz.

Sadly, the man explained, it was probably Hamburg's last blitz of the war.

THIRTY-THREE

She was privileged to see a rare sight: Gottfleisch in a plastic apron, washing up. The first, discarded apron had had ties of normal length, but the second could be stretched around his girth. On Gottfleisch the apron seemed small, like a French maid's pinny in a farce, but he stood at the sink, shirt sleeves rolled up, and seemed to be enjoying the unfamiliar experience.

'What I don't understand,' he said, brandishing a mop, 'is that after these appalling experiences you defend the Nazis.'

'It wasn't the Nazis who bombed my house.'

'Nevertheless—'

'And I don't defend them. Don't you see?'

She paused till Gottfleisch glanced round from the sink.

'But I don't condemn them either.'

He nodded guardedly and leant his back against the sink.

She said, 'That's too easy. We delude ourselves that Germans were a breed apart, totally different from the rest of the human race, certainly different from *us*. But rather than condemn we must understand. To understand is not to condone.'

Gottfleisch pulled a wry face and turned to gaze across the sink into the garden where the blackened scar still seemed to be smouldering. After a while he heard her continue.

'We cannot say blithely that the Nazis were evil, and that's an end to it. They were not. The Nazi leaders were efficient and charismatic men who *believed* they could revitalise their country. Like many politicians they thought they had the cure for the nation's ills. Initially, their cure succeeded – but it was too strong a medicine, and could not be continued. Like any strong medicine it should have been used only to arrest the decline. – If a patient has a cardiac arrest, for example, a doctor might give digitoxin or electric shock. If a patient is in extreme pain he might give morphine—'

'Or for gangrene,' Gottfleisch suggested, 'he might amputate.'

She snorted impatiently. 'But in each case, extreme measures must be followed by more gentle treatment.'

'A gentle Nazi? Sounds a contradiction in terms.'

'Strong remedies can be addictive. A dramatic political cure may achieve remarkable results – for a time. The bright-eyed advocate of extreme measures may rescue us from hardship – for a time. Every nation has had such heroes, but can you imagine Robin Hood or Wyatt Earp living on to be elder statesmen?'

Gottfleisch had finished the washing up. 'So this is your solution – Hitler and his gang should have been put down in 1938?'

She traced her finger across the kitchen table.

'Like the Sun King, killed ceremoniously after each harvest, before winter came? Perhaps.' She concentrated on her doodle on the table-top. 'You know, at the Berghof, Hitler confessed that if the French had opposed him on his first attempt to recapture German land – on the bridges of the Rhineland – he would have been forced to turn back and yield. So perhaps he *could* have been checked, right at the beginning. But the French missed their chance – as did Hindenburg and the rest in Germany, as did Britain later. But that's not my point. History has failed to teach us the lesson of those days; in fact, we've learnt the opposite. We believe that evil is easily recognisable and must be stamped out – or we *say* this, because we never practise it – while the truth is that real danger comes from giving charismatic leaders too much power.'

'Charismatic?'

'The Nazi leaders were charismatic. Joseph Goebbels had the most beautiful voice – did you know? He was Minister of Propaganda, as you are aware, and today we are disgusted by his message – but at that time people deliberately tuned in their wirelesses to hear his mellifluous, persuasive voice. He was charming and amusing. He had some splendid jokes about the Jews.'

'I'm sure.'

'But he made one laugh. Isn't that where danger lies? Beneath his charm and wit lay zealotry and hate. He taught the rest of us to share – or at least to accept – his view of life. He persuaded us that the Nazi way was the only true philosophy. By following it, Germany had become prosperous and powerful. It was the way, the truth, the life.'

Gottfleisch frowned, as if her phrase had struck a chord.

She said, 'But of course there is no single way. There is no single solution. My husband – a clever doctor, a good well-intentioned man – became persuaded at his medical school of the clean, single solution offered by eugenics. Hindsight tells us the very word eugenics is evil, but in those days our clear-sighted 'modern' enthusiasm told us differently. Eugenics works for farmers, for dog breeders, for race horse owners – it works, in fact, for every living thing on earth. How

304

can it *not* work for man? Are we unique? Consider: human races are visibly different, aren't they? – Not only black and white races, but any nation: Italians are different from Norwegians; Englishmen different from French. *English*men are visibly different, indeed, from other races in the British Isles. There are men you need only glance at across a street to recognise as Irish, Scots or Welsh. Let's not deny these differences. Science won't be advanced by our pretending the world is not as it is.'

Gottfleisch had intended to sit down but changed his mind and began stacking things in the fridge.

'At his medical school in Alte Rehse my husband learnt that since races differ, then it follows that some races must be better, some be worse. If, for the finest of altruistic reasons, we wish to improve the human stock – as we do for race horses and cattle, just as we do for apple trees and cabbages – we must weed out the poor stock and breed the best. But how can we be convinced it works on humans? By experiment. Experiments on humans! That seems perfectly logical. And which humans should we experiment on? Ah, Hugo, are you still with me? Do you see the step-by-step reasonableness of this argument?'

She paused and Gottfleisch, reaching into the back of the fridge for a tub of yoghurt, realised she was waiting for a reply. He closed the fridge door and said, 'It may seem reasonable – or logical – but it isn't right.'

'Why not?'

Gottfleisch raised his eyebrows. 'It's obvious.'

'What's your rational counter-argument?'

He chuckled. 'You have me stumped for words.'

'Beware logic, Hugo. Beware the step by step reasonable development of a simplistic argument. As my friend Hermann might have said: when you hear the word 'logic' reach for your gun.'

Gottfleisch tore the foil from the tub of yoghurt and said, 'Gosh.'

'You know, since the war there must have been thousands of books written exposing the horrible acts of Nazism. They're still being written. Each book, each film, each painting tries to outdo the previous in the supposed realism of its portrayal. The descriptions get more horrific as each concerned young artist tries to bludgeon our sensibilities. By doing this, they claim, they help ensure that 'The Holocaust Will Never Happen Again'. What rubbish! What conceit. Those artists *have* bludgeoned our sensibilities. They reduce flesh and blood evil to the level of cartoon melodrama. They make it harder for us to see that evil and horror are *human* characteristics that we certainly shall meet again.'

The policeman who led Cy from the cell looked tired. Without a word he marched the boy to a bleak interview room. A sergeant sat at a table, but Cy had to stand.

'Last time, son: your name?'

Cy didn't answer.

'Address?'

The sergeant wrote something on a form, then glanced up at Cy with no more interest than if he were selling him a train ticket. 'I'm surprised you ever *heard* of a right to silence, son, because they abolished that when you were in junior school. And you never did have the right to withhold your name. That's obstructing the police. Understand? So what's your name?'

When Cy again showed no reaction the sergeant lifted a sheet of fax paper which had been face down on the table before him. Though it was turned away from him Cy could make out the general image through the flimsy paper – a photograph and text.

'Well now, Cy,' the sergeant said. 'This is you all right.'

He turned the paper round so the boy could see it. Cy shrugged.

'A bit of a record for one so young. Now you've added to it, haven't you?'

Not a word.

'A stolen car which you wrote off. Dangerous – no, reckless driving. Possession of an offensive weapon. And let's see: how old does this say you are? Fourteen. So there's no point asking if you've got a driving licence.'

The sergeant grinned coldly. Cy looked around the room.

'You know what, son? We're going to sort you out. You'll stay here tonight – as our guest, of course. You'll be in court tomorrow, first thing if you're lucky, then you'll be taking a trip to – what does it say here? – the Merryview Children's Home. Or as you and I know it, Cy, the Young Offenders' Custodial.'

The sergeant briefly caught his eye.

'Merryview,' he said. 'Don't that sound nice? Dare say they've been missing you, and they'll be glad to have you back.'

✳

'I've been thinking,' Gottfleisch said, 'about your story. Don't you think the newspapers would revel in it?'

'I told you this in confidence.'

It was nearly lunchtime, and they were sitting in her garden across the lawn from the charred remains of her summerhouse. Whenever a breeze blew they could smell ashes and acrid wood.

'I suspect we could sell your story for a tidy sum.'

'A few hundred pounds at most. No, Hugo, it would ruin my life.'

'Oh, we'd get rather more than that. But perhaps you're right – we'd earn far more from a single picture.'

'I notice you say '*we* could sell' and '*we* would earn'.'

Gottfleisch reached down to the grass for his glass of sherry. He smiled contentedly. 'For better or for worse, Naomi—'

'Miss Keene.'

'Yes, point taken. Perhaps Miss Keene would be wiser – not Naomi; she doesn't exist. Well, we are now bound together, you and I – for better or worse, for richer or poorer. I prefer richer, of course.'

'That sounds like an implied threat.'

'You judge me harshly.'

She lifted her face to the watery sun. 'I have always been a realist.'

'Very wise.' Gottfleisch rubbed his hands. 'So tell me, when will you return to that lucrative easel of yours?'

She sighed. 'I have grown weary, Hugo – painting what I can dredge from fading memory, leaving a coded message no one understands.'

'Painting can be therapeutic, I understand.'

He drained his sherry and ignored her withering glance.

'I am eighty-five – no, eighty-seven; it was Sidonie who'd be eighty-five. Anyway, my execution isn't what it was. That young critic you dislike so much, Miss Strachey, was correct: my line has grown shakier after all these years. It no longer has the confident sweep of the young Naomi Keene. It looks like the careful work of a competent copyist.'

'Strachey doesn't matter.'

'She has taken a position on this. She will be asked to vet any new painting which appears.'

'Let her. Your painting will be genuine.'

'But if Strachey insists it is not, who will people believe?'

Gottfleisch gazed at her calmly. 'You must vouch for its authenticity as you've done before.'

'My word against hers. The old battle-horse against the young filly. Who would you put your money on, Hugo?'

＊

The Merryview Children's Home had electronic gates, and when the police car stopped, the driver had to get out of the car to use the intercom. In the back seat Cy sat slumped beside another uniformed officer. Cy didn't look out of the window. He knew where he was.

The high gates swung open and the driver eased the car forwards onto a tarmac drive. He cruised between the trees till they reached the barrack square on which the parking spaces were marked in white.

When they were out of the car Cy sniffed the damp air. Country air smelt different. Somewhere in the distance a man was shouting commands. They went inside. Cy recognised this smell too.

In the Housemaster's office the two policemen surrendered their charge into the custody of Mr Cardew and another man Cy had not seen before. The new man dealt with the paperwork.

Cardew smiled at Cy. 'You've had quite an adventure, I hear.' He glanced at the policemen. 'We'll keep him occupied.'

'Just keep him here.'

The other added, 'Those white lines outside could use repainting.' He sniffed. 'With a toothbrush.'

Cardew examined the boy, who was staring at the carpet. 'Cy is not the artistic type, are you, Cy?'

He didn't seem to have heard. The driver asked, 'Is the kid always this talkative?'

'Oh, is he in a sulk? We'll sort him out.'

'I wish you luck.'

The paperwork was finished. As he replaced his pen the uniformed officer said, 'You won't mind if we don't stop for tea, sir? We have more pressing business.'

'Glad to be shot of him,' the driver said.

Cardew responded with an oily smile. 'Cy isn't so bad. Here at Merryview we can make a man of him.'

'Teach him some respect.'

Cardew saw the police to the office door. 'I dare say you regard these boys as tigers on the streets. But we turn their destructive energy into a force for good.'

'Tigers should be shot.'

Cardew kept his hand on the door knob while he made his point. 'We remould our boys to give them a sense of responsibility toward family and country. We help them understand that they are not alone. If they contribute to society, then society will look after them. They will become stakeholders in society.'

'We'll be going now, sir.'

Cardew, unconscious of their haste, leant against the door and looked across at Cy. 'Young boys have a surfeit of energy, a thirst for action which we meet with a carefully designed programme of energetic activities. Here at Merryview we believe in competition. We arrange all sorts of competitions – sport, of course, but also bed-making, story telling, and work they can do with their young hands. These boys are part of our nation's future.'

'Good-bye, sir.'

Cardew moved from the door and the policemen stepped outside. As he glided back across the carpet Cardew fixed his keen gaze upon the waiting boy. He took a position in front of Cy, looming above him to emphasise his power.

'You seem taller, Cy. Perhaps you've grown up a little, while you've been away.'

✳

On Election Day morning she dressed carefully, put on her warm coat, and walked half a mile to the polling station. She cast her vote, not because she had any real interest in the outcome, but because it was her duty. People had died so others would have the right to vote. To toss that aside should be unthinkable.

The walk to the church hall took fifteen minutes. She marked her cross, saw no one in the polling station that she knew, then slowly walked the quiet lane home. The return journey took twenty minutes, and when she passed through her garden gate she felt warm, ruddy and out of breath. Her calves trembled.

While making her morning cup of coffee she listened to the radio. Now the election had arrived there was a sudden lull in the endless clamour of political small-talk which had saturated the media in recent weeks. To this morning's analysts it seemed inevitable that Labour would win with a majority of thirty to forty seats. The fight was done. Normal programmes could resume. The excitement and urgency had died and the sudden calm was as if the election result were already known. It was like a respite in frantic sex, the *petit mort*, in which the pounding, striving participants collapse in peace among tangled sheets.

To ease her throbbing shins she wandered out into the garden. It was May Day – beautifully warm and sunny – and the forecast for the next day, Friday, the first day of a new government, was even sunnier.

When she re-entered the kitchen she was carrying a metal paint-box distorted by fire, salvaged from the wreckage of the summer-house. She took it to the upstairs bedroom which she now used as a temporary studio. The room had a steady northern light.

She knew that even if she could prise the paintbox open the charred tablets inside would be unusable – but they had sentimental value. They could join other odds and ends she had retrieved. Several times already she had wandered through the blackened carcass of the summer-house, kicking her feet through ashes while she scoured the ground.

309

At half past nine that evening the converted bedroom was lit by a flat artficial light. The curtains were drawn and an unshaded lamp hung above her easel. Sir Walter Sickert had told her many years ago that artifical light showed colours without deception. In those unflattering conditions the artist could ensure that the light *inside* the painting revealed its subject. Art did not benefit from reality and daylight.

In the room behind her a radio burbled. As studio pundits chatted, awaiting first results, unofficial exit polls were forecasting an astonishing 150 seat majority for Labour. A male voice – presumably Tory – was dismissing this as extreme and not in keeping with his party's own polls on the doorstep, but there seemed no disguising that New Labour was bound for an overwhelming victory.

She felt tired and drained. It had been a long day. Her pot of Viennese coffee simmered on its warming plate and filled the room with a comforting fragrance. She stood with a Delft mug in her hands and examined the watercolour a final time. A final glance at the final portrait, before she fixed it. If she believed in Fate and all that Seventies nonsense, she thought, she would have taken the loss of the studio as a portent that it was time to stop. But Gottfleisch insisted she continue. The old woman sighed. She could have refused, but this was a simpler route. One more painting was so quickly done.

First results were being declared at the hustings. Sunderland South had declared first, returning a staggering 10.5% swing to New Labour, giving them a huge majority of more than nineteen thousand. But that result might be untypical: Sunderland had always been a Labour stronghold. The voice of British Conservatism had yet to speak. As the first hour ticked by, Tory majorities came in savagely slashed or lost altogether. Forecasts of the possible Labour majority rose by the minute. The wildest was that Labour might claim over 400 seats while the Conservatives might fall to less than half of that – perhaps to as few as 170. Other political parties scrabbling for crumbs at the victory table were hardly mentioned. Tony Blair was the man of destiny. He would lead the nation into a glorious new millennium.

This was becoming the greatest swing since the second world war, somebody said. No, since the turn of the century, claimed someone else. The British people had spoken more decisively than ever before. These were extraordinary events, in which the old Conservative government was being anihilated by a new party of unclear persuasion. Only that morning, Labour's majority had been predicted at 30 to 40 seats; now it was forecast at over 200. Yet this was a party which till recently had seemed unelectable. Labour hadn't won an election for twenty-three years, yet it had now crashed in from nowhere like a tidal wave smashing on the shore, scattering the battered Conservatives like so many sagging deck chairs. Where had it come from, this unstoppable shock wave? How could a country change its mind so dramatically, so quickly?

She shook her head and switched her attention to the watercolour before her.

Was it finished?

Like her earlier works, it was a soft-toned, sympathetic portrait, demonstrating again that if the Devil existed he would not proclaim himself. 'The banality of evil' – those words said it all. Evil *was* banal. It was not dramatic. It was not performed to a thunderous Hollywood soundtrack. Evil dripped as insidiously as spilt blood.

In her watercolours she tried to recreate the perpetrators of that evil as they had appeared to her, to show how their ordinariness blended deceptively with charismatic zeal. She didn't try to recreate the deeds themselves. Reminders of those appeared every day. Well-funded institutions existed solely to perpetuate the horrors and to present them to succeeding generations as terrible lessons of the Second World War. Such sins were endlessly revisited – almost reverentially revisited – so that they might never happen again. But they did happen again, almost every day.

She recalled a primary teacher once telling how she taught children to beware of strangers. The teacher had explained that while a frightening stranger found it hard to lure a child, an unknown man who smiled and held out a puppy persuaded the child to smile back and say, 'I like that man. He is not a stranger.' But the smiling man might be the real danger.

In the upstairs room, her final portrait was of a vulnerable, wryly sardonic man – vulnerable because he had taken off his spectacles to clean them. Bereft of those stern round metal frames his face revealed an unexpectedly soft aspect. The man looked kindly, almost familiar – certainly not a stranger that one should fear. He was Heinrich Himmler.

As the radio commentators became mildly hysterical at the unstoppable progress of New Labour, Naomi lifted an old wooden frame from the floor and checked its size against the portrait. It seemed just right. She placed it back on the floor, and in the plain white border beneath her watercolour inscribed a signature where it would be concealed by the wooden frame. Once mounted, the signature would disappear out of sight, hidden where only Jane Strachey, eventually, might find it. Gottfleisch did not know that this would be the final portrait – he looked forward to a succession of hugely profitable sales. He also expected more than his previous dealer's commission. He thought he could force his will. He smiled and seemed avuncular, but his air was deceptive. He must be stopped. She would phone him tomorrow and ask him to collect this last painting by Naomi Keene. She signed the portrait *Hugo Gottfleisch, 1997*. Then she hid the signature with the frame.

∗

In the dark moonless night a faint wind stirs the windless leaves. A threat of rain hangs in the air. Though the high clouds look invisible they hide every star.

The wall is ten feet high, yet when the boy appears on it he emerges so effortlessly he could be a snowy owl. He perches a moment, one foot either side of the brick wall, his hands resting on the coping stones. He wears a Death's Head ring. Beneath his leather jacket is the thick woollen sweater that has been part of his uniform. Strapped inside his jeans he has a sharp knife stolen from the kitchen.

From his high vantage point he looks back inside the grounds, then both ways along the empty road. No one is out there. In this lonely spot so late at night it would be surprising if someone were. He swings over the wall, hangs for a moment, fingers curved across the coping – then drops lightly down.

The jolt surprises him. But he is young. He stands up, shakes himself, then sets off along the country road. He begins to jog. For the next few minutes he must concentrate on getting out of sight of the detention centre. A mere five minutes should be enough. Then, out of earshot, he can acquire a car. Out in the lonely countryside there will be no parked cars, yet the loneliness will help him. Away from Merryview he can hitch a lift. It doesn't matter that it is late, because Cy reckons that at this time of night he need only wait forlorn and appealing at the roadside. He need only smile. Any driver who catches his pale young face in the headlights will surely stop to offer him a lift. It is all he needs: someone to stop.